# The Moon Runners

# The Moon Runners

## Mary Lennox

Five Star • Waterville, Maine

First Edition
First Printing: January 2004

Published in 2004 in conjunction with Tekno Books and Ed Gorman.

Set in 11 pt. Plantin by Ramona Watson.

Printed in the United States on permanent paper.

---

**Library of Congress Cataloging-in-Publication Data**

Lennox, Mary.
    The moon runners / by Mary Lennox.—1st ed.
      p. cm.
    ISBN 1-59414-107-X (hc : alk. paper)
    1. Atalanta (Greek mythology)—Fiction.
2. Thessaly (Greece)—Fiction.   3. Princesses—
Fiction.   4. Macedonia—Fiction.   I. Title.
PS3612.E55M66 2004
  813'.6—dc22                2003064228

# The Moon Runners

# Prologue

## Macedonia, 1350 B.C.—Year 24

## in King Kryton's Reign

Melanion burst out of the nightmare as he always did—teeth clenched in an effort not to scream, skin drenched in sweat. He rose and staggered to the window, breath rasping as though he'd raced away from a pack of wild dogs. Pressing his hands against the stone wall on each side, he stared into the night. The moon rode almost full and the stars, beautiful and remote, dotted the heavens. Slowly, he forced his jaw to loosen.

From the great hall below rose the courtiers' drunken laughter. Ironically, it soothed him. It was reality, just like the whores and the sycophants who gathered now at court since Polymus had become Lord Commander, second only to Melanion's father, King Kryton. No matter how corrupt life had become at court, it was better than the dreams that left him shaking because he didn't know how he could choose.

Melanion's earliest remembrances were of his mother weaving the conflicting threads of his fate tight within him. Above all, he was to protect Thessaly, the beloved country of her birth.

As a child, he'd stood with her before a great altar on a mountaintop. There, Melanion's mother had bound him with her prophecy and her demand for one other vow.

"When you are grown," she said, "you will battle your

own father, never ceasing until you free Thessaly." That was the prophecy.

And then she demanded his vow. "Swear," she told him, "by the Mother and the gods, that you will do so without harming a hair on your father's head."

After her death, the dreams assaulted him. Even now, as Kryton and his generals planned the invasion that would pound Thessaly into the ground, visions writhed in his head when sleep took him. Filled with blood and violence, they were all the same. In every one, he was too weak to save his mother, to save her homeland, to even challenge his father.

Awake as he was now, he understood what had caused them. He remembered the night they'd fled the palace. He recalled his mother's bruised throat, the pain lancing through his ribs with each breath, and his own voice coming from some cold well inside him.

"When I am a man, I shall kill him."

Melanion pressed his palms to his ears, as though he could block out the words. Muttering a curse, he grabbed a towel and wiped the sweat from his chest. He reminded himself he was grown, now, strong enough, and, at least when awake, more understanding than he had been that night.

But the questions haunted him. How could he keep both halves of the vow? Was he caught in the pattern of the loom like Orestes, like Oedipus? Must he, in fulfilling one charge, succumb to his true fate, no matter how he struggled against it?

Would he in the end murder his own father?

Melanion rubbed the back of his neck. Crossing the spare room to a small table, he poured water into a bronze basin and splashed his face. He threw on a chiton, belted the short tunic, and wrapped the thongs of his sandals up his calves. Thrusting open the door, he passed into the corridor. The guards gave him the sign of respect due a crown prince. He nodded, striding past guttering torches and armed men, and then climbed to the palace ramparts overlooking the city and the river that flowed through it.

Dawn approached, rosy streaks threading the dark sky. As he lifted his face to the cool eddies of early morning air, he heard his father's rough voice from the archway behind him.

"The guards told me I'd find you out here. Pretty sight, eh?" Kryton gestured to the city below, now visible in the first light of morning. "It'll be a lot prettier when we've brought the gold home from Thessaly to fancy it up and put food in the people's bellies." Pleasure and anticipation filled his voice.

"Council meets soon, boy. Come with me to the Megaron and sit beside me while we plan the campaign."

Melanion bowed his head. "I would be honored, Father."

He knew he should be grateful for any influence Kryton gave him if he could use it to avert the bloody conflict. But he also understood that Kryton's hatred of Thessaly made peace a difficult goal. The truth was, until last year when Melanion returned from Myron's school in the mountains, he hadn't known Kryton as a man at all.

As they walked toward the great hall together, Melanion realized he was pledged to a path of diplomacy with a man he barely understood, attempting to avert a disaster that man was bent upon. He needed words that would sway the generals. He had to at least mitigate the misery his father would soon inflict upon thousands of helpless souls.

Entering the Megaron, he saw that the generals had already assembled. His father took his seat at the center of the table.

"A chair for my son," Kryton shouted in a voice that would raise the dead, and a slave skittered forward to produce it. Melanion sat beside his father amidst the greetings of several older generals. These men had been loyal to the Lion Throne since Kryton took his first town in his conquest of all Macedonia.

Someone placed a map of Thessaly on the table before the king. As his father studied the map, Melanion studied his father. Aside from the gray streaks in his dark hair and beard, Kryton was still broad through the chest and shoulders. He looked every inch a strong man in the prime of life and he made a powerful adversary. Kryton shoved the map over to Melanion with an anxious eagerness he quickly concealed behind a grin.

Then Polymus stood. He grasped the scepter and, with it, the right to speak in council. Melanion stared at him, wondering how such a man had risen to prominence in his father's court. The high commander's strangely ringed amber eyes homed in on each general with the cold concentration of a hawk sizing up his prey. His eyes and reddish-gray hair set Polymus apart from the dark-haired, gray-eyed Macedonians. He came from a village north of Macedonia, the first small hamlet Kryton's army took. Polymus had thrown himself on Kryton's mercy, claimed absolute loyalty, and then proved himself indispensable.

"We'll be ready to march before mid-summer," he said. "Once we've taken the capital, the rest will fall into our hands like ripe fruit. The mines in the south of Thessaly will be ours within the month.

"We'll wage a campaign so brutal they'll never dare to rebel. Don't think we'll merely enslave them; they're expendable. We want that rich land and the gold it contains. We should cleanse Thessaly of the men, leaving only the women for breeding purposes."

The barons muttered among themselves. Then Myron stood, reaching out his hand and wresting the scepter from Polymus. Melanion hid the smile of support he wanted to give his old teacher. Since Polymus had gained so much power, council was no longer a place for open expression.

The white-haired veteran stood tall. The black patch he wore over the socket of the eye he'd lost in battle gave him the jaunty look of a brigand. His three sons, solid, well built men, stood beside him.

"Polymus' plan brings shame to us all and unnecessary death to many of our own as well as their fine men. What good will it do to decimate a population? If the two countries combine, if the noble houses intermarry in the peace that follows, the Thessalians will support us willingly, and the cost in lives will be low. If not, they'll hide out in those hills to the south, working their strange magic against us. We want their wealth and their knowledge, not their destruction."

The barons murmured, but Melanion couldn't tell whether Myron had swayed them or not. Kryton, giving nothing away, held out his hand. Myron bowed and placed the gold scepter into it. The king turned to Melanion and held out the scepter.

"What do you think?" Kryton asked, studying him closely.

Melanion accepted the scepter, rose and squared his shoulders. "If you must fight at all, do so honorably." He kept his voice quiet. The generals leaned forward to listen— a good sign.

"Join the lands after your victory. Rule so the people of both prosper. Make a name men will speak long after your death—with respect," he said. Then he bowed to his father and offered him the scepter.

Kryton shook his head. "Why do you call this *my* victory? You'll be a part of this war, Melanion. I want you to enter the city of Iolcus at the head of the army—right beside me. When we've settled the land peacefully, it will be yours to rule as my representative. If we decide in favor of Myron on this, will you ride by my side and rule in my name? Will you dispense Macedonian justice in a way that will prove once and for all that we're not the barbarians they've mocked all these years?"

Kryton waited for his response with an expressionless face, but there was something hungry just beneath the coolness there. He wanted an open pledge of loyalty and offered Melanion enormous power to protect Thessaly in return.

Melanion could choose to dishonor his father publicly by refusing his offer. Then Thessaly would fall to Polymus' brand of justice. Or he could accept, openly choosing his father's side in this war Kryton waged against his wife's people as a substitute for the war he had waged against her before her death.

He was sick of measuring every step he took. But he could see no other choice—this time.

"I'll ride beside you, Father, and I'll rule in your name afterwards, and they'll acknowledge Macedonia as a civilized nation-state, and you as a just and honorable king." He offered the scepter again and his father took it, grinning in triumph. As he sat, Kryton slapped him on the back, and it was no mean tap. His father was a stocky man with enormous muscle and strength.

"We follow Myron's plan. Enough said for this morn, my friends." Kryton snapped his fingers and a slave began to pour the wine. Kryton shoved the chair back and stood, feet braced wide, silver cup raised. "Macedonia!"

Chairs scraped as the old generals came to their feet. Scarred by past battles, unfailingly loyal, they were a powerful force to pit against an enemy. Melanion knew each one of them would fight to the death for his father. The generals raised their own cups. "Macedonia!" they shouted, and tipped their heads back, draining the wine in one draught.

When they'd settled again, the talk turned to last summer's blighted crops and the need for snow and rain to fill the mountain streams before planting. A young bard, a prisoner from a skirmish with the south, played softly in the corner. Melanion turned to his father.

"I need to go the mountains. The spring games in Iolcus—the ones you wanted me to enter—they'll be upon us before we know it. I'm out of shape, Father, living so well."

"Aye," Kryton grinned. "Myron saw to it you and the others worked and lived hard, didn't he?" He poked at Melanion's upper arm. "Still like a rock, boy. You'll win glory for Macedonia among those coddled weaklings."

"I need wind for the footrace, Father. What with training for battle, I've not gotten in enough hours running. Will you let me go?"

"Alone?" Kryton scowled. "Into that borderland? Take some men with you, lad. I need you safe."

"It's harder for me if I go alone. Better. I'll have to live off the land, Father. A good thing to learn if one is going on campaign."

Pride gleamed in Kryton's eyes, and fear.

"Nothing will happen to me. I'll return," Melanion said, and some of the desperation that thundered through him must have reached his father.

"Go," the king said. "Make your camp and train. But

come back to me by the next moon, do you hear? You've been years at that school of Myron's, and only a few months with me. I've lived without a son too long."

Melanion knelt and placed his fist on his chest. When he looked up at his father's weathered face, his heart twisted.

Fool, he chided himself. Kryton's clever, driven. He can be an animal. That's all you really know of him.

Plunged deep in thought, he made his way to his chamber and grabbed a traveling cloak and hat, his quiver and arrows. From his store of arms, he took a hunting knife and exchanged his sword for his prized possession, the fine one of bronze, fashioned by the metalsmiths of Thessaly. Shouldering the quiver, he made for the window and looked out again at Hamalclion. The capital stirred to life below the palace, the shapes of the tradesmen and their wagons indistinct in the swirling mist. Soon the sun would rise and clear it from the valley.

He thought of his mother, whose body lay in the mountains, and the answers he prayed he'd find close to her grave. He thought of himself, helpless to stop Polymus from gathering more power every day with his father's active support. He thought of everything he didn't understand and couldn't accomplish due to the claustrophobic bonds of honor and fate.

Melanion strode toward the courtyard. He walked out into the morning, past the guards and the scurrying courtiers. He knew his father would send men after him to keep him safe, but he was certain he could evade them. The sun broke through and shone on the steep path down to the river. Under the brightening sky, he breathed deeply and felt his shoulders stretch, relaxing into an animal state of unfettered motion. The air was sharp and cold. He had chosen wisely to go now, before he went mad.

# Chapter 1

## Thessaly, the Palace at Iolcus

"Atalante!" Her little brother Hyperion tugged at Atalante's tunic, his green eyes dancing with excitement.

"Let go, Little Mite." Atalante circled Nestor as Hyperion jumped back out of the way of the wrestling ground. Her eyes narrowed in concentration, searching for the right place on Nestor's sweating torso to grab hold. He was at least four inches taller and outweighed her by more than she cared to acknowledge, but he was slower. She smiled as she observed his stance and the weakness in it that would allow her to topple him.

Lunging in and gripping his left wrist with both hands, she twisted him off balance and clipped his heel from behind. He fell with a satisfying grunt and lay sprawled in the dust at her feet.

A lock of blond hair had come loose from his club and lay over his left eye. Nestor pushed it back with a dusty hand and squinted up at her.

She supposed her old friend didn't appreciate the way she stood above him, hands on hips, legs outstretched, mouth curved in a wide grin. "Next time you brag you can beat me, you'd better work harder on the exercise field," she said.

Nestor's scowl turned into a lazy smile, and he purposefully lay back, arms stacked beneath his head. "You managed to win for one reason alone—the ridiculous amount of

15

time you spend training with that fanatical uncle of yours. Meanwhile, I've been drinking my wine neat and chasing the prettiest girls in the kingdom."

Atalante snorted through her nose. "You're impossible. First you say you're the better wrestler, and when I prove you wrong, you say you never gave a damn for the sport."

"What kind of language is that for a princess?" Nestor gripped the arm she offered and rose to brush off the dust from his tunic.

"Perfectly fine for one who's a war leader, and that's what I'm to be. I can curse with the best of them, if I please."

Nestor gave her a long, mocking look. "Maybe that's why I never see any of our youths swarming about you. I told you two years ago that you'd better begin cultivating a ladylike attitude."

"And I told you marriage and children weren't for me."

Nestor quirked a brow. "Only because you refuse to learn gentleness."

"I suppose I should affect a giggle and borrow some of your effete gold chains," Atalante said, staring pointedly at the heavy necklace Nestor's father had given him for his birthday. The waspish scorn in her voice made her ashamed, but Nestor had touched a nerve.

"You could be kinder," Nestor said quietly. "That in itself would be a vast improvement."

Atalante knew she'd gone too far and hurt him. The flush of her wrestling victory turned to ashes as Nestor walked away, leaving the field to her.

"Damn," she whispered. "Damn, damn, damn." Recently, it seemed she and Nestor did nothing but antagonize each other. He didn't miss an opportunity to expound upon her lack of "womanly softness," and she responded by striking out at him. Most of the time, she went wide of the mark, but today, she'd landed a solid blow.

In part, Nestor wore those chains out of respect for his father, who showered them upon him, and in part, he wore them out of a sense of regional pride, for the chains were fashioned from the gold in his father's mines. But with all his pride, Nestor was sensitive, and more so if it was Atalante who laughed at him or disapproved of him.

If the prophecies held true, Thessaly would need Nestor in the coming year, for he had one superb gift. He knew every forest, mountain, and valley in Thessaly. A rebel force with Nestor on its side could wreak havoc on an enemy and melt away quickly. She couldn't afford to antagonize him. Also, she hated the personal sense of loss she felt over their feuding. Until this year, she and Nestor had been close friends.

Atalante grabbed her cloak and quickened her pace. Staring fixedly at the ground, she wondered why it was that Nestor could so easily see her flaws beneath the confident façade she wore.

All this year, she had wondered, too. Would a man ever . . . care for her? When the goddess laid her hand on Atalante's head, had she scarred her so badly that men were repulsed, or even worse, pitied her? Because of the oracle's warning, she would never know what they saw when they looked at her.

Atalante felt like a child frightened of a monster beneath her bed, wanting to look and prove it wasn't there. Only she was the monster, and she was forbidden to look.

"Wait!" Hyperion's voice cut through her thoughts. He panted after her, caught up and tugged at the short skirt of her chiton again for her attention. Atalante stopped, conscience-stricken. She had completely forgotten her little brother in the middle of the wrestling match, and after-wards had made him run to catch up with her. She stooped down to rub his back until the harsh little breaths deepened and slowed.

"I'm sorry, Little Owl."

"There's nothing you can do about it, you know," he said, his sea-green eyes gazing seriously up at her.

"Of course there is. To begin with, I can walk slower."

"No," he said patiently. "What Nestor said—you can't do anything about it."

She started as though a rather large horsefly had bitten her. Hyperion's ability to read her mind always came as a shock. Somehow, hearing priestly pronouncements from a little brother all of eight summers in age did that to her.

"It's because you're more than, not less than, the others."

She shook her head with an angry laugh. "Don't you think Mother would have said something—just once—if there were any chance of that? I am what I am, Hyperion—a warrior. I must learn to take pride in my duty, and that's all there is to it." She flushed, then felt the familiar pain of guilt and sorrow.

Her little brother, who was too weak for sports and games, who lived his adventures secondhand through her, was the soul of patience. And here she was, bitter about the lack of something she managed to ignore most of the time, unless Nestor got under her skin. She smiled down at Hyperion and took his hand. They strolled toward the palace.

"Why did you come for me?" she asked him.

"Father sent me to fetch you. He wants us in the Megaron and knew you'd need time to bathe."

"The Great Hall! We'd better hurry. Climb up. Perch on

18

my shoulders." Atalante bent over while Hyperion climbed on her back and clung to her, his arms around her neck. She tucked her arms through his thin legs. He was easy to hold, she thought with a pang. He felt so light and frail on her back.

"Ready?" she asked him.

"Yes. Go as fast as the wind, Atalante."

She flew along the path, her feet sure and swift, his shrill whoops of excitement sounding in her ear.

Her father was already seated on the High Throne when Atalante entered the Megaron with Hyperion at her side. She had hurriedly bathed and changed into a gown of corn-flower blue. A maid had finished the job of dressing her hair into a quick knot and had placed the serpent diadem on her head.

Hyperion took his seat to the left of his father. Atalante sat on his right in the familiar ivory chair inlaid in a wild-flower pattern with semi-precious stones.

"Who won?" her father asked.

"Who do you think?" She gave him a quick grin. Beyond the great shaft of sunlight streaming down through the clerestory above the hall, the crowd milled.

The herald announced the first case and two women stepped forward, darting poisoned looks at each other.

"Iasus, High King, hear me," the first said. "I am a widow from Oram. I grind grain for Ariston, miller in our town. But he died this summer owing me six moons' wages. Now his widow refuses to pay me. She means me to work for nothing, like a Macedonian slave. Make her pay what she owes me."

The other woman stepped forward. "Majesty. I have three young children and no means to feed them but what little my husband left me. If I could sell the mill, I'd pay her, but nobody in town has the coin to buy it. What else can I do but ask her to wait?"

"Huh!" the other spat. "What am I to eat in the meantime? A rumbling belly has no patience."

"Well?" To Atalante's surprise, her father turned to his children for advice.

"Give the poor woman the money she's owed," Hyperion said.

"No." Atalante grinned. "They live on the baron Niko's land. Make him give them both work with his goats and make him buy the mill. Then the widow will be free of debt, and the other woman will have honest work and wages."

"Your brilliant idea wouldn't have anything to do with the fact that Niko is Nestor's father, would it?" Iasus eyed her closely.

Atalante shrugged. "Nestor just got a team of beautiful blacks and a chariot carved and painted by masters. All this plus a heavy chain of gold for his twentieth birthday. He was just bragging to me that his father has grown rich these last two years. The gold is flowing from his mines."

"Atalante." Hyperion's voice took on a resonance beyond time and place. "Do not resent Nestor, but be kind to him. One day, you'll owe him a great debt."

Atalante shivered and stared at her brother. Then Hyperion blinked twice and shimmied back in his chair, like any other eight-year-old.

"Could you . . . be a little more specific?" she asked him.

"Of course not." Hyperion rolled his eyes. "You know that's not how it works."

"All right, I'll let it go," she said, ashamed of mocking Nestor for the second time that day. "About the women," she asked her brother. "Should Niko be responsible for them?"

Hyperion nodded. "But don't command Niko, Father. Ask him. Like his son, he has a good heart. It will be a matter of honor to him."

Iasus looked at one child and then the other. Atalante could feel her father's love, steady and comforting. "I am pleased," he said.

But Atalante wasn't pleased with herself at all. She had been curt to her brother. She had been mean-spirited with her friend. When night fell, sleep eluded her as she struggled with a growing sense of shame.

Her father was a great leader because he had a great heart. Hers was growing smaller and pettier by the day.

She tossed and turned until dawn the next morning, then rose and walked to the doorway of her mother's chamber, knocking softly to wake her parents.

"What's wrong?" Alarm sounded in her mother's voice.

Her father stirred in the great bed and raised himself on one elbow to look closely at her as she stood in the doorway holding a lamp. "Is Hyperion sick?"

"No, he's fine. I just had to talk to you."

Her mother slumped back against her father and yawned. "Couldn't this wait until morning?"

"No, Mama. I have to go—to the northern mountains. Please let me go, Father."

"The northern mountains!" Her mother's voice was sharp. "You're looking for the altar of Artemis Great Mother, aren't you? What are you going to do—demand to know why you were chosen?"

Her father pulled her mother close. "Clymene, calm yourself."

"How can I, when she plans to run off to the very border! Do you have any idea what would happen to you if the Macedonians find you and your friends?" Clymene took a deep breath and narrowed her eyes suspiciously. "Who's going with you at this hour?" her mother asked.

Atalante emitted an impatient sigh. "Nobody. Winter's coming and they don't want to camp."

"Just as I thought! You're going alone, skirting that nest of barbarians, flirting with disaster from beasts as well as Macedonians. No. You won't dare the goddess to tell you why she took you as her own. You won't sacrifice yourself when your duty lies here."

Something potent and hot burst inside Atalante, searing her lungs as she drew breath to speak. "Yes," she said bitterly. "*My duty.* You needn't worry that I won't survive to do my duty. You were there that night, Mother. You claim to have seen her, too. Every day, you see how she marked me, even though I am forbidden to look. Well, if it's true, and not just some drug-induced dream, then I belong to her, and she won't let anything happen to me in the mountains, or the city, or the battles ahead, until I have fulfilled my *duty!*

"I'm going, Mother, with or without your blessing. I have to go." Atalante couldn't keep the desperation out of her voice. "I have to make peace with myself before I can lead the people." She hated the tears choking her voice.

Her mother sat up, clutching the sheets to her. "Atalante. You are more . . . vital than either your father or me," she said in a softened tone. "You will accomplish more than we can. That is your destiny. Don't play with it on some foolish whim to know more than you must at any one time."

"Hush, Clymene." Her father stroked his wife's back in a soothing motion. "Where will you sleep? What will you eat?" he asked.

"I can find a cave, build a fire, and snare game. I can eat

the berries and roots that grow in the forests and hills.
Uncle Miletos thinks I am quite capable in these skills."

"Yes," her father said. "You are most competent."

"Mother," she said softly. "You have to let me go sometime."

Iasus looked at Clymene, who sighed and bowed her
head.

"Three weeks, Atalante. No more."

She threw her arms around his neck and hugged him
fiercely. "Thank you, Papa," she whispered. She hugged
her mother then, with a careful self-consciousness she had
never outgrown. Clymene had raised her with strictness and
patience combined, but since the goddess had marked her,
Atalante had never again felt the same warmth that her
mother showered on both her father and Hyperion.

Clymene spoke as Atalante bent over and picked up her
pack. "Say good-bye to your brother," she said.

Atalante gave her a smile. "I already have." And then she
was out the door.


Melanion found the cave again with no trouble. Two
days before arriving in the mountains, he had slipped away
from the guards his father had ordered to follow him. He
made camp and cooked a fine stew of lentils, dried carrots,
onions, and a dove he'd brought down earlier that day. He
even gathered pine boughs and threw his himation over
them, turning the fine wool cloak into a sheet. The moon
rose, still just a sickle in the glimmering sky. It was time. He
rose, and walked the path he'd trodden so many years ago,
until he came to a small mound of rock. He'd brought a
wine cup with him and stood before the mound, tipping it
until the rich red libation flowed from the cup to the stones
and the earth below.

"Mother," he whispered.

He thought of their flight to these mountains in the dead of night. From the great distance of his memory, he heard her voice, saw her bend over his six-year-old self as she put him to bed on a pallet of pine boughs wrapped in a white wool himation. She tucked a snowy blanket about his shoulders and stroked his hair.

"What you saw was more a battle between your father and me than . . . it looked. You can't understand, yet. Someday you will."

"I don't want that dream anymore," he muttered.

She lay down beside him, gathering him in her arms. "It won't come back tonight."

It hadn't come back all that summer. It only haunted Melanion's nights after his mother began to cough, and all the firewood he gathered couldn't warm the chill that killed her.

He opened his eyes, stared at his mother's grave, and squared his shoulders. Perhaps in the next month, he would learn the secrets that would vanquish the dream. That was why he'd come back—to understand, now that he was old enough and strong enough. She had told him to swear two heavy oaths and, trusting, he had done so. Now, somehow, he must live by them. Only the Great Artemis, at whose altar he'd sworn, could give him the answers he sought.

Melanion turned and walked back toward the cave. He could only hope that Artemis would find him worthy of her aid. Tomorrow he would begin to seek her.

Atalante stood by the lake at the base of the mountain and watched the flush of dawn spread over the sky. The contented munching of her tethered pony on the rich field grass was the only sound she heard. She was glad she'd come to the mountains. She felt young and fierce, as though she weren't quite human. Here, so close to the world of wild things, she needn't worry about the foolish concerns that marked her days and nights in the city. It didn't matter what she looked like to the butterfly that alighted on her head. It didn't matter to the fish that jumped in the stream beside her camp whether she would ever hold a child to her breast.

She played with the string of her bow and heard its soft twang in the quiet.

"Goddess of wild things, send me a buck," she whispered. "I'll give you much of my kill."

At the snap of a twig, her chin jutted upward. A stag slipped in and out of the trees, more shadow than substance in the early light. Atalante began to climb, keeping her feet quiet on the narrow path. The flash of a white tail sent her heart racing, and she began to run.

The stag hadn't scented or heard her. He climbed upward, leaping easily over the deadfall of the forest. Atalante quickened her pace, glad that her breath came slow and quiet in spite of the long climb.

The buck stopped for a moment by an outcropping. He sipped at a stream, then began to trot toward the crest of the mountain. Atalante pushed forward. Ignoring the brambles raking her thighs and calves, she leaped over brush and fallen limbs, pushing hard to gain ground on the buck.

Melanion knelt by the stream beside the cave and watched the drops of water cascade from his hand. Brilliantly, they reflected the first rays of morning. The light slanted through the forest and the mist rose from the mountains to meet it. The world was hushed, on the edge of something green and hopeful. Even the smallest creatures must have paused to listen.

He rose slowly and braced his feet apart. Lifting his arms as his mother had done those many years before, he looked up at the sky. "Goddess of the Hunt, I am here. Mother taught me that you have compassion. Tell me what to do. Give me a sign, no matter how terrible, and I will obey."

He waited, barely breathing, and the silence crystallized about him. Everything brightened and clarified, until it hurt to look.

Suddenly, the world burst alive with a crashing of branches and a flash of white. A great stag leaped onto the path and flew past him, its wide-sprung horns blazing gold, its neck and chest a pure, snowy white. The creature was large and strong beyond mortal possibility—and beautiful.

Melanion ran through a dream forest following the great stag's hoofbeats. When King Stag slowed to trot the path, Melanion unlaced his bowstring. Even to approach such a creature armed would be impiety.

Joy rose in him. Here was the sign; surely the Huntress walked beside him now. If he proved worthy, maybe he would find the answers, and peace. He ran forward to embrace his moira.

Following the magnificent stag to a small meadow on the mountain ridge, Melanion waited at the edge of the meadow, still as stone. With a mixture of awe and excitement, he watched King Stag toss his head, golden antlers flaming in the morning sun. The stag's snowy neck lifted in glory against the morning. He looked straight at Melanion.

Melanion stepped into the meadow, arms at his side. With a single look, the stag called him closer, until he was only a few feet from him. Pausing, he knelt by a bed of succulent clover and pulled a fistful for an offering. He slowly approached the king, awed by the aura of power shimmering around the magical beast. He stood so close he could smell the clean scent of its sun-warmed coat. The lordly gaze of the stag rested on his and then it bowed its head and ate from his hand.

Atalante looked past the brush of the forest. Halfway across the meadow, in easy range, stood the buck. She pulled an arrow from her quiver and fitted it to the bowstring, smiling. Maybe she would please the goddess with her offering. Maybe Artemis would send dreams that made sense of life, and give her strength not to want what she couldn't have. More pragmatically, she would eat for many days. Less time hunting meant more time to train for the games.

The buck bent its head. Atalante took aim. Her bowstring sang in the silent air. A cry rang out in the meadow as the arrow found its mark—a strangely human cry, high and hoarse, and then it broke off. The buck bolted and disappeared into the dappled green of the forest. Atalante dropped her bow and flew into the meadow.

A man lay like a sacrifice on a bed of gold flowers. His long, muscular limbs were still as marble and just as pale. Flowing down from his shoulder, staining his tunic and the crushed flowers, was the bright stream of his life's blood.

# Chapter 2

## Enemies

"Have I killed you?" Atalante whispered. She bent over the man while color shimmered—a river of rust over gold, still flowing. She blinked; maybe if she looked again, her buck would lie dead before her, and not this impossibly beautiful man, his long limbs slack.

His eyes opened. They were gray like a storm over the sea, ringed with incredibly long black lashes. He stared at her for a moment, the iris dark and wondering. The good arm rose in a weak salute.

"Hail, goddess," he whispered, and then his eyes rolled back in his head.

The acrid taste of panic rose in her throat. Judging from his ridiculous reaction to her, this man was in the throes of a vision brought on by his encroaching death.

"What have I done? What have I done?" she muttered, kneeling, her fingers gently touching the flesh around the wound. The arrow had pierced through the meat of the muscle on his upper arm and missed the bone. Grateful that he was unconscious, she lifted his arm. The arrowhead had come clean through and showed on the back. She had to get it out before she could bandage him and stop the bleeding.

She took a deep breath, grabbed both sides of the shaft and snapped. The feathered back broke cleanly.

"By all that's holy, sleep on," she said, tearing strips of her chiton to make a thick bandage. When she had what she wanted, she rubbed her hands along her sides to wipe the sweat away. Gritting her teeth, she set her foot against his shoulder and grabbed the head of the arrow. She heaved with a thrust that left her muscles aching, and the shaft slid out, spurting bright blood.

Quickly she knelt beside him, lifting his arm and wrapping it as tightly as she could. He groaned, then fell silent again. Her shoulders slumped and her head bent. She tried to take deep breaths and calm herself. Out of the corner of her eye, she saw something moving by her waist. Atalante glanced down. Her hands shook like leaves in a strong wind.

"Idiot!" she castigated herself. "To mistake the flash of a man's white chiton for a buck's tail!"

She forced herself to look at the man again. He was pale, but his breathing was deep and steady. Maybe the blood loss seemed larger than it was. Who was he? What was he doing in this wilderness?

He looked like a warrior, an athlete. His legs were long and muscled, his hips lean, and his shoulders wide. His face—oh, his face was noble. High cheekbones, strong chin, fine, straight nose, and those eyes . . . He was far too beautiful to die. That inane thought brought her back to her own sore lack of knowledge about healing.

She had to get him to somebody who could help him. Not knowing the first thing about salves and ointments, powders for healing and sleeping draughts, she had to make haste to—where? She hadn't seen a farm within a day's ride on her side of the mountain. There was nothing for it but to go north and take her chances in the foothills of Macedonia. The very thought of crossing the border chilled her blood.

She glanced down at her victim. His eyes were open, half clouded in pain, but the look he gave her was steady.

"You're not the Huntress," he said.

"Of course not." She kept her voice brisk like her mother did when Hyperion was ill. "How can you tell?" she asked, checking to see how lucid the man actually was.

One brow quirked; his gray eyes gleamed with amusement. "She wouldn't be wringing her hands."

Heat stole up her cheeks. With concentrated effort, she dropped her hands to her side.

"A gift," he said. "Or a charge. Either way, I accept."

"What?" He was back to talking nonsense, now.

He closed his eyes against the pain, or perhaps the sinking weariness. "This morning I promised Artemis that I would accept whatever she brought me, be it good or evil. Obviously, she brought me you. In spite of either your very poor eyesight or questionable archer's skills, I accept the gift."

"You are as vain as you are handsome," she muttered. "An unappealing combination."

His face blanched so only his sculpted lips showed color, along with his dark, questioning eyes. She heard his breath hiss out as he tried to ease his arm.

"Don't move. You've lost enough blood for one day," she said in fresh alarm.

"I have a horse," he whispered. "Just down the mountain path by the stream. Help me mount and I can make my way without bother to you."

Worry sharpened her reply. "By the gods! I've almost killed you, and you talk of going on alone. Rest here while I fetch the horse. Understand?"

Atalante ran down the footpath until she reached the cave. She loosed the black and leaped on his back, trotting him smartly into the meadow. The stranger had obviously not heeded her. By the time she reached him, the man had struggled into a sitting position, his head in his good hand. She jumped off the horse and tore at her chiton, fashioning a sling out of the material.

"Truly, can you ride?" she asked him.

"Of course," he said irritably. "Bring the horse and help me mount." Leaning heavily on her arm, he rose to his feet and stood swaying as she led the black to him. She knelt. He placed his foot into her cupped hands and leaped astride, gasping as his arm jerked. But he was on the black, and she could lead him down the mountain now and mount her own pony.

And then she'd take him north. Where men tortured and mutilated Thessalians for sport.

At noon, they had just crossed into Macedonia when the stranger slumped against the black's neck and began to sway. Atalante leaped off her pony and ran to him. "Don't you dare fall!" she shouted. "I can't lift you back on. I can't mount behind you and hold you on. You're too damn big."

The man shook his head like a punch-drunk boxer. "Blind as a bat, a poor shot, and a voice like a fishwife. Maybe I should give you back to the goddess."

"Hold fast," she said more softly, lashing him to the horse's neck with the lead rope, finding another to affix to the black's bridle, and mounting again. As the sun's chariot rolled slowly across the sky, she glanced back a million times, expecting to see him crumple to the ground any moment. Oh, gods, wasn't there a hut, at least, in this miserable land? The man needed rest, and broth, and dear gods, a healer.

The sun was setting when she peered ahead, and felt the first tug of hope. Was she wishing, or did smoke curl upward into the distant horizon? She pulled gently on the black's reins, moving him and her pony at a quicker walk towards what she prayed was a farmhouse that would take them in.

As they drew closer, she could see it—a hut nestled in the trees with small neat fields of corn and barley spread before it. As she approached, a family toiling in the fields paused and leaned on their tools and then came forward, first at a walk and then at a run. A large man in his mid-twenties with a bearded, friendly face and a head of blond hair separated himself from the group and approached them.

"What happened to him, lady?" he asked, pointing to her charge.

"I—he was shot through the arm. He's lost too much blood, and I don't know how to heal him, and his wound may fester if I don't find help. Is there a healer nearby? Or at least somebody who knows simple herbs and cures?"

"My mother, Maia, has the gift. Please, come inside."

Her knees went weak with relief. The gift!

The others ran to the hut, shouting for their mother, who appeared at the doorway. She was gray and thin in the way of country women, with muscled hands and keen eyes.

The farmer loosed the rope, easing the man to the ground. His legs buckled as soon as he touched the earth and he groaned. The farmer lifted him gently and carried him into the house.

"Thank the gods he's still alive," thought Atalante, and her own legs gave way. She landed on the ground with a jolt and sat there between the two horses, her head on her knees.

"Erytes!" shouted the farmer from the doorway. "Bring her water." The youngest, a boy of about ten summers with a mop of black curls, raced to the well in the yard. After he'd brought a cupful of the clear, sweet liquid to Atalante, he somehow convinced her to let him take care of the horses.

It felt like bliss to drink deeply and rub the knotted muscles at the back of her neck. But she couldn't sit slumped in the farmyard like a child with no duties. Brushing her hands on her chiton, she rose and walked into the hut. A hall led to a doorway where the family had gathered. They moved aside as she passed into the common room.

The stranger lay upon a polished oak table in the middle of the room beneath a woolen blanket. Maia raised her head from the wound on the man's arm as the shufflings and mutterings at the doorway threatened to become a thunderstorm of sound.

"All but the lady, out! The lad needs peace, and so do I." The rest crept away, and Atalante leaned against the doorway, watching the healer in tense silence.

Maia's fingers were sure and gentle as she cleaned the wound with hot water from a water pot that steamed on the brazier beside the table. She stitched the wound, smeared an ointment all over it, pressed some mossy mold over that, and re-bandaged the shoulder with clean cloth. The man moaned and shook his head from side to side, as if to get away from the pain.

Maia reached for a cup of some dark brew and signaled her forward. Between the two of them, they got his head up and poured most of the liquid down him. Within moments, he lay relaxed on the table.

"Will he be all right?" Atalante asked. Her voice trembled as badly as her hands had earlier—aeons ago—today.

The woman looked up kindly. "He needs rest, and somebody to nurse him through the first nights, when the fever may strike. He'll carry the scar for the rest of his life, but if luck goes with him, he'll have full use of the shoulder. Did you remove the arrow?"

"Yes," she said.

"You did a good job." The woman nodded her approval.
"It wouldn't be smart to move him for a while. He'll have to
stay here. We'll give him my sons' room. You, my lady, are
welcome, too, if you don't mind a bit of rough living."

"Oh, not a bit. I'd be glad to stay—anywhere would be
fine. Outside, or in the barn. I can take care of myself. I
won't be a problem. If I could just, maybe, help with the
nursing, or bring him broth, or maybe I could help in the
field, or . . ." Atalante raised a hand to her mouth, stopping
the words that wanted to rush on and on. Maia looked at
her. Beneath that careful scrutiny, Atalante blinked very
hard. The strain of the day finally crashed in on her. Tears
gushed from her eyes, and an uncontrollable shaking took
her.

The mother's arms came around her shoulders, and
Atalante began to sob. The older woman held her tight.
"There, there," she said. "It's all right, now."

"It won't be all right again, ever!" she sobbed. "I—I did
it! I thought . . . it doesn't matter what I thought." She
stared up in horror at the woman. "How can I face him?"
she whispered.

"Tell me exactly what happened," said Maia. Atalante
told her everything, while Maia listened with more care and
more concern than Atalante had a right to expect. When the
story was done, Maia poured a cup of wine and handed it to
her. She drank, and handed it back with a small hiccup.

"You'll stay and nurse him," Maia said decisively. "He's
young. He'll heal. And when he does, you'll say how you're
sorry, and ask how you can make it right. Because you're
tied to him, now. All right?"

She thought of the man's jest—that she was his gift from

the goddess, or a charge put upon him. She shivered as a wave of superstitious fear and something else, a sort of hushed hope, coursed through her. She had come to mountains looking for a sign from the Huntress—something that would tell her what the goddess meant for her future. Certainly, it couldn't be this stranger, with his beautiful dark-fringed eyes.

Atalante pursed her lips, angry that she had become so emotional as to give way to impossible dreams. This man wasn't for her. The goddess had seen to that long ago, when she had marked her. Abruptly, she nodded her agreement to Maia's suggestion. Nursing the stranger was the only way to make what she'd done right, and she accepted the responsibility with a strange sense of relief. The knot in her stomach loosened and she took her first deep breath since early morning.

With the weight of her guilt lifted somewhat, Atalante could concentrate on other things. For the first time since they'd stopped at the farmhouse, she looked about her and saw a neat, clean kitchen. Taking another deep breath, she smelled charcoal smoke from the brazier, fresh herbs and flowers drying as they hung from the rafters, and the sharp, medicinal sting of unguents and powders in the open jars beside the table. This was a good house.

"I am honored that you'll let me stay," she said to Maia.

Melanion awoke in the night with a loud cry. The old nightmare again, this time bathed in the red hues of fever behind his aching eyelids.

Someone pressed a damp cloth against his forehead, wiping the burning heat away.

"Shh," a woman's voice whispered, running through his consciousness like cool water. "You're safe."

He couldn't open his eyes to see where he was. He was almost too weary to ask the questions floating just below the surface of his consciousness. Was he back in the cave? Who touched him so gently? Peace stole over him as she bathed his chest, then covered his own restless hand with hers. It was small, but there was strength in it—calluses from hard work or exercise. He shouldn't give in to this sense of rightness, of safety. He shouldn't trust it. He might give too much away.

He thought of his mother, the only person other than his friends from Myron's rough school who had not failed him.

"Tell me the story of the Twins," he said, testing. Nobody in Macedonia knew the history of the gods. Nobody believed in them enough to do more than give lip service to the priests on festival days. He had learned the story of Apollo and Artemis from his mother. Somewhere deep in his memory, the tale was connected to everything good. If this someone who tended him knew the tale, he could sleep knowing Polymus' people hadn't found him.

"How they were born?"

"Yes."

The words came in that same pleasing, cool voice, soothing him with a warmth he had not known for a long time.

"Leto wandered, heavy with child, from country to country. But each land, fearing Hera's wrath, refused her until she came to the little island of Delos . . ."

With a sigh, he cradled the small hand against his cheek and relaxed into sleep.

When Melanion woke alone in a cool, dark room, he felt a moment's pang, as though he'd lost something priceless. But then, he knew where he must be, where he'd awakened for the last few days.

The cave on the mountain, he thought, groggy from sleep. He must have dreamed the golden woman who'd stood over him in some meadow, and the sweet, musical voice that spoke of gods and courage. He attempted to rise. Pain shot through his shoulder and arm, shoving him rudely awake. He grunted, and dream-like memories rushed back in a confusing puzzle of color and sound.

A curtain slid open and he saw a strong, tall figure of a man silhouetted in the light. The big blond hurried forward with a cup of something steaming in his hands. He hunkered down by the bed and smiled at Melanion.

"For the pain," he said, offering the cup.

"My thanks." Melanion drank slowly, trying to piece together the events of the last day. His host sat back on his heels and remained silent while Melanion sorted out his thoughts and then turned his gaze to him. The man had a heavy beard a darker blond than his hair and an open, pleasant smile.

"Where am I?" Melanion finally asked.

"You're in our farmhouse on the Macedonian border. The lady brought you here three days ago."

"Three days!" He jerked upright, only to feel the pain spike through his arm.

"Easy, now." The farmer rose and helped him lie back against a bolster for his head. "You were feverish at first, but the wound is healing well, my mother says."

"The wound," Melanion said, beginning to remember events so bizarre that it was not surprising he'd thought he'd dreamed them in the last days of fever.

"You are with the family of Amphitrion, who was my father. I am his oldest son, Linos. We've lived here time out of mind."

Melanion stared at the farmer and suddenly, he was back

at the cave, a young boy who had just buried his mother and awakened beside her grave to find his father's troops looming over him. Polymus had led them that day. Only one man had been kind to him and that man was Linos, son of Amphitrion. Linos had ridden beside him, loosened the bonds Polymus wrapped about his wrists, and treated him with honesty and respect. He had spoken of this very farm, of how, when his time was up, he'd come back to the mountains that he loved.

"Linos. By the gods! I would have known you but for the beard. Did you become a farmer then, the year after you took me back to Hamalclion? Did you never go soldiering again, as you swore?"

The farmer's eyes narrowed as he stared down at Melanion. Slowly, never taking his eyes from Melanion's face, he sank to one knee and made the sign of respect with his fist against his chest.

"I thought perhaps I knew you, the first time I saw your eyes. They haven't changed, my lord Prince, although much else has," he said with careful formality.

"I hope I am enough the same to remember kindness from a friend."

Linos' face relaxed into the good-natured smile Melanion remembered. "How goes it with you? Even here, we learned of your adventures at that school for the barons' sons. There are whispers that you made a brotherhood based on honor. Is this true?"

"I didn't do anything. They wanted to be heroes. They looked to me to show them how, because I am the son of a king." Melanion gave a wry grimace.

"I think they had other reasons to pick you."

Melanion shrugged his good shoulder. "I didn't do anything special. There are ways a man should act. Once you know them, there's no choice left but to act that way."

"I know others who'd choose different," said Linos with an ironic smile.

Melanion thought of Polymus and he frowned. "So do I."

"We in the hills hear more than you'd guess," Linos went on. "And we worry, for we're the ones who'll get called up if the rumors are true." Linos' eyes narrowed. "Is the king preparing for war? And do you stand with him?"

Melanion was used to making quick decisions. The times were too uncertain to do otherwise. He'd learned when to hide his mind and when to talk truth. Partly from gratitude for old favors and partly from observing Linos' courage in asking his questions straight out, he decided to reveal his thoughts. He could always use a stalwart friend, particularly one who knew how to fight.

"If the choice were up to me, there wouldn't be war. There'd be trade with Thessaly, and fast ships to Troy soon after that. We'd trade goods from all over the world to put coin in the people's hands and food into their bellies. But Polymus is lord commander now. If I wish to alleviate the suffering he's planning for the Thessalians, I have to ride with my father."

Linos turned his face to the side and spat. "That demon—deciding all our fate."

"He leads the left flank of the army. The king believes in him. I daresay you know what he's capable of."

"Aye. I had enough of him on that trip returning you to Hamalclion to keep me in nightmares for the rest of my days."

"I stand against him, but I must be careful. The court grows dangerous for men who speak their minds. A good man, my teacher from the boy's school, stood up in council against Polymus. I sent him into Attica before I came here, ostensibly on a mission to the High King of Mycenae. I couldn't think of any other way to keep him safe."

Linos shook his head grimly. "I'm a simple farmer. All I know is, Polymus is a greedy bastard. If he gets enough power, he'll destroy us all, yourself and your father included. I think you'd better plan your stand against him, and we'd better stand together, high- and low-born alike. When the time comes, much as I can't stomach the killing, I'll put down the plough and go soldiering again."

"If I can't stop him, I'll fight beside you, Linos. My hand on it."

Linos grasped the hand he offered. "You've the look of a good soldier. Mother says you'll heal well. So you be careful against that snake. It's the only way you'll live to honor your pledge."

Melanion nodded and rubbed his burning eyes. As quickly as it had come, the strength of the last half-hour seeped from his body. He had learned a lot from Linos— what the reaction of a good farmer was to the present power struggle at court, how little the common men wanted the coming war. He gathered his wilting wits for one last conversation—with the woman who had held his interest from the first day of his injury.

"The maiden who brought me here—where is she?"

"Out hunting with my little brother, Erytes. He follows her around like a puppy, can you imagine? She seems to like the company well enough—and she a lady of some distinction, I'd guess."

"Has she told you her name, and how she came to be hunting on a deserted mountaintop?"

"She's said nothing, but her manner screams noblewoman. She seems a little scared and very eager to help, especially with you. I think she may be Thessalian, and has heard all sorts of stories about what monsters Macedonians are."

"Aye. The barbarian hordes poised to sweep down on Thessaly and destroy her. I can't say she's wrong." Melanion rubbed his eyes once more.

Linos must have caught the gesture, for he picked up the cup and headed for the door. "When you're awake again, I'll bring the lady to you. Maybe she'll trust you after talking to you awhile."

Melanion had just enough energy left to nod before he closed his eyes. His last thought was of his gift from the goddess, and he drifted off to sleep with a smile.

Atalante returned from hunting with two plump rabbits for Maia's cooking pot. She sent Erytes ahead while she bathed off the morning's dirt in the clear stream close to the cottage. It had been a good morning, the first she had known since the accident three days back. The stranger's fever had broken last night. Even though the danger had passed, she had remained with him enjoying the simple pleasure of looking at his face. He was beautiful and a little bit stern, even in sleep. And he looked like a man who never let his guard down. She wondered why. After a while, she'd laid a cloak on the floor beside the bed and stretched out on top of it, listening to his even, untroubled breathing until it lulled her to sleep.

Hunting with Erytes had been another pleasure. He was a wonderful lad, the same age as her brother and a diverting companion. Erytes' black eyes always seemed to be smiling. Finger to his lips, he showed her where a nightingale nested, and they watched, silent and still as shadows, while the bird's young had their first lesson in flight. Atalante found herself wishing Hyperion could meet him.

As she returned from the stream, Atalante felt thankful the hunting had gone well. They'd used snares for the rabbits. After what had happened on the mountain, she still couldn't trust herself with the bow. Atalante approached the cottage and stopped outside the kitchen window. Inside, Linos slumped on a stool, his cape pulled comically over his head like a small boy playing hide and seek. She wasn't the only one amused.

"Quit hiding," Maia said, and laughed.

"I want to hide from it, Mother. I hate these god-begotten things. I'm a farmer, not a priest—how am I to interpret all of this? After my stint in the army I vowed never to think too much again. And now Erytes tells me the lady wears a gold ring with two serpents twined together, which means *she's* that Thessalian princess, and *he* . . ."

With a groan, Linos pointed toward the back room. "*He's* the prince Melanion. How am I to deal with this?"

At Atalante's choked cry, Maia's head turned sharply toward the window and Linos threw down the cape and stood up, a helpless look on his face as he stared at her.

"Come into the house, your Highness. Don't be afraid. Your secret is safe with us," said Maia calmly. "Indeed, I have guessed who you were from the beginning."

Atalante's fists clenched as she approached the kitchen. The son of her enemy—*her enemy* in this house!

As she entered, Maia bowed to her, and so did Linos. She wondered if everything had changed and if now these Macedonians, who had treated her as a friend for the past three days, would look upon her as a stranger, a threat, or a hostage.

As though she had read her mind, Maia straightened and smiled warmly. "I am honored to have you as our guest, my

Lady. Please, don't run from this situation, as my son wishes to do." Maia led her to a seat and, as she had the first day, offered her wine. Atalante took a deep gulp, feeling the fire all the way down to her stomach. It did little to calm the rage and horror surging through her.

"I can't stay here," she said, rising and walking toward the door.

"Please, your Highness," said Maia, running after her and laying a hand on her arm. "I've got only a little of the Sight, but it told me from the beginning that there was something . . . necessary about your meeting with the son of Kryton. Don't leave before you've spoken to him."

Atalante shook her head to clear it. Blood beat against her ears, making it difficult to think about anything but getting back across the border as soon as possible. "You don't understand. I'm a valuable prize for his father, whose reputation for killing Thessalians has traveled south before him. Even if he kept me alive in some scheme to humiliate my father, I'm needed at home. We know in the first days of summer, he'll ride with his father, leading his troops through the passes."

Slowly, an icy determination cooled her brain. "At least I'll know his face and therefore which man to aim for on the battlefield."

As Atalante strode past her, Maia gave her a stern look and she laid a hand on Atalante's arm. "My son was right," she said. "This meeting between you is god-begotten. You can't run from it. Linos," she said to her son. "Tell her what you know about the prince. My Lady, it behooves you to listen, if just in repayment for the healing I've worked to set right your mistake. Please. Before you decide to leave, listen to Linos."

At the reminder of her own shameful part in this

meeting, Atalante decided not to shake off her hand, but to turn back from the doorway.

"You must know Prince Melanion is the son of the lady Althea of your own country," said Linos. "When he was a boy of six, the lady fled the palace, taking Melanion with her. I was a raw ephebe in the guards at the time."

Linos began to pace the small room, clearing his throat and knotting his forehead. He seemed unhappy about having to tell the tale.

"There had been rumors for months about the king's drunken rages in his wife's chamber, about the other women he took to his bed, about her coldness to him. Indeed, I saw him once coming from her chambers and the look on his face was one of a man going through the deepest pits of Hades.

"Well, in the end, she fled with the boy. King Kryton discovered her missing in the morning. His outcry brought us running. I have never seen a face so tormented. He demanded we find them at once and put Polymus—you've heard of him? No? He's a snake, the lowest scum, raised to power because he had no conscience and so always got results. Well, Polymus was to lead us."

Linos grimaced and rubbed his jaw. "It took us four months, but we finally located a farmer who knew where they were. 'Course, it took him a long time to betray the queen and her son, but Polymus liked taking his time. The man didn't talk when Polymus killed his wife. It was only when Polymus hanged his children, one by one, that he finally broke."

Linos' hand trembled as he grabbed a cup of wine and held it to his lips. "When we got to the cave on the mountaintop, we didn't find the boy right away. I was the one to spot him first, asleep on a pile of rocks behind the cave. As I got closer, I could see the blood on his hands and arms. It was a grave, you see. He'd just buried his mother." Linos took another sip and wiped his mouth with the back of his hand.

"I found out later that it had taken him three days to do it. Well . . ." Linos shook himself. "Polymus bound the lad's hands and told me to ride beside him. If he gave any trouble, I was to report it at once. We rode down past the farmer's land. 'Don't look,' I told Melanion. But it was too late. He saw the bodies, all of them, including the farmer. He looked long and hard."

Linos paused. In the profound silence, Atalante heard only the soft crackle of the charcoal in the brazier and a bird's trill from outside. "I knew how terrible that sight must have been to such a young boy. By Zeus, I was sickened by it, and I was a man of eighteen summers.

" 'Please, your Highness, look away,' I said to him. He turned to me. You should have seen his eyes. They burned. 'No,' he said. 'I want to remember this. Forever.' And I knew one day, he'd avenge them and I realized that Polymus had made an implacable enemy."

Linos cleared his throat and turned to her with a pleading look. "There's one thing more, my Lady. Every night when we made camp, Polymus told the boy that his father was crazed with fury at his betrayal. Polymus said that soon as they reached Hamalclion, the king would kill him. When we took him into the palace at Hamalclion, Polymus herded the lad before him like a young bull calf to slaughter, goading him with his sword. Melanion walked straight as a spear into his father's hall.

"King Kryton sat on his throne and motioned the prince forward. He stood before the king, his hands bound, filthy and scratched from his labors and the long journey. 'Kneel,' Polymus said, and shoved him down on his knee. Kryton drew his knife from his belt and Polymus smiled, looking like a jackal when the lion brings down a deer and he knows he's going to get the leftovers. The boy must have seen the blade flash. He straightened his back and raised his head, looking his father straight in the eye. Seemed to me he wanted to face his death like a man, not a slave.

"Back then, I was a youth who just wanted to survive and return home. The gods know I didn't want to die a traitor. But there was something about that boy. And I wasn't the only one whose right hand went to his sword and whose legs tensed to spring at the king. We were too late. The knife sliced down, and the rope that bound Melanion's wrists slithered to the ground.

"The king pulled the boy into his arms and raised his head. I was close enough to see the tears glittering on his cheeks. 'At last,' he said, 'here is my son, come home to me.' "

Atalante stared at the coals hissing in the brazier for a long time. She took a deep breath. "Why did you tell me all this?" she asked Linos, finally.

"Well . . ." The farmer rubbed his beard. "You might think on it, my Lady, before you judge the character of that man lying yonder. The way I see it, he's the only thing standing between that bastard and your people."

Atalante nodded curtly and walked out the door of the cottage. She took three steps toward the forest and broke into a run. "Lady!" a shrill voice called. "Wait for me." It was Erytes, she thought dimly, and increased her pace. Her heart pounded and her blood raced through her veins. She ran faster, and faster still, eating the distance over deer paths, leaping streams and rocks in her way, dashing through briars. She ran until she thought her heart would burst in her chest. At last, gasping, she sank to her hands and knees on the forest floor.

Her enemy. She had almost killed her enemy, and then, at some peril to herself, taken great pains to ensure that he lived. Soon he'd be well enough to ride into the plain before Iolcus, assault the capital, and kill her friends, her family, herself. In spite of this, Maia told her to speak to him—that the gods decreed she *must* speak to him.

Very well. She would see him. But only to show him that she knew what they planned. Only to tell him they wouldn't have an easy time of it.

Slowly Atalante walked back toward the farmhouse. She didn't bother to scrub her face in the clear stream again. Let him see that she valued his kind so little that she didn't care how filthy she looked.

The anger simmered just enough to give her mind a sharp edge. She was sorry she'd wounded him, for if he was whole, she'd challenge him now and get it over with. As it was, she must hold back until he could fight her in full strength. The shadows made by the herbs planted in the cottage yard had lengthened. It must be late in the day. If she wanted to leave this place before nightfall, she must see the man now. Squaring her shoulders, Atalante entered the farmhouse and walked the corridor to face her enemy.

# Chapter 3

## The Altar

Melanion raised his head at a sharp rap on the door to his room. "Enter," he called, pleased with the interruption to his thoughts, which had been considerably wearying since he had awakened this morning. It seemed that the further he traveled toward health, the more troublesome his concerns. At this point, they stemmed from his conversation earlier that day with Linos and his musings about the elegant creature who had wounded him on top of the mountain.

The woman herself burst into the room, her color up and her blue eyes blazing. He was transported again to the meadow where he'd first seen her. It was not surprising that he'd mistaken her at first for Artemis. She had looked like the goddess, with her bow in one hand, her short white tunic glowing in the sun, and her hair a halo about her face. Even the crescent moon above her brow marked her as the goddess's own. He had felt then that his prayer had been answered and that his life was now irrevocably intertwined with this mysterious, glowing nymph.

But her first words to him now roused him quickly out of his musings.

"Will you wage war on Thessaly?" she demanded.

"What? No 'Greetings, stranger?' No 'And how are you feeling today?' " Melanion quipped, viewing her warily as he struggled to sit up. She stood by the doorway, golden hair flung over one shoulder, glorious, enraged, filthy, and scratched. His gaze traveled over her as he sat against the wall at the head of the bed. With narrowed eyes, she folded her arms across her chest and tapped her foot impatiently.

"You heard me. Will you invade my country?"

So. She was Thessalian. He might have guessed, with that shining halo of hair. She seemed to know exactly who he was. Nobody but a prince from the House of the Lion could have aroused such ire where he had sensed nothing but gentleness during the days of his fever.

"When my father goes to war, I'll go with him," he said in a quiet voice. "I can't persuade him otherwise. I've tried."

"The people will fight you every minute you remain in Thessaly. Maybe they won't win at first. But they'll never give up and they'll sap your will."

"Why do you say '*my* will?' " he asked, plucking at the blanket in his irritation. "If it were my will, we'd stay home and trade with Troy and even farther east. That would feed the people. War will only bring death and devastation to both nations."

"You're deceiving me. What Macedonian would have taught you this? Certainly not your father!" She almost spat the word.

Weariness swept over him with her vitriol. He was tired of defending his father in his own mind while he tried to sway him toward the honorable path. He was sick of seeing himself through the eyes of Kryton's victims. He leaned his head back against the wall and tried to speak gently, to allay her fears.

But in his attempt to cover his frustration, he spoke in the high tones of formality, and feared he widened the distance between them even when what he wanted was to bridge the gap.

"My mother, the lady Althea, taught me. She taught me that the people need a king who will watch over them as a shepherd leads his flock. She taught me that there is always the moment of choice, and that my duty was to stay alive until the time when all lay in the balance." His eyes ached. He rubbed them and then raised his head to look at her.

She had stopped tapping her foot. The fire in those striking eyes had cooled a little, but she studied him from the emotional distance he had set up. Her face gave nothing away. "Word has it your father's a heathen. How is it with you? Do you believe in anything more than yourself and this mission your mother gave you?"

"I believe in the Twelve, just as you do, for my mother taught me to love them as she taught me to love honor. Of these, I follow Artemis. My mother was her priestess, and years ago, on the mountain where . . . you met me, she dedicated me to Artemis Great Mother."

She put her hand out to grab hold of the doorframe. Color stained her cheeks and then, just as quickly, drained from her face, so only the crescent-shaped scar above her brow was a purer white.

"Why did you come back to the mountain?" she whispered.

Somehow, bitter and mistrustful as she was, he could only give her complete honesty. "I hoped to approach the goddess, to find out how I should act. If I lead the army into Thessaly, I am dishonoring my mother. If I don't, I leave Thessaly to a crueler fate—Polymus, a man not fit to walk the earth. He plans to rule your country afterwards. I can't begin to tell you what terror he's capable of inflicting."

Melanion watched her face. She didn't flinch or shake her head to deny the brutal truth of his words. No, she drew herself up, standing tall and proud as she heard him out.

Finally, she nodded, once. "Swear by the goddess you follow that this is the truth. That you have no desire to hurt my people."

He raised his good hand. Watching her all the time, he said, "I swear by the Huntress, whom I serve, by the gods and the Mother, that I wish only good to Thessaly, and that all I have told you is truth." He almost smiled when her eyes widened. He had taken her by surprise when he swore to Mother Dia, Thessaly's highest deity, whose worship was banned in Macedonia.

"Aye," he said. "My mother taught me to honor Her, as well as those that dwell on Olympus."

The sun setting beyond the narrow window bathed her in a shaft of light, illuminating her face, caressing the crescent scar. Her hair, fallen from the loose tie she wore, crowned her head and shoulders like a golden nimbus. She shone in its light. The last rays set the room on fire.

The room grew dim in the approaching dusk. There was no sound, as though the whole world were listening.

"I am Atalante, daughter of Iasus, king of Thessaly," she said. "I would learn more about you, and about your people. I hope you will do the same. Let us break bread together this night, and pledge to try."

"Atalante," he said softly. "My gift, my charge."

"So you said right after I shot an arrow into you," she said with a weak attempt at sarcasm. Through the darkening shadows, he could still make out the wariness that wavered in her eyes. It didn't matter that she was reluctant to trust. He had enough certainty for both of them. So slowly that at first, he didn't even notice, a weight lifted from Melanion's shoulders. This grave, shining creature was truly his answer from Artemis. He had a path to follow now, and a destination. All he had to do was convince her that they must follow it together.

"I'm bored, the scar itches, and if you don't get me out of here soon, I'll run into the night howling in another few days."

Atalante sighed. "You become more difficult every day. I've played dice with you so often, I've lost half my kingdom. I've sung you all the tales our bard has ever fashioned, I've described the palace and our family to you, and still you complain of boredom."

"I know." Melanion quickly quelled a twinge of guilt. True, he had become an impossible patient in the past days as his health returned. He did hate being cooped up in the cottage. But he also had a new, troublesome worry chewing at him. There was the very real possibility that Kryton was upset after Melanion slipped the guards he'd sent after him. The king's next step would be to send troops out searching for his son. If they found Atalante here, they would take her as hostage. He had to get her back across the border as soon as possible.

Furthermore, he had to convince her that in order to save Thessaly, their path lay together. The only way to accomplish both goals was to bring her to the mountain and let the goddess tell her so. He never doubted the outcome of petitioning Artemis on the subject.

Atalante fascinated him. He caught glimpses of the soft woman hidden beneath the proud warrior, and his body responded in a most immediate and obvious manner. Part of it was that his health was returning. Although he could deny his appetites, Melanion knew he had rather pressing needs. Watching Atalante from a sickbed with the unwelcome additional company of Erytes or Linos was a torment designed, no doubt, by the king of Hell.

Some of his frustration must be getting through to her. Yesterday, she'd caught him staring at her, his fingers smoothing the sheet in an unconscious caress. She broke off whatever she'd been saying, her mouth dropped open, and then she blushed and looked elsewhere. She seemed totally confused.

His sense that they were losing valuable time together combined with his frustrated attraction, made him, he was sure, unbearable.

Today, finally, Atalante came in with only a bouquet of field flowers accompanying her.

"Where's Linos?" he asked.

"He had to go to market." She kept her eyes glued on the vase and fussed with the flowers.

"What about Erytes?"

"He's gone, too. They all have." She flushed. Her lashes swept downward, shielding her eyes from his scrutiny.

"You've braved the lion's den alone," he said, not bothering to hide his irritation.

Her lashes swept up, and so did her brow, making her look haughty. "Bear's den is more like it. Maia must itch to kick you out of here, you've been such a tyrant these last days."

"It's time she does. I'm sick of sitting around all day like an old man."

"With that shoulder, you can't take care of yourself yet," she flared. "Somebody needs to make camp and see there's food and . . ."

He stood up and leaned against the wall, studying her. "You could do that. As a matter of fact, you owe me that much." He found her scowling up at him. "You're the reason I'm cooped up here, patched and bandaged like a trussed chicken. I want to go back to the mountains. I can ride back better than I rode here. I can sleep out in the open. By the gods, I'm not sick. I'm merely wounded. It's different."

"It's too soon. I'm . . . you're not ready."

"We're both ready," he said, "and there's more." Quietly but clearly, he told her about his fears. "I won't have my ally turned into a hostage," he finished. "The mountain is the best place for both of us."

"You're right," she said. "But I could leave here by myself, today. You don't have to come with me."

He shook his head firmly. "I want to, and you owe it to me to take me. And that's all there is to it. We'll start off tomorrow."

"Impossible man," she muttered, glaring at him. Fascinated, he watched the struggle between conscience and defensiveness play itself out on her expressive face. As he expected, conscience won.

"I do owe you," she said grudgingly.

He didn't want her backsliding. His gaze held hers for a long moment. "Tell Maia when she returns tonight. We'll leave tomorrow morning."

When Maia sailed into Melanion's room that evening, she had a satisfied smile on her face.

"I'm pleased to hear you finally convinced the princess to leave with you," she said, changing the bandage on his arm for the last time.

"It's past time we left. We've caused you and your family no end of trouble," said Melanion.

"Don't be foolish. You've been a lamb with all of us— except Atalante, of course. But that's understandable. I know you'll set it all straight once you've had a chance to make her see clear about everything."

Maia's perception startled him. He wondered for a moment whether the healer had the gift country people often whispered about, but which he'd never seen before. Sight, prescience—that strange sensitivity to see what muddled mortals should do or would do in the future seemed as strong in Maia as her gift for healing.

"You've healed quickly—better than anyone I've seen with this kind of injury. Give it an easy week, and by the next, you can use the arm, but take care with it for at least a month—let the muscle heal up the right way."

Atalante peeked in. "You can see he's not ready, can't you?"

"Nonsense," said Maia. "He was walking the fields yesterday before we went to market."

"I—we'll need help," Atalante said.

Melanion knew they were perfectly capable of taking care of themselves. He wondered how much of his eagerness to have her alone she sensed and vaguely understood.

Atalante blushed. "Could we . . . would you allow Erytes to go with us?"

"I might." Maia looked at her long and hard. "Are you sure you need him?"

"It would be easier if he were there." Atalante seemed to have trouble looking her in the eye.

"I don't think you'll need him after you settle in, but you can take him," said Maia, looking at her pointedly.

Atalante looked back in confusion. "Thank you. He'll be an enormous help to me. But I have another reason for asking for Erytes' company. I hoped, perhaps, to take Erytes into Thessaly. My little brother, Hyperion, would like him so much. Erytes can teach him things he'll never learn—wonderful things about animals and plants, and how to be a boy instead of a wise old man." She gave Maia a look that pleaded for understanding.

Melanion knew if she looked at him that way, he'd have a hard time refusing her anything.

"Could you spare him?" she asked.

"I must think. Stay with me and give me your hand."

Atalante did so, with a swift, questioning glance in Melanion's direction.

Melanion shook his head, as puzzled as Atalante.

Maia opened her eyes and stared beyond the window. A long silence followed. The healer's eyes went dim. Her face tightened, as though she were in terrible pain. The tendons of her arm strained, but Atalante held on tight, seeming to support her. Melanion stared at the two of them and felt a chill pass through him.

Maia shuddered several times. After a moment, the tremors ceased and she took a long, unsteady breath. Finally, she spoke. "My youngest, only eight summers. Though I wish with all my heart to keep him here, I must let him go. And you must take him. No matter what happens, try your best to keep him alive."

The next morning, Erytes waited beside the horses while Melanion bid Linos and his family good-bye. The boy's eyes snapped with excitement, and he could hardly keep from jumping up and down in his eagerness to be off.

Finally, Linos laughed. "Enough thanks, Highness. My brother will fall into a fit if you don't mount up and take him off on his great adventure."

Erytes gave his brother a grateful grin and hugged his mother once more, hard. "Atalante says she'll send a messenger with a tablet telling how I am until I can learn to write it myself. I'll be fine, Mother. I promise."

"Go with the gods, love," said Maia, holding him. He squirmed to get loose.

"Mama, you're hurting my ribs. I'll be fine."

Maia's arms loosened. "Of course," she said smiling down on him. To Atalante she said, "Remember your promise."

Atalante nodded and took Erytes up on her pony before her.

Melanion felt like a truant out of school. The day was bright with a frosty tinge to the air. He grinned at nothing in particular—the way the sun felt against his face, the way his horse felt beneath him, the way Atalante's hips swayed as she rode ahead of him on their long climb up the mountain.

They reached the cave at dusk the first night. It was just as he'd left it—set up for one man. It took little time for them to unpack their supplies and start a fire. He'd left plenty of deadfall wood stacked neatly beside the cave.

Erytes was exhausted. He crawled off into the cave and his sleeping skins after a hasty dinner of oat cakes, apples, cheese, and wine. Melanion simply felt . . . happy. He realized that he hadn't felt this way for a very long time.

"Your mother brought you to this place?" Atalante's voice was soft in the darkness.

For the first time, he felt like telling somebody about her. "When I was six. It was a wonderful summer. A farmer lived down there," he said pointing toward the lake. "He gave us honey cakes and goat cheese and milk. His son and I were friends—we'd search for berries and then later, nuts to gather. My mother taught me to write in the dust with a stick, and she told me all the stories about the gods.

"She was beautiful, my mother. Not the kind of woman

whose looks strike you like an arrow." He gazed at Atalante for a moment. *Like you,* he added to himself. "Soft, graceful, like a doe. She was gentle. I never knew her to raise her voice, or to laugh for that matter. But she was happy that summer. She was free, and she loved it. At least she had that summer before she died."

Atalante didn't ask for more. He was grateful to her, and the silence was easy between them. She poked the fire up a bit and settled beside it comfortably again, supporting herself on one elbow and staring into the flames. The firelight illuminated the soft curve of her cheek and he stared at her, fascinated by the sheer perfection of her features.

She must have sensed his perusal. "What?" she asked, straightening up. The wine cup at her elbow fell over draining its contents into the ground.

"Quit rubbing your nose. There's no dirt on it." He took such pleasure in her occasional self-consciousness that he should be ashamed of himself. He wasn't. He liked knowing he affected her enough to make her movements, usually so graceful and sure, abrupt and coltish.

"Then why are you looking at me like . . . that?"

He smiled, feeling amusement deepen into something more luxuriant. "I like to look at you. Why do you mind?"

He could see her blush in the firelight. "It makes me feel . . . strange all over. Like I can't get enough air all of a sudden."

"Why would you feel strange? Surely men have looked at you before."

She bit her lip. Her brow furrowed in what looked like puzzlement, and then pain. "Not like that."

Melanion shook his head, not believing her apparent reaction. "Either you lack a certain honesty, or my original assessment of your eyesight was correct, and you're blind."

He watched her turn her head away and saw the trembling in her shoulders. "Atalante?"

She rose, and he stood up, as well. She had her back to him, hands curled into fists at her side. "It's cruel of you to mock me, and I don't have to listen to it. I'm leaving now."

"Atalante!" He reached out and took her wrist in his hand. He could hear the soft plea in his own voice, and hearing it too, she half turned.

"Men look at other women that way. Never me. Are you satisfied?" she said to the ground. In the silence that followed, she threw a swift, mutinous glance at his face, a look that made him ache with tenderness the way a soft smile never could. He lifted her hand and stared for a long time at the supple wrist, so strong and yet so vulnerable. When he bent his head and laid his lips against the pulse speeding there, she gasped.

"I was wrong, Atalante," he said. "The men in your country are the blind ones. Maybe the Huntress blinded them, to save you for something else. Or someone else."

She tugged. Reluctantly, he loosened his grip and her hand slid from his. She backed away from him, staring with wide, frightened eyes. He wasn't surprised when she wheeled and ran off into the forest. He was only sorry.

Melanion awoke with a sore shoulder. He'd tried to chase after Atalante the night before. But she left him in the dust moments after she'd torn out of camp. He spent the rest of the night cursing softly as he paced, waiting.

All he could think about was her puzzling refusal to acknowledge her very obvious feminine power. Atalante plainly prided herself on her athleticism. Why, then, did she seem so blind about her allure? The gods knew he was aware enough of it for both of them. So much so that sleep eluded him for a long hour after she'd returned and slipped into her sleeping skins.

Atalante seemed to be in a much better mood this morning. She and Erytes returned from hunting with two plump pigeons, which she gave to Melanion to dress and spit. He could manage this quite well by now. Only a small bandage remained about his arm and he would remove that in a couple of days. As he worked, he thought how best to explain his need to bring Atalante with him to these mountains. He needed to tell her soon—tonight—that she was here with him for another purpose.

In the meantime, he presented her with nuts and grapes he'd found that morning in an abandoned field halfway down the southern side of the mountain. Atalante roasted the pigeons over the fire and buried roots in the coals. When baked, they tasted like toasted wheat. Replete from the food and wine mixed with water, she seemed much friendlier than he feared she'd be after last night.

"I was thinking," she began. "There may be no answers for us on this mountain. You wanted to learn what you should do. Perhaps I'll take you home with me."

"To Thessaly?" He felt the blood speed through his veins. His mother's land—to walk its roads and see its people!

"Aye. I want you to see my father. You should see how he rules. Every week, he sits in the Great Hall and gives justice to the people. They come from everywhere to Iolcus for this. They speak to him as if he were their father, and he is in a matter of speaking."

"Do they come for food? We've got beggars in the citadel, but they don't dare approach the palace."

She shook her head. "They come for his judgment, and they follow his decision after he gives it."

Melanion raised a skeptical brow. "High- and low-born alike?"

"Of course. He can make them reveal themselves. It's really quite an art—he can teach you how. They tell him things they wouldn't say to the ones they love the most. Well, he's priest, as well as king. Maybe that accounts for it."

"Maybe." He thought hard on this Iasus, this priest-king. "I want to see him. I want to see a lot that I haven't been able to see. I want to sail fast ships to Crete and Troy. The cities must be full of sights and smells so different from my city. I want to bring home goods from their finest craftsmen, so my people can copy them. I want to learn all about their culture and all their ideas, so I can pick and choose."

"I know some of their ways—I'll tell you. Last spring, a bard came from Crete and gave us their songs. I haven't told you those tales yet." She bent her knees and propped her chin on them, staring out at the cool shade of the forest.

"They're very vain, you know. They think Crete's the center of the world. They're immodest, too. The men wear very little besides gaudy jewelry and a short cloth wrapped around their waist. The women go without bodices. They wear flounced skirts like their goddess, whom they worship as the Mother. But I don't think she's really the same as our great Goddess. She's small, and very feminine—more a flirt than She who loves all things."

Atalante settled back on her elbows, long, shapely legs stretched out before her. She smiled as she told him more about her young brother, half boy, half seer and priest. She spoke of his odd visions, his strange, adult understanding of the world he could never experience because of his ill health. It was obvious to Melanion that she loved him fiercely.

As she talked, she forgot herself. The deep blue of her eyes sparkled with each animated word. She gave him a real smile. Melanion made the delightful discovery that she had a dimple. This was a pleasure he'd never even thought existed—to simply talk to a woman with ease.

When later that afternoon, she went off with Erytes to hunt, Melanion walked for miles through the forest, working to increase his stride, pushing against the limits of his returning strength. Toward evening, he readied the campsite, gathering wood and starting a fire. He took pleasure in bathing off the dirt and sweat of the day in warm water, and put more on to heat.

Tonight, he thought. I'll tell her tonight, when she's relaxed and easy with me. Eagerly, he waited to hear Atalante's voice calling out a greeting.

Atalante had had a good day. She'd shot a buck, small and plump, the first notches of its antlers showing. To her relief, it was a clean kill, swift and painless for the buck. She'd been so afraid her nerve and her hands would fail.

As they carried the meat back to camp, Erytes shyly pointed out a bird's nest. The fledglings gave out raucous cheeps when he got within hearing.

The boy grinned. "They're baby nightingales. I adopted them the other day. The mother must have died, for she's nowhere to be found and the babes are hungry. I feed them lots and lots of worms. They've got a terrible huge appetite, but they're almost old enough to fly off and find their own. I'll show you the prettiest one. She's named Aphrodite and she sits on my shoulder now. You'll like her."

"I know someone else who'll like her even better—let's bring her to Iolcus with us to show Hyperion." Atalante grinned. How happy her brother would be.

She returned to camp full of eagerness to be off to Iolcus. After dinner, Erytes went to sleep, leaving her alone with Melanion. The tension she'd felt the night before curled upward around her spine. She rose and moved to the other side of the campfire, staring into the flames in order to avoid staring at Melanion's face. He wanted something from her—the same thing he'd wanted for nights, now.

It had to do with the trust she couldn't quite give him, and the way he moved, with fluid strength and the grace of a big cat. It had to do with the solemn expectation in his eyes. She hunched her shoulders and faced the truth. She was afraid of him. And she was jealous.

"What's wrong?" he asked, startling her out of her thoughts.

"Nothing," she said after a long moment.

"Nothing? Are you turning girl on me—cold and aloof, and when I ask what's wrong, that's all you give me?"

She gritted her teeth. "This girl will best you in the games, both in running and in archery. And why would I want to be like a man, anyway? Do you really think you know all the secrets of the universe, just because you're a man?"

"What do you mean?" Melanion sounded genuinely puzzled. That was one of the things that scared her so much about him. He always sounded genuine.

She felt hot irritation overcoming her fear, and welcomed the anger. "You pretend the buck I saw was this King Stag, and a sign from the Goddess. It was no such thing. It was just a medium buck and maybe the rising sun glinted off its horns and made you think they were gold, but you're dreaming if you think they weren't the color of bone, pure and simple. It may have bolted when it heard me nock the arrow. It probably went loping off into the forest. But it didn't just . . . disappear. It couldn't have."

"Certainly," he answered, in a maddening, even tone of voice. "Just like the buck you downed at the stream today. You're such a loud, clumsy hunter."

"The stag you describe is sacred to Artemis. He is a sign of her favor. Why would it appear to you?"

A flush of anger stained Melanion's cheeks. His eyes went dark. "Why shouldn't it? Because I'm too much a barbarian?"

She'd hurt him—she could see it from where she sat, as far away from him as she could and still be in the same clearing. It made her feel mean and small and full of contradictory, shifting emotion. "Of course not," she said staring at her hands. They seemed to waver as though they were underwater. "You're not a barbarian."

She stopped, blinked against the sting in her eyes, willing herself fiercely to regain control.

"Why wouldn't she let me see the King Stag too?" she asked in a voice that quavered, and was ashamed.

As the silence dragged on, Atalante kept staring at her hands. She didn't want to stand up until she'd gotten herself under control.

She heard a soft footstep and then he sat beside her, his shoulder warm and hard against hers. He took her hand and lifted it. A lone teardrop sparkled on it in the shifting light of the campfire.

"Who can say what she wants of us, Atalante? Maybe that we face our fate together. I only know that, before and after the arrow ripped through my arm, I felt absolute peace. I knew I was in the hands of the Huntress, and that she would bring me what was necessary." He lifted her chin with finger and thumb. His intense gray gaze held hers, and she forgot to breathe.

"Atalante. She brought me you."

It was too much. He was too close, his smoky gaze a gentle caress. She reared back and pushed away from him and the ground, trying to use the small distance she gained from him as a protective armor.

"I am no man's prize," she said.

He gained his feet, and his hand locked around hers, pulling her inexorably closer. With the other hand, he touched her cheek, and rubbed the wetness away with a gentle thumb.

"Why are you so angry? What are you afraid of? Look at me—don't hide your head. Tell me."

She swallowed hard against the lump in her throat. She stared at their joined hands. "When I was five, I saw her, Melanion—the Huntress. She chose me, herself. She put the mark on my forehead, and it was a time too wondrous for words.

"But it meant I would never belong to the Mother. I would never have the Sight, the way my grandmother and my brother have it. I wouldn't have the deep understanding of the old ways and the healing arts to help my people. I would be a war leader, not a priestess."

She paused to stop her lips from trembling. "I'd never be the kind of woman a man could love, or one he'd wish to bear his child."

"Did she tell you this?" His voice was hushed, with a note of pain in it.

She shook her bent head and gave a shrug. "My grandmother and my mother told me, when I was old enough to understand. But it was an honor—the choosing," she rushed on. "Only . . . I never saw her again. And now there's war coming, and I can't save the people by summoning Mother Dia's power the way a priestess can, and my goddess speaks not to me, but to you."

His hand brushed a loose strand of hair back from her face. The other rose to her neck, kneading low near the shoulder. His fingers were so delicate, she wondered if he could charm a frightened bird into trust simply with a stroke of his hand. Even she felt a loosening in the cramped muscles of her neck.

"I'll tell you a secret," she said. "I came here to train for the Games. But I wanted to be alone in the place of the goddess, where she might come to me, and tell me what I should do, and how I should accept my fate. And I see now that she's forgotten me."

"And you think she prefers the son of your enemy. Don't try to deny it. Apollo listens here, too, demanding truth from us."

She raised her head and let him gaze deep into her eyes, searching out the secrets of her soul. "When the war comes, Melanion, will the Huntress help you conquer my country? Do the Immortals forsake Thessaly?"

The smile on his face had something in it of tenderness and something of triumph. "These are matters too deep for us. Come." He held out his hand. "Let us ask the goddess."

"Do you know where to find her?"

He nodded. "I sacrificed at her grove with my mother years ago. We brought branches of apples to her then, but now we'll bring only ourselves. We'll ask for a sign. You have to trust her, Atalante. If not, she'll withhold herself from us. Remember, she not only gave you to me, she gave me to you, as well.

"Atalante, this is why I asked you to come here with me. You have to trust me. Can you do it?"

It had come to this, then. She knew enough of these rituals to understand what Melanion was asking, and she shivered in sudden fear. If she agreed, and if the Huntress gave her blessing, the risk would be terrible.

He would take her. Not as a shy bride on the eve of a sanctioned wedding, but in a primitive ritual where she could hold nothing back, for she must be true to the claiming. She pictured herself helpless beneath him, giving him something of herself she could never get back again. How could she trust him? she thought wildly. He was a near stranger, an enemy. He might destroy everything she loved. They might die at each other's hands in battle.

He was too handsome for his own good.

Her pulse pounded in her throat. She saw him probing her soul as he drove himself into her. She might reveal every hope and dream she'd ever had.

He stood with his hand outstretched, waiting for an answer. Could she do it—open herself to a man she hardly knew, a sworn enemy? If she didn't, what other way did she have to save her beloved country? She looked about her wildly for a way out of this trap. With a sinking sense of despair, she knew there was none.

Atalante put her hand in his and raised her chin. "I must," she said, and followed him into the forest.

# Chapter 4

## Uncertain Bonds

The moon led them, limning the forest path with silver light. With a rush of wings to the left of them, an owl flew upward seeking his prey. Around them the forest creatures stirred and squeaked, rustling through the bracken. With every step, they entered deeper into the night. Atalante looked at Melanion and wonder filled her. He was bathed in silver, like a god's statue come to life.

After a long while, the forest opened into a glade, silent and round like the moon, itself. They approached a giant stone about half the height of a man. Round and ancient, it rose in the very center of the glade—an altar put up by Titans. There was no darkness on it, no sign of blood sacrifice. Melanion turned and leaned toward her. Her whole body froze.

"Where's your knife?" Melanion's voice was but a warm breath in her ear. She shivered and pulled her dagger from the sheath at her waist. Melanion bowed his head before her.

"Take a lock of my hair, and then give me the knife."

With tentative fingers, she lifted a lock of his hair. It seemed somehow cruel to cut something so surprisingly soft and warm to the touch. But she did it quickly. When he loosed the strip of cloth holding her hair back, the heavy locks tumbled onto her shoulders. He reached for one curl and snipped it. While she sheathed the knife, he laid the lock next to his on the altar stone. It glowed in the moonlight beside Melanion's darker lock.

Melanion raised his arm to the shining disk in the night sky. "Goddess, we are your hunters. We're afraid, not of what comes, but of choosing wrongly. If we must not go forward together, withhold yourself from us. But if we walk the right path, give us a sign."

He seemed to vibrate with a power she had only sensed in him before. Time telescoped out in waves of silence that caught her up, so she didn't know if she stood for an instant or an hour.

Suddenly, the wind plucked the branches of the trees circling the glade. The leaves sang like a swift chord on a lyre. A cloud scuttled across the moon dimming her light, then fled with the wind, and she shone into the glade with a blinding brightness. Atalante blinked against silver fire, then froze, her hair rising at the nape of her neck. Unbidden she made the sign of deepest respect, hand raised to the goddess, and knelt on the springy moss beside Melanion, who had done the same.

From the edge of the clearing stepped King Stag, regal and strong, his chest gleaming pure white, the horn of his wide sprung antlers pulsing with a golden light. His eye held hers in its calm and noble grip as if to say, "Daughter of Iasus, why did you doubt?"

He glided to the center of the glade in a stately cadence and stopped before the altar where the two strands of hair lay intertwined. Dipping his head, he delicately sniffed their scent. Gold and bronze rays shot from the strands as they feathered lightly with his breath.

King Stag raised his head and looked at them long. Slowly, he dipped it in acceptance, once, twice, three times. Then he wheeled and trotted out of the glade. His hooves struck fire against the ground.

The crystalline silence gave way to small noises. From the forest, low and solemn, the hunting owl repeated his cry. Dazed, Atalante reached out for the ground. She didn't think her legs could hold her. An outstretched, steady hand appeared in front of her. She grasped it like a lifeline and rose slowly, overwhelmed by what had just happened. The goddess had spoken, not just to Melanion, but to her. Artemis still favored her, in spite of her lack of faith.

Melanion drew her toward the altar. "See how she has answered our prayer," he whispered.

She looked at the pulsing gold of her hair, now changed into a graceful swirl of that precious metal. It wound about Melanion's bronze lock like a vine, melded so tightly to it that there was no way to pull it asunder or destroy their perfect bond. Even melting them down would only mix them more perfectly.

Melanion turned her to face him. With the tips of his fingers, he gently brushed her cheek and slowly, he lowered his head. His face swam above hers for an instant. Then his lips covered hers and he drew her toward him the way the moon drew the tide. She tasted his mouth, warm and sweet, velvet soft lips and hard purpose beneath as the kiss deepened. It didn't matter that she knew nothing, that no man had ever touched her before. She didn't feel shy or self-conscious or ugly. She only wanted him to stand there forever, holding her, surrounding her with his heat, his strength, his sensitive lips roving over her mouth, her face, until all she felt was this loosening of all her tight muscles, this breathless warmth. She clung to him, she who had never held fast to anyone, and felt the solid strength of his chest against her breasts and the hard columns of his thighs as he pulled her up against him.

Still holding her in the circle of his arm, he drew his face back and she almost moaned from the loss of his mouth against hers. He smiled, his teeth a white gleam against the darkness of his lips. The scar on his shoulder was a burning brand in the moonlight.

She could feel the hammering of his heart. But his voice was curiously formal when he spoke.

"We have been dedicated, Princess," he said. "We're in the hands of the goddess. It's fitting that we dedicate ourselves to each other. Is this your will, Atalante? Will you be one with me, in body and in spirit, to show your trust?"

Atalante nodded slowly and cleared her throat. "I will."

Melanion smiled again. She caught that same look of tender triumph in his eyes. "And I will be one with you, in body and in spirit, and never betray your trust in me, until the thread of my life is severed. If this oath be broken, may the Mother and the Daughters of Night take note, and pursue me even beyond the grave. So do I swear."

She didn't understand. He had given her so little to promise, and had bound himself to her with a heavy oath, indeed. What did he mean by it?

Moonlight filled her eyes and swept into the marrow of her bones, racing through her blood until it obliterated all thought. She gazed at Melanion and saw only his hard, beautiful body and her own desire. The moon filled her lungs, so she must breathe in the night as deeply as she could. They began to run, feet sure upon the moon path. Melanion led. His feet pounded a light rhythm against the ground that echoed in her quickening pulse. Sometimes he shone like silver, sometimes he was dark and shadowed.

They wound swiftly through the forest, searching. The wind rose and Melanion's cloak flew back, exposing his shoulder. His scar blazed in the moonlight like a perfect crescent. Atalante ran behind him, pierced with a bright recognition, as though she had run behind him before,

71

staring in inconceivable joy at the scar on his shoulder.

Checked by some instinct, Melanion slowed and grabbed her hand. She felt as though the pull of his blood was so strong that her own leaped in her veins to meet him. Swiftly, he led her into the shadows until she stood in a thicket hidden from the eyes of night. He threw down his cloak on the soft, dry leaves and slipped from his chiton. Her lips parted in a gasp of awe-filled, primal recognition.

With a flash of joy, she understood, and her heart skidded wildly in anticipation. Artemis had given her this night, this magnificent lover. She wouldn't die without knowing a man's touch. She straightened and raised her head as she loosed the girdle from her waist. Her chiton fluttered to the ground. Wordlessly, she came to him and they twined together, falling on his outspread cloak.

The madness was on them. Melanion cupped her breast. His face was strained, as though he suffered. But his eyes were still tender. He knew who she was. He bent his head to her breast and touched the nipple with his tongue.

She gasped. This intense pleasure was hers. For tonight.

Under the shaft of moonlight, she felt something break free inside her and flow up through her veins, as sweet as nectar from the gods.

Atalante's eyes flew open with a start. The moon had sunk toward the horizon and the last of the stars were dimming. Melanion murmured something unintelligible, pulled her closer against his body, and was asleep again instantly. She stared at the dim trunks of trees surrounding the thicket, her brain feverishly racing backward into the night.

She stifled a moan of humiliation at the thought of her response to Melanion's lovemaking the night before. At least it had been dark in the thicket. Too dark for Melanion to see her face and draw away from her. Unfortunately, no amount of darkness could hide her wanton cries.

Not that she regretted their first mating. That was a ritual in honor of their vows before the goddess, a symbolic joining of their purposes and their countries. He had made it so easy—like slipping into a warm, rushing current that carried her to unimaginable bliss before she felt fear or the sharp sting of loss for the land. Their joining had been her gift from Artemis, to cherish forever.

What made her hot with shame and a terrible, secret thrill of remembrance was her eager delight when he reached for her again. She had surged back into his arms, her body hot and open to each subtle stroke, arching to him, moving urgently to take more of him. His hands, his mouth seemed to know just how to propel her higher until the world spun away and she clutched his shoulders, reeling with the intensity of the sensations he so easily brought forth. Even now, thinking about it made her want him again. Still wrapped in his strong arms, she fought the desire to move closer into the warmth of his body, to turn and touch the muscled contours, to feel him grow hard with desire.

But it was growing light. Soon, he would see her face clearly, and his desire would ebb, leaving only embarrassment for both of them.

She felt like a beggar who'd been given a feast—grateful for the marvelous textures and flavors of the delicious food, longing for more to the point of debasing herself. And begging.

What would she say? *Take me in the dark, when you needn't look at me. Don't turn away after giving me a taste of what a man can do to a woman.*

The dawn crept closer with every minute. She didn't want to see Melanion's face when he first saw her. He would look like a man trapped in a situation with no diplomatic way out. Better to keep busy, to show him she'd accepted what happened last night as part of the ritual. She rose from under the cloak he'd spread over them in the night and hastily wiped her tears.

Her jaw jutted out. She was a princess of the House of the Serpent. She begged no man for love.

As soon as Melanion felt the cold air, he reached for Atalante and woke completely to find her gone. Rising on one elbow, he peered across the thicket, discerning her dim outline at the edge of the little clearing. She dressed with jerky movements.

He lifted the blanket in invitation. There was no doubt she heard the movement. Her whole body froze for a moment when she did, but she didn't turn around.

"Come back to me," he coaxed. "It's nice and warm under the cloak."

"No. Erytes will wake up soon and wonder where we are."

"It's long before sunrise. Come here," he said.

"We have to get an early start for Thessaly." Her voice was clipped, cool. Averting her face, she walked toward him. He lay there like a supplicant, still holding one edge of the cloak open as his mind slowly assimilated the realization that she had changed toward him, utterly. She dropped his chiton into his lap.

Melanion jerked upright and grabbed the tunic. A few of the threads ripped as he slipped it over his head. What in Hades was wrong with her? He had wanted her from the first moment he saw her, but the taste she'd given him last night was not nearly enough. Now he craved her, and she made it painfully clear that she wanted nothing more to do with him.

Melanion yanked his chiton over his hips. He remembered the look of revulsion on his mother's face on that last night when his father tried to work his will on her. That was what this Thessalian princess would feel for him, the barbarian from the north who lacked the graceful manners of her courtiers.

He was no barbarian. He was a prince, and he knew good from evil. He wouldn't force her, nor would he beg. No matter what happened between them, he had a realm to rule and decisions to make in the present situation. He needed to meet with King Iasus, her father. But if she ever wanted him again, she would have to be the one to ask.

Atalante was silent as they set off. Erytes who'd found his balance in just a few hours of riding, sat behind Melanion. He had the young nightingale perched on his shoulder, and he busily chattered at both of them. Melanion was grateful for the diversion.

As the day wore on, they traveled down from the mountains and into a fertile valley, approaching a vineyard where young men and maidens gathered the last grapes for the new wine. Atalante waved and they waved back. When a boy sitting on a mound of sun-warmed grass began to play a cithara, she jumped down from her pony and threw Melanion the reins.

"Princess! Here!" called several voices. She ran toward the group forming two circles, men on the outside and maidens in the center. The youths began a hymn to the god, keeping time with hands and voices. The girls wound about each other like vines, their steps light with the rhythm of the music, their arms weaving and then interlocking in the pattern of the dance.

They pushed Atalante into the center of the circle, weaving and spinning about her and the lush, purple grapes at her feet. Her lips parted in a smile as she wheeled, beating out the rhythm, her arms raised toward the sun. The men's eyes followed her in the dance, and no wonder. She'd changed in the night. Melanion could tell from her sensual, heady response to the music. As he watched her, the blood beat heavy and hot in his veins.

The pony's head jerked up and Melanion glanced down at his hands to find them clenched about the reins. Notes soared higher and faster in a reverberating crescendo; the men's bodies swayed in toward Atalante, their arms out-stretched as though to grab her. He could see the lust stamped on their faces. The women's clear voices sailed up-ward, and Melanion froze, remembering tales of Bacchants, the passionate followers of the god, who celebrated him with lust and murder.

Sensing the frenzy and tense with possessive heat, he felt for the knife at his belt. A wild cry echoed in the air from the maidens. A shout rang out from the men. Silence fol-lowed, and then the sound of the cithara, slow and sweet, as Atalante began to sway. She sang in the clean, sunlit air, and her song must go straight to the listening god de-scending into his realm of darkness. Her voice was pure and heady, like the grapes.

When it was over, each helot touched her, as though she were their luck for the year to come. Not only did she put up with their insolence, she seemed to welcome it, gifting each one with more smiles than he had gotten from her in weeks of knowing her.

His chest was tight with an edgy irritation when she fi-nally waved her last good-bye and they could ride off. Atalante, maddeningly unaware, sat her pony with a back more relaxed than she'd had all day.

"How could you be so free with them?" he demanded. "They're nothing but low-born peasants, yet you gift them with your smiles, with your modesty." The vision of the men surrounding twisted his gut. "And all for a god who makes men drunk and violent!"

Atalante's face went pale. She stared at him, biting her lip, and then her eyes narrowed. "The people mean everything to me, Macedonian. And the god doesn't make men beasts—they do that very well all by themselves."

She turned her face away and took the lead. Melanion followed, seething with frustration. She had to know what effect she had on the men—on him.

Erytes must have noticed the tension that shimmered between them, for he spoke quickly, as though to divert their anger. "Why do you dance for the god?" he asked.

"The people love Bacchus." Atalante's voice had softened. For Erytes, of course. "It's because he dies for them. Look at the vine each year—its cruel pruning. Of all the Immortals, he understands our suffering, because he suffers like we do. And he is the god of inspiration. We dedicate our plays and pageants to him. He deserves all the honor we can give him."

Melanion spurred his horse into a trot, and Erytes gave a joyful whoop.

The wind stung Melanion's eyes as he urged the black into a canter. Damn. That woman had a sweet word for everyone but him.

With Erytes clinging to his back and laughing, he raced against the wind until his dark mood lifted enough to turn the black and meet Atalante again. As she cantered her pony toward him, she shot him a wary look.

"I'm sorry," he managed in a cool voice. "I'm not very fond of the god. I've seen too much misery due in part to his 'gifts.'" It was true enough, he thought, remembering his father drunk and reeling outside his mother's door.

She seemed content with that, and made way on the road so they could ride side by side past rich fields where the reapers worked, their loins covered with skirts of rough linen. The men and women paused in their work to call after them. Many knelt as they passed, fists on chests in homage.

"Soon we'll be home," Atalante told him in a more friendly tone. "It's just beyond there." She pointed ahead and upward. Squinting into the setting sun, he rode on, and at the crest of the hill, he saw it.

The great citadel of Iolcus rose like a vision above a large plain where cattle and sheep grazed. The sky poured out a red-gold light, limning the carved serpents on the tall gates with fire. The high walls glowed dark gold in the setting sun around the city. On the fourth side farthest from them, he could just see the shining, ever changing sea. Just above the wind he could hear its call, a roiling chorus of freedom and distant shores.

The city must have been three times as large as Hamalclion. He followed Atalante to the outer gates. The gatekeeper knelt on one knee and pressed his fist to his forehead. Melanion glanced up at the massive, arched entryway with its carved serpents. The colossal stonework dwarfed him and made him feel like an insignificant rube. He straightened his back at once. He had much to learn, but he was a prince.

Once through the gate, they wound down a bustling street full of people dressed in bright colored robes. Unveiled women strode about as freely as the men, calling boldly to Atalante as she passed.

"Back early, Princess!" one shouted. "We didn't expect you for another week or two. Your father and mother'll be right pleased."

Several of the people stared at Melanion and pointed to

Erytes with open curiosity. Erytes waved and the nightingale on his shoulder burst into brilliant song. The crowd laughed and applauded. Melanion had never seen such open ease between nobility and townsfolk.

Another archway rose before them, crowned with two stone serpents forming a ring, head to tail. Melanion looked through the gate and saw the great columns of the palace.

"My great-great grandfather came from the northern plains with his barons," Atalante said to Melanion. "He married the reigning queen and took the Mother's serpents for the sign of his House. Come. You must meet my father."

"Your people conquered this land," he said slowly. Of course. All of Greece had a history of conquest. The smaller natives had all once ruled the lands until the stronger, taller insurgents had taken them. Deep in thought, Melanion rode through the archway and dismounted in a large courtyard. Had Atalante's people made a better transition than the one Macedonia intended to force on them?

Grooms wearing chitons trimmed in blue embroidery quickly led the horses away to the stables and Melanion followed Atalante through another set of high open doors into the huge Megaron. It made the great hall of Hamalclion look like a room in a helot's cottage.

Erytes gaped. "Look at those," he called to Melanion as they passed the gleaming swords and shields of the house barons. Thessaly's master artisans were famous throughout Greece for their intricately fashioned shields. These bore scenes from the lives of the gods and goddesses. Further down on the wall, artists had painted delicate murals of men and women gathering the harvest, competing in races, hunting, and wrestling.

A man in a white robe trimmed in red bustled past, carrying several tablets. He stopped and bowed, his face wreathed in smiles. "Princess," he said. "The king will be happy to see you safe home. I'll announce you as soon as the next case is settled."

"How good of you, Lasos. I'll present my guests after I've greeted him."

Atalante greeted other servants as they walked forward past a huge fireplace below a high clerestory drawing the smoke from the middle of the great hall. She seemed to know them all by name. Beyond the marble fire pit, Melanion saw a raised platform at the far wall where a man sat on a marble throne inlaid with semi-precious stones. His gray hair was neatly cropped, as was his beard. He was older than Kryton by a good ten years.

Two men in fine, colorful robes stood before the king, bristling at each other like boarhounds over table scraps. From the look of their clothing and jewelry, they must be barons. They both tried to speak at once, gesturing in agitation. More men in white robes trimmed in red embroidery hurried about the place, while one sat below the throne writing on a tablet with his stylus.

The king held up his hand and both of the combatants quieted immediately. Iasus spoke. One of the men looked down at the flagstones and the other squared his shoulders. Iasus waved them away. Both men bowed and placed their fists on their chests in a sign of respect. Melanion watched them back away from the throne, clearly accepting the judgment.

It seemed the king had absolute authority over his barons, Melanion mused. Yet he saw no large force armed and ready to put down insurrection in Iolcus. How did Iasus manage it? He felt a tug on his arm. Atalante pulled him forward and he walked beside her toward the throne, following suit when she dipped into a graceful bow. He was close enough now to see the lines in Iasus' face, the glints of white amidst the gray in his hair. The king smiled, and Melanion found himself included in that warm kindliness. He rose and took his daughter in his arms, kissing her brow.

"Well, well. Here you are again, as you promised. Safe and sound, thank the gods." He turned to a servant and said softly, "Eumaeus, go to the queen and tell her our daughter is home."

Then he turned to Melanion and gave him his hand. His grip was firm and steady. For the space of an instant, the king studied Melanion with a sharp perusal, but he said only, "Be welcome."

Including all of them in a broad smile, Iasus led the way toward the fireplace in the middle of the great hall. "Come. First we'll eat, and then we'll talk. And who's this?" he asked Erytes who walked beside him, pointing to his shoulder.

"Her name's Aphrodite." Erytes lifted her off his shoulder with one delicate finger. "If you pet her just on the tops of her wings, she'll like it." The king bent solemnly to his task and stroked the bird's wing.

A pat of sandals sounded on the stairway above the Megaron. Melanion turned his head to see a slender young boy flying down the staircase, an excited flush crimsoning his cheeks. He must be Atalante's brother Hyperion. Sliding to a halt beside her, Hyperion threw his arms about her waist and hugged her.

An older woman walked into the Megaron with a regal step. When she came within several paces of Melanion, her dark, questioning eyes fixed on his face. "Oh," she said, and raised her hand to her cheek. "Oh, my." For a moment they stared at each other while Melanion wondered what she saw in his face that would cause her to blanch and her eyes to fill with tears.

"Clymene," the king said quietly, and the queen drew a deep breath and straightened her shoulders. Nodding regally to Melanion, she motioned for him to sit in an ebony chair inlaid with semi-precious stones.

"You must be weary after your long journey," she said, clapping her hands and murmuring something to an older servant who had approached her with a tray of cups and a jug of wine. "Sit, please, all of you." She motioned Melanion into the seat at Iasus' right. As he took it, the servant bowed, presenting him with the ritual first cup of wine.

"My Lady bids me welcome you, sir. You are our hearth guest, and wish that you will spend many days beneath this roof."

Melanion held the cup, waiting for the king to be served, and then, with a bow of his head, drained the cup. "The Queen honors me," he said. "I am grateful for the hospitality of this great house."

Meanwhile the boy, who had, some time ago, slipped into a seat beside Atalante, glanced first at Erytes and then at Melanion. His gaze was as grave and assessing as a man's, and he stared at Melanion for what seemed a long moment. Then he smiled, and his face took on such a look of unearthly sweetness, that Melanion smiled back at him.

"Welcome," he said in a quiet voice. "You are in a safe place, sir, where none wish you harm. Learn what you can from us."

Startled, Melanion narrowed his eyes at the boy.

"Hyperion," Atalante said softly. "You make our guest uneasy."

The boy rolled his eyes at his sister. "Don't be so protective, Atalante. He'll get used to me soon enough."

Atalante cast Melanion an apologetic look. "I told you

my brother sees things a little differently at times. And," she added with a rueful glance at Hyperion, "when he does, he has a tendency to . . . blurt."

Servants laid platters of bread and sizzling meat on the polished ebony table where they sat. A silent servant poured more wine into his cup. Iasus motioned to Melanion to take the first helping of bread. Hyperion, seated opposite Erytes, stared at the rustling motion inside the boy's cloak.

"Want to see my nightingale?" Erytes asked, pulling her from that warm protection and holding her out to Hyperion. "Here. Take her. That's right—just one finger. See? She'll perch there. If you wait long enough, she'll sing for us."

Hyperion's hand never wavered with its precious burden. Iasus speared the choicest cuts of meat on his knife and held them out to Melanion. All the while, he spoke of the work going on in the kingdom—a road through the mountains to the lake palace where the queen's mother lived, the plans for the spring games, and how many of the great Greek houses were sending athletes.

Melanion couldn't quite relax as he ate the warm, nut-flavored bread and sweet cheese the king offered him. From the end of the small table, he felt the queen's troubled gaze. As if she realized he was aware of her scrutiny, Clymene broke into the conversation, suggesting in a casual tone that the stranger might wish to see some of the more interesting sites of the city, or asking after the journey from the mountains.

"Did you pass any of the vineyards on your way?"

"Indeed," said Melanion. "The harvest looked abundant."

Clymene nodded. "I was in the region at mid-summer to bring the Mother's blessing. I thought it would be good."

At a lull in the conversation, Hyperion looked up from petting Erytes' bird and turned to his sister. "Did you make camp? Are you even faster than the wind? Was the hunting good?"

"Finally, my only brother remembers me," laughed Atalante. "I'll tell you everything tomorrow, but the quick answer is yes, yes, and yes."

Melanion felt something give in him. He had never imagined people lived like this—at least not kings and their offspring. Aside from the watchful queen, the rest of the little family exhibited a natural ease and delight with each other.

Erytes' head bumped against his shoulder. Melanion reached out an arm to circle his shoulders and keep the sleeping boy from pitching into the table.

Atalante turned to Hyperion with a smile. "Will you show Erytes where he'll sleep tonight? He's had a hard ride, and no doubt he's beginning to feel it."

"If someone will show me the way, I'll take him," said Melanion. He rose and lifted Erytes in his arms.

Atalante watched Melanion mount the stairs behind a servant, his strong arms holding the boy with such gentleness, she felt her eyes sting. She shoved the tenderness that tugged at her heart deep, deep down and forced herself to deal with reality rather than dreams of an impossible future where Melanion would carry a child of theirs with just such gentleness. Atalante glanced at the other servants still in the Megaron.

"Father," she said quietly. "Please send them out." Her heart accelerated its beat as her father did her bidding. She looked up. Through the clerestory windows she saw the stars flung out on a velvet sky. The great hall loomed over them in silence broken only by the licking flames of the torches and the crackling of the fire in the hearth.

She took a deep breath and swallowed the lump in her throat. "The man I've brought home is a prince, the son of an enemy. He's here because I asked him to come, to learn what we are and how we deal with each other. He put his safety in my hands simply because I told him to trust me in this matter."

"I knew it," said Clymene with a gasp, rounding the table. Atalante tensed and watched her father rise to fold her mother in his arms.

"He's his mother come to life again," Clymene said. "I thought my heart would stop when first I saw him. Those eyes, Iasus—they are hers looking at me after all these years. But his father!" Clymene said, fiercely holding Iasus with hands desperately kneading his shoulders. "We must send him away."

"My love." Her father spoke gently, stroking her mother's cheek. "What will come will come, no matter how bitterly you try to deny it. We must be ready to meet fate. We must do everything we can—*everything*—to prepare for it. The prince is barely more than a boy. We have heard the rumors of how he inspired honor and courage in a ragged band of Macedonian youths. If we fail in battle, this is where our people's fate lies—not in the hands of his father, but in his."

"We can't fail, we can't," Clymene moaned, rubbing her cheek against Iasus' chest and clinging even more tightly.

Iasus kissed her brow. "Beloved, you know the strength of our army and the strength of the Macedonians as well as I. Please. See that Hyperion has gone to his bed." Her mother opened her mouth to protest, but her father raised his hand to her in a gesture that, though gently done, held the weight of authority. She nodded once, abruptly.

The king gave her a look of understanding. "Clymene, my love. Come back to us as soon as he is settled, and I promise to discuss my decision with you. Immediately."

She nodded again. Atalante watched her walk toward the stairway with the hesitant tread of an old woman. For the first time since rumors of war had washed down from the north, Atalante felt the cold tremor of real fear.

Iasus studied her, then held out his hand. Her father, too looked older and wearier in the flickering torch light.

"Come," he said. They walked together across the great hall to the foot of the throne dais. Her father drew her up the short rise and motioned to the Serpent Throne.

"Sit, my daughter." Her gaze flew to his face in uncertainty. "Do so. Look before you. I want you to think, Atalante. Think about this palace, a great monument to a civilization that began well before the Huntress gave the land to our people. For all their sense of honor, our ancestors were wanderers, barbarians with only the simple blood laws and the force of the priest-king to keep faith among them."

She raised her eyes to her father's beloved, wrinkled face and gathered strength from the serenity and love that shone there—for her.

"This young man comes from such a people. What does he need from me?"

"If you teach him, he could become a ruler to reconcile the kingdoms. When—if the worst comes."

"What does he fear? What does he want? If you can tell me this, I'll know how to teach him."

She rubbed the scar above her brow in deep concentration, and thought of the days and nights she'd spent with Melanion. How wary he was, how little he knew of trust between the people and the monarch. But there was one thing that overrode all these. She had sensed it when he lay deep in fevered nightmares.

"I think he's afraid of his strength—afraid that he'll use it to do evil. We spoke of the future—how he must lead the Macedonians if he can't persuade his father to call off the war. I think Melanion hates himself because he's got the power to lead men and draw them to his cause."

Iasus stroked his beard and remained silent for a moment, deep in thought. "Kryton is a charismatic leader. Perhaps Melanion believes his power comes to him from his father. Perhaps he is ashamed of resembling Kryton. Is it possible?"

Atalante shrugged. "We never spoke much of his father— only of his mother. Power isn't evil, Father. It's just a force that can be used for the Good. This is what you'll teach him. Please."

Iasus tipped her chin until he could look deep into her upturned face. "For whose sake do I help him, Atalante?"

She dropped her gaze and felt the painful blush begin at her scarred forehead and travel downward. "For our kingdom," she said.

"Look at me."

She raised her eyes and met her father's gaze for a long moment, willing the pain not show on her face. "There's more than my . . . affection at stake. I have been to the mountain. I have seen the sign of the goddess. I am convinced the fate of our kingdom rests on Melanion's choices, and perhaps mine, as well. That's why I brought him here."

Iasus' expression softened, and she wondered how much of her unhappiness her father could see.

"I have never tried to force you into marriage, my dear. I won't try now. But you do realize that a match between the two of you might solve this problem. Have you any tenderness toward Melanion at all?"

She was sick with shame. If his father agreed to the marriage between them, Melanion would do it. He would wed her, treat her kindly, and bring his soft, pretty women to Thessaly to sweeten his long nights of misery.

There must be some way to avert both disaster and the humiliation of a reluctant husband who couldn't bear to look upon his wife.

Footsteps sounded behind her. Her mother's voice broke the silence. "It's impossible. Even if this . . . Macedonian prince is a decent man, his father has hated us from the moment he took Althea as his bride. Don't you remember when we found Althea sobbing in the garden right before the nuptials?

"You brought Kryton to Althea's father and accused him of owning an uncontrollable fury that would destroy Althea. In front of Kryton, you told her father to renege on his pledge. Kryton will never consent to a marriage between your daughter and his son."

"Still, if his son wed into the House of the Serpent, he'd have what he wanted—Thessaly united with Macedonia," said Iasus, still obviously enamored of the idea.

"Listen to her, Iasus. If there's any chance the youth is like the father, we would never forgive ourselves."

"He's not like his father," Atalante said hotly. "He's gentle, and he would never hurt me—not deliberately. But I won't let you force him. Do you understand? You won't make me a pitiful supplicant, begging a man for his . . . to give me children. Artemis has chosen me. I'm a war leader. I must have faith in myself. Unless there's no other way, don't take it away from me. Not yet."

Her father stroked her cheek. "I wouldn't force you into marriage with the Macedonian, my dear. We still have time."

She shut her eyes and heaved a deep sigh. "Thank you, father. For not shaming me."

"Majesty." Melanion's voice carried to the throne as he paused uncertainly on the stairway. Atalante closed her eyes. If she could shrink into the flagstones of the floor, she would be grateful. How much had he heard?

Iasus was the first to recover. "Come forward, Prince of Macedon," he said formally.

Melanion squared his shoulders and approached the throne.

"I know you, Melanion, son of the House of the Lion," Iasus said. "You are welcome in my kingdom and in my home."

There ensued a rather long, impromptu audience with Iasus that turned out to be less a formal inspection of Melanion's character and more a spirited philosophical debate. Atalante listened and watched, knowing she'd made the right decision to bring Melanion home. Already, she could tell that he admired her father. And why not? Her father was wiser than all the kings of Attica.

Melanion, following Atalante to his chambers after his interview with Iasus, acknowledged that the king had certainly seemed more accepting of him than had his daughter.

She hadn't spoken a word to him since he'd entered the Megaron to hear her rejection of a marriage alliance with him. That her father had thought of a marriage between them didn't surprise him. He'd thought of it—hoped for it, himself, before they approached the altar of Artemis Great Mother. Indeed, that night, he'd assumed she understood the will of the goddess. In spite of what Atalante now thought, the ceremony of dedication at the altar had been a marriage, and the arrival of King Stag had signaled Artemis' sanction of it.

What had changed Atalante's attitude toward him? How could she assert that such an alliance would shame her? Did he disgust her? He began to understand why his father resented the House of the Serpent. Half of a mind to leave in the morning, half of a mind to confront her with her betrayal of her vows, Melanion followed Atalante down a wide corridor to a large door trimmed in priceless ebony.

He turned to open the door and felt a soft hand on his shoulder. It touched him with hesitance and yet lingered a moment, as though reluctant to let go. He froze, undone by the simple touch of her soft fingers on his skin.

Slowly, he turned and fixed his narrowed gaze on her face. She looked up, swift and, by the gods, seemingly eager. "I'll *shame* you?" he said, his voice tight with controlled fury.

She turned as red as the tiles on the floor where they stood. "I belong to Artemis," she said with a stubborn jerk of her chin, as though that explained everything.

His hand cut through the air between them, negating that tawdry explanation. "You belong to me."

"I and a hundred other women you'd bring with you for your pleasure," she snapped, and cast him a look so full of rage, he thought she'd clenched her fists to keep from striking him.

He found himself eye to eye with her, his own fists clenched. "How dare you insult me like that? You don't even know me, and you're making judgments about my honor?"

Her gaze dropped to her toes. She shook her head slowly, and the flush of her rage paled. "I don't know you, Macedonian. And neither do you know me. That is the problem, isn't it?"

The flash of his anger drained, leaving him shaken by its force. "Perhaps. Or maybe it's your reluctance to trust me."

"I mean no disrespect, Melanion." The flame rose in her cheeks, but it looked more like embarrassment now. She refused to meet his gaze as she pleated the skirt of her chiton with nervous fingers.

"I'm glad I met you. I'm glad you consented to come with me. I know you did this for the sake of your kingdom and mine. I'm grateful."

Her hands gripped each other. He bent his head to see her more closely. She was worrying her lip. Then with a sigh, she raised her head and looked straight at him, lifting her chin proudly.

"I have been worrying about how you might view my behavior on the mountain that one night when we . . . when we sought guidance from the goddess. You needn't worry that I'll impose upon you in any way that would threaten you, or demand anything more from you but a sincere friendship, which I hope you can give."

Melanion blinked in complete befuddlement. What in the world was she about? One thing was certain. Atalante was afraid. Of what, he hoped he'd learn in the next week.

Melanion gave her a courtly bow. "I am also glad that I have come. I'll not importune you again, Atalante, until you trust me more. But that day will come. For the sake of my country and yours, it had better come soon." The latch of the door to his chamber turned in his hand. He walked into the opulent quarters Iasus had ordered prepared for him. With a quiet click, he shut the door behind him, leaving the woman he wished to wed alone on the outside.

# Chapter 5

## The Sacrifice

Except for meals—at which she was unfailingly polite, Atalante barely saw Melanion in the next week. Tonight would be the first time he had a chance to talk with her alone, at a banquet Iasus had arranged to introduce him as a "cousin from the north". Actually, the description was a true one, for his mother and the queen were, in fact, cousins.

His days in Iolcus had been very busy, and what he'd learned from the artisans, ministers, priests, and above all, Iasus, made him think of other things besides his frustration with one very sweet, very maddening princess. Each day, Iasus and he sat together in the king's study discussing the workings of a prosperous kingdom.

Now, in the late afternoon before the banquet, Melanion sipped the spiced wine Iasus offered him and perused the tablet before him from a northern official reporting the present harvest.

"This land has seen other conquerors before you and your father," Iasus said, and Melanion flushed.

"The strong wrest the land from the weak, but time merges the cultures and slowly, the inhabitants teach the new rulers. In the end, they become much like the conquered, with the same values and the same dreams."

"Why must this take generations?" Melanion asked him.

"Observe the average man who does evil to another man.

He doesn't beg forgiveness or try to make up for his cruelty. No, he hates his victim—tries to crush him until he destroys him. Why do you think he does that?"

Melanion shrugged. "Because he's filled with evil, and loves to make men suffer." A face with odd, rimmed eyes of a hawk rose up in Melanion's mind.

"I'm talking about the average man, the one who was taught the difference between right and wrong. The one who gets trapped and has to do what the mob around him does. A soldier during a massacre, for instance. Or a reasonably decent man who does great harm in a moment of weakness."

The king gently tugged at a lock of his gray beard while he thought. "I think a man like that will hate the one he's harmed. His victim reminds him of the evil he's done, of his weakness and wickedness. If he can destroy that man, he no longer has to look at the ugliness of his own soul.

"So a soldier in a conquering army, worked into a frenzy of rape and murder, will call the conquered stupid, inferior, less than human. He'll enslave them and humiliate them."

"Then his crimes have made him, not his victim, less than a man," said Melanion in disgust.

"I believe that in the heart of the night, he knows this, and despises himself. In the loud, bustling light of day, he can hide from himself. And to keep from facing the truth, he pretends that his victims are hateful."

Melanion sat, chin in hand, and stared at the brazier. A coal hissed softly and broke apart.

"I think that's what takes so long, Melanion. A man must think himself worthy before he learns the worth of others. It takes generations for the shame and the self-loathing to end."

Iasus' lips tugged into a small, wry smile. "Of course, we

must consider the thoroughly understandable resentment and rebellion of the oppressed. It's a wonder they ever reach understanding."

Iasus stood and stretched his limbs. "Look," he said, nodding his head toward the window. "The sun is setting. I have sat long enough, and you must be eager to get some fresh air. Enjoy a brisk ride and then ready yourself for the banquet."

Melanion bowed and withdrew, closing the door behind him.

Iasus sat again and perused a tablet for a moment, then looked expectantly at an inner door. It opened without more than a perfunctory tap.

A gray-haired man a few years younger than Iasus swung into the room. He had the same aquiline features and deep blue eyes, but he carried himself with the gait of a soldier and he strode to a seat in one of the wooden chairs arranged about the oak table.

"He could be a spy, Brother," he said.

"No, Miletus. He's exactly what he appears to be."

"And what's that, pray?"

"The answer. If only it can come soon enough."

The general shrugged. "We'll hold him hostage until Kryton can be made to see reason."

"He's my guest. If I foreswear my oath, the Huntress will loose her wrath on Thessaly."

Miletus waved an airy hand at his brother. "You're too persnickety about these religious details. Get some priest to prepare a rite absolving the people."

Iasus' mouth quirked into a wry smile. "You're forgetting. I'm the priest, and I know what the gods will and will not allow."

Miletus' brow shot upward and he snorted. "Have you

consulted Hyperion about this?"

Iasus gave his brother a long look. "I didn't need to."

The general frowned. The lines in his ruddy face creased deeply and made it look suddenly old. "Then let's pray this Macedonian can turn his father from his mad purpose. Time's running out."

Atalante entered the Megaron on her father's arm, greeting barons and their clans as she walked. Now that the harvest had been brought safely in, many had returned to court in the last week, but she'd seen barely anyone. She chided herself for a coward, hiding with Hyperion and Erytes in their rooms near the women's quarters. But the thought of running into Melanion, of seeing the coldness in his eyes, in his very stance, kept her from all but her duties and the exercise field.

In spite of everything, she scanned the hall now several times, looking for Melanion. He appeared at the far doorway dressed in a dark blue tunic belted in gold. Armlets of gold enclosed his strong wrists, and his winter sandals of fine, soft leather, laced up his calves. His auburn hair was lightly oiled in the Thessalian style, holding the curls down against his neck. His eyes swept the hall and immediately homed in on her. They seemed to burn and he held her gaze relentlessly. Her heart pounded so loudly in her ears she could barely hear what the woman beside her was saying.

"Well, that's somebody new. And a god, by the looks of him."

"His name is Melanion," said Iasus. "A distant cousin of ours from the northern border."

"What's he looking at so long?" asked the lady, smoothing down her flounced skirt. "Atalante, is he looking

95

at you?" she asked in surprise.

"I—I must see to my guests," murmured Atalante, and escaped into the crowd, her cheeks flaming.

"Atalante!" Astrid, tall and slender with bright locks flowing down her back, ran to her and gave her a hug. "Korone," she called to Atalante's other close friend. "She's here."

Korone strolled gracefully toward them. Dressed in a bright red gown girdled with a chain of silver, her tiny figure radiated an unconscious sensuality Atalante had only recently noticed. So had most of the young men in the Megaron tonight.

Korone patted her black hair, which her maid had plaited with red ribbons and wrapped like a crown on her head. She looked Atalante up and down and reached up with one hand, flexing Atalante's biceps. "How are the legs? Strong as the rest of you? I can't see in that gown. And wasn't I right to tell you to have that material made up? Just the right shade of blue to set off your eyes," she said, nodding approvingly.

"Yes, I'm stronger," Atalante said, ignoring the last. "I'll take every contender at the games this spring. Now, what about you?" She turned to Astrid first.

"How are the horses? Did the mares all conceive?"

Astrid shook back her shining hair. "Every one. Remember the bay you liked at the summer fair? She's in foal to your stallion as are five of the others. You can have first choice of the offspring as stud fee, if you like."

"If there's a quiet one for Hyperion, I want it," said Atalante. She pictured her brother's delight in learning to ride a fleet horse when he couldn't be fleet himself.

"I'll help you find him a pony to learn on this fall," said Astrid, always quick to understand her moods.

Korone nudged Atalante. "Look. There's the stranger who was eyeing you as though he could see right through your gown."

Atalante glanced up and caught her breath. Melanion moved toward her as inexorably as the tide. "He did no such thing!"

"He's coming this way," Korone whispered.

As she tried without success to keep her heart from beating too quickly, she vaguely heard the sound of metal, and realized that Korone had idly begun to twirl the buckle of her silver belt.

"Behave, Korone," she whispered back in a hiss of breath. "Don't you dare embarrass him or me, or I swear by Poseidon's trident, I'll make you pay."

"I'll be on my best behavior, my dear," Korone said. "I'll only flirt a little with him."

Astrid sighed. "That's about the best behavior we can expect from Korone."

Melanion approached their small group. Korone eyed him like a sleek black cat that had spotted a particularly succulent mouse. She tossed her head and smiled as Melanion stopped in front of her. "Introduce me to your cousin, Atalante," she said in a purr rich as honey.

Melanion bowed gracefully, first to Korone. He turned to Atalante and inclined his head again with cool courtesy. While she could barely put words together to form a sentence in his presence, he moved on, elegant and careless, to the next flirtation.

"Korone, daughter of Baron Lexias. Astrid, daughter of Baron Admetes. My cousin, Melanion from the northern borderlands." She tried very hard to keep her voice cool as she made the introductions. But afterwards, she couldn't look at Melanion, and Korone, sleek and gleaming, took over the conversation.

"It's been forever since a newcomer graced these halls. Tell me, Melanion, what do you think of Iolcus?" Korone asked.

"Impressive. We have nothing like this where I come from. I have never seen women so garbed." Atalante cast a look at the women in the hall. She had supposed Macedonian women also wore bright colors, tight bodices, and flounced skirts.

"They have so much gold hanging from their necks and belts," Melanion went on. "The men, too, are very fine and different from our men. Most of our men still wear their hair long and bound into clubs when they do battle. Few have the rich embroidery your barons sport, as well as the colorful cloth.

"And what are those?" he asked Korone, pointing to the jeweled and gold symbols hanging from chains the men wore around their necks.

"Symbols of their households. See the older man over there?" Korone pointed. "That's my uncle. He wears the sign of our household patron—the bull of Poseidon, for we live beside the sea. The man next to him, Nestor's father, in fact—you'll meet Nestor sooner or later, for where Atalante goes, Nestor follows."

"Korone!" Atalante felt an altogether unexpected heat in her cheeks. What was Korone talking about? If gossip about Korone's mischief reached Nestor, it would only embarrass him.

"Nestor's father wears the hammer of Hephaestos," Korone said, blithely ignoring her. "His lands are rich in ore, so the god favors his family. Just as your cousin wears the crown of the serpent, because the Mother watches over her family."

Korone homed back in on her first question. "You live close to the border, Melanion. You must hear things. What chance do we have against the Macedonians?"

"It depends upon how badly you want to win," Melanion said. Even though he still smiled, Atalante saw that the smile didn't reach his eyes.

Korone swiveled her belt buckle impatiently. "What an uninformative answer from one who lives almost in the enemy's pocket," she said. "And useless to the men and women who intend to shed their blood for this state in the near future."

"What a penchant you have for stiff-necked pride," came a voice close to Atalante's ear. She could hear the smile in it.

"Nestor!" She turned and took both his hands. It was a relief to see him give her an open grin and know all was forgiven.

"You should have told me you were going to the mountains alone. I would have come with you, even if it meant giving up the pleasures of a soft couch to sleep on." He turned to Melanion, wrapping his arm about Atalante's waist, casually, as though he did it every day. As though she would allow such familiarity. Atalante glanced up at him quickly, wondering what particular scheme he was weaving in that clever brain of his.

"Is this your famous cousin?" Nestor asked lazily, pulling her an inch closer to him. Atalante tugged back to escape his hold but Nestor held on, smiling at her in a proprietary manner that made her want to shove her elbow into his ribs. Hard.

Melanion seemed to draw himself up even taller. His smile grew cold and assessing as he stared pointedly at the hand Nestor clamped about her waist.

Nestor bristled, the very imitation of an accepted suitor who senses a rival. Atalante squelched the urge to slap him. Showing her aggravation would only encourage Nestor to play more ridiculous games.

Nestor's gaze went from Melanion's face to Atalante's waist. He shrugged, gave her a squeeze, and withdrew his hand, only to bow politely to Melanion, who sent him a wary look, then inclined his head.

At least Nestor's foolishness had given Atalante the time and the temper she needed to speak with self-possession. She repeated the introduction, hoping that was the end to all mischief her friends were intent upon making.

Nestor's gaze returned to her face. "I expect you'll get a chance to see my team of blacks. Astrid's family bred and raised them. They're the fastest in Iolcus."

"Is that a challenge?" Atalante felt a grin tug the corners of her mouth. Scoundrel and clown that he was, Nestor still roused her to compete, much as a brother close in age would have done.

"Only if you have a team you think can best mine." Nestor's brow quirked, again teasing her, again luring her into their private competitive game.

"I'll stick to wrestling. Care to try again?"

"Not on your life." Nestor laughed and pulled her close enough to say in a mock whisper that traveled to the group, "However if you care to risk your cousin, I might have a go at him."

Melanion's hands curled into fists at his sides. From the first moment he'd spotted Atalante across the great hall, that blue gown clinging to every curve and hollow of her body, he had found it almost impossible to keep from grabbing hold of her wrist and pulling her away from the crush of courtiers. He wanted to explain to her clearly what she had accepted at the altar of Artemis Great Mother.

And flirtation with a handsome popinjay with three heavy gold chains around his neck and hands that clasped her waist in too familiar a manner was not any part of it.

"Look," said Korone. "They're bringing the food." She reached out for Melanion, tugging him toward a table filled with men and women his age. Melanion found himself seated next to Astrid on one side and Nestor on the other. A youth moved aside to make room for Korone on the bench across from Melanion. Someone called Atalante to the end of the table and pushed her into a seat before he could make room for her beside him on the bench. It irritated him that, with an amused laugh, she accepted the invitation.

Servants scurried among tables, carrying huge platters of roasted lamb and freshly baked bread. The banter among the young courtiers was free and jocular. Although table manners were excellent and the use of finger bowls and linen towels prevalent, the men and women at his table had the general air of students who might just start a food fight at any minute.

"We've been together since we were weaned," explained Astrid with a delicate lift of the brows when the teasing got somewhat rough. "We know each other's strengths and weaknesses, and believe me, nobody gets away with anything in this group."

"True," said Nestor. "But we also make a good fighting team, for we each know how to make up for what another may lack."

"Forgive me," Melanion said. "Are you saying that all the women at this table will fight?"

"Aye," said Korone, her brows drawn together in a frown. "What of it?"

"You'll be fighting an army comprised only of men.

What will happen when you confront men filled with battle rage? Are you aware of the horrors a marauding army can wreak on women they've caught?"

In the sudden silence, Korone rose slowly to her feet and leaned both hands on the table, bending toward him. Her arms shook from some strong emotion. "Women aren't the only creatures the beasts have caught and played with. Our men have been tortured to madness, then killed by slow degrees for no greater sin than hunting close to the border with Macedonia in a time of supposed peace. Do you think we'll allow those barbarians into our country without a fight when our fathers, our brothers . . ."

She put her fisted hand to her lips and spun, walking swiftly to the door.

"Her brother," Nestor said shortly. Suddenly, he was no longer the suave courtier, but a soldier, curt and intent. "Her twin. Slaughtered last year by a troop of Macedonians on our side of the border. Believe me, she'll fight."

"What is this talk of battle, when half of you have not been to the exercise grounds today?" Melanion heard a gruff voice from behind him and turned on the bench to see Miletus, commander of Thessaly's forces. Iasus had introduced them earlier in the week. "Less talk and more sweat is what Thessaly needs now."

Miletus glanced down at Melanion and clamped his right arm, lifting it to get a better look at the scar. "You've healed enough to wield a spear. Meet me tomorrow at dawn and I'll put you through your paces with the rest of the ephebes."

The next morning, Melanion stretched out his legs and arms before he left the exercise field. Muscles he'd not used for a month were sore from the workout, but he had been impressed with Miletus' training methods. Nestor stopped beside him, waiting for a word with him.

Melanion rubbed the knotting muscles in his right arm.

"Hurts, huh?" Nestor said. "I've got a liniment that'll take the ache out. Follow me to my rooms, and I'll get it for you."

Melanion gave him a long look. "Tell me first. What claim do you have on Atalante?"

Nestor raised a brow and affected a look of amusement, but there was heat in his eyes. "You take a rather possessive tone for a mere cousin, sir."

Melanion regarded him steadily. "I do not assume to hold Atalante in cousinly regard alone. What claim?" he asked again.

Nestor gave him a long look and jerked his chin once, as though he'd made a decision. "Friendship. She will permit nothing else."

Melanion nodded. "I'd be grateful for that liniment."

For a moment they walked along in silence.

Then Nestor cast a glance at him, almost a silent question. "What do you really think of the troop we've formed? Don't give me the answer I want to hear. Give me the truth."

Melanion took a deep breath. "You're strong. You'll fight like demons. But there aren't enough of you."

"They'll come, won't they?" Nestor said.

Melanion stared into the distance through the gates of the city. People were just beginning to set up their booths in the marketplace. Neighbors jostled each other and laughingly apologized for it. It seemed impossible that soon this plentiful peace would be turned to fire and devastation.

"Yes," he said. "Unless the Macedonian prince can convince his father otherwise."

Nestor stopped and held his gaze. "How possible do you think that is?"

Melanion looked back into brown eyes that saw more than most. "There's a chance—a slim one, and there's still some time before the summer. In the meantime, train as many soldiers as you can."

Melanion left Nestor's sumptuous rooms carrying a jar of liniment and an uneasy sense that the man knew more about him than he should. Nestor had already challenged him last night, when he held Atalante closer than was fitting. Now, the baron's son accepted him, as though he'd given himself over to a goal greater than personal desire.

*Friendship and nothing else,* Nestor had said. How much did he know? Had Atalante told him anything—everything?

Melanion knocked at Hyperion's open door. "Where's your sister?" he asked poking his head into the room.

Hyperion looked up from the clay soldiers he was stacking. "Father let you out already? She's meeting with Nestor."

"I see." Melanion scowled and turned to go.

"Wait! I want to talk to you anyway." Hyperion jumped off the bed and joined him in the corridor. "Here. This way."

He led the way outside then turned left and skirted the palace walls until he reached a tall hedge facing the ocean below. Dropping to his knees, he burrowed into the hedge like a ferret.

"Come on," he said.

Melanion dropped on all fours and followed through. In the narrow space between wall and hedge, Hyperion was standing and lighting a lamp. He pushed gently on the wall and it metamorphosed into a door that swung open sound-lessly.

"Come *on*," he said, and Melanion followed through.

"Atalante found it. It must have been built as an escape route for the royal family. They could climb down the cliff and take a fast ship if the palace was invaded." The lamp's flame bobbed, throwing their shadows high on the walls of the underground corridor.

"There's even a way straight to the Megaron. A secret door like the one we just entered, right behind the throne."

They came at last through the gloom to a rather large chamber holding a great shrine. Torchlight glimmered off walls of pure white, revealing an altar that stood at the far wall beneath a large statue of the Mother. She was formal and stiffly carved, unlike the serpents that wound at her feet or the bulls that lay at her side holding the moon in their horns. But an ancient power emanated from her, mixed with a gentler compassion. Melanion made the sign of reverence and turned to follow Hyperion, who stood watching him.

The boy led the way out of the shrine to a storage room full of chariots. Pushing aside dusty cobwebs, Hyperion sat down in a chariot of strong oak with intricate carvings on the sides and front. Melanion settled next to him, stretching his legs out on the floor behind the back of the chariot.

"I wanted you to see the Mother's shrine. You felt the strength there?"

"Yes. I felt it."

"If you're born of the House of the Serpent and you have the Sight, you go there many times to perform the rites. Sometimes, the Mother gives you a vision, but most of the time, you only get a headache from what the priests make you drink before you go in. Sometimes the vision is very clear, and many times, it's only a flash of a picture, or a scene.

"Three days after Atalante went to the mountains, I dressed in the holy robes and went to the sanctuary by myself. I didn't even tell Father. I drank the potion and performed the ritual. Then I asked the Mother to show me my sister. I wanted to make sure she was safe.

"I didn't see Atalante at all. Instead, I saw a great stag. It was so beautiful. It had golden antlers and hooves. When they struck the ground, they made fire.

"Suddenly, it sank to the ground, shot through with an arrow. I saw its blood spill out of its shoulder like a bright red river on a field of golden flowers. I asked the Mother, to what god or cause was such a magnificent creature sacrificed? But She was silent and sent me no more visions."

Melanion sat still as stone, the small hairs at the nape of his neck prickling. Hyperion looked at him solemnly, troubled questions shadowing his eyes.

"The night you came, I sat opposite you in the Megaron. When you stood beside Atalante, I saw golden antlers of the stag molded right into the hair on your head and you became the stag. Melanion. I hadn't drunk the potion, but I saw clearly."

Hyperion gently brushed the scar on Melanion's arm, and his fingers gave off an odd charge against the meat of his muscle. "Why were you the sacrifice for Thessaly, Melanion? For I know the Mother's worship is forbidden in Macedon, yet She knows you, and follows your fate. Does She speak to you?"

Melanion shook his head, then paused, as a picture of a bright, hot day filled his mind. "Someone spoke to me— once, at school. I'd made a bet, a stupid, reckless wager with an older boy who constantly challenged me. I bet all my coins for the term that I could dive into a pool at the base of a very high cliff. I was angry, restless. Things at

106

home had been . . . difficult."

It all rushed back to him—the feel of the sun on his back, his friend Theas arguing with him, the older boy and his gang sauntering over to make the bet.

Theas had grabbed his arm, trying to stop him, but he'd walked to the edge of the cliff without a qualm. Pausing at the edge of the precipice, he'd shut his eyes.

"Great Mother, take me to Your home beneath the waters," he'd whispered. He sprang, arching off the edge of the cliff and dove down, down into the abyss, thrilling with the light and shadow speeding past him, the cold spray and thunder rush of the waterfall. He was an arrow flying straight at the center of the pool.

As he hit, the force of the water stunned him. He cut deep into the mere, the water ringing in his ears. The world turned black and he welcomed the darkness.

But a voice in the darkness mocked him. "For shame, son of the Lion, to seek the easy way. Live and struggle."

A force greater than his own helped to push him upward, out of the darkness. His lungs strained to hold on and he shoved with a great heave of legs against the water's resistance. The air rushed into him and when he opened his eyes, the light blinded him. He had not felt full of fresh purpose, or fervent with a sense of the Divine. He had only returned to his studies and eventually to his father, understanding that he could never take the easy way out.

"My friend Theas wouldn't speak to me for a week. It was the first time that I realized I affected more than my own pitiful existence."

"Was that when you became the leader of those boys?"

Melanion shrugged. "They were my friends already, especially Theas and three others. But after that, I saw a way to do more, and tried to do it. I felt—caught in something I didn't understand. But I was driven to play out my part with honor. That's my biggest fear, Hyperion—that I'll choose the wrong part, because there are so many contradictions. If I could see my loyalties clearly, I would rest easier."

The boy clasped his arm. "I'll ask, and I'll listen to my dreams as carefully as I examine the visions."

Melanion felt the goose bumps rise on his skin. He'd been so wrapped up in discussing these matters that it never occurred to him until now that he was revealing his soul to an eight-year-old boy with the uncanny power of the Sight, a gift he didn't understand.

Hyperion gave him a sidelong glance. "I believe there's one more thing to discuss before you find my sister," he said.

Melanion gave a bark of laughter. "Haven't we had enough for one day?"

"I don't think so. You'll be leaving soon—probably tomorrow. You must ask Atalante to run with you at dawn in the hills above Iolcus. You must ask her why she never looks into a mirror." Hyperion jumped up and started for the door of the chariot room. "Better hurry up," he called over his shoulder. "We'll be late for dinner."

The hills around Iolcus were alive with birdsong in the dawn light. Melanion had managed to speak with Atalante at table the night before. He'd actually caused her to blush when he reached for her arm and pulled her down to sit beside him. As though she, too, had sensed that his time in Iolcus was coming to an end, she'd given him her full attention, albeit with downcast eyes. When he asked her to run with him in the morning, she'd accepted without argument.

She was in high spirits this morning, teasing to the point

of recklessness. She ran ahead of him, breathing light and steady, then returned to run circles around him, showing off. Saucy as a yearling mare kicking up her heels, she returned again, thumbing her nose. Before he could attempt a sprint to catch her, she'd flown ahead, disappearing into the trees. He ran steadily, breathing hard, glad to feel the healthy pull of muscle and sinew in arms and legs.

She must have determined that he'd had enough, for she returned and slowed to a walk. He bent forward, gulping great breaths of air. As they walked side by side, they came to a clear pool. Atalante knelt beside it and drank. Melanion cupped the water in his hands. It was cold, pure, and sweet.

"You'd better keep this up if you want a chance at the laurel next spring," she said. "Even if you work all winter, I'll probably take you in the sprint." Her eyes gleamed like sapphires at the thought. It seemed that neither of them wanted to think ahead beyond the spring. Just for this day, the dawn's beautiful promise forbade dark thoughts.

"Not in archery, and certainly not in wrestling," said Melanion. Just as he'd hoped, she rose to the bait.

"You think not, Macedonian! I've had practice throwing oafs as large as you."

He rose to his feet and arched a brow at her.

"Try me," he challenged. His arms beckoned, and he wagered she'd answer the challenge rather quickly.

She didn't disappoint him. Atalante lunged from her crouch, counting on the element of surprise. She jabbed for his left ankle with her foot, but he dodged handily and they circled each other. When she came in low for the knee, he anticipated the move and swooped her up in his arms. She kicked and squealed, laughing, all warrior gone and all girl for the moment. Melanion tumbled her to the ground and followed her down, pinning her beneath his body. Laughing, he pressed his length against her. In the silence that followed, he could hear her breathing hard, and knew he was doing the same thing. Neither one of them moved. She stared at him, wary, then lowered her lashes.

"Oof, what a move! You'll show me the way of it, now, won't you?" she said, attempting a light tone while looking somewhere in the direction of his collarbone. Her voice came out in a breathy whisper.

Melanion refused to be put off. He could feel the softness of her breasts crushed beneath his chest, the firm curve of her hips. He ached. It was so evident that even a recently initiated virgin couldn't mistake it. He bent his head and covered her lips in a hard, branding kiss.

Atalante made a low sound, perhaps of protest, but he didn't care. He kissed her again more softly, his tongue teasing at the corner of her mouth, and heard her sigh as her lips parted, letting him in. She was pliant and warm beneath him. It was all he could do not to devour her. He tasted the curve of her throat, sweet scent and salt in the hollow between shoulder and neck. And he breathed in the mysterious musk of desire. She clung to him and gasped softly.

He wanted her here—on the springy grass surrounding the little pool. He could take her. Thank the gods, she was willing.

He lifted his head to look at her, to let her know this was the consent he had been waiting for from her. To take this day with him, for all the nights he would need to remember her pledge. Her face was flushed and her eyes were the deep, dreamy blue of a midnight sky.

He didn't want her surrender. He wanted her knowing acceptance, an entirely different thing. Thus, everything between them must be clear. "I have to leave today," he said. "I want this to happen between us under the open sky, with your full consent. Like the last time."

Her gaze sharpened, narrowed. She shoved against him with both fists, and it was no love tap she gave him.

"Like the last time?" She rolled away from beneath him, jumped up, and strode from the clearing. With a lunge, he caught her by the elbow and whirled her around to face him.

She looked fierce and stubborn. He felt it return—that bewilderment, that anger he'd felt at her rejection after they'd pledged themselves, and again the night of the banquet.

"Lie to me all you want," he said, grabbing her wrist to keep her from running. "You felt something, now and on the mountain. It's that fussy popinjay, isn't it? You want me to release you—for *Nestor?*

Her mouth dropped open. "Nestor?" She shook her head. "You must be daft. Nestor likes the pretty girls. He'd never . . . And even if he did, I should not want him. He's my friend, not my lover." Her eyes burned, her lips curled, scornful. Beneath it, she had a hunted look, as though she were bracing for—what? Humiliation? Rejection of some sort?

The heat of anger left him as suddenly as it had sprung up, and Hyperion's advice came into his mind from nowhere.

"Why don't you use a mirror?" he heard himself ask.

"What?"

"Why don't you look in a mirror? Hyperion charged me to ask you."

"I see." Her lips quivered. "And if my brother tells you to do so, I must answer." She pulled free and turned away

111

from him, but she couldn't disguise the hollowness of her voice.

"Before the goddess marked me, I was apparently a rather vain child. I liked pretty clothes. I had a beautiful polished bronze mirror and after my nurse dressed me, I would run to see how I looked."

Atalante turned slowly and raised her hand to touch the scar. "After I received this, my mother was at a loss as to how to deal with me. I am sure my parents worried over the problem as soon as it happened, because I was an only child, and used to my pleasant life of admiration and petting. How were they to tell me of the change in my appearance without breaking my spirit? For I was to be Artemis' warrior, her huntress and runner, not a pretty girl that Nestor would flirt with. Not a princess whom my father could give in marriage to some wealthy king." Her voice was cool, distant, but he heard the quaver beneath it.

"When I was still recovering from the effects of the drug I had taken and from the goddess' touch, my mother went to Delphi to petition the god. The oracle told her I must never look into a mirror again, or words to that effect. I knew then that the change in my appearance must have been rather horrifying."

She stared down at her hands. "I had another indication, as well. My mother . . . changed toward me at that time. She was always good to me. But there were no more hugs, or special days together. Of course," she hurried on, "I had my father's approval, and that was more than enough for me. And then Mother had Hyperion to worry about. He was sick from birth."

He had noticed the difference in Clymene's manner toward Atalante and Hyperion. With Atalante, she was kind, but cool. But she clucked and fussed over Hyperion like a tender hen over her favorite chick.

Atalante shrugged. "Since that day, I never have been tempted to look at myself, and my family has helped me deal with my disfiguration. There are no bronze mirrors in the palace."

"Has no man ever asked for you?"

"Haven't you been listening?" She gave him a look that clearly questioned either his hearing or his intelligence.

"Yes. I still want to know. Has any man asked for your hand?"

"Some. They came themselves to look at me. And what a surprise—the first thing each one stared at was my face, particularly my scarred forehead. I watched them approach me, looking hard at it every time. Sometimes I think they came simply to see if the rumors about my poor, ruined face were true. Some of them practically ran from the Megaron, muttering about how they dared not take the goddess' favorite. A few, particularly the more powerful kings, were very good at pretense. They remained and sued for my hand."

She gave a mirthless laugh. "Some of these actually told me how beautiful I was. One had a bard sing of it to me at a feast in his honor. You can imagine how I felt, sitting in the Hall, compelled by honor to remain and hear all of that . . . infamy."

"How did you feel?" he asked softly.

"I was furious. I wanted to kill the blasted liar."

She didn't look furious, he thought, and his heart twisted. She looked devastated.

"If these men insisted on pursuing you, how is it you're not some high king's wife?" he asked, but gently, clasping her wrist again. Her free hand fussed with the folds of her chiton.

She gave a hollow little laugh. "I told them they could have me if they could outrace me. None ever did."

"I see." And finally, he did.

By the god's will, she wasn't permitted to see herself, and it was obvious now what she thought of her looks. And anything he did or said to mitigate the misery she felt might turn the god against them both. He thought of the king who'd praised her beauty and recognized what her reaction would be if he said even, "You are beautiful to me." He would send her running in the other direction, forever.

He suppressed the urge to howl in frustration and took a step closer. As soon as he raised his hands to her cheeks, Atalante froze like the ground in winter. She turned her head away, but he wasn't going to stop. His fingers stroked the scar and her winged brow, then the delicate skin on her lids, learning the feel of her face. They drifted across the high bones and the softness of her cheeks, and her lips. With finger and thumb, he turned her chin up. "Look at me," he said in a voice that would brook no disobedience.

She opened her eyes, and they burned with unshed tears and defiance.

"I'll wait for you. For as long as it takes you to understand."

She gazed straight up at him, a princess and a war leader. "You have no obligation to do that."

"No obligation! Woman, you'll drive me mad." He shook her lightly. "Never forget. You belong to me. The goddess who marked you chose you for me. Nothing—no god, no war—can separate us. And just as the stars circle in their course each night, I'll be back for you."

He bent to her again, letting her see his purpose, and laid his mouth upon hers. And kissed her until they both were breathless, and all the sounds of the earth receded into a hush. When he broke the kiss, her eyes burned with a hot, blue flame, and she stared at him as though she were branding his face on her memory, along with his command.

"Good," he said, and gave her one curt nod. He held out his hand imperiously. Without a word, she slipped her hand into his clasp, and they walked toward Iolcus together.

# Chapter 6

## The Red Bands

There's a strange objectivity that comes with travel. What was once familiar and unexamined stood out bright as a new painted mural to Melanion on his return home.

He saw the soil of Macedonia and realized how thin and rocky it was compared to the rich, black earth of Thessaly. The rags of the Macedonian poor were little protection against the northern wind compared to the sturdy wools of the Thessalian helots he had passed just a day ago. And the begging urchins surrounding the black stallion he rode tore at his heart. The glaring differences oppressed him long before he saw the mountains surrounding Hamalclion.

It was evening when he reached the capital. A light snow fell, dusting the cloaks of the guards who let him pass with friendly greetings as he made his way to the palace. Handing his horse to a groom, Melanion walked into the smoky Great Hall. The scar on his shoulder still throbbed, especially in the chill of night. The last thing he wanted was a fuss over the wound, and all the questions that would follow his father's initial worry. He kept his chlamys on; the short cloak hid it from curious eyes.

The steward caught sight of him and strode to the dais where Kryton drank with some of his generals. When the steward bent and whispered in the king's ear, Kryton rose eagerly from his seat and strode to meet Melanion.

He knelt before his father, felt Kryton lift him by the

shoulders and throw his burly arms about him. Pain shot
through the wound. Melanion stiffened against it, and his
father stepped back, his mouth set tight in what looked to
be fury.

Melanion gritted his teeth. The throbbing ebbed a bit as
he studied Kryton's face and saw that the king was suffering
himself from some kind of pain. Maybe pondering
Atalante's confusing behavior gave him a deeper understanding, for suddenly he knew that his father had inter-
preted his action as a rejection.

Melanion did what he never would have done willingly
before. He took his father's right hand and placed it on his
own heart. It was a relief, after Kryton's initial look of
stunned surprise, to see the lines of disappointment ease on
the king's face.

"Back from the wild lands, are you? And safe, no thanks
to the guards I set to follow you. Slipped them right away,
didn't you?" His father was grinning now, clapping him on
the back, for which Melanion and his shoulder were
grateful.

"Where have you been, boy?" asked the king, turning to
the table to pour him a cup of wine with his own hands.
"Not hurt, are you?"

"Nothing that a little exercise won't cure. Father, I need
to talk to you. Privately."

"Not when you're stiff from the journey, eh?" Kryton
looked him over critically, like a fussy nurse. "You've lost
weight, Melanion. You need a warm bath, feeding up, and
then rest." He motioned to a server. "Hey, woman! Make
up a bath and fetch the oils and salts for my son. Send for
the herb woman and be quick about it.

"So. But first, I've a surprise for you. Hey!" He summoned another slave, who bowed low to both of them.

"Rouse the Companions. Bring them into Hall. Hurry up!"

"Companions?" Melanion pictured a group of hatchet-faced guards assigned to follow him and told that to lose him would be worth their lives. How was he to return to Iolcus before spring if he was spied upon with the vigilance inspired by a death sentence?

"That's right, boy," Kryton told him, beaming. "Just for you. Are you happy?"

"I'm fine by myself. Really. I need to talk to you, Father. And I'd rather not put up with . . ."

Kryton's bluff voice took on a note of steel. "Things've changed in the time you've been gone. Traitors strike from every end of the realm. You're in peril more than anyone, maybe more than me, even. I've sent for men you can trust with your life. By Hades, they were loyal to you before they could see any profit in it. They'll protect you now."

His father's arm snaked around Melanion's head and pulled him close as his voice hissed in his ear. "By the gods, you go nowhere without them. Do you understand?"

Melanion nodded wordlessly.

The king gave a snort of satisfaction. "That's all right, then. Here—look sharp! They tumble into the Hall like a pack of green hounds ready for training. I leave it to you to drill them into shape."

Melanion took a step forward as he stared at the twenty young men eagerly striding into the Megaron. A slow grin broke out on his face as he recognized the friends of his youth.

"Melanion!" A familiar voice shouted. "When did you get here? We've been waiting for days." Philip, white blond like the northern tribesmen, with ice-blue eyes and a build like Heracles, strode forward, followed by the rest, that now-grown gang of boys who had followed him soon after he'd entered Myron's school.

"I told you he'd return safe, you idiot. Philip thought you'd come to grief alone in the mountains." Before him stood gray-eyed Theas, dearest of all. With his steady mind and unswerving sense of honor, Theas gifted him with logic when he was most inclined to be too reckless.

"I did not," said Philip in answer to Theas' set-down. "I just got bored. Snow for three days, and nowhere to go. The waiting made me itch for a full blown war." In the year since Melanion had seen him, Philip had grown even more. Standing with hands on hips and a scowl directed at Theas, Philip looked so formidable only a fool or a friend would challenge him.

"You damned know-it-all," Philip muttered to Theas. "You're the one who said we'd organize a search party if he didn't get back tomorrow."

"That was just to keep you from tearing down the palace, you great lug." Theas' clear gaze rested on Melanion, and his lips curved again in quiet welcome. "How do you fare, friend?"

"I'm well. And you?"

"Quite well. Now." Hands clasped arms, and Melanion's spirit lightened.

Niko wormed his way in beside Philip and stood tall as he could next to the giant. "I've grown. Six whole inches."

"So you have." Melanion tactfully neglected to add that the rest of them had also grown, with the result that Niko was still the smallest of the group. However, he was well muscled, and his movements were, as always, the quick and clever dodges of a wrestler.

"Move over." Alex shoved Niko to the side and stuck his head into the circle of friends. As suited the bard of the gang, his features had grown even more dramatic. Alex's eyes were a deeper violet and his hair the color of Astrid's, now—a shining mop of pure gold. The ever-present lyre hung over one shoulder.

They were clear-eyed and fresh, not one past twenty years of age. Melanion looked from one to the other slowly.

These could be brothers to the men and women I met at Iolcus, he thought. Iasus would say a ruler could build a shining civilization with a kingdom of such youths.

They crowded around him, pushing against each other.

"Come sit with me." Melanion motioned to a table below the dais of rough oak with benches on each side. Behind him, his father spoke a word to a slave, who brought a small chair of inlaid ivory to the head of the table and bowed toward him.

"Father." Melanion turned to Kryton, filled with emotions he couldn't completely understand.

"No need to say anything." Kryton's voice was gruff and his grin wobbled a bit. He cleared his throat and gave Melanion a push in the direction of the table. "Best begin at once with that pack. Going to take a lot to get them into shape."

As a slave brought cups and poured out a warm and spicy smelling wine, Melanion looked down the table at twenty pairs of eyes all fixed on him. "What have you been told about your duties?" he asked.

"Why, to protect you, with our lives. When you are about the palace, or when you leave for the mountains, we're to go with you," said Philip.

"The king worried when you went away for so long. He was adamant that we accompany you on any trips you might take. Personally," Theas lowered his voice, "I think your worst threat is in Hamalclion."

Melanion felt the confines of the palace settle like a shroud. Iolcus with its unguarded corridors and its trustworthy courtiers was very far away. "Did you take an oath of any kind?"

"Your father demanded that we take one. But only to you, and none other. Not even to the king, himself," said Alex.

Melanion saw his father across the smoky hall, bent over the table. Polymus, looking more forceful than before, stood and spoke. It seemed that the generals swayed in time to his gestures. In only one month, Kryton's beard looked greyer. The lines about his mouth and eyes cut deeper.

Why? He wondered, staring at his father. Why did you give me a guard pledged to me alone? What are you saying? He wished the anger would come and erase this softening, but all he could feel was confusion when his father glanced his way and grinned at him.

The conflict between them was far from over. The man who seemed to trust him would crush Atalante's people beneath his heel unless Melanion could stop him.

He had to fight against his father's resentment and ambition. He must, or all that he honored—his integrity, his oath to his mother, Iolcus' rich civilization—was lost. A vision of horror rose in his mind—Atalante, lying dead on the plain of Iolcus after a fierce and bloody battle. He raised his head and scanned the small, upright army looking up at him, trusting him to shape them to his own sense of honor. He would *not* let it happen.

"Well, then," he said to his men. "We'll renew our vows before the gods, and make a beginning." To himself, he thought, *Tomorrow. I'll find a way to reach him tomorrow.*

"Hold on!" Theas grabbed Melanion's arm later that night. He pulled away and plowed forward through the corridor. As the others pounded after him, he shook his head in exasperation and wheeled at Theas.

"Can't a man walk in the halls of an armed fortress without a bodyguard of twenty dogging his heels? I need to think for a few minutes on the parapets. Could I kindly do it alone?" He'd left his rooms just a moment ago to plan his meeting with Kryton the next day, only to find the Companions racing after him down the hallway. By this time, he was surrounded on all sides—again.

Theas jerked his chin to the right. "Your answer's over there."

A beefy six-foot man leaned against a doorway that led out to an alley behind the exercise yard. He wore leather breeches and a slow, stubborn stare. As they passed, he saluted at the last possible moment with a sly smile. The gesture was an affront. A bright red band circled the meaty biceps of his left arm.

"Polymus' private guard," said Theas with a frown. "He must have searched the brothels and alleys of Greece for the swill he's brought here. Oh, but they're loyal to him. He's promised them gold and spoils once they've taken Thessaly."

"I see." Melanion had a fearsome vision of Atalante imprisoned and surrounded by animals like the one they'd just passed.

Theas, thinking out loud, slowed his walk. "Question is, how far will they go for their great leader Polymus? Would they kill the king's son for him?"

Melanion halted in mid-stride and stared at him.

"Surely, you've understood what that snake wants?"

Melanion gave a sharp nod.

"It would be so easy," Theas went on meditatively. "A fall from the palace ramparts, a stab wound in the citadel . . ."

Theas' hand clasped his shoulder. "I'm afraid you're

stuck with us all, until the gods or some clever twists of fate rid you of this inconvenience. I take it that you have a few things still to do before you're content to die?"

Thus next morning he awoke behind a bolted door, with twenty prone men twitching and snoring in sleep. Amusing, though, how knowing a man wanted him dead did wonders for the quality of his life. For breakfast, he knew he'd have a hearty appetite for food tasted beforehand, he would run and exercise in the afternoon, and now he carefully planned what he would say to his father this night. And when dreams came to him, he had a feeling they would not be the nightmare again, but more like the one he'd had the night before. He smiled, remembering a runner's long, slender limbs wrapped around him in abandon, and her soft cry of surrender and ecstasy.

In the Hall that evening, Melanion studied the generals gathered at the board. Some members of the old guard were gone, and new men with crafty, smooth expressions had taken their place. Polymus and his red-haired son, Xuthus, sat in a place of honor. The redhead had the same hawk-like eyes as his father. He wore a robe of Syrian blue embroidered in gold and red thread. Even Nestor would have hooted at its gaudiness.

Polymus lounged in his chair, playing with the heavy gold chain of rank that hung from his neck. When he made a joke, many at table laughed uproariously. Xuthus' eyes slid from face to face, noting who remained silent. Several men glanced uneasily from Kryton's face to Polymus'.

Finally, Kryton rose. "I'll take wine in my chambers with my son," he said, motioning to the Companions. They rose as one to follow while the company bowed them out. Kryton slung an arm about Melanion's injured shoulder as they climbed the stairway. What bothered Melanion wasn't the pain, but the fact that his father's weight rested heavily on him. How much had Kryton aged in the last month?

The Companions fanned out about the outer doorway as he entered Kryton's chamber and escorted him to his seat. The king dismissed the slave who'd followed him in with the wine. Drinking deeply, he gestured with the cup for Melanion to be seated. His face was flushed, and as he relaxed, it took on the old expressions of cunning, command, and charm.

"I watched you with the troops today," he said. "You have the makings of a fine warlord."

"Not like you, Father." It was true. Kryton had a rough charisma that the warriors loved. His men would follow him anywhere.

Kryton drained the cup and poured out more for himself and Melanion. "The men say the cub favors the lion. By late spring, you'll command a great force on the right wing."

"And Polymus?"

"The left."

Melanion squared his shoulders. "I know a way to share the riches of Thessaly without a man dying."

Kryton stretched his legs in front of him. His eyes glinted in amusement. "And how the hell would you manage that?"

Melanion leaned forward eagerly. "Make a marriage. Between me and the princess Atalante. She's unwed, but of the right age. We could easily avoid all the misery ahead."

His father lurched to his feet, knocking the wine cup to the floor. He strode to the door. It shuddered on its hinges as his fist crashed against it. Melanion leaped up, his fists clenched at his sides. When he whirled on Melanion, Kryton's eyes were as red as his face—he looked like a monster ready to strike.

"That bastard Iasus and his queen Clymene—she especially despised me. I can still feel her cold eyes on me at the wedding feast. They fought against me from the beginning of my suit. Right after the wedding, Iasus told Cleon to send me back without my bride. In front of me and all my men, the pig."

Kryton pounded his fist against the wall again. His knuckles bled.

"They didn't know me at all, but they took one look at me and treated me like a piece of scum. Like an animal! And do you think that son of a bitch would accept my suit for his daughter, boy? If it hadn't been for the two of them, maybe your mother would have learned to accept . . ." Kryton bowed his head and covered it with his hands.

Melanion didn't know where to look. A long moment passed. Then the king wiped his face with both hands and turned to his son. "Well, that was long ago. But that pissy old man will look down his nose at me for as long as he lives—which, I swear to you, won't be long. So put that idea out of your head, Melanion. It won't work." Kryton motioned for Melanion to sit again and picked up the overturned wine cup. Wearily, he slumped back into his seat, staring into the cup.

Melanion's head whirled. His father's feelings for Iasus went much deeper than resentment. How had Thessaly's wise king been so foolish to insult another monarch to that extent? It was surprising that Kryton hadn't invaded Thessaly the spring after his wedding. Had he stayed his hand all those years out of consideration for Melanion's mother?

His father's mouth clamped in a grim line, but his eyes told another story. Shadowed by ghosts, bewildered by hurts too old and deep to name, Kryton seemed almost fragile.

How could he say to his father, "Yes, I have been in your enemy's home for the last two weeks. I have betrayed and hurt you in every way with him—I even thought of foreswearing my vow of loyalty to you. And, oh yes, he may despise you, but he'll accept me. He may have humiliated you at your own wedding, but he'll dance at mine."

He looked at the lined, craggy face brooding over the wine. The silent, passing minutes stretched him taut as a bowstring in his fear for Thessaly. If he couldn't avert disaster immediately, at least he could begin by ridding both nations of Polymus.

"Father," he said at last, thinking of the generals who would at least keep their troops from the worst atrocities. "Where are Myron and Tyrenos, and Dion, and—"

Kryton waved his hand airily. "Polymus urged me to send them back to their estates. He thinks they're good for battle, but too squeamish to plan a winning campaign. When they return in the spring with their armies, they'll follow orders, like all good soldiers."

"I know what plans he has for Thessaly. I watched tonight. There are still many men who'd cheer loud and long if you broke with him before the campaign. And the force he commands, the Red Bands. Get rid of them before they grow too strong. Even now, they're like the heads of the hydra."

Kryton's fist crashed down on the arm of the chair. "I *need* him."

"You can't trust him. Listen to me."

Kryton's face relaxed into a grin. "Dismiss him because I can't trust him? Oh, Melanion! You've the soul of a priest. It must come from your mother's side. The gods know mine were all plotters from the days we were horse tamers."

He poured out another cup of wine and passed the

pitcher to Melanion. "You think I don't know that viper plans to see my shade in hell after I take Thessaly? That he would find a way to slide a knife between your ribs before we even enter the south? Why do you think I sent for the Companions—to keep you company while you drink and wench?

"Pah! I've held this kingdom against harder cases while you were robbing beehives with the rest of those boys you've got around you now. Talk about not trusting. What's wrong? Do you think I've lost my touch—that the old man can't outsmart a piece of horse shit like Polymus?"

"Father. He's surrounding himself with an army of thugs. He gains power with the generals every day. I'm not the only one worried that he'll win this game."

"They should all understand. I'll take every ounce of strength Polymus can give me, and I'll win in the end." Kryton's eyes held Melanion's gaze. They burned into him.

"Don't ever forget, boy. I am king. My will and my grasp are stronger than any man's. And if I will this victory, not even you can stop me."

Kryton's face relaxed into a smile. "Now out with you. I've got a late supper with a beautiful woman. Don't want to keep her waiting."

It only took walking through Hamalclion for Melanion to see the rot eating the kingdom. The Red Bands roved everywhere and the people were afraid. The marketplace was eerily quiet. Vendors sold only the barest necessities— sour wine and plain bread dipped in low grades of olive oil heretofore used only for cleansing after exercise.

The people's faces were pinched and hungry. When Melanion reviewed the palace records, he found that the citizens had been taxed almost beyond endurance to supply the growing army camped around the palace.

Kryton dismissed his objections with an airy wave of his hand. "A half empty belly now will make them fall all over themselves to thank us after we conquer the south with her rich harvest."

Melanion drilled his small guard and pushed them beyond themselves. He saw them stand the taller for it. They sent home for brothers and cousins, who came to the city to form an army under his command, ostensibly to win glory in the campaign, but more, he soon realized in gratitude, to present a show of force against the swelling ranks of the Red Bands.

Melanion saw them for what they were—green and excitable, but honest. They longed for glory and a bright path to follow. Melanion sent them about the citadel in night patrols to protect the people from Polymus' brutes. He kept them on the exercise field for hours because they had to become strong as well as quick. Many of the Red Bands were beefy towers, difficult to overwhelm by force but slow-witted.

There were about a hundred of these youths gathered around Melanion at first. Even after their ranks tripled, they were called "the Hundred."

The commander's chamber was dark save a single lamp that burned low. The soldier stood in the doorway peering into the darkness.

"Shut the door, Simeon." The voice came from a corner of the room, sibilant and soft as a whisper. The small hairs on the Red Band's arms rose at the sound.

"Walk to the lamp." The soldier shuffled forward uncertainly until he stood beside the light. After the darkness, the light made him squint. He definitely couldn't see the figure shrouded in the darkness. He was sweating like a pig and hoped it wasn't showing in the lamplight.

"Do you know why I sent for you?" The soft voice set the soldier's teeth on edge. "There's a problem. I am sure you can solve it for me."

"Yes, sir." He croaked, half strangled with tension, and swallowed bile.

"You are aware that nothing ever escapes my eye."

"Yes, sir."

"I am concerned about the prince. He's surrounded by a gang of thugs these days. Wouldn't you agree?"

The Red Band let out the breath he'd been holding and moved slowly from animal terror to relief. The commander wasn't about to kill him.

"They hound us, Commander. They got no respect."

"Yes." The word was a hiss. "It grieves me to see my men in such danger from these bandits. And you, Simeon. I hear you're excellent with a knife."

The Red Band straightened his shoulders and stood at attention. "I am that, sir."

"Perhaps you can think of a way to rid us of these inter-lopers—something that happens naturally. An insult from one of them, for instance, that must be answered with blood."

The Red Band caught the drift and pumped his head up and down. "Yes, sir. I can do that."

He could feel the fine chill of Polymus' smile as it reached out to him in the dark. "I'm sure you can." The commander waved dismissal and he bolted for the door.

At the sound of that sibilant voice again, the soldier's hand froze on the latch. "I'll be watching, Simeon. The man who gives me satisfaction is never forgotten." Through an ominous pause, the Red Band tried to keep his shaking at bay. "And neither is the man who disappoints me."

★ ★ ★ ★ ★

As the weeks drew on, the earth in Hamalclion turned iron hard and cold underfoot. Winter forced the Companions into the confines of the palace. The Megaron was full of soldiers and guards who gamed, ate, drank, and often slept there. Several of the old generals and their troops from northern Macedonia came into the capital for the winter, as well. These threaded their way between the two camps of Companions and Red Bands.

The newcomers were tough. Seasoned from border skirmishes and cattle raids to the north and east, they were bluff, but honest. Melanion liked their rough humor and their wild dancing on winter nights, when their oiled bodies gleamed in the firelight. They drew blue kohl around their eyes and on their cheeks beneath the slits of their helmets.

Polymus strolled the Megaron with his son Xuthus and a guard of Red Bands on this particular winter morning. He stopped to speak to a group of northern soldiers near the fireplace just as young Niko passed by. A hulking guard with tiny eyes and a scar searing one side of his face lurched forward as Niko passed him.

With a roar, the Red Band threw Niko to the floor with enough force to crack bone. Melanion ran through the crowd, trying to get to Niko's side as the Red Band straddled the boy. Philip was nearer and struck just as the soldier's hammy fist ripped into Niko's face.

Philip's arm locked around the Red Band's throat. He shouted to Melanion to drag Niko out of danger.

Pandemonium broke out in the Hall. It took both Melanion and Theas to drag a sputtering, struggling Niko out of the circle of men surrounding them.

"My fight!" Niko shouted. "I can take him, damn you."

"Shut up," hissed Theas. "If Philip is lucky, he'll down

him. You, we'd be burying tomorrow."

Niko struggled against their restraining arms and yelled to Philip. "Let be! This is none of your business."

Philip, elbowed in the kidneys by the flailing Red Guard, grunted and redoubled his efforts.

The two camps were shouting and seizing whatever weapons were handy. As they tore shields and spears from the walls, the northerners formed a circle around the pair struggling on the floor. Melanion managed to shove his way into the circle, but brawny arms held him back from the heaving figures.

" 'Tis a fair fight, Cub," said one grizzled veteran.

Philip flipped his body like a big fish landing on shore and lay hard across the Red Band, pinning his arms to the floor. The man kicked and wriggled, but his ragged breath revealed ebbing strength.

"If we end it here, you leave with your life," said Philip through his teeth.

The man nodded and Philip eased his grip. He went to his hands and knees, shaking the blonde hair out of his eyes. Silver flashed beneath him. As Philip rolled, the knife grazed his belly, leaving behind a thin trickle of blood. With a full-throated cry of rage, he grabbed the wrist holding the blade. The crack of bone echoed through the silent hall.

Philip flipped the Red Band face down on the cold stones. He shoved his knee into the guard's back and grabbed him by his long hair. The Red Band's throat arched. Melanion saw the man's face. Except for the dull red of the scar, it was white as chalk.

Philip's knife flashed in the torchlight. The Red Band choked as blood spurted from his neck in gushing waves. In a moment, his struggles ceased. His head lolled over

Philip's forearm. The young giant shoved the body aside with a grunt. He spat and rose.

Shouts clashed in the Megaron. Polymus had Kryton's arm, and he shouted something in the king's ear. Melanion tensed as he saw the outrage on Kryton's face. The king strode toward the circle of northerners and broke through. Philip stood panting above the Red Band's body. The knife dripped in his hand.

Kryton's face seeped with red from his neck to his hairline. "I've seen scuffles in the Megaron before, but no man's done murder until now. I understand your man attacked Polymus' bodyguard for no reason and slew him. What say you?"

The northerners looked from the king to Melanion with a certain expectation. Melanion made a quick decision and prayed it was the right one. "Ask these men, Father," he said calmly. "They saw it from the beginning."

"Well?" said Kryton roughly. "Speak."

"Not him, Majesty," said one, pointing to Philip. "T'was the other one—the one dead."

"Deserved it, he did. Snuck a knife on 'im when it was to be fists." Rough voices rose from all sides and Philip was taken in, clapped on the back, and made to drink neat wine from somebody's goatskin. His hands shook as he raised the skin and gulped the wine.

Kryton stared at Philip for a long moment and nodded. "His first kill," he said, half to himself. "Find him a woman tonight," he told Melanion. "Somebody young and still unused enough to be kind, if there's such a thing in this palace. He'll need to forget."

The grizzled veteran who'd spoken for Philip gave his king a look of pride and approval. Melanion knew this man would die for Kryton at a moment's notice. The soldier turned his gaze on him and jerked his head in the direction of the men toasting Philip.

"A word, Cub. Don't worry about us. But don't turn your back on that crowd there." He looked towards the Red Bands gathered in a corner whispering to Xuthus.

"He knows," said Kryton. He and the soldier exchanged a silent conversation with a long look, in which a promise was asked and given. Melanion knew then that the northerners would defend not only his father, but him as well, with their lives.

Kryton took him by the elbow and walked to an empty corner of the hall. He spoke in a low voice.

"This blasted weather makes for too many men in a small space. Take your lads to the mountains until all this is forgotten. Keep them busy. Keep them fit. Who knows what they'll have to do someday to protect you?"

He stroked his beard, thinking. "Go southeast to Kalydon, if you want. Oineas has been nagging me for months to help him get rid of a boar destroying his vineyards. Now he's sent through Greece for men to hunt it down. War leaders, the sons of kings, are coming from everywhere. It'll do you good to know these men. Someday you'll have to treat with them. When better to begin than now, when you're all young and out to prove your worth to each other?"

Melanion felt the whole world expand. Freedom and Thessaly beckoned. "All right. Tomorrow, then. I'll take the Companions and leave the Hundred here under someone I can trust. I'll get busy now and set up everything."

"Good," said Kryton. As Melanion turned to go, the king grabbed his arm. Melanion turned once more to face him. "Someday, it won't be like this. When you come home after we've won Thessaly, you'll bring your sons, maybe even your wife. We'll talk—we'll have the time then. After Thessaly, everything will be better."

Clouds scudded across a winking sun as the Companions climbed into the southern mountains. They rode for much of the day in an uneasy silence. Niko, usually bound to Philip, studiously avoided him. He'd barely greeted Melanion before setting off.

"Got his back up?" Melanion asked. He and Theas rode side by side, leading the Companions as they had always done at school.

Theas rolled his eyes. "He says he'll never forgive us for dragging him away from his own fight."

"Damn. How long is he going to brood?"

Theas shrugged. "He'll keep it up until he finds some way to prove himself."

"This'll wreak havoc with morale."

Theas nodded. "Got any solutions?"

They were almost at the mountain peak now. Melanion grinned and pointed ahead. Maia's neat cottage stood beside a well-turned field. Over both lay a dusting of snow. "Indeed. I'm leaving you to handle it," he said.

The cottage door opened. Linos stepped into the sunshine, a wide grin breaking out on his bearded face. "Prince!" he said, bowing one knee, his hand lifted to his chest. "Why come you here?"

"I bring gifts, and hope to take a great deal," Melanion said.

"And which'll we have first?" Linos' brow quirked as he came forward and scratched the chin of Melanion's horse. The black nuzzled his shoulder, knowing an old friend when he scented one.

Melanion slid to the ground and gave the reins to Theas, who exchanged looks with Alex. He gathered several bundles of herbs and spices from his saddle pack and entered the hut with Linos, greeting Maia and her children. A short time later, he stepped out again beside Maia and Linos, facing his men.

"This is Linos, son of Amphitrion. He'll command you for the next week. Obey him as you would me, and you'll learn all we'll need to know in order to survive. How to eat with no supplies, even now when the ground lies frozen. Which roots to boil, where the rabbits and deer hide in the hills, which wood will blaze quickly with little smoke.

"And Maia, his mother, is a great healer. She'll show you some of her craft. Learn which herbs keep wounds from going bad and which keep pain from killing a man. I'll return at week's end."

"Melanion!" shouted Alex. "Where are you going? We can't leave you."

"I command you to stay. This is the first test of your oath, Alex. Would you break it so soon?"

"This is stupid," Theas muttered.

Melanion reached up a hand to cover Theas' hand clamped on the reins. "Have some faith in me, for once. This isn't the waterfall." He gave Theas a smile, and Theas opened his mouth and shut it again. Then he nodded imperceptibly.

Philip was shaking his head, and many of the others looked grim.

"I'll meet you by the cave in the mountains. Linos will take you there. In the meantime, learn all you can. We'll need it soon."

Linos called them. With a look from Melanion, all but Theas gathered around him. At first they looked doubtful, but as he spoke, they began to listen. Melanion raised his hands for the reins, and Theas, with a last question in his eyes, gave them over.

"I'll be back," Melanion said, and flung himself up on the black. He turned his horse, felt excitement rise in him like a tide, nudged his mount into a gallop and shot towards the south and Thessaly.

# Chapter 7

## The Boar Hunt

Atalante dreamed that she wanted to twirl and sing, she was so happy. She was in the mountains with Melanion, and Hyperion was there, too, because Maia was making his heart better. It was warm. Hyperion's face was no longer pale, nor was he as breathless as he'd been all winter. Erytes wouldn't have to bring him squirrels to feed. He could find his own.

In her dream, it was night. Melanion covered her face with kisses, and he said she was more beautiful than he'd remembered. She wanted to tell him he was daft, but he'd covered her mouth with his own. His breath was warm. She opened her mouth to taste it, and his tongue slipped inside. She tasted the sweetness of warmed wine, smelled pine trees, and cold night air.

"Beloved," he said. "My love."

She reached for him, but he was gone.

She woke to an empty room. Outside her window, dawn crept across a clear sky. Coals hissed softly in the brazier, warming the air. She felt her cheek, her eyelids. They were cold. Her lips were swollen and soft, and the taste of mulled wine lingered in her mouth. With fumbling hands, she threw on a gown and a wide shawl. She walked the stairway and entered the Megaron.

At the far end, her father clasped Melanion and gave him the kiss of formal welcome. They looked up as she approached. Both smiled at her with a look so alike, she put her hand to her mouth and felt again Melanion's words against her lips.

As she walked toward them, Iasus clapped his hands and called for breakfast. The servants quickly brought a warm porridge topped with honey and goat's milk, and hot, crumbly oat cakes on a large platter.

"What news?" Iasus asked Melanion after he sat down beside her. His arm was only a hair's breadth away from hers.

"None good," he said. Melanion told him about the Red Bands and Polymus.

"This is our true enemy. Even my father can't destroy him now."

Iasus drew a hand across his eyes. "Then there's no way out of this."

"The Companions and the Hundred stand firm against him. The old generals won't break with Kryton, and Kryton—he's resented you all these years. I can't avert it. There'll be war come summer."

Melanion stared out the window. In the sunrise, the sea sparkled below the citadel.

"I could stay," he said. "I could call for the Hundred, and they'd slip south to hold the pass through the mountains." He looked down at his hands.

"Stay," Atalante said.

For the first time since he'd begun, Melanion looked at her. He gave her a smile, but it was tinged with bitterness. "If I do, I'll break a heavy oath." He turned to her father. "Majesty," he said in a ragged voice. "What shall I do?"

"Keep your oath," said Iasus calmly, and Atalante wanted to shout at him. She held herself very still instead, and forced herself to listen to her father.

"Keep your honor. Battle Polymus. When the time comes, you must fight at your father's side. If the gods are good, you'll rule this land someday, and there will be an end to the horror."

Atalante followed her father's gaze to the window. In the crashing waves below, she saw only destruction and blight.

Iasus shook his head, as though to clear it. "A man who dwells on hopelessness does himself no good. Tell me about these Companions, and the Hundred."

Melanion drew a deep breath. "They're not seasoned, but they're willing enough, and steady. With time, they could be a force to fear."

Iasus nodded thoughtfully. "So could the young of Thessaly," he said. His eyes brightened with the look of a man who'd just had an idea he liked.

"Melanion!" Hyperion's clear, high voice rang out across the Megaron as he hurried breathlessly through the hall.

Melanion lifted him up and gave him a rib-cracking hug. When he set Hyperion down again, he looked at him carefully.

Atalante saw that Melanion's smile didn't hide the worry in his eyes. She gazed at her little brother and understood what she hadn't allowed herself to see in the last months. Hyperion's pale, delicate skin had a translucent quality. His green eyes were shaded. And he was tired. Simply crossing the Megaron had been a struggle for him. He sank into his chair and panted.

"You've come just in time for the excitement," he said a few minutes later, when he'd caught his breath. "Atalante's going hunting." He tugged her arm. "Tell him about it."

"King Oineas sent a message to Father," she said, and pulled Hyperion close. If only the gods granted wishes, he would be straight and strong and going with her, if just to watch.

Melanion nodded and his beautiful mouth broke into a smile. "King of Kalydon."

"He's got a huge boar—*huge*—eating up all the grapes. And trampling the vines, too. My sister's going to kill it. Don't you want to go, too?"

"I don't know," Melanion said. "If I stay here and talk with the king, maybe I can learn enough to plan for the time ahead."

"There is need for you to go," Hyperion said in his different voice, the commanding one of a priest and an oracle. "Go. The future will catch up soon enough for all of us." Hyperion's gray eyes lost their clouded look and gazed at him solemnly from his small, pale face.

"The little priest has spoken," Melanion told Atalante. "I must go. But I hope you will not. The Kalydonian men are a morose lot, and they have very set ideas about women. What will they do when they see you dressed to hunt?"

She didn't like it when he used that condescending tone with her. She narrowed her eyes at him. "Oineas knows that Thessalians honor their women. And he's desperate. He'll take help where he finds it, and that includes puny women who ought to stay home and weave while the men have all the fun."

Melanion frowned. "Whatever you wish," he said. "Try to stay quietly in the background, if that's possible for you. I know men like these Kalydonians, and believe me, if they're outraged by your behavior, there'll be havoc ahead, and not just for you."

This day was not beginning well, Atalante thought. There was the dream, and then here was Melanion ordering her about. Wondering what was real and what was just her own desperate wish had frayed her nerves from the start. And now Melanion acted as though she were a troublesome creature who would make life difficult for him. She didn't want all these raw feelings and jumbles of fears and hopes.

"I plan to bring both men and women to Kalydon," she said, trying for some common ground. She would hate it if Melanion were cold and distant with her for any longer than a minute. "The ones you met when you were here before. Why not bring these Companions of yours, and join together?"

He thought about that. "It's a good plan," he said, and his eyes softened.

As her father turned to speak to a servant who held a tablet in his hands, Melanion's lips curved up at one end. "You and I would have to spend many days together," he whispered. "Do you think you could bear such prolonged . . . intimacy?"

Good. He was back to teasing. Even as she felt the heat rise to her cheeks, Atalante made an attempt to speak lightly. "I'll suffer it, if only to have the pleasure of watching Korone make mincemeat out of your Companions."

Early that afternoon, Hyperion met Melanion as he left the king's library. "Come meet my cub." The boy sounded so excited, Melanion couldn't say him nay, even though he had planned to ask the queen for an audience immediately.

"Your what?" Melanion hoisted Hyperion up on his shoulders and began to walk toward the prince's rooms.

"My lion cub. Erytes found him in the woods. His mother was dead, and he was crying, so Erytes brought him home. Here," he said as they reached his rooms. "Put me down and I'll introduce you."

A deep, rumbling purr greeted them as soon as they entered. Erytes, seated on Hyperion's bed, waved and grinned. One hand held a cloth that he dipped into a bowl of what looked to be goat's milk.

The cub, standing to suck, rubbed his head against Hyperion's side as he sucked from the cloth. He was tall—his tawny head already came to Hyperion's thigh. When Hyperion climbed into his bed, the lion cub followed, and proceeded to lick the boy all over.

Hyperion shrieked with laughter, doubling up to get away from the cub's rough, tickling tongue. "Here," said Erytes, handing the prince the cloth. "Take it before he rubs the skin right off you."

Hyperion took the cloth and the bowl. The cub settled beside him and resumed his feeding.

"He looks big for his age," Melanion said, looking at the cub's paws.

"He is. He's *huge*. It's all the milk and no competition."

"What's his name?"

"Heracles."

"Maybe you should try eating like Heracles, to get stronger. I'll tell you what. Atalante said there are oranges and dates in the bazaar. I could go and get you some right now. Wouldn't they taste good?"

Hyperion smiled up at him. In the bright light of the chamber, the dark shadows under his eyes were even more pronounced. "Food won't make me well, Melanion. It's that my heart struggles to beat."

Melanion sat down on the bed next to Hyperion and stared down at the cub. He wished so many things. That his father would retract his vengeance. That Atalante would understand how beautiful she was. That Hyperion would get well. Bored with the cloth, the cub awkwardly lapped at the milk in the bowl. Hyperion covered one of Melanion's hands with his.

"Don't feel bad. I've known ever since I could know anything, that I wouldn't grow to be a man." He gave Melanion a child's sweet smile. "This isn't all I'll have. There's more to life than this span of days."

His eyes grew unfocused. "I've seen it in visions, along with the darkness I'll go through before my time ends. You, too, Melanion, and my sister. There's suffering ahead for all of us. And for you, almost the worst. Shame and exile, and a deep pit. But you must hold hard to what you know is true, for the kingdom and for your love."

Melanion stared down at the green, unfocused eyes. A shiver threaded its way down his spine. Then, as quickly as it had clouded, Hyperion's vision cleared, and his sweet smile lit the room.

"Now is the time for joy. Heracles is strong and healthy. He'll live to sire beautiful cubs. It makes me glad to be with him. Because when I look at him, I see hope."

Melanion asked the queen for the private audience he'd wanted after leaving Hyperion's chambers. She sent a servant to fetch him immediately, and greeted him with courtesy in a small chamber within the women's quarters.

"Please, sit down," she said, motioning to a chair. Clymene did the same, and, settling her hands quietly in her lap, bade him speak.

He had given a great deal of thought as to how he wished to approach the subject, for Clymene, although she had treated him with courtesy, had an aura of distance about her that only her husband and her son seemed to penetrate. Melanion decided to be blunt. "I wish to know something about your daughter," he said.

"Yes," said Clymene. "Hyperion told me you would come sooner or later with your questions. I am prepared to answer them."

"Thank you. Atalante tells me you consulted the oracle at Delphi after the goddess marked her. I wish to know exactly what the oracle told you."

Clymene smiled, and her lips trembled slightly. "Do you know, prince of Macedonia, that eyes like yours—I mean that clear gray, without a hint of blue or green in them, are very rare in Thessaly? Indeed, I've only known one other to have them, and she was my dearest friend. Do you remember your mother's eyes?"

Wordlessly, Melanion nodded.

"Hers were almond shaped and black fringed, like yours, and her brows were straight, too. When I saw you for the first time, I knew exactly who you were." Clymene laughed, and there was something painful in it.

"I didn't know whether to call the guards or fall on your neck and cry. You're my second cousin, you know. She was my first. We played together from the time we were old enough to toddle. I loved her."

Melanion sat back in his chair and stared at the queen, who sat quietly, her head bent. "You must have known everything about her—what she liked, the things she did . . ."

"I'll tell you everything I remember, and I remember a good deal. But I stray from the subject. As I was saying, there are none in Thessaly with eyes the color of yours." Clymene smiled at him and proceeded to tell him what the oracle said.

After dressing for dinner, Atalante dismissed her maid. She hadn't seen Melanion since breakfast that morning. Part of it was her fault. There were so many contradictory emotions and questions swirling through her brain, that she spent the better part of the day in the hills running away from them. And when she returned, Melanion had been closeted with her mother in her chambers.

From what she could gather, Melanion had visited with her father, her mother, her brother, Erytes, and even the market, of all places, but he'd had no time for her. She flung away the foolish hope that had haunted her since early morn and came to the only logical conclusion. Melanion had not visited her chamber before dawn. He had not kissed her. He had not called her his love. She had merely been dreaming of him, just as she had all winter long.

She shrugged and walked to the window. The sky was going black. Below, the tide sighed against the shore. He probably had a woman in Hamalclion. A pretty one. They probably made love with all the lamps lit. She wondered if he'd gone to buy his woman a trinket, a bracelet or a piece of jewelry. Pretty girls liked pretty things.

At a quiet knock on the door, Atalante turned, but she didn't call out. It opened anyway, and there he was, dressed for feasting in a chiton of fine maroon wool banded in blue. His arms were even more developed than they had been in autumn. She could swear his chest was broader, too. His long, muscled legs showed to advantage tonight. Every woman in the Megaron would be looking at him.

She raised her chin and gave him what she hoped was a cool look. "I hope you had a pleasant day," she said, and cringed at the snappish tone in her voice.

He smiled, as though her bad mood pleased him. "I had an informative day. Would you like to know what I learned?"

"Of course. I'm always pleased to hear of your progress."

He stepped forward. He came close, but didn't quite

touch her. "This particular tidbit concerns you. I wonder how much you know yourself."

She began to move away, but his hand snaked out and clasped her wrist. Her gaze flew to his face. He was staring at her, and his gray eyes were warm, like a banked fire. "What were the oracle's words concerning you and this odd mirror prohibition?"

*"I'll be back,"* he had said, yet he couldn't spend more than a moment with her the whole of his first day. And now, in the most cavalier fashion, he wanted to delve into *that* again. Atalante flung off his grasp and strode toward the door, but he was there before she could reach it, and shot the bolt through.

"Open that door!" She was on him in an instant, nails set to rake his face, his neck.

He gripped her wrists hard and whirled her around, pinning her with his body to the wall beside the locked door. "You little hellcat! You'll listen or I'll truss you up and keep you here until you're ready to listen."

Atalante stilled instantly. If there was one thing she recognized, it was an opponent who was stronger and quicker than she—and just as angry. Eyes locked on his, she nodded slowly.

He backed away, shaken, it seemed. He looked at his hands. "Did I hurt you?" His voice was a little unsteady. Silently, she shook her head. He let out a breath he must have been holding for a while.

"Atalante, answer me. Please."

She wet lips gone dry. The oracle. Right. "You know how these priestesses are, always rhyming." She shrugged and stared at the far wall just beyond his shoulder. "Mother never told me the exact words, but just that I must never look in a mirror again."

He smiled suddenly, and the sweetness of it almost took her breath away. "Your mother gave me the rhyme.

*Until you see yourself through eyes of gray,*
*From your mirror look away.*"

She frowned. "I had blue eyes, not gray. They haven't changed in the last twelve years, have they?"

He lifted her chin with a gentle tug of his thumb. His smile was broader now, but just as sweet. "I have gray eyes, Atalante. Not green, not blue, not brown, which I learned are the colors of Thessalians' eyes." His hands stroked her forehead, and the outline of her face.

"Your face is oval. You have a dimple in one cheek that's quite fetching when you smile. Your eyes are a deep blue, the color of the sea beneath a clear sky in late afternoon. Your brows are like wings." He gave her a considering look while his fingers smoothed her brows, sending shivers through her.

"They're an odd color, given that your hair is gold. Sort of a soft brown. Your nose is straight and small, and it has just the hint of a stubborn tilt at the bottom. And your lips—they're the best, Atalante. They're darker than pink, lighter than red. Your upper lip is a perfect shape, like a bow, and your lower lip—don't bite it, and look up at me again—it's so lush a man wants to do terrible things as soon as he sees it. Your mouth—I've dreamed of it all over my body for months."

His words. She should think they were too raw. But she had never heard anything as beautiful as his words.

"Atalante, your skin is smooth, soft as a petal, except for the scar right above the center of your brow. The scar's this big." He held up the tip of his finger, then touched the tilt

147

of her nose with it. "And it's a perfect crescent, just like the one on my arm."

He reached into the top of his chiton with one hand and pulled something from it, a package wrapped in a length of bright blue cloth and a ribbon. He held it out to her. "I would have been here sooner, but I couldn't find the right thing until the market was almost closed."

She hesitated, staring at the package.

"Take it," he said, and pushed it into her hand.

"For me?"

He looked at her in surprise. "Who else?"

She shrugged. She wasn't about to tell him that no man had ever brought her a gift. She unwrapped the ribbon and the cloth. "Gods," she said, and stared at the object in her hand as though it were a snake.

Melanion, meanwhile, was circling the room, lighting all the lamps in it until it seemed as bright as day. "It won't bite."

"How can I keep this?" she asked, suddenly cold and hot at the same time as she stared at the highly polished bronze oval she held. It was beautifully crafted, with an intricate leaf pattern circling it. The artisan had carved a stately stag on the back.

Every nerve in her body twitched. She wanted to fling it away. She wanted to look into it.

Melanion took her hand and led her to the brightest corner of the room, where he'd placed several lamps on a tall chest. His arms wrapped around her from behind, and he held on tight. Slowly, her rigid muscles relaxed and she leaned back against him. He was solid and strong.

"It's all right." His lips were warm on the nape of her neck. "We've done the will of the oracle. It's time you looked into a mirror again."

Atalante raised the mirror. She wished her hands would stop trembling so she could get the first look over with. If she was going to be struck by lightning, she wanted it to happen before she could get any more frightened.

In the depths of the mirror, a face appeared. A perfectly ordinary face, just like the one she'd had eleven years ago, only grown up. The same nose, the same eyes her father used to tell her were so beautiful, the same mouth, only fuller, maybe more . . . womanly. And right above her brow, the small, white crescent scar. Melanion slipped his hands from her waist and moved around to face her. Her gaze rose from the mirror to his face. He was smiling a little. His eyes, the ones that helped her see herself, were tender.

But she didn't feel like smiling. She frowned, pointing to the scar. "This is *it?*" she said. "After all these years, this is *it?*"

Melanion blinked. Slowly, his smile widened, became a grin. "Oh, Atalante." He began to laugh, and he laughed harder and harder.

It was too much, on top of everything else. She put the mirror on the chest and stalked toward him, fists clenched. He backed away, holding up his hands, still laughing like a madman.

She lunged at him and her fists pummeled his chest, but he just kept laughing, pulling her into his arms and holding her so tightly she couldn't hurt him.

"Stop it," she said. "What's so funny, anyway?"

He shook his head. "Atalante. You are by far the most impossible woman I've ever known. I solve a problem that's made you miserable for years and years." He nodded toward the mirror on the chest. "Knowing how little you trust words, I present you with proof that you're the most beautiful woman in the world, and what do you do? You get angry."

"You don't understand," she said against his chest. She didn't know what made her cry when she was so angry. "I saw a woman once, who'd been disfigured in a fire. Her face was—it looked horrible. Children ran from her in the marketplace. She killed herself, and I understood. I thought how good the people were, because they could look at me and love me, in spite of my disfigurement.

"It was like the monster under my childhood bed. I wanted to know how awful it was, but I wasn't supposed to look. And after a while, I was too scared to look. Only, for years, the monster has been me. As I passed every still pond, I'd avert my eyes. If I wanted to drink from it, I'd throw a stone into it first.

"And now, to finally see myself and all that tormented me and frightened me, and made me asha—well, anyway. To find it was nothing, nothing at all. Nothing but a celestial joke. I hate her, Melanion. She's cruel, and she doesn't care."

"Hush." He put his hand over her mouth and made a sign, averting evil or a goddess' revenge. "There is always a reason, a good one, for our suffering. If you had known, would you have worked so hard on the exercise field all these years? Would you have said yes to the King of Mycenae when he asked for your hand? Would you be here to lead your people now that they need you? Would you be here for me?"

She searched his face, afraid to concede, afraid not to. His eyes burned with conviction. As she watched, the intensity changed. He smiled, a little upward curve of the lips was all. His gaze glinted with something that made her shiver. It traveled down from her face, and he said in a voice that purred like Hyperion's lion, "But I haven't finished."

Her laugh was a little breathless. "You look just like Hermes must have looked when he stole Apollo's cattle." She backed away one step, but his arms were tight around her waist, and the look in his eyes excited her, too.

"What a thing to say, when I mean only to continue the task the goddess sent me. I have not even begun describing you, lady." His hands slid beneath the clasps of her robe at her shoulders, and before she realized what was happening, her bodice was about her waist.

"Melanion!" she hissed, tugging it up and backing away. "Someone will come!"

"Nay. The bolt will hold. Now, where was I?" He followed, until she felt the wall against her back. He took her wrists and pulled her hands out at her sides. The bodice fell again. His smile was still there, but his gaze held no mischief now.

"Aye. Your breasts."

She shivered again, and not from cold.

"Soft as the white dove's. But see, even in lamp light they glow."

The gown slipped further down, lightly circling her hips. "Here, you're a sapling, slender, pliant," he said, hands outlining her waist.

The gown fluttered to the floor. "As to your hips. They're graceful, with a tempting curve. A man wants to smooth his hands over them, feel them against him, as close as they can go. Turn, please." She shocked herself by obeying him, glad to hide her face, grateful for the coolness of the stone against her hot cheek. He hadn't touched her, yet she ached.

He was silent for too long; she had enough time to realize what he was looking at.

When his callused hands caressed her buttocks, she

wanted to scream, and not from shock, but hunger. "Round. I think these alone are driving me mad." He sounded as though he were clenching his jaw. "When you run ahead of me, I burn." He stroked the muscle where the curve of her buttocks met her thigh. She heard him swallow. ". . . Strong here, sweet. Except when you stick your nose in the air and walk away in a snit. Definitely tart, then—saucy, just like you."

He cleared his throat. "Atalante. You'd better turn again."

"No," she said on a tremor.

"Yes." The single word was a command, not a request. She turned because she wouldn't have him thinking she'd hide from him in fear.

He didn't look as though he knew he had the upper hand. His gaze burned into her, branding her. "Your legs aren't soft. They're smooth, muscled. The legs of a warrior, of an athlete."

It was too much, to watch his gaze travel down her body, and fix upon the very center of aching heat. "Douse the lamps, Melanion," she said, and her voice was a low moan, a plea.

He shook his head slowly. As he stepped closer, his arm slipped beneath her knees, and the other clasped round her back. He lifted her and carried her to the bed as though she were no heavier than a breath of air. And she knew then that he controlled everything tonight.

"I want to see you," he said. "No more hiding in the darkness, Atalante. From now on, there's only you. Only me. Only what I can make you feel. I want to see it all."

His chiton fell to the ground. He stood naked before her, handsome as a god, powerfully aroused. She raised her arms to take him, and he came, covering her with his body, holding her down with his warm weight. She buried her fingers in his curls. Turning her face against his neck, she breathed in the scent of him, clean soap and heat and male. His skin was sweet to taste, to touch.

And then there was nothing but his hands, his mouth. He kissed her mouth for a long time, tasting her deeply, teaching her to do things with her lips, her tongue, that she'd never suspected existed. He acted as though they had all the time in the world, while her blood beat heavy and insistent. He stroked her neck, her shoulders. She shivered when he caressed her collarbone and lightly traced the rise of her breasts. Then he began all over again.

"Melanion," she sighed. "I'm dying."

"A little longer," he whispered. She stared up at him, begging with her eyes. But he only smiled and shook his head.

When he bent and took her nipple into his mouth, she arched off the bed and gasped. His hands stroked downward, over her hip, to the juncture of her thighs, and he found the heart of her. There was no escape from the feelings his knowing fingers aroused. She writhed beneath him, unable to hold back anything—her thighs opening wide for him, her body arched higher to him, the moans deep in her throat. She turned her face to the side, trying to hide, but she knew she was more exposed now than she had been standing before him without a speck of clothing on.

He turned her face up and his eyes burned into hers. "Mine," he said. "Forever."

She had no words. Passion, delight, a feeling of rightness were as close as she could get to her emotions. She kissed the scar on the front of his shoulder, a perfect crescent, just as hers was. There was war ahead, and the enmity of his father for hers. Would it be enough, this rightness, to counteract the indomitable will of fate?

She shut her eyes to all of it and just felt. Felt his heat slide into her, the tight burn as she adjusted to his fullness, the first thrill of friction as he stroked her, pulling her hips higher. He groaned, bent to her breast, and suckled there in rhythm to his strokes. She clung, joined him as he thrust harder and faster, until the tension built so high she was sobbing with it.

"Gods!" she heard her own voice cry out. "Please."

His hips ground against her, urging her higher, and burying her face in his shoulder, she muffled a scream of ecstasy as she burst over the pinnacle and flew with him into the wild, moonlit night.

She lay beneath him for some time, savoring the weight of his body as it covered hers. Then he rolled, taking her with him, until she lay beside him all along the length of his body. His eyes were shut and he smiled. She studied him, filled with wonder. He really was beautiful, with his dark lashes fanning his cheeks, and the strong bones of his face. His auburn hair was surprisingly soft when she drew her fingers through the curls.

She wanted him to be this way always—content, happy, with no trace of caution or cynicism. With a start, she recognized the truth. At that moment, gray eyes flew open and fixed on her.

"Atalante?"

She must look as troubled as she felt, for his face tightened. With the wariness of a wild stallion, he seemed to gather himself for something bad to happen. She shook her head and gulped down the lump in her throat.

"I love you," she whispered. And knew it was the worst thing in the world that could have happened to her.

★ ★ ★ ★ ★

Atalante didn't want to go to the banquet, but Melanion insisted.

"They'll know," she'd whispered after he'd helped her dress and pinned her hair up.

"After I washed you most tenderly with my own hands?" he said, turning her to see that her girdle was fastened properly. "Although it would have pleased me to know that beneath that very lovely gown you still smelled of me, and what I was doing to—"

"Hush!" She placed her fingers over his lips to keep him quiet, and he grinned down at her just to tease her. He wished it was obvious to everyone that she belonged to him. But policy demanded tact. One didn't brand a princess his, even when a goddess had as much as wed that princess to him.

He kissed the fingers that silenced him, then turned Atalante toward the door. "You look as you always do, so beautiful and remote the men will try to look at something else before they all succumb and fall at your feet."

"Don't make a joke," she said, and he realized that it would take her a long time to believe what she'd seen in the mirror tonight.

By the time they entered the Megaron, the hall was filled with courtiers. Laughter and the din of many voices greeted Melanion's ears. He took Atalante's elbow and led her to the group of youths and maidens standing against the far wall. As they walked, he noticed the courtiers were less richly garbed than they had been three months before.

"We have better things to buy than silk from the east," said Korone, when he mentioned this to her. "We're training war horses now. Swords, breastplates, and helms occupy the trunks where we used to keep our finest clothing."

"Beyond war, only the games in spring occupy our thoughts," said Nestor, who joined the group moments after Melanion led Atalante to her friends. Nestor's smile of greeting was replaced by a look of bewilderment.

He stared at Atalante. Slowly, his gaze shifted to Melanion and then back to Atalante again. Nestor's expression darkened. Melanion moved closer to Atalante, and gravely looked back into Nestor's eyes. Nestor's mouth set in a grim line. But after what seemed a long time, he gave Melanion an infinitesimal nod, and smoothly commented on how crowded the exercise field had become in the last months. By the time the servants entered with platters of bread, cheese, and spicy wine, they'd begun discussing the boar hunt, and Nestor seemed himself again. He joked with Melanion about his skills, challenging him with his usual cheekiness.

"In spite of Atalante's recommendation, I have it on good authority that you move at the speed of a madly terrified tortoise," he said.

Melanion grinned. "You sound sure enough of my lack of skill to place a small wager on the foot race at the spring games."

"Gladly, since I'll be betting on the fastest runner in three kingdoms." Nestor raised his cup in a silent toast to Atalante.

Talk turned to the horse races. "Who's Astrid bringing for the race over obstacles?" a youth down the table called to them.

"I've got two or three stallions in training," Astrid turned to call back. Her long, shining hair was clasped in a tail that flowed down her back tonight. "Probably Hermes'

Arrow will do it for me by race time. He's got the heart and the wind."

"Don't bet on her," Nestor told Melanion. "You'll win no coins. Even the odds makers are certain she'll take the day."

"And Korone," Melanion said to the dark-haired flirt across the table. "Will you dance?"

Korone shook her head. "Only for the opening ritual. After that, not until the war is over. Till then, I fight."

As the talk turned to Kalydon and the boar hunt, a chill crept through Melanion. The gaiety in this brightly lit hall seemed forced. The room seemed haunted by the specter of war.

The next morning, Melanion visited Hyperion's chambers. A servant stood at the door with a breakfast tray for the boy. He'd caught a chill the day before, and although he was mending, his mother had ordered him to remain indoors for the next week. Melanion took the tray and entered.

A charcoal brazier warmed the room where Hyperion lay beneath a blanket, a clay tablet on his bent knees. The lion cub sprawled across the foot of the bed.

"What are you writing?" Melanion asked, setting down the tray beside the bed. "In Macedon, only the scribes write and it's usually tiresome details like how much grain was harvested." He bent over the boy's shoulder, expecting to see drawings, riddles, or such things as children might enjoy when recovering from an illness.

Hyperion bit his tongue in concentration as the stylus darted on, making quick neat marks in the clay. "I'm writing down my father's reign and my sister's courage. If we are all destroyed, maybe this will live, and men will know how a kingdom can be ruled."

"I see," Melanion said. The boy had rendered him all but speechless. He sat for a while in silence, watching the strict concentration on Hyperion's face as he wrote on, ignoring the porridge and milk on the breakfast tray. If writing gave the boy hope, let him make the effort. But if Polymus got hold of the city and found the record, he would destroy it.

"Hide the tablets, Hyperion. Hide them in a good place," he said.

The boy's stylus paused. For a while, he sat silent in thought. "I understand," he said. "I'll do it."

They both turned their heads as the door opened and Atalante entered. She was carrying something long and curved, wrapped in a deerskin. Hyperion climbed down from the bed and walked to her side, inspecting the package.

"I'm just the messenger. Melanion asked me to bring this present to your room, as his hands were full with your uneaten breakfast," Atalante said with a meaningful glance at the tray. "And how do you know it's for you, Little Owl? Maybe it's for me."

Erytes followed Atalante into the room. He grinned at Hyperion, his black eyes dancing. "Maybe it's for me," he said.

"I know it's for me," said Hyperion, staring at the gift.

"How?" Erytes asked.

"If it were for Atalante, she wouldn't be holding it, and if it were for you, Melanion would have told me all about it, just like he told you."

Atalante came close and put her hand on Melanion's arm, laughing softly. "Give it to him," she told him.

Melanion grinned, warm from her touch and the pleasure he got from surprising this wise little boy. "I know

when I'm outfoxed." He took the package from Atalante
and handed it to Hyperion. "Sit down with it. There are too
many pieces."

Hyperion sat on the bed and unrolled the skin. "A bow!"
he shouted. "Just like the large bows, but small enough for
me to handle. Melanion, you are the kindest man in the
world!"

The small horned bow was a graceful piece, intricately
carved with swirls on the handgrip.

"Keep looking," said Melanion. He could feel his grin
spreading all over his face.

"Arrows, and a quiver! And what's this painted thing?
Oh, a target. What will we stuff it with?"

"Straw."

"When can I try it?"

"See if you have the strength to string your bow. I think
it will just bend to your hand, but you'll have to do it each
day just to keep it pliant."

With a minimum of huffing and puffing, Hyperion managed to attach the cord to the notches at both ends of the
bow. "What next?" he asked breathlessly.

"Now you rest while I set up the target," Melanion told
him. "Then . . ." He paused for a moment, enjoying
Hyperion's shining eyes. "We all hide under the bed while
you take your first shot."

Later that night, Atalante crept into his room and drew
him into the dark corridor. Stopping at a tall wooden cupboard, she touched the tail of a carved snake in the center
of the piece. The wall beside the cupboard opened without
a sound. She took his hand and they slipped past the
opening, into a silent hall. The door swung shut again as
soon as they had entered. She lit a torch from the wall

sconce and started walking.

"There are hidden corridors all through the palace," she said softly as she led him down an incline into the bowels of the palace. "There's one right behind the throne in the Megaron."

Eventually, they came to a door. Atalante doused the torch and pushed the door to. As they entered, he made out a small chamber holding a bed, table, and a lamp already glowing. She must have made up the room some time during the day, for the bed was laid with fresh linen and fragrant lavender filled the air.

"Do you like it?" She was studying his reaction, her eyes luminous and slightly uncertain in the light of the wavering lamp.

"Like it? After wanting you every moment at the feast? After making do with stolen kisses in a darkened hallway? After lying alone and burning for you last night, knowing I couldn't risk coming to your chamber again?" He pulled her to his body, his mouth hot on hers for a long moment. "Yes. I like it very much."

She had done this for him. She had done it for herself, as well. He lifted her and whirled around, so her gown billowed out like a sail behind her.

She laughed, then caught her lower lip in her teeth as he set her down and lowered the sleeves of her gown from her shoulders, baring her breasts. He bent his head, his breath lingering over the pink nipple until it peaked to meet his lips.

"You taste of flowers," he whispered. "Hyacinths and lilies, sweet oils and eastern fragrances and Atalante." She smiled, and lust surged through him. How had she learned that teasing, secretive look in so short a time? And then he knew with a surge of joy that he had given her this new pride with the mirror and his lovemaking. When he unlaced her gown, she let it fall to the floor and stood before him, shoulders straight, eyes full of mystery.

Turning, she walked toward the bed. Her hips swayed and beckoned. Artemis become Aphrodite. One slanted glance over her shoulder created a whirlpool of desire. He pushed her down onto the scented bed, groaning as she arched her hips and rubbed her belly against him. Following her down, he entered her with one deep thrust, feeling the welcoming heat enfold him. He thrust again, watching every changing expression on her face. She looked fierce and tender at the same time. She looked as though she fought to reach a goal she still wasn't quite sure of, and it was only a little beyond her reach. Deliberately, he slowed the pace, and when she gave a low moan of protest, he covered her lips with teasing kisses.

She was fascinating, this vibrant young butterfly hatched from her chrysalis at last. Even though she'd lain with him twice before, her sensuality had a touch of innocence she'd probably keep when he'd loved her a thousand times.

She humbled him. Maybe it was because she gave everything of herself. Maybe it was because she only knew truth. Her eyes were half shut, blue flame glinting beneath tender lids. The scar glowed above her brow. Going to his knees, he brought her with him, lifting her hips high to bury himself and all his doubts as deeply as he could go. He felt every flutter pliant and tight around him. He hung on to control by a thread.

He sensed that she wanted something more than mastery. Something greater drove her, for he felt as though he made love to light and fire. She wrapped her legs high around him and he burned in a sensual conflagration. Her cries were all he could hear above his own gasps. All he could see were her eyes, open now, compelling. As the explosion shook her, she arched upward, and he lifted her against his chest. Her arms wrapped around his neck. He groaned, burying his face against her hair, and joined her in the conflagration.

It took him a long time for his breathing to slow down, longer for him to lower her away from his body. He sank into the bed, covering her like a blanket. Spent and sated, they lay in a tangle of arms and legs.

"Why?" he asked her, when he had breath enough to speak. He didn't quite know what he was asking. Maybe why she'd gifted him so generously with her body, or how it was that Atalante had so joyfully cast aside wariness in the space of a single day.

She snuggled closer, as though she wanted to absorb him. "Did you see Hyperion today when he shot the bow for the first time?" She looked up at him, her eyes limpid as the sky on a perfect spring day. "He's very ill. He knows he hasn't long. But he makes every moment count. He devours life with absolute joy.

"We don't know how long we have either, do we, Melanion? It would be foolish of me not to do as my brother does." Her arms tightened around him as though she could hold him that close forever. He felt the wet warmth of her tears against his chest.

"I'm making memories, my love. When my shade crosses the river and enters the land of the dead, I'll have this to warm me."

"Oh, gods," he whispered, and pulled her even closer. He had no soothing words that would take away her fears.

Or his own.

They didn't move, as though they feared to be severed. They lay like that until the gray hour before dawn.

"Macedonian!" Korone spat the word, pacing the room the next day. Atalante turned to Astrid and Nestor, but they were silent and their eyes were troubled.

Korone whirled, her loose black hair flying about her pale face. Her eyes glittered with a fury Atalante had never seen before. "How dare you bring him here, into the center of the kingdom? Has he had time enough to take inventory of all the treasure he intends to seize? Does he know enough about how large our army is, how well trained, or must he spend more time with us to accomplish that? Perhaps I should invite him to my father's lands, so he can count the cattle and the horses he'll take."

"Mind your tongue!" Atalante reared back, primed for battle. "There are reasons for him to be here. Whether I share those with you will depend on your ability to control yourself."

"Don't pull rank with me! You expect me to travel to a land under the curse of a goddess where, according to all reports, I may be gored or killed outright, and I am to trust twenty of *his* kind to watch my back? No, thank you. I'm going home. Send for me when the heat of your lust no longer blinds your reason."

"Korone! You go too far." Nestor held her while she struggled against the strength of his hands on her arms.

"Atalante . . ." Astrid's voice pleaded with her for understanding.

The room went silent. The only sound in it was Korone's deep, jagged breaths. Atalante unclenched her fists.

"Don't you think I know what it's like to love a brother?" she asked in a softer voice. "I fear for Hyperion's life every day, Korone. I don't ask this of you lightly."

Korone drew a deep, shaking breath. "Talk. I'll listen."

Atalante motioned to Nestor. He let Korone go and took a seat, as did Astrid. Atalante drew close to Korone and wrapped her arm around her shoulders, drawing her close and rubbing away the shaking.

"There, now," she said in the gentle tones of a mother soothing a frightened child. "This is what happened when I went to mountains . . ."

That evening after dinner, there were outraged grumbles among the rest of the Thessalians when Astrid, Korone, and Nestor told them who Melanion was and that they were expected to ride with his Companions. But the three leaders quelled most objections.

In the ensuing silence, Atalante rose to her feet. "I speak of Melanion's friends. You know him to be a gentleman, and my hearth guest. He who will disgrace me with crude gossip in front of the Macedonians should remain in Iolcus."

The group went about the business of preparation without open complaint. Korone, with a set, calm face, insisted on no open rebellion. The rest, knowing she had the most cause to object, followed her lead.

By the time they set out on a frosty morning, Melanion felt fewer of the cold looks the Thessalians had been giving him for the past few days. The horses' hooves rang against the hard ground, and the boar hounds brayed on their leads. He rode with Atalante at the head of the group, eager to meet with the Companions and begin the business of melding the two groups.

They reached the cave in the mountain in a day and a half. The Companions, gathering firewood and water, stopped in their tracks and gaped at their approach.

"Hey, Philip!" Melanion shouted, noting the giant stood like a statue and stared at Atalante. "I bring a princess and you goggle like a buffoon." Philip stammered something and bowed to Atalante. Theas stepped out of the cave. He greeted them both with a bow and held the reins while Atalante swung off and walked back to speak with her Thessalians.

"She's got a rather frightening beauty," Theas told Melanion. "Philip thought she was the Huntress, herself."

"Indeed," Melanion said, his gaze following Atalante. "She's Thessalian, isn't she?"

Melanion tore his gaze away and turned to Theas. "They're all Thessalian."

"So that's why we're here." His brow wrinkled.

Melanion clapped him on the back. "I never have to explain to you, do I?"

Theas shrugged. "You'd better make it good for the rest of the Companions."

"Gather them so I can."

Theas frowned. "I assume you know what you're doing."

"I do."

Theas took a step toward the Companions, then turned back. "That explanation? It had better be a good one."

Melanion sighed. If Theas found the prospect of close proximity with Thessalians troubling, he'd need his wits about him to make his plan work.

The Companions received the news about their new comrades with as little initial grace as the Thessalians had. Furthermore, there were now boar hounds snuffling and milling, horses—now forty-three to tether and feed—and the immediate need to mold the two groups into a cohesive whole.

Atalante set them all to work unloading the pack horses and comparing provisions. By nightfall, an uneasy truce existed between the Thessalians and the Companions. Atalante found herself worrying that it wouldn't get any better, ever. When Melanion held out his hand to her, she rose and took it, following him down the path they'd taken one moonlit night months earlier. Melanion had caught a hare earlier that day. They made a little fire before the high altar and sacrificed the hare; its entrails were healthy and clean scented.

"It's a good sign, isn't it?" Atalante's whisper caught in her throat.

Melanion's hand squeezed hers. "Yes."

Although they waited for a long time, King Stag didn't appear.

They bowed once more before the altar and made their way into the forest, walking silently as Atalante's fears skittered through her mind. Melanion stopped and took her into his arms. Atalante recognized with a shock that they stood in the deer thicket where they'd come together the first time.

"The others . . ."

"Let them wait," Melanion said. His eyes burned with the unmistakable fire of need.

"It's been three days. Three days and twelve hours. I need you, my heart. Will you take me?"

She nodded as heat and yearning engulfed her. He could do this to her, with only his voice, his words.

He wrapped the wings of the warm woolen himation around her and pulled her to his body. When he touched her, she forgot everything—her home, her people, her duty. All she knew was Melanion, strong and hard against her. She followed him down, just as she had followed him from the beginning. If only she could keep him like this, bound to her forever.

But afterwards, when he held her against him, the doubt crept close again. His hand cupped her breast, stroked her side.

"Why so melancholy?" he said.

She searched for words. "Korone said I was too lust-filled to see you clearly. She said you were planning to destroy everything in a few months' time, and I was helping you find the way to do it."

"You know that's not true," he said, kissing the nape of her neck.

"Yes. I know. But you will stay, and call the Hundred to you in Thessaly, so we'll have better odds against the army? You'll do that, won't you?"

He was slow to answer. Frightened, she sat up. "You'll do it," she said, and heard the note of panic in her voice. He sat up beside her and took her hand.

"Atalante," he said in a voice laced with sorrow. "Even Iasus told me I have to fight for my own father, not yours."

She grabbed at his shoulder. He winced at her tight grip and she drew her hand back from the scar. "You know how he plans to conquer us. He'll kill my father! Without the king, the troops will be like hounds without the huntsman. You can't possibly fight beside a madman bent on such carnage as we'll see on that day."

"I took a heavy oath, Atalante. One my mother insisted I take. I cannot fight against him."

"My father could have killed you," she cried. "But he treated you like a son, taught you everything he could. You can't allow him to die—it's as if you struck him down with your own sword! Tell me you'll fight to defend him against this evil. You must fight with us."

"Don't!" He leaped to his feet, his face a mask of pain and struggle. "You're asking me to betray my father!"

"So instead, you slay mine." She skittered away from him, buried her face in her hands, and sobbed.

"Atalante. You're tearing my heart out," Melanion said softly. He reached for her, but she backed away.

"Don't touch me!" She fumbled for her chiton, grabbed her sandals, and crashed out of the thicket.

"Wait." She heard his cry as she pounded through the forest, running like the wind away, as far away as she could get from her dying dreams.

She didn't return to the cave until the dawn threatened. Melanion walked toward her with the stiff gait of an old man. Without a word, he folded a cloak around her heaving shoulders.

"No, thank you." Atalante pushed the cloak off her shoulders. She didn't want it. She didn't want anything more to do with him.

"You're overheated and the air is cold. You can't lead your people if you take a chill," he said in an even voice, and wrapped her in it again.

As the himation enclosed her, Atalante felt sweat dripping down her breasts and thighs. She didn't want him to be right about anything—even the heat her body had generated in a futile attempt to outrun her misery. Nodding numbly, she kept the cloak and walked away from him, to talk with Astrid about the needs of the coming day.

# Chapter 8

## Kalydon

Atalante spoke to Melanion only when it was absolutely necessary. His frustration mounted, driven by his realization that the Companions and Thessalians kept to their own camps, eyeing each other warily when they passed. It couldn't go on.

The following morning, he waylaid Atalante on her way to hunt with Astrid and Korone.

"Send them ahead," he said, grabbing her arm.

"Let go. You're hurting me," she hissed.

Melanion eased his hold, but kept her arm in his grasp. Her eyes were shadowed, but as he had been tossing for the last two nights, he had no sympathy.

"This snit of yours can't go on," he said.

"Snit! You think my refusal to turn my country over to your tender mercies is a mere snit?"

"I think you don't trust that I'll find a way. In my blacker moments, I agree with you. But I can't believe that the gods brought us together only as a celestial joke. I can't believe we're meant to waste this opportunity. Look about you."

Her frown didn't change, but she turned her head and looked at the campsite.

"They're two separate units, mistrusting each other as much as you mistrust me. We're going into a strange and brutal land where only the gods know what will happen to us. Think clearly for a moment, not about six months from now, but about tomorrow. Do you want two bands of twenty or one of forty defending each other?"

She turned to him with haunted eyes and a pale face. "I understand. I want them to know each other. Then, when war comes, perhaps these of your men will recognize them, and spare them the worst. We'll go forward together. For this time, but no other."

There was a cold pain near his heart. "Don't do this," he whispered.

Her voice was like ice. "Let me go, Macedonian."

He dropped his arm, and she walked back to the camp. He followed. After all, he was more than himself, just as she was. And that part called.

"I will not work with that self-satisfied little bitch." Theas felt the heat rise in his face, in his whole body. Two days with that girl had driven him mad. Surely an assignment where the two of them were together for the gods knew how long would send him howling through the forest.

"Korone shoulders her share of the load and more," said Melanion.

How could he possibly not understand the wench? Theas sighed and lowered his voice. "She flirts like a harlot with those men your princess brought. She has a stare designed to freeze a man's testicles. I wouldn't put it past her to slice 'em off, bit by bit, for the fun of it. Just station me far away from her."

"I can't do that, Theas."

How could Melanion look so determined about this travesty? "Change the order. I'd be glad to ride with Nestor. He's a gentleman, at least."

"He's gone with Niko and Alex. I'm telling you, there's

nobody else to find grain for the horses."

"Melanion, I swear by Zeus, if you make me ride with her, I won't be responsible for my words."

Melanion sighed. "There's more to this hunt than meets the eye, Theas, and I can't have you, the most rational of us, shouting and storming at one Thessalian maiden who's done nothing to warrant your anger. So I must order you to be polite."

"Gods! I'm beginning to regret taking that damned oath your father laid on us." Theas stalked away fuming. Halfway to the hobbled horses, he whirled around, suddenly curious about Melanion's last words. He walked back.

"What more is there to this hunt?" he asked softly.

Melanion raised a brow and gave him a mysterious smile. "You have a day alone with Korone. Try to figure it out."

When he turned back to the horses, Korone was mounted on a small horse she couldn't seem to keep from grazing while they stood. In her right hand, she held the rope halter of a pack pony who was fast learning her horse's bad manners. In spite of her predicament, that snotty little nose of hers was already in the air. "Hurry up, Macedonian. I don't have all day to wait for you."

Theas smiled to himself. He was to be polite to the little brat, was he? By the gods, he'd be as meek as a priest. "My apologies, lady." He gave the minx a courtly bow and leaped on his own horse. He grabbed the lead rope of another pony from Astrid and sat his mount, waiting.

"Well," she said sharply. "Why aren't you going?"

"I live to follow you, my lady. Please. If you'll lead, I'll attempt to keep up with you."

As they entered the forest at a snail's pace, Theas' mood

improved considerably. Whoever had decided to give Korone the Macedonian horse they'd ironically named Windfleet deserved a cask of the finest wine he could find when they returned to Hamalclion. As herd-bound as a mare in season, the horse wouldn't lead away from its stable mate without a strong rider on its back. Korone was obviously no strong rider, and Theas was mounted on Windfleet's stable mate.

Theas petted his horse and slowed him down to a crawl. Windfleet turned his head and whinnied every two steps. Korone kicked and pulled the reins in what looked like a misery of frustration from behind while Windfleet slowed to a halting walk.

"A crop," Theas heard her mutter aloud, and watched with pleasure as she pulled Windfleet into a clump of trees. She loosed the reins and lifted her arms to break off a branch. Windfleet, sensing her hands elsewhere, turned and trotted back to Theas. Korone scrabbled for the reins, just catching them in time to halt him four paces from the other horses. Meanwhile, the pack pony, rope trailing, cantered off ahead in search of a nice meadow.

Korone squared her shoulders and glared at Theas.

Theas shrugged apologetically.

Korone turned her horse forward with a swift and vicious tug at the reins. Somewhat chastened, Windfleet broke into a shambling canter, held at it by the furious and constant drumming of Korone's heels in his sides. They traveled in silence to the edge of a meadow, where the pack pony gobbled at a high patch of brown grass. Korone slipped off her horse, grabbed the pony's lead shank, and jerked its head up from the strand of grass. By this time, Windfleet buried his head in the grass patch. Korone took a deep breath, jerked hard on both reins and rope. She sent Theas a look that might have melted a less . . . polite man, but Theas simply bowed from his horse's back and gave her a puzzled look.

Korone's lower lip—quite a fetching lower lip, Theas noted—trembled, but she squared her shoulders again and led the horses to a tree stump. Somehow, she managed to jump up on Windfleet's back without losing the pack pony's rope. She turned the horse so she faced Theas. He felt exceptionally pleased with the way the day was going.

"Macedonian," she began in a subdued tone.

Theas stared at her blankly and didn't answer.

"Macedonian. Please."

"I'm sorry, my lady. There are so many Macedonians. Were you talking to me?"

Korone took a deep breath. "I . . . don't know what to call you."

"I am Theas, son of the Baron Alcestis," he said, and gave her a cool look.

"Theas. Would you—"

"And what is your name, Lady?" he asked.

"I am Korone, daughter of the Baron Lysis." She lifted her chin and stared at him, blue-black eyes boring into his. He hadn't realized how lovely her eyes were.

After a moment, he said, "You were asking something of me?"

She sat straight and lifted her chin. Even in defeat, she was proud, he saw, and he liked her better for it.

"I am a poor rider," she said, and her lips quirked, just a little. "If I continue to lead, we'll get the grain some time next spring. Will you ride in front of me?"

"I'll lead gladly, for a price, my lady."

"What price?" she asked, those fascinating eyes flashing.

"A real smile, and a thank you. Do you think you could spare it?"

"Gladly," she said. She had a dimple in one cheek, he noticed.

"I thank you, Theas, son of Alcestis."

He felt his own grin starting, bowed as best he could on horseback, and took the lead. They set off through the forest at a brisk pace, Windfleet gladly hurrying to keep up with the horse in front of him.

When it came time to leave for Kalydon, they broke camp and set off long before sunset. Where the path was broad, Linos traveled between Atalante and Melanion, reporting on his week with the Companions, as though she had every right to hear of their progress.

Atalante was glad for the interruption. Melanion and she had maintained a cold silence broken only by their need to communicate as leaders. At night, alone in her bedroll, she stared at the stars. A dull pain enfolded her as she fought herself, missing Melanion's warm arms, wanting to beg his pardon, wanting him to swear he'd fight to keep her father safe.

The others seemed to make peace with each other, although she'd noticed a hint of defiance and almost shyness when Korone greeted Theas after their mission together.

"They can live off the land in winter," said Linos to Melanion, breaking into her thoughts. "In summer, they'll eat like kings in the woods. They're good lads. How many more do you have in Macedonia?"

"About three hundred at last count," said Melanion. "They come with wild ideas about how they'll cleanse the country of the Red Bands, but when they see the king won't sanction it, they stay anyway. That gives me some hope."

"They're a beginning. But not enough, Melanion," said Linos.

"I know."

"I'll talk with the helots and the small land holders—they know Polymus, and several would take up arms against him. But sometime in the next year, he'll strike for the throne," said Linos in a worried voice.

"I know."

*"This is the enemy."* Atalante shuddered, remembering Melanion's words to her father. They were talking about Polymus, not King Kryton. She glanced quickly at Melanion and the grim lines of his face frightened her even more. Oh, gods, what did fate have in store for her beloved country?

They rode east and north into the Pindus Mountains. Kalydon lay at their base, surrounded by forest and marsh. There had been singing, and even some good-natured jests between the two groups. But as they rode through a vineyard in the hills overlooking the city, all voices stilled.

The air wafting up to meet them held the stink of rotted vines. They rode by many trampled vineyards. The horses slid on sickly, overripe grapes littering the soil. A dark mist enveloped the riders. Atalante strung her bow and slung it across her shoulder. Melanion's hand went to his sword.

Theas rode up to speak to Atalante and Melanion. "Something unclean has happened here. Will it cling to us, as well as the Kalydonians if we agree to this hunt?"

"He's right," a Thessalian said.

"Maybe the goddess hates this land. Maybe she'll destroy anybody who tries to cleanse it," a Macedonian agreed.

The others murmured their assent. Atalante held up her

hand. Horses and hounds came to a halt.

"We must ask her," she said to Melanion.

A dove flew up and settled on a branch of a gnarled oak to her right. She moved faster than she ever had before, readying her bow, nocking her arrow, and sending it flying to the heart of the bird. It fell to the ground, a quick, painless kill.

"Artemis has sent the sacrifice," she told their people. Reaching into her traveling sack, she pulled out clean clothing and walked to a clear stream she spotted to her right. Before she sacrificed, she must cleanse herself to honor the goddess. While the group gathered wood for the fire, she dressed in a ceremonial white chiton girdled with a gold rope.

Melanion had dressed the dove by the time she returned. She took the offering and raised it to the darkening sky, then placed it on the altar they'd made of crossed green branches above the fire. A goodly aroma purified the air, and the smoke from the offering rose in a thin, brave column to the heavens. As they watched, the full moon rose from behind the hills to greet the sacrifice. A sigh escaped the group, both of relief and resignation.

But Atalante didn't hear them. The moonlight pierced the night, holding her prisoner in a clean, cold silence. Her head hurt as though someone had placed a lead fillet upon it and strung it tight as a bow. The pain radiated down to her chest and settled like an arrow in her heart.

"Delian Artemis," she whispered. "What doom awaits me here? Give me an answer. Send me a sign, so I can prepare myself." The crown of lead dug into her forehead, and the darkness settled into her heart. She knelt, neck trembling with the strain of a burden heavier than she thought she could bear. And just as suddenly as it had come, the pain was gone. But the darkness remained, wrapped snugly about her heart. And there was no sign. Her goddess, as she had so many times, ignored her pleas.

She rose on trembling legs like a child fresh from the sickroom. Melanion lurched toward her, but she shook her head. "Put out the fire," she whispered. "We're to go on." He nodded wordlessly and doused the flames with a libation of wine.

By the time she had mounted and begun the last of the journey, Atalante's strength had returned. She led the others until at last they came to a clearing filled with the boisterous sound of men's laughter.

By the light of several fires, she saw many men lying back on rolled skins. For the most part, these hunters were bearded, at the peak of their strength—heroes, from the look of them. Their arms and chests shone with oil. Most of them glanced at the newcomers and then turned back to the others sitting beside them, interested more in their tales and drinking than in these youngsters from where ever.

One of them had risen at the approach of the horses. He was a well-built man, shorter than Melanion but heavily muscled. He had a pleasant face, with neatly cut blond hair, and a fair beginning of a beard. He looked to be in his early twenties. He strode up to Atalante and gave her a deep bow. His eyes were a dusty blue in the firelight. Atalante's father had described this man as the crown prince of Kalydon.

"You are Meleagros?" she asked, sliding from her horse. "Your father sent to mine for help. My name is Atalante, daughter of Iasus. We come with a band from Macedonia, as well. This is Melanion, son of Kryton."

To her amazement, Meleagros knelt at her feet. His blue eyes were laughing. "Are you Atalante or the goddess, herself, come to join our hunt? No mortal maid has such beauty." He looked at her as though he wanted to eat her. Inside the dark place, her heart gave a frightened leap. Melanion stepped closer to her. His arm touched hers. It felt rigid as iron.

"I am a mortal maid." Atalante's cheeks burned. "Get up, Prince. You embarrass me."

With a laugh, Meleagros rose and bowed to both Atalante and Melanion. He beckoned them to the fire. Atalante stole a glance at Melanion. She had never seen such narrow-eyed fury.

Two men in their thirties sat drinking, their backs against a boulder near the fire.

"My mother's brothers, Plexipus and Toxias, princes of Pleuron," said Meleagros. "Uncles, may I present Atalante of Thessaly and Melanion of Macedon?"

The two brothers raised their dark heads. " 'Tis not the custom to hunt with a woman. Why didn't you keep her home?" the elder asked Melanion, and spat at Atalante's feet.

Meleagros sprang forward, his fists balled, but a young man came out of nowhere and pulled him aside.

"It's all right, my friend," she heard Meleagros tell the young man. "I know not to let them push me too far."

Melanion responded to the surly brothers in a cool voice, "You will be hard pressed to claim the spoils while Atalante and her maidens hunt the boar. The goddess guides her spear."

Plexipus, whose eye slid to the left as the other looked straight at Melanion, called out to his nephew. "The Dark Mother decrees it's bad luck to hunt with a woman. Only men move about under the open sky during the day. Your mother fed you this knowledge with your first milk."

Atalante was so furious, she didn't have time to be afraid. She stepped into the clearing and raised her voice so all gathered could see and hear. "In my land the Mother and the gods talk to their children. If the gods of this place wish me to leave, tell me so. I will not offend them. Otherwise, we're here because your king asked me for help. Let us do what we agreed to do."

A tall warrior stood up. He shot her a flirtatious look and bowed as though she were a great queen. Then he turned to his companions. "I speak reason, so listen to me. What do you have to fear? The Maiden sent this boar. It won't hurt to have a maiden hunt it." Several men grunted. The sound seemed encouraging.

Another stood. "The omens foretold doom with this hunt, but we all came anyway. Perhaps the princess can avert some decree of the gods, not bring it on."

"Listen to him," said someone from the shadows. "He knows the ways of the gods."

Men nodded assent, called out a welcome. Meleagros walked into the center of the clearing and bowed again to Atalante. "It is decided. You are most welcome, daughter of Iasus."

Atalante heard one of the Companions calling to Melanion. He gave her a questioning look.

"Go on. I'm all right," she said.

As soon as he was gone, Meleagros pulled her aside beneath an outcropping of rock in the hillside. "There is no restriction in Kalydon to women hunting, Atalante. But where Plexipus and Toxias rule, men fear their women, who are filled with Dark Magic. My own mother, sister to these two I must call uncle, knows the ways of the Dread Mother, and all the curses. My father tried to wean her from the old ways, but to no avail.

"To tell the truth, she scares me. There's no form of suffering she can't call up with her spells and incantations."

The darkness throbbed around Atalante's heart. "I must be certain there'll be no trouble here. I'm responsible for my people," she said.

"Of course. All of you are welcome." Meleagros waved a hand to include the Companions and Thessalians, who had drawn nearer to each other as they approached the clearing. "Please, sit down and join us."

The young warrior who had pulled Meleagros away from his uncles appeared again with a wine cup.

"My thanks, friend." Meleagros gave the cup to Atalante and bade her drink.

When she returned the cup to his hand, Meleagros lifted it so all could see. "This princess and her maidens are my hearth guests. Let no harm come to any of them, for I am sworn to protect each one." As the warriors cheered, Meleagros drank from the cup, his lips on the same spot where Atalante's had been. She wanted to squirm, to run away from his bold grin.

"There's wine, there's fresh meat," Meleagros said to the Thessalians and Companions. "Be at ease. You have my oath on it that all of you are safe."

Theas settled the group into a corner of the clearing. He listened to the men, all of them hardened by experience in war he'd never known. One of them talked for a long time about finding a hollow ship after the winter storms to gain gold and glory.

He lounged on one elbow against his blanket roll, a cup of wine in his hand. A lithe movement from the left caught his eye. Korone walked toward the wineskin nearest a group of Kalydonians, her lush body moving in a sensuous glide. Theas sighed in exasperation and jumped to his feet.

"Go sit down," he said under his breath, grabbing the wine cup.

"I can get my own wine," Korone said with a sniff. She took a step toward the Kalydonians.

His hand closed on her arm like a vise. "I said sit," he repeated in a voice that brooked no disobedience.

Her gaze flew to his face and then to her arm. Without a word, she nodded and walked back into the shadow of a rock.

She was waiting for him there when he returned with the filled cup. He looked at her glittering eyes, then offered the cup. She took it and flung the contents into his face.

"You may have women who play at life where you come from. I am not one of them," Korone said in a furious whisper. "I tend to my own needs, Macedonian. I wish no man to fetch for me."

Theas was so hot, he thought he could feel his skin sizzle. By the gods! She made him regret that he had been raised a gentleman. "Look around you, woman," he said through gritted teeth. "Are you in Thessaly now? These men would as soon rape you as look at you. How many of us are there to defend you when a score of hardened warriors come to take you in the middle of the night? Had you sidled up to that wineskin, you'd have put us all at risk."

"I did not sidle!"

"You most certainly did. You can't seem to make a move without stirring a man's blood, you cheap little flirt!"

She stared at him, wide-eyed. Right before those blue-black eyes narrowed, he saw hurt on her face. What the hell had he done now, besides give her the truth? He'd done it for the sake of their band. Hadn't he?

"You think I'm too stupid to understand we're in a strange land, outnumbered ten to one by warriors in their prime?" she said glaring at him. "You think I move—whatever way I move—to arouse men in a situation like this?"

"Maybe not." Sense won out over exasperation, and maybe a little guilt crept in after that. He'd never lost his temper so completely with a woman. What the hell was wrong with him?

She put her hands on her hips. "I don't know how I move, Theas. I'm a dancer. I move like one, that's all."

"Around these men, try to move like a boy," he said.

Korone folded her arms across her chest and tapped one foot.

"What?" he asked.

"That apology you're thinking about making—I'm waiting for it."

He glanced down at that pretty arched foot, and then into her cool, dark gaze. "I'm sorry," he said softly.

Korone lifted the edge of her cloak. She wiped his face and neck clean of the splattered wine. "I'm sorry, too. I didn't realize what I was doing, Theas. I'm glad you warned me."

He tried a smile with her, and liked it when her lips curved a little. "All right," he said.

She held out the cup. "For the time being. If you would keep it for me."

He took the cup. He felt much better. This time, her smile was a real one, surprisingly sweet. She turned to join the others in the shadows.

"Korone?" he said softly. "One more thing."

She looked at him over her shoulder, all unconscious sensuality.

"If you so much as touch that damned belt of yours, I'll confiscate it."

"Come closer to the fire," Melanion heard one of the warriors call to Astrid and Alex, who were listening to their talk from the shadows. "This is a bitter night without the blaze to warm you." The men obligingly made room for them.

As Alex moved into the light, the skin he carried over his shoulder swung to a muffled sound of strings.

"A bard, are you?" a man said. "Give us a tale, lad. Something bold for men used to great deeds."

"I'll give you the story that began the journey of the Argo," said Alex. He pulled out the lyre and began to tune the strings. The men leaned forward, waiting, Melanion knew, for some pretty tale praising the hero of that adventure. He smiled, waiting for Alex to surprise them all.

Alex, satisfied with the chords, began to sing. His tale was not what they'd expected. He sang of a king who scorned his queen, and the king's mistress, who plotted to kill the queen's two children. The mother cried out to Father Zeus.

"For myself, I ask nothing. Take pity on my children."

The Lord of the Thunderbolt heard her cries and sent a golden ram with horns of silver. The queen placed her babes on the ram's back. Up it sprang, far above the conflicts of men.

With a clanking of armor and greaves, the king's soldiers came for the queen. One thrust of a bronze blade ended her life. But before death closed her eyes, she saw her children soar free and unafraid.

Alex's voice was strong enough to reach the farthest campfire, and sweet enough to break one's heart. Men stared at the ground. They seemed to be thinking of their own mothers and wives, and of the hundred little kind acts that each had never acknowledged. They looked at the women sitting around the fire, and Melanion saw that their eyes were gentle.

Atalante, sitting beside him, stared into the fire.

"What are you thinking?" he whispered.

"I wish I could place my brother on the back of a golden ram. I wish it would leap across oceans to a land where he can grow up strong like other boys. What are you thinking?"

He couldn't speak past the lump in his throat. All he could do was shake his head and stare into the fire.

"I wish your mother had lived," she said, and her voice was gentle. "If she had, maybe none of this . . ." Her gesture took in the clearing, the sickly, rotting fruit, the blasted land. "None of this would be necessary now for either of us."

Atalante believed that none of her friends knew of her feelings for Melanion, but somehow Meleagros must have guessed. The next morning, he asked Melanion to form a scouting party. No one knew the boar's range for certain, and on the face of it, Meleagros' request was reasonable, even prudent.

"I don't like this," Melanion said before he left.

"We'll be fine. The visiting warriors as well as Meleagros have given us protection. Everyone will heed them, even the Evil Eyes and their men." She glanced at the Pleuron campsite and Melanion nodded.

"Go on," she said quietly. "Return safely."

He nodded and squeezed her hand. Since the night before, they'd developed a tentative truce. Amidst the loneliness of this place, she was grateful for it, and watched him go down the forest path until she could see him no more.

Meleagros approached her a few moments after the scouting party had left. He spent the rest of the day with her, and all of the next. His eagerness to please her made her feel like a penned-up animal, and his extravagant compliments sent her into spasms of embarrassment.

Atalante stared into the fire early the next morning. The others were still asleep, but anxiety had chased her from her blankets. A twig broke behind her. She turned, only to find Meleagros taking his seat, an expectant look on his face.

Meleagros gave her a broad smile and settled back on his elbows. "This is wonderful. I've had more pleasure in the last two days than I've had—maybe ever."

"You must enjoy hunting a great deal," she said, inching away from his recumbent form.

He sent her a laughing glance. "It's not the hunting I'm enjoying, Atalante."

"How is it that the men of this region have such contempt for women, but are controlled by them at the same time?" she asked in an attempt to change the subject and escape his pointed compliments.

"They're not contemptuous, exactly. The men of Pleuron respect women who stay close to the hearth and loom. And they fear women who, like my mother, can hold back the harvest or bring sickness through black magic. But you—you are something very frightening. They think you and your maidens have broken the sacred laws."

Atalante shuddered and stared at the ground.

"When my father married my mother, he joined the two kingdoms together," Meleagros said. "For many years, he's wanted to stop the evil—to allow only the practice of the Mother's healing magic, and to teach the people only that side of Her that is good. My mother must hold something over him, some threat that keeps him silent when she takes her women to the forest to sacrifice to the Dark Mother. No man is allowed to see what they sacrifice, but it chills the blood to think about it too much.

"And I . . ." He shrugged and looked down at his hands.

"I've always been torn between my parents. They war on earth just like the sky gods war with the Dark Mother. Honor spurs me on to take up my father's side, but I'm a sorry sort of son."

He gave her a self-deprecating smile. "I fear pain more than death. And my esteemed mother is quite capable of cursing me with both."

His face grew very serious as he looked at her. One large paw groped for her hand. She swallowed the lump in her throat and allowed him to take it. "If I had a reason to fight her, I would do it. If I had a woman beside me for inspiration, I would take this country and make something great of it."

Meleagros' large hand squeezed hers and the pressure was like a vise. "If that woman needed me and my soldiers—and believe me, Atalante, I have a powerful army—I would come and destroy her enemies."

The world grew dim around her. The dark spot around her heart expanded until she drowned in black. This was what the goddess meant, when Atalante had made the sacrifice to her. She must sell herself for the promise of a strong army to protect her people. She forced herself to stay still, when all she wanted to do was run, run as far and as fast as she could, away from this cursed place.

Her blood pounded in her ears as she looked at Meleagros. His gaze was hot and eager. Carefully, she took a breath, knowing that with the slightest movement, she might shatter, begin to laugh, or gibber hysterically. She had to do it.

Meleagros spoke urgently. His hand gripped hers harder. She forced herself to concentrate, to make out his words.

"Atalante, when you came, I took you for a vision at first. Now I know you're a sign to me from the Huntress,

who calls me to the gods of my father. I know I can free myself, if only you'll help me. With you, I can be strong
enough."

Atalante took a deep breath against the nausea welling
up inside. "Come to Thessaly. I'll show you how the gods
and the Mother live together in harmony."

He took her other hand as well. She forced herself to accept his touch. "If I come, it will be with gifts and music.
Do you understand?"

She looked straight into his eyes. He meant he would
come as a groom. "Then come," she said.

He raised her hand and put it to his lips. She suppressed
a shudder as she stared beyond his bent head, thinking of
the years to come. She hoped he wouldn't beat her. She
hoped they didn't have to live with his mother. Gods! She
would have to live in this terrible place. The Kalydonians
would despise her unless she hid everything that made her
life worth living.

As a shadow fell over them, Meleagros dropped her
hand.

"The scouts are returned. Time to make ready," his
uncle Plexipus said in a sour voice.

Atalante crept away from the rest, who shuffled out of
their blankets and yawned over their mead. She found the
small stream that ran nearby and sank onto a mossy rock.

It was done. To live as Meleagros' wife, to feel his hands
on her body, to be imprisoned in his household, bearing
him the children that should have been hers and
Melanion's—how could she endure it? Better to die in
battle than to live in such hell.

Cold sweat ran from her neck and face; her chiton was
damp with it clear through. When Atalante was young,
she'd thought it a glorious thing to give her life for

Thessaly. She'd thought it would be easy—one quick death, not endless days of misery. The sun rose flat and dull in a steel gray sky. She rose, washed the sweat from her face and arms, and returned to camp.

Melanion searched for Atalante as soon as he entered camp while his men shouted for the hunters to arm themselves. Early this morning, the scouting party had caught sight of the boar in the distance. It took a little more time to find the beast's lair close to the foothills in swampy land. Their hunting ground lay in a dying forest with underbrush and roots that could trip a man, caves in which the boar could hide and then charge, ground interspersed with muck that could give at any step. His men had set the nets, pounding the pegs in very deep, for, even in the distance, the boar looked like a monster.

As they loosed the hounds, Melanion saw Atalante break into a run at the edge of camp. Feathering out to catch the scent, the boar hounds soon found the line and bayed their discovery. Melanion ran toward the swampland, catching up with Atalante. He was still worried about the strength of the nets.

Then, quite suddenly, the hounds lost the scent. Melanion took a deep breath and signaled the hunters to draw back and wait. Men fanned out as best they could in the uneven, swampy terrain. The land was dangerous in the best of times, but even more so on a hunt for a maddened boar whose movements were lightning fast. Melanion frowned looking at the thorny underbrush. It would impede the hunters' movements and hide the boar at the same time.

An unnatural silence settled around the hunters as they took their places in groups of twos and threes, not knowing when the hounds would push the boar toward them. No birds sang, no field mice or squirrels rustled the leaves lying on the spongy ground. Melanion stared in each direction for any hint of trouble. His ears strained toward the distant hills, where the hounds worked for fresh scent.

Suddenly, the hounds belled, this time, furiously. Meleagros shouted and sprang forward. Atalante winged past him through the marshy underbrush. A chill rose along Melanion's backbone. He shot after her, foreboding spurring him on, but she'd gotten a head start on him. Moments later, he spotted her in a copse somewhat ahead and to his right. Atalante waved once and signaled him to stay where he was. At the same time, he heard Philip's call to stop and wait. The others caught up; he could hear their straining breaths.

Melanion stood at the far edge of a cluster of low bushes to the east of the nets. He didn't like being so far from Atalante. He was too far away to divert the boar from her if it came through on a mad dash for its lair.

The clearing that led to the lair was close ahead. With startling speed, the hounds sprang into it in full cry.

The boar burst out of a thicket towards the lair like black thunder. The stories were true. Three times the size of an ordinary boar, he was a monster sent by an angry goddess— too strong for the nets, and too dangerous for mere men to hunt. His breath blew fire, hot and stinking, and his tusks were sharp as a sacrificial knife. He paused, snorting. His tiny red eyes took in the men. The hounds bayed madly and snapped at him, then raced back out of reach.

The hunters fanned out again in a semicircle, still grouped in twos and threes. Two of the heroes waited for him to his right, spears at the ready. He raked the earth, fiery eyes swerving from man to man. The boar charged and the hunter thrust his spear. Too late—the boar wriggled like a snake through the underbrush and was on him before the spear began its downward plunge. The man clutched his side, stared down at the red flowing blood and collapsed to the ground.

The hunters shouted, the hounds screamed, the boar raked the earth with his sharp hooves.

"He's mine!" one hunter called out. His javelin flew but the boar shot to the side and the weapon buried itself in the back of the second man who was stationed on the path to the lair. The man groaned and fell.

Melanion heard the boar coming again, but he zig-zagged, and . . . disappeared. In the eerie silence that followed, Melanion heard the groans of the two injured hunters. To his left, another hunter limped away leaning on his spear.

Suddenly, the underbrush ahead moved like a giant wave.

"Nestor!" Astrid cried. Nestor reacted instantly, leaping and grabbing at an overhanging bough, raising his legs beyond the reach of the murderous tusks as the beast shot through beneath him.

Philip stood a little way from Melanion, close to the lair. He must have decided that the boar would keep going for it, and he stood at the ready. But the boar slowed, then wheeled to the right and slipped through the brush. Melanion clutched his spear tighter, his eyes on Atalante.

Beside and a little behind him, Philip relaxed. He lowered his spear and looked disappointed. Suddenly, Melanion heard the sound of brush snapping right behind Philip and shouted a warning. He saw the sick look of understanding on Philip's face as his friend realized it was too late to protect himself. From the right, a flash of white thudded into Philip. He tumbled and crashed through briars and brush.

"What the hell?" Philip yelled. Niko lay sprawled on his stomach.

"You were a dead man," Melanion heard him say, pointing back with a limp hand to the clearing full of trampled brush. "And now you're not. We're even."

"How'd you do that?" Philip stared up at Niko, who'd risen and was wiping mud and dead leaves from his chiton.

Niko offered him a hand. "You're stronger," he said. "But I'm faster."

Ahead, men and hounds began to clamor. They were trying to drive the boar into the nets, but this was no ordinary beast.

He wheeled again, pinioned a hound on his left tusk, and dragged it for yards. With a snap of his neck, he flung the hound free into the muddy marsh and wheeled back again, headed directly for Atalante.

"Atalante, draw your bow!" Melanion shouted. His voice trumpeted out over the shrieks of the hounds as the beast tore through their ranks with supernatural swiftness.

"Apollo of the silver bow, give her time," he whispered, and ran toward her, spear upraised, shouting to turn the boar to him.

The boar paused in his mad rush. It must have seen him streaking toward it. But Atalante, clean and shining, was closer and a quicker kill. The monster plunged at her.

Atalante shot without hesitation and the arrow slid neatly between shoulder and rib. But the beast didn't go down. He waded toward her, madly squealing with pain, bent on her blood.

"I've got him!" Meleagros shouted from an outcropping above her. Just as Melanion reached Atalante, Meleagros jumped, pushed Melanion aside, and speared the boar. It turned on the spear, and writhed forward in fury to get at Meleagros. The prince hung on to the shaft as it whipped and bucked like a ship in a gale. Melanion scrambled up and thrust in his spear with all his strength. The boar's eyes dimmed and it sank, foaming and grunting as his life winked out.

"Hai, hai!" shouted the Kalydonian hunters and they leaped down into the marshy soil, circling Meleagros, pushing Melanion and Atalante aside. She looked up at Melanion and cocked a brow. Her hair had come loose from its thong. He brushed golden strands back from her hot cheeks with trembling hands.

"He was too big," he said with an almost steady voice. "Two men are dead and the gods know how many hounds."

"Atalante!" Meleagros shouted and pushed his way out of his relatives' circle. His hands were bloodied from the boar's carcass. His eyes blazed from the kill, and another urge, just as predatory, when he looked at Atalante. Melanion's blood began to race again. He clenched his fists and moved even closer to her.

Meleagros held up the boar's tusks for the hunters to see. "The spoils go to Atalante. It was she who downed the boar."

"No!" Plexipus, the elder uncle roared. "You bring dishonor to your House! Are you so besotted by this female that you have forgotten your mother? The spoils go to her from you, the dutiful son who rid his land of the cursed boar." The circle parted. The uncles grasped their swords and spears, standing over the carcass with menace emanating from every muscle.

Meleagros' face flushed a dusky red. His sword flashed as he drew it. His friend, the one who had protected him from the uncles when Atalante and Melanion had first met Meleagros, appeared at his shoulder, and drew his sword. Their friends threw them spears. The circle fell away completely in dead silence. Meleagros and his friend took a step toward the Keuretes.

"Stop," Atalante cried. "For shame. Give the spoils to Meleagros, who dealt the death blow."

"Hold your tongue, woman. This quarrel concerns only the men of this house, and it's been a long time coming," said Plexipus.

"You shame me with your insults to this woman and steal from her the rightful shares of a hero—yes, a woman hero, just as you steal my father's power. You want me to dance like a puppet upon my mother's strings. I am of Kalydon, not Pleuron. I tell you now, before all assembled, I serve my father, not her or you." Meleagros grinned and turned to give Atalante a triumphant look. Melanion felt her shrink from Meleagros' burning gaze.

Meleagros turned to his uncles and raised his spear. "Release me from your ceaseless demands, or death waits for some of us now."

"Never!" shouted Plexipus. "In your lust, you desecrate the dark law. Better you meet your death than betray our House and our city."

The uncles raised spears and swords. Meleagros and the slender youth by his side circled back to back. Plexipus lunged at the prince. Meleagros feinted. The spear glanced off his ribs, leaving a trickle of blood behind. He grunted, swerved, and his spear hand thrust forward. Plexipus, pinned between the spearhead and the hillside at his back, arched against the sharp point and grinned madly.

"Do you know what your mother will do when she hears of this? Torture and death await you. Make your choice, infidel. Your time grows short."

Meleagros pressed the spear forward just enough to dimple the skin on Plexipus' chest. "Your taunts mean nothing to me. She knows my father will have her put to death if she kills his only son. Yield, Uncle, and accept the end of ignorance and fear in our kingdom."

"Blasphemer, I die to ensure the price you'll pay." Plexipus drew a great breath and flung himself forward on the point of the spear. The shaft slammed through his ribs. His eyes dimmed, his breath gave from the clenched teeth. As his head lolled, he slumped to the ground.

Meleagros pulled out the spear and turned. His companion was locked in combat with Toxias, the younger Keurete.

"Uncle!" he shouted. "Stop now."

"Make me, you rutting, foul-minded beast."

Meleagros groaned and sprang at him. His neck was knotted in strain as he rang blows down upon his uncle's sword, pushing him back through the clearing. They stumbled over the boar's carcass and righted themselves, cursing. Meleagros fought as one possessed. His iron blows clanged against a weakening sword. Toxias retreated until his feet touched a cliff edge high above a marshy lake.

"Uncle. Don't make me do this." Meleagros' voice broke.

"Child of damnation, you've killed my brother. Fight," sobbed Toxias, and thrust.

"Let the gods judge us," cried Meleagros. He lunged left and forward at the same time. His sword spitted his uncle's chest. Toxias slid earthward and died.

As the hunters stared at the bodies of the uncles, a cold dread settled over them all. Men from Pleuron picked up the fallen brothers and carried their bodies out of camp.

Meleagros said not a word as he mounted his horse and
led the rest of the company to Kalydon. He looked straight
ahead with lifeless eyes. His friend leaned toward him,
speaking urgently, but he rode on unheeding.

The sun was a blood-red ball low in the sky as they entered the city. Melanion leaned over on his horse and
wrapped Atalante's flapping clamys close about her, but
she didn't seem to feel anything, not even the raw north
wind that had blown up from nowhere. As they entered the
city, Melanion looked toward the end of the square where
a silent palace rose, waiting, it seemed, to swallow them
all.

Meleagros led them into the Megaron. What little light
the lamps gave off was smothered by the shadows. On the
great hearth, a log, half-consumed, glowed a dull red.

Atalante and Melanion followed Meleagros until he
stopped. Melanion looked past him to the woman who
stood before the hearth. She was tall, cloaked in black, with
long, dark tresses crimped above a tight bodice. Bracelets of
coiling serpents banded her arms. Atalante shuddered to
see her. Atalante, thought Melanion, who called the House
Snakes her brothers.

The woman's eyes slid over her, then shot to Meleagros
standing dead still, watching her with doomed certainty.

"You were my son, my treasure, and I loved you so
much that I begged the Dread Mother to grant you long,
long life. She did. But if you proved so hateful that I wished
to destroy you, she gave me magic to take back the gift.

"Do you see the log on the fire? It's your life. When the
log is consumed, you will die. Just as I am filled with hatred
for you, you will be devoured by death." The queen swayed
like a snake. Her voice hissed and echoed in the hall. For
the first time in his life, Melanion was cold with fear.

Meleagros fell to the floor writhing. The log cracked in half. Sparks exploded.

"No," cried his friend. He threw himself on Meleagros. "Lift the curse," he begged the queen. "He didn't want to kill them. They forced him."

The queen drew herself up. As Meleagros' screams rose, she seemed to loom larger. Her black shadow towered higher on the wall behind her, like a cobra right before it struck. Meleagros' screams turned to whimpers of anguish. And then there was no sound at all.

"See the brand?" she said. "It crumbles into ash. It is finished."

His friend cradled Meleagros' head with his arm, and sobbed.

"At-a-lan-te," the queen intoned in a trance-like voice. "Girl with the beauty of the goddess. You have brought down this House, with your bright hair, with your long limbs. You think to outrun your fate.

"Listen to me," she hissed. "Your beauty will be a curse to you. It will bring death to many who seek your love, while havoc and destruction whirl around you."

The queen raised her arms. The black cloak fell away from her shoulders as she swayed. The fire leaped in the hearth.

"Much killing will you witness, and much blood will be on your hands, until you wish that the goddess had given you an eye that wandered, or skin marked with the pox."

Melanion leaped forward to shield Atalante, making the sign against evil on her brow. She stood like stone. He tried to wrap his cloak about her, but she cried out and broke away, running faster than a gazelle, out of the palace, out of the city, across the marshy plain. Thessalians and Companions raced to the courtyard and mounted their horses.

Melanion was the first away, cropping the black until they flew after her.

He found Atalante at the edge of a marsh lake, kneeling in the mud. She didn't seem to notice him. She sobbed as she rubbed filthy bracken and decaying marsh dirt over her cheeks and hair. He grabbed her hands and held them still. She struggled against him, but he shouted her name and shook her until, finally, she looked at him with tormented eyes.

"See the irony of the goddess," she whispered. "I wished to be beautiful for you. And she gave me that gift, so in my hubris, I could destroy everything. I betrayed—"

She hid her face in her filthy hands. "Don't ask me. I can't tell you what I . . . Don't look at me, Melanion. I'm not fit for you to look on. And now my people will pay for my sin. The slaughter to come . . . it's on my soul."

He found the edge of his chiton and dipped it in the lake. Washing her face and hands, he murmured over her as though she were a fever-sick child. When the worst of her sobbing was over, he lifted her onto his lap. His heart cracked while she clung to him. She was so fragile, so devastated.

He cradled her, looking blindly into the distance. "Do you believe that poison—that the goddess made you beautiful so you could destroy your own people? She gave you beauty, and more, so you could be a hero to lead men up from destruction—to help them see the way to the good.

"How many times have you told me the Mother isn't cruel or terrifying? I swear to you, she'll soften the curse, giving us only what we can bear. Come with me. We'll leave this blighted land and go to the hills. We'll breathe pure air and walk in the sun."

Atalante slumped against him. For the first time since he'd met her, she seemed helpless. He lifted her onto his horse and swung up behind her. Their people followed him out of Kalydon, and they didn't stop until they reached Melanion's cave beside the clear stream. Before they slept, Melanion insisted they make libations to Artemis and Apollo. Holding Atalante close, he offered thanks that they still lived, and before all present, he kissed Atalante's brow and begged Apollo to heal her whom he loved.

Their provisions were running low, but they shared what they had, and the simple meal seemed to cheer them. As Melanion covered Atalante with another himation, he overheard Nestor and Philip.

"It's not the worst thing to be born a Macedonian," Nestor said as he rolled over in his blankets.

"Nor a Thessalian," Philip replied. Then there was silence under the stars. The little company slept while Atalante tossed with troubled dreams. Melanion held her, making soothing sounds. And knew that, in Macedonia to the north, the queen's curse brooded and fed upon itself.

# Chapter 9

## The Spring Games

When Melanion arrived in Hamalclion several days later, he saw that the city had become a center for war and warriors. Everywhere, the flames of the arms makers rose high in the air. Anvils rang day and night. Swords, greaves, shields and helmets piled up beside the forges. Farmers and vintners filled the marketplace with their grain carts and booths of huge wineskins. The army's provisioners shopped daily.

The Megaron overflowed with mercenary soldiers. Tall, black-haired Assyrians with hooked noses and long curls rode in on their war chariots with spiked wheels. African men in leopard skins shivered in the northern winter air. Small, dark Etruscans from beyond the western sea lounged about, throwing quoits and playing drinking games. There were too many of them for the palace to hold. A tent city sprang up outside the citadel. At night hundreds of fires blinked on the plain.

As soon as he'd bathed off the grime of the trip, Melanion received Kryton's summons to meet him in council. He offered him a seat at his right hand, but had no time to greet him, for the generals and councilors were in an uproar.

"Outrageous sons of bitches . . ."

"The stupidity! When they know we'll be upon them in a few months!"

Kryton rose, grabbing his wine cup, and glowered his

councilors to silence. "Come walk with me," he said to Melanion. "I feel the need to clear my head."

They found a deserted spot on the battlements. Melanion gave his father a questioning look. "What's going on?"

His father drained his wine cup. "A Thessalian raiding party crossed the southern border three nights ago. They burned down Baron Alexias' manor, stole away his young wife and the more comely of the slaves. We found her the next morning." His eyes narrowed. "They'd tortured her, raped her, and then slit her throat."

Kryton shook his head wearily. "I always thought they were cowards. But I never expected this—butchery from them." He sighed, stared out at the plain below, where hundreds of watch fires burned. "I have my hands full, let me tell you. Half my men demand that we take Thessaly now. But we have to wait until the spring rains are over."

Melanion's mind ferreted about, looking for a reason. And found one.

"How do you know this is a Thessalian crime?" he asked, leaning close and speaking so low there was no danger of being overheard. "I was with them in Kalydon. They could never have done anything like this."

"We found a tablet by the wife," Kryton said. "The killers said they were avenging the torture and murder of a Thessalian nobleman a couple of years ago. It was Polymus' men who killed him, but Polymus swears they did so without his knowledge. He claims he was riding ahead with scouts when his soldiers caught the young man. By the time he returned, they'd killed the boy. Polymus says he disciplined the men severely."

"A fine story. Did you question the men individually? Thessaly's fate shouldn't depend on a liar and a schemer like Polymus."

Kryton dismissed his objections with a sharp wave of the hand. "Listen to me, Melanion. I need that land. The bastard who rules it deserves what he gets. Whether Polymus ordered the torture and murder of one Thessalian youth and one Macedonian wife means little in the long run. Especially if the lie serves me well. The generals are so furious, they'll make short work of our campaign."

Melanion fought the hot rush of rage that threatened to engulf him. For a moment, he saw nothing but Polymus' throat and his own hands tightening around it. "You can't do this." His voice quivered with the fury he felt. "Your men will destroy every Thessalian they find if you allow this lie to go unpunished. Think what will happen to the innocent, to the women and children, the male servants, the shopkeepers and farmers. Stop Polymus before he destroys everything, including you."

"That's enough!" Kryton's face was purple. "I send you off for a few weeks to treat with other princes, and all you've done is develop a fondness for the enemy. What the hell's wrong with you, Melanion?" Kryton rubbed his eyes. When he looked at Melanion again, the rage was gone, leaving only a weary looking king with a troubled frown.

"Get some sleep, boy. You're tired, that's all. Tomorrow, you'll see things more clearly." Kryton clapped his hands and the Companions emerged from a near doorway. "Take him to his rooms and see that he gets a decent night's sleep, there's a good lad," he told Theas.

*Do no harm, do no harm, do no harm.* The vow he'd sworn to his mother and the gods drummed through his head as he walked to his rooms. How could he protect Thessaly without harming his father? Why had his mother bound him so his soul was cleaved in half? Was this pit what the bards called fate?

★ ★ ★ ★ ★

The next morning, Melanion watched his father drill his troops. At Kryton's command, they moved into massive formations with the precision and delicacy of dancers. Few men could rival Kryton as a tactician. He knew where each force would march, what defense the Thessalians would mount against them, how to move his vast army in phalanxes that would overwhelm any variation Iasus might add to his defense.

That night in the Hall, Polymus, sitting at the king's left, turned a smile on Melanion like that of a crocodile pleasantly contemplating dinner. His son, Xuthus, gaudy in gold and green, sat beside Polymus, directly opposite Melanion. He fingered an ivory handled knife with which he occasionally stabbed a piece of meat.

When the platters were cleared, several of the commanders left the Megaron, but Polymus and Xuthus remained.

"Father, I need to speak with you tonight," Melanion said softly to the king.

Kryton nodded. "Soon," he said.

"Prince Melanion, your adventure in Kalydon has made you familiar with the Thessalian royal household," Polymus said. "I am much interested in the Princess Atalante. Word has it that she is a courageous woman with a beautiful body and face. What is your impression?"

Melanion stiffened. A chill raced down his backbone. "Why?"

Polymus shrugged and smiled more broadly. "I have plans to make her part of my household this summer."

Melanion willed his hands to remain relaxed and easy as he slipped out his own dagger and reached for a winter apple from the burnished bowl. "You'll make her a slave if

Thessaly is defeated?" he asked.

"Only until she breeds. If she rewards my son with a superior child or two, I shall reward her. Instead of his concubine, I shall make her a second or a third wife."

Xuthus gave him a bone-chilling smile and stabbed through an orange at the navel.

Melanion's answering smile was a baring of teeth. "Think twice about it," he said softly. Staring at Xuthus, he buried his dagger in the wood of the table with one jerk of his hand.

"The princess was cursed in Kalydon," Theas said from his post behind Melanion. Obviously, he was trying to protect Atalante. If Melanion's jaw wasn't clenched in rage, he'd be grateful.

"She'll be the cause of death and suffering," Theas continued in a quiet voice. "I don't believe you wish your son such a fate, do you, Commander."

"Who gives the curse power?" Polymus asked.

"The Dread Mother," Theas said.

Polymus shrugged. "After we take Thessaly, there'll be no more talk of the Mother, in any of her aspects. I'll personally put her shrines to the torch. When you destroy the wealth of an enemy, man or god, you destroy his power. But what say you, Prince? Shall I claim Atalante for my dear son?"

Melanion jerked the knife out of the table. "You've presented the princess in a flattering light, Commander. I've a mind to claim her for myself." Dimly, he heard Theas suck in his breath.

Melanion forced himself to sit back in his ebony chair, to drink as though his blood didn't boil with the urge to end it, now. He stared at Xuthus' hands, playing with the knife. It would be so easy to slam down his wrist and fillet him with his own knife. But Polymus would be at his back, ready to stab him if he even moved toward Xuthus. And Polymus, the real threat to all he held dear, was just far enough away from Melanion to survive the fight.

Melanion concentrated on the fine grains in the table—anything, to keep from murder at his father's high table. Finally, Kryton rose and signaled him to follow. As soon as they were alone in the king's chambers, Melanion turned to his father.

"Atalante is everything Polymus says, and much more. If I could be certain of the future, I would protect her with my life from that monster and his spawn. But I don't know what will happen to me in the coming battle."

He gripped Kryton's hand hard. "Father, I swore a sacred oath to protect you and to stand by you, even when I opposed your will. Now I ask the same of you, but not for myself. Swear to me that you won't give Atalante to Polymus. Swear you'll protect her."

Kryton stared down at their joined hands. He laughed. "You think I'm some sorry fool, boy? That I don't know this man—what he'll do if he gets the power he seeks? Pah! I understand the girl would have a poor time of it under his thumb. If you want her that badly, you can have her soon. But I'm not fool enough to wake this man from his dreams of glory until he's given me a victory."

In desperation, Melanion gripped his father's hand harder. "Not good enough. Swear."

"Let go of me, Melanion." Kryton's voice was deadly quiet. "Nobody forces me to take an oath."

Melanion's blood seemed to turn to ice. "Very well," he said in a voice that held nothing—no anger, no sorrow, nothing. He turned and headed for the door. If he got to his rooms, he could take the Companions and fight their way out of the palace. Perhaps he'd make it to the border with all of the Hundred if he was swift enough.

He had his hand on the latch when Kryton called, "Wait!"

As Melanion turned back from the door, his father sighed in what sounded like relief. "Very well," he said, "if it means that much to you." Kryton crossed the room, placed his left hand on Melanion's shoulder and his right on his heart. "I swear by the gods above that I'll protect the princess Atalante from Polymus and any other as long as I shall live. If I foreswear this oath, may the Daughters of Night destroy me." His gaze sharpened as he looked at Melanion. "Happy now?"

Melanion nodded in one jerky motion. When his father pointed to an inlaid chair, he sank into it, his muscles suddenly weak in the aftermath. Did his father realize that he'd come within a hair's breadth of committing treason?

Kryton massaged his reddened hand and gave him a rueful smile. "Must have really liked this woman to champion her the way you did. The way you were in the Hall, boy! For a while, there, I thought I'd be one commander short. Don't do that again around Polymus, hear? It's dangerous to show that snake anything you're thinking."

Melanion nodded and stared down at his drink.

"I need him a little longer," said Kryton in a quiet voice. "Just give me that time. After Thessaly, we'll de-fang him. Together. All right?"

Melanion stared at his father in despair. "Please. Do it now. Fate has a way of making a man sorry he waited to get rid of something as evil as Polymus."

Kryton gave him a smile of great warmth. "My own son. You're right about Polymus, but you're wrong to have so little faith in your father. Think of me as a juggler, with three, four swords in the air at one time. I've been at this game too long to get slashed. By the time all this is yours, Macedonia will be done with poor peasants and greedy barons. There'll be enough for everybody in Thessaly—gold to build ships, harbors to send them trading that'll bring in more gold.

"You'll have wealth and power and a huge standing army. Do you want this princess? Take her, then. But you'll have your choice of brides after Thessaly. She's only the daughter of a weak-livered, smug, pissant. The High King of Mycenae has a daughter, as well, you know."

"Just protect Atalante, Father. Don't forget."

Kryton rose and wrapped Melanion in a great hug. "I never forget an oath, son. Especially the first I've ever had to make. Go to bed. That damned hunt's got you lashing out at anybody fool enough to get in your path. I should never have sent you to that cursed country."

Later, Melanion stared into the black night. His father's promise hadn't eased his sense of foreboding. If only his dreams weren't full of terrible visions—Atalante in tears, Iolcus beneath the heel of Polymus and the Red Bands, Xuthus in red and gold, claiming Atalante before the Serpent Throne. He shuddered as a cold sweat broke out on his neck and brow.

Very well, Melanion thought. If he was the only roadblock in Polymus' way, he'd be very, very careful. For he had no intention of making it easy to remove him.

Turning abruptly, he called for the Companions. They posted a guard and threw down their skins around Melanion's bed. From that night on, they only ate in the chamber. The slave who delivered the food tasted everything in front of them. Wherever Melanion went, his friends surrounded him. In a world he didn't trust, he was as safe as he could hope to be.

Winter slipped from the land, giving way to spring's clearer light. The Hundred grew in number until they equaled a small army. Each man was related in some way to one of the twenty Companions.

Melanion stood beside Theas in the Megaron one warm evening. In a week, the spring games would begin. Foolish as it was to lose his concentration, Melanion was pondering the many ways a man could make love to woman and which one he'd teach Atalante first when something brushed against him. Startled, he glanced up to find a serving woman smiling at him. She was small with doe eyes and soft hair. Her body gave off the musky scent of sandalwood as she rubbed her breasts against his chest.

He stared, trying to place her. She looked young and innocent, but he'd seen her in the corridors with Xuthus recently. Certainly, the look she gave him was bold as a hetaira's. But her lips trembled. With another look of open invitation, she moved away to pour wine for someone else, and he thought no more of it until later, when he and several of Philip's cousins caught sight of her in the corridor to his chambers.

She waited as he approached, wringing the pleats of her gown between her fingers.

"What is it you want?" he asked, as she shifted her weight from side to side.

"Only to be with you," she whispered, and moved closer.

He wanted nothing to do with the woman—not her obvious fear or her sad attempts at seduction. He reckoned he knew who'd sent her. But why?

He pulled her in front of him, where he could see her every move. "Come," he said. He and all of Philip's cousins followed her to his chamber. At his knock, the door opened wide. Twenty pairs of eyes stared at the serving woman as Melanion pushed her into the room.

"What does she want?" Theas asked him.

"Maybe just Melanion, you ninny," said Alex.

"I don't think so." Eyes narrowed, Theas looked her over while the others formed a circle around her.

"Who sent you? What are your orders?" Melanion rapped out. The woman trembled like a sparrow caught in a net.

"It doesn't matter. It's too late," she whispered in a pain-filled voice.

A pang of pity shot through Melanion. "Tell us who sent you and what he told you to do. We'll arrange safe passage far away from here. You can start a new life, a better one," he said in a gentler voice.

The woman twisted, looking around the circle, perhaps for some way to escape, and then covered her face. "He'd find me anywhere." She reached into her gown. A small, ivory handled dagger flashed against her arm, and a thin trickle of blood dripped on her gown. She groaned and sank to the floor writhing like a snake. Her eyes rolled in her head. As her gasp turned into a choking, dribbling wheeze, her face turned the blue-gray cast of death. The last breath rasped out of her.

Niko gaped. "But it was only a scratch." He bent to pick up the dagger, still clutched in her hand.

"Careful," Theas said pulling him back. "I'll wager there's poison on the tip of the blade. And it was meant for Melanion. Take it by the handle and throw it into the brazier."

Niko did so. The charcoal hissed around the knife blade.

"Hmm. She chose to die rather than to escape." Theas looked thoughtful. He lifted the girl's gown.

"By the gods, man," Alex said in a shocked voice. "Have some respect for the dead."

"Look here." Theas pointed to the girl's thighs. On the tender flesh between her legs there were raw, bleeding sores and searing burns.

Melanion clenched his jaw. "Who would do something like this?"

Theas stared down at the dead girl. "Not Polymus. It's too close to the campaign. He wouldn't risk dissention and an accusation of murder. No."

Theas' gaze found Melanion's. "Odds are Polymus will wait until the battle to kill you. Then, it's easy—a javelin in your back during the chaos—a state funeral afterwards and nobody the wiser. That's his style."

Suddenly, Melanion wanted to be sick. "Xuthus?" he asked softly.

Theas nodded. "I agree."

Xuthus. Melanion stared numbly at Theas. "He wants Atalante." Brutal rage replaced the nausea. "I'll kill the bastard," he said. "I'll announce it now, before my father and all his men. And then, I'll kill him." He grabbed his sword and lunged for the door.

Theas grabbed his arm as he swung by. "What'll you tell them?" he yelled. "That a bold piece of baggage took her own life in your chamber? Did she ever make a move against you? Hell, it's just another sad story—the celibate prince of Macedon refusing another lovelorn beauty. There's not a shred of evidence that Xuthus sent her. And what do you think King Kryton will do when you challenge his commander's only son? Cheer you on?"

"Gods!" Melanion crashed his fists into the door. The oak cracked with the blows. He was choking on the rage, going under a tide of red that blinded him. "I should kill them now. Both of them. Why not?" His voice sounded like something inhuman, feral. "A knife in the back, poison in their food. Their methods are easy enough to copy."

The Companions stared at Melanion as though he'd metamorphosed into some monster they'd never seen before. The red tide withdrew slowly. He looked down at his bleeding knuckles and drew a jagged breath. Then he gazed around the circle, and had his answer in the shocked faces of the men who'd followed him because he insisted they live honorably.

Melanion swallowed hard. "Alex," he said in his own voice. The young bard snapped to attention.

"Bring your cousin Clisthenes and two more of your kinsmen from the Hundred. Take the girl into the forest and bury her. For pity's sake, observe the rituals. Say nothing of this to anyone so Xuthus will wonder what became of her. It'll keep him off balance. Let the Hundred know. We'll be leaving again, as soon as I can arrange our provisions."

As the Companions quietly laid out their sleeping skins, Melanion stared out the windows of his chamber into the darkness. If only he could kill them cleanly, in open combat. He shook his head impatiently. "If onlys" never solved anything. He needed to think, to plan. He needed to get to Iolcus, to warn the king and convince him to use a particular strategy. And he needed help.

Thus it was that two days later, he and the Companions stopped for the evening with Linos and his family. Melanion pulled Linos aside after the evening meal.

"I need you now," he said.

Linos nodded. "I am yours."

"Guide my men until I return. The times are dangerous. The Hundred need a seasoned leader. Ask for Clisthenes,

Alex's cousin." Melanion slipped off the heavy gold ring with the lion's head seal—the heir apparent's ring. "Take this," he said, holding it out to Linos. "They'll follow you as they would me."

Linos nodded and took a leather thong, slipped it through the ring, and tied it securely round his neck. Melanion nodded. He'd done what he could.

Iolcus shone like a jewel above the glittering sea. As Melanion and the Companions made their way through the city, sounds and sights stirred their curiosity and fascinated them. Jugglers and tumblers in bright colors flipped, somersaulted, and danced on wagons parked at street corners. The taverns were filled with travelers. Parents proudly bragged to strangers about their children's chances at the games. Men and women who loved sport had come from their rich estates beyond the southern mountains. Odds makers argued over the athletes.

Melanion approached the Serpent Gates and dismounted. He greeted the groom who rushed forward to take his horse and the man colored in pleasure. As he made his way into the Megaron, his blood almost leaped in his veins. It felt so good to breathe free air.

Melanion passed through crowds of courtiers and southern landholders who had come to ask the king's judgment. His eyes raked the huge hall and found Atalante immediately.

Instantly, she turned as though she'd heard him call out her name. He felt his grin widen so much it seemed to split his face. But she didn't smile at him. She looked at him with eyes that seemed to die a little death, and his stomach twisted in sudden fear.

Still, she came toward him. The crowd parted as she

walked forward. Finally, she was close enough to clasp his hand, but she still said nothing. Instead, she turned and led him back through the crowd, out beyond the walls of the palace to the small door behind the hedge. She kept her silence and his heart began to pound against his chest.

What was wrong? Had Hyperion died over the winter? Was her mother ill? Had her father lost faith in him? When they finally reached the small room they had shared in autumn, he opened his arms to take her, but she held up a hand to stop him. Her eyes pleaded, deep indigo pools in a dead white face.

She crossed the room and looked out the high window to the plain beyond. What had happened that she couldn't even face him?

"I can't live with it any longer. I wish—oh, gods! I wish I could lie to you. But I have to tell you. About Kalydon."

An icy hand grabbed his heart and twisted it. He stepped toward her but she wheeled at the sound, staring at him with wide, frightened eyes.

"Stay where you are." She even sounded afraid of him.

"Meleagros. It was my fault he died." She bit her lip, wrung her hands. "When he asked you to lead the scouting party he—he did it to get rid of you. So he could tell me things."

Blood began to beat in his brain. "What kinds of things?" he asked. Her chin came up to meet whatever threat she must have heard in his voice.

"He wouldn't leave me alone, Melanion. He told me he loved me. He said he'd bring his warriors to stand with us against Macedonia. If I'd marry him."

"No!" Melanion heard the roar that ripped his throat. Atalante's expression changed from tension to blazing defiance.

"Do you remember when we asked Artemis if we should remain in Kalydon? I'd seen something in the smoke of the sacrifice—some terrible burden just for me. I thought this was it. He looked at me as though . . . as though he wanted to eat me, Melanion. I didn't want to, but I thought the goddess had charged me to say yes. So I did."

The rage Atalante saw in Melanion's face burned so hot she feared his touch would scald her. The room was silent for so long, she could hear her own heart beating a fearful tattoo. She thought she'd better finish the recitation before he made the first move to throttle her.

When she opened her mouth to explain, he cut her off. "Did you lie with him? Did you cry out the way you do with me? How did you keep your moans from the others, or did they all hear you and keep your secret?" He sneered as though she were a piece of offal brought indoors on someone's sandal.

His fury sparked her own. "I didn't let him touch me. But by the gods, I would have, and more, to save Thessaly."

"Damn you!" he shouted. "What did you think of me, to dishonor me like that?" His hands gripped her arms, hard, and he gave her a shake that rattled her teeth. Suddenly, he went dead still, staring at his hands. He dropped them and backed away. His face drained of all color. Whirling, he laid his forehead against the wall. The muscles of his back knotted beneath his chiton. His hands clenched and unclenched.

She couldn't bear to see him like this. "Melanion." Her skirts rustled as she walked closer.

"Don't touch me!"

"Please."

"Atalante. When everything else in my life was murky, you were clear light. You betrayed me without even giving me a chance to find another way."

She took a deep breath. She reached out a hand to his shoulder.

He whirled on her, towering over her. Fury twisted his face into the dark mask of a fiend. "Get the hell out of here before I hurt you."

Atalante steeled herself not to leap away. It wasn't a difficult thing to do as her legs trembled so much, she couldn't have taken a step. She raised her chin and gave him what she prayed was a look of utter calm. "If I leave now, we'll never find our way back. Do you understand? I'm more afraid of losing you than I am of what you'll do to me."

Atalante took a deep breath. Somehow, she made the trembling stop. Deliberately, with both hands, she reached out and grabbed his arms.

His biceps corded like hot iron. He jerked her to him, staring down into her eyes, his own burning, his lips just a breath from hers. She held his gaze, past the fury, the sense of betrayal, and saw a terrible, lost agony that wrenched her heart. And as she looked, the color seeped from his face, leaving only the lines of strain, the nostrils flared, as though it took effort to breathe.

"Oh, gods," he said, his voice broken. He pulled her to him, one hand cradling her neck, the other holding her close against him. "I can't—even when you tell me this—I can't touch you in anger. But I must touch you. Do you understand?"

Her knees went weak with relief. "Yes."

"I can't . . . There's no grace in me, only need. I'm drowning in it."

She raised her hands to his face, then to the ties on her gown. "Yes." The gown slipped from her shoulders and pooled on the floor.

He swept her up and laid her on the narrow bed, murmuring unintelligible, tortured sounds as his lips traveled across her face, and down, into the crook of her neck. Her hands trembled as they slipped the ties of his tunic and pushed it down over his hips. His body covered her, his heat warmed her where there had been only coldness before.

She pulled him to her. "Hurry."

He groaned. With one thrust, he slid into her. She felt the shock of pleasure through her whole body. His eyes locked with hers. Rising on his elbows, he found her nipple, stroked once, with just his thumbnail. She gasped, lifted her hips to take him deeper. And he began. With every stroke, he cleansed away the poison that lay between them. And he watched her, holding her gaze, stripping her naked down to her soul, and letting her see him, in all his pain and all his vulnerability. It was too much—everything she felt was too intense—the passion, and the depth of that wordless communication.

"Listen to me," he said. "Never again, do you hear? Swear it. Not for anything—country, kin, anything. You never forsake me."

Pinned in extremity, aching for completion, she felt something shift, and it might have been the whole world. She saw Melanion in all his aspects: hero; tender, enraged lover; a lonely man attempting the good against overwhelming odds.

He had trusted her and she'd betrayed him. He needed her, not only as war leader, but as the keeper of his heart.

She saw her sin for what it had been—her refusal to trust the one true point in a life fraught with uncertainty. What she must believe in was not her country, not even her father's wisdom. It was this man who had never broken trust with her, who needed her in every way a woman wants to be needed. Who suffered even as he made her suffer. Who controlled his fury even though she had taken away her trust.

The tears ran down her cheeks, but she didn't care anymore what he saw. He was entitled to all of her. "I'll never forsake you," she said. "Never again."

He must have sensed the change, for his eyes blazed with triumph. She was filled with ineffable tenderness and sorrow, because he couldn't really feel the love that flooded through her for him. He thought only that he'd won the least victory, her body's fidelity. But if the gods gave them time, she would make him see what he was to her, and believe.

She wrapped her arms around his neck, and kissed his throat, then bathed it with her tears. "I love you," she whispered, and knew that wasn't enough to even begin to explain.

With a groan, he buried his face against her hair and thrust his hips, plunging. She locked her legs around him and gave to him, letting him take her, trusting him with all of herself. He thrust deeper, faster, and it was enough. It was everything.

Melanion woke in darkness, Atalante's warm body pressed against him. He thought she slept, he couldn't be sure. He had not been a graceful lover—there had been few, if any, preliminaries. But then, she hadn't seemed to miss them, and she'd given as good as she got. He smiled a little and felt the sting on his shoulder—a love bite he'd carry for a few days. That's what came of wedding a warrior, he thought.

In the moonlight, her limbs looked like living marble,

tangled with his. But she was warm and soft, and in the end, something had changed between them. The fury and the hurt had disappeared. He was still too raw to question why. His lips sought the pulse in her neck, felt it trip faster, knew she was waking.

In the aftermath of lovemaking, his troublesome mind slid into questions again. "In the end, before the altar of the gods, would you have done it?" he asked.

She sighed. The hand that stroked his hair pulled him closer. "And when the time comes, will you choose my father or yours?" Her voice was soft, accepting, filled with pain.

Now that rage no longer blinded him, he understood. She had struggled between two forms of treason and had chosen as her honor bade her. He remembered the revulsion in her voice when she described Meleagros' attentions. Melanion hated the fact that she'd been willing to condemn herself as well as him to such misery.

"I brought the curse on all of us," she whispered. "Meleagros' death, the war to come—all of it is my fault. I—I don't sleep well, knowing what I've done."

He felt his heart twist in an agony of tenderness. "You think Polymus and my father and all the Red Bands will invade Thessaly because you agreed to . . . ?" The words still stuck in his throat.

She shook her head. "Meleagros would never have rebelled against his mother had I not accepted his suit. His mother would never have killed him, would never have cursed me, and with me, all of Macedonia and Thessaly."

She lifted her face to him. Tears spilled down her cheeks. He had forgotten that, in this land of magic, a curse had as much power as a prayer.

"Atalante," he said stroking the tears away from her cheeks, "the gods and the fates decree our lot long before we are born. But we have a right to act as though we can weave our own pattern. And in the end, perhaps, our courage will soften their hearts. You must believe this, and you must keep strong. For whatever comes, it will be your moira to work the loom."

A shaft of moonlight illuminated the bed. His gaze traced the faint bruises on Atalante's arms—his doing tonight. He thought of how close he'd come to acting like his father, and shuddered. Looking down at Atalante, he wondered whether his father's brutality with his mother had been fueled by the same emotions he'd felt a short time ago—rage and deep, devastating hurt. For the first time, he wondered if Kryton had loved his mother. If Atalante were his queen, if she had shunned his advances, hated his touch, called him barbarian, how would he have responded? Would he have beaten her? Would he have raped her?

Melanion rolled to his side and studied her face. "I'm sorry for these," he said, softly touching the bruises on her arms. "I had no right to hurt you."

She shrugged. "I've had worse on the exercise field. I gave worse tonight." Her lips quirked as she traced the bite mark on his shoulder.

"That's no excuse. I have no right to touch you in anger."

She smoothed her fingers over his lip, frowning. "How will this end, Melanion?" she asked in a weary voice.

"I don't know," he said, tasting despair. "Gods, I hate this helplessness. But I made two heavy vows at that altar in the mountains. I must believe that I can keep one without betraying the other."

At times like this, he wondered if she somehow knew what he was feeling. For when she smiled, her lips trembled, but her eyes were calm again as she lifted both hands and drew his head to her breast. "It's all right, Melanion. Whatever comes, I love you."

The next afternoon, Atalante and Melanion visited the king in his library. Hyperion stood at his father's left and General Miletus at his right. The boy's eyes were huge on his pale, thin face. He was robed in the long white garb of the High Priest, and his gaze was old with wisdom.

"It'll come soon," Melanion began without preamble. "My father has too many men. Like waves of that sea in storm, they'll come at you again and again at the first battle. No matter how many you kill."

Iasus gave him a long look. "I can't walk out on the battlefield and say, 'Take it all, it's yours.' "

"No, of course not. But Iolcus will fall. I'm asking you to save back half your men from the first battle. Send them south. A group of zealots who can fight in the mountains will wreak havoc on Macedonia's troops and supply lines. In time, Thessalians can circumvent the city and go north through the back trails in the mountains. A few men on the passes could cut off the Macedonians. They'd be stranded in an empty city with no supplies and no way to either the south or the north. Many of the men are mercenaries. They'll not have much desire to stick it out when things get rough."

"I see." The king began to pace the floor. Grim lines appeared on each side of his mouth.

"There's a chance Polymus will kill my father right after the battle," Melanion said. "If so, I'll be free to commit all my men to your command. The old generals will desert Polymus if he's trapped in a frustrating war here. The resistance will only have to contend with the Red Bands, Polymus' troops. They're brutal, but they're stupid, too. A

219

strong underground force could defeat them with time."

"This gamble leaves my country too vulnerable," Iasus said. "What if you and I are both killed in the first battle? Who will lead the rebel force then?"

"I've thought of that, sire. I have men I trust, but in truth, this is my battle more than theirs. I don't like the odds, but there's no other way that will save Thessaly."

General Miletus pointed an accusing finger at Melanion. "How can we trust him? Unless you've forgotten, he's the son of your enemy."

This kind of thinking was the last thing they needed, Melanion thought irritably. "I'm right in the room, Miletus, so kindly speak to me and not about me. The king knows I've been against this war from the beginning. I respect and honor him. I love this city. If that isn't enough, I love your niece."

Miletus' mouth dropped open. Atalante chose that moment to move closer to Melanion and Miletus stared from one of them to the other. With a jerk, he turned to Iasus. "Did you know about this?" he demanded.

Iasus slowly grinned. "I've had my suspicions, yes."

Miletus turned back to Melanion and gave him a searching look. "You could take the city and have her easily enough. That's what your father would do."

Gods, how they hated his father! Melanion had to force himself to refrain from defending him. Although Miletus' argument stung, it had truth on its side. "King Iasus knows what I am," he said. "I ask this because it's the only path. If you divide your forces, your men will win back Iolcus. Otherwise, we're all doomed. I beg you to believe me."

Iasus gave a weary wave of his hand. "You have both spoken. It's on my head, now. The gods grant me the gift of right action. Leave me, all of you."

Atalante took Melanion's hand as they left the library. Hyperion tugged at his chiton to get his attention. "I need your help, Melanion."

"Anything, Little Owl," he said.

"I can't walk to the edge of the forest. Will you take me?"

"I would have carried you," Atalante said. "Why didn't you ask me?"

"I'm older," Hyperion said. "I'm getting too heavy for you."

Melanion looked down at the little prince and his heart twisted. Hyperion was no taller, and even lighter than he had been a few months ago. "You're right," he said. "Your sister would definitely pull her back out if she carried you all that way."

They entered Hyperion's chambers and the great cat lying on Hyperion's bed stretched, leaped down, and nuzzled the boy's hand. Melanion looked from lion to master and understood.

"Hyperion, he guards you well. He might even save your life, if it comes to that."

Hyperion shook his head but didn't speak. Melanion wondered if that was because the boy was afraid he'd break down and cry. He didn't argue further, but took the little priest up in his arms. Atalante walked with him as he carried Hyperion across the plain to the edge of the forest. The lion strode out beside them the whole way.

When Melanion lowered Hyperion to the ground, the boy knelt and took the lion's great head in his hands.

He spoke softly, and the creature never took his tawny gaze from Hyperion's face. "Heracles, if you stay, you'll try to protect me. There are too many of them, and you'd die for nothing. You don't really belong in the world of men.

And if you live, I'll have left something good behind."

Atalante stood silently beside Melanion. Her hand crept into his.

From the depths of the huge beast came a rumbling vibration. He laid his head in Hyperion's lap and gave a sigh that sounded human. Then the cub lifted his head, looked long at Hyperion, and nodded once in consent.

As the big cat turned and padded into the forest, Hyperion stood straight. He didn't move a muscle when the lion turned once to look back at his master, sighed again, and disappeared behind the low oaks and scrub of the forest. When Melanion bent to pick him up, Hyperion made no sound as he wound his arms around Melanion's neck.

Melanion carried him back across the plain. Hyperion was painfully light in his arms. And as the boy laid his head on Melanion's shoulder, something cracked inside him and something else sprang free. In a blur of visions, he saw Iolcus shining in the sun, Hyperion, wise and innocent, Iasus all kindness in the face of disaster, and Atalante, love shining from her eyes. And he knew he would never raise his hand against any Thessalian when the time came. His family was here, his purpose was here, all his love was here. *Do no harm,* he thought. *It goes both ways.*

That night, Melanion drew Atalante against him, as they stood in the silent amphitheater. He rubbed his chin against the soft warmth of her hair. "Hyperion told me to ask you about the foot race."

"Oh. Yes. I'm not running."

"Why not? The people are expecting you to do your best for them."

"Hyperion had a vision. The Macedonians must not know how fast I am."

He studied her face carefully. "After all that training. You're not sorry, are you?" he said.

"No. In the face of what's coming, this is a very small disappointment. Besides, I like the training better than the actual race. But Hyperion says you must run in my place, and you must win." She knelt and felt his calf. Her hand paused. Then, with a wicked smile and eyes full of mischief, her fingers slid upward and caressed his thigh.

Just like that, he grew hard. "Vixen!" He lifted her and crushed her against him, so she must feel exactly how she affected him. She laughed, a giddy, slightly breathless sound in the still air of the stadium.

"I just wanted to make sure you'd been exercising all this winter. I can see you'll acquit yourself quite well, on the field and off," she said. Then she grew serious, all mature responsibility.

"With me out of the race, there's only Nestor to beat. You can do it, if you understand his strategy and work around it. I can tell you everything you need to know."

Atalante was a terrible taskmaster, Melanion decided a few days later. She'd wake him hours before dawn and run before him in the hills beneath the cool, silver disk of the moon. She told him how to use his breath and his legs to increase his staying power and when to pull ahead. She checked her stride to the speed she though Nestor could reach. He was clearly the front runner. His odds improved daily with the gamblers in the taverns.

The Companions had already joined the young Thessalian nobility on the exercise field. Astrid convinced Philip to try his luck in the discus throw. Niko was entered in the light wrestling competition. The first time she saw him stripped on the exercise field, Atalante nudged Melanion.

"There'll be many a woman watching his match," she said. Niko hadn't grown an inch, but his muscles bulged from the exercise he'd done all winter.

Melanion pulled her closer with a possessive hand. "And you, my lady?" he asked her.

She gave him a slanting glance. "I have eyes only for the runners."

He tugged her even closer and she smiled. "One runner in particular," she added, and he felt light, and young, as though, just for this moment, the whole world was happy with him.

Korone had been absent from the exercise field for days, Theas knew. He couldn't understand why she refused to enter any of the games. His first glimpse of her was in the Megaron at dinner several nights after they'd arrived, and he was already out of sorts.

She sat not far from a tall, handsome youth leaning over his fellows in the rudest manner to keep talking to her. She liked it, the little flirt. She encouraged him, of course, by answering all his questions, and even offering some of her own. Theas knew he must have been scowling at her, for suddenly, she blushed and glanced down at her lap. If that wasn't a sign of guilt, he didn't know what would be.

"You ever going to eat that? You picked it up aeons ago." Melanion nudged him and pointed to a piece of roast lamb suspended in his fingers. He shrugged, bit into the meat. That was all he needed, to have an occasional lapse of attention pointed out to him in front of everyone.

"How's rehearsal going?" Astrid asked Korone from across the table.

"Better than I expected," she answered. "With any luck, the lifts will be smooth enough by the day of dedication."

She gave the blond down the table from her the melting smile of a courtesan. Theas frowned at his plate this time.

"What's wrong?" Korone asked, all seeming innocence, the little witch. "Don't you like watching the dancers?"

"I don't know anything about it," he said.

Alex grinned at him. "Theas has never understood music or dance," he told Korone.

"I can speak for myself," he said, irritated beyond belief at this ridiculous scene with all his friends—former friends, make that, who couldn't wait to embarrass him further. "I'm tone deaf," he said. "I hate listening to music. I have to sit still—no tablet to read, no friend to puzzle over a problem with—while it drones on and on."

"What a shame," said Korone with a little toss of her head. "Music and dance are what I do best. I can understand that you would consider my work of little importance. I would hate to bore you. Perhaps you'd prefer staying in the palace until after the dancing." She turned her back to Theas and renewed her conversation with the tall blond. Theas found out a moment later that the blond was to be her partner.

Theas grabbed his wine cup and took a deep swallow. If Korone thought for one moment that he was about to miss their performance, she was gravely mistaken. Someone had to keep an eye on her, or she'd flirt herself right into a disastrous match with a blond, for instance, who knew nothing about what she really needed.

On the first morning of spring games, the athletes were dedicated to the goddess Artemis. Theas sat beside Melanion and Atalante in the princess' stand. The view was perfect across the circular floor of the amphitheater.

Some said the Titans had set up this amphitheater as a

stage upon which the tragedies and triumphs of the human drama could be played out for them. The stands were benches carved from the stone of the hillside that rose to form a natural bowl. The flat, grassy track of the bottom was natural as well. The place was filled to capacity with aristocrats, merchants, and peasants.

A life-sized statue of Bacchus as a slender and beautiful youth stood on a pedestal on the green in the middle of the floor. Men and women entered to form a chorus behind the statue. Several of them held citharas, flutes, and drums.

Korone entered, her black hair unbound and swinging against her hips as she moved with that sensual, swaying walk of hers. She took the hand of the tall, damnably handsome blond he'd seen the night before at table. Bowing first to the statue of the god, then to the king, and last, to the spectators, the two parted. Heads bent, they waited.

The drums took up a steady beat. This much Theas could understand. When the music began, he could make out the singer's words telling how the god found Ariadne deserted on the island of Naxos, and how he fell in love with her.

Korone began to dance, acknowledging the blond dancer. Her body swayed and turned in the figures of the dance, at first formal and shy as she played a mortal woman in the presence of the god. But as the chorus rose, the blond grew bolder, acting out a drama of pursuit to Korone's hesitance. As the couple grew closer, Theas heard women sighing in the audience. And when the blond embraced Korone, lifting her high above him in exultation, Theas gripped the low stone wall in front of his seat until the joints in his fingers protested.

He leaned forward, his gaze locked on Korone, a transformation of perfection as she leaped and whirled. He had never seen anything like this in his life. He wanted to be the one who captured that look of radiance on her beautiful face. He wanted it to go on forever.

A hand tugged at his arm and he shook it off, but it tugged again. Aggravated whispers behind him brought him entirely to himself. He was standing upright, leaning toward the dancer on the green.

Atalante gave him a questioning look, but Melanion merely grinned at him in a way that made him go quite hot in the face. The little dancer ran across the green and leaped into the arms of the blond. He caught her against his chest and ran out of the stadium, a study of erotic triumph.

Theas gritted his teeth. Melanion smirked at him.

He glared back. "What's so interesting?"

Melanion shrugged and turned his gaze to the empty green. "I'm delighted to see you've developed such an over-whelming interest in music. It's commendable of you to accept new . . . experiences."

The foot race was among the first contests. Atalante led Melanion to the Athlete's Gate. They paused beneath its deep shade and she clasped his hand.

"Remember. Keep steady until the last turn before home. Never mind about Nestor. He'll pull out too early and ruin his pacing."

"I'll remember."

"Try to win. I want the people to know exactly who you are."

He nodded and squeezed her hand. His stomach seemed to be jumping about in a most undisciplined manner as he stepped out into the green. This race was somewhere between the long race and the sprint. Stamina and strength wouldn't be enough. He'd have to use his head.

Blinking against the sunlight, he found himself in the middle of the track. An official pointed out his starting stone and he went to it.

Glancing around the stadium, he seemed to see everything with unusual clarity. Up in the stands, children leaned out across their mother's laps for sweets their grandmothers held out. Men stood behind the wall separating the crowd from the track with toddlers on their shoulders, pointing to him, among others. The babble was almost deafening. He had never been in a place this huge, this filled with humanity. His heart beat so loudly in his ears, he couldn't hear Nestor's first greeting.

The starter shouted above the crowd. Melanion rose against the stones. Dead quiet filled the stadium. A whip cracked, and Melanion shot from his block.

Suddenly, his body belonged to him again—body and mind together. They passed the end stave for the first round. Melanion found himself in the middle of the group. Nestor ran a few feet ahead of him. Melanion pulled behind and let him cut the wind for both of them, as Atalante had told him. A couple of youths had broken early to the front and ran full out. They'd never last the time.

For three more rounds of the track, the runners stayed in place, like figures on a vase. Melanion began to use his lungs and his legs harder, but his breath came deep and easy. The sunlight was blinding. A sense of completion filled him, as though he ran with the god's urging. He blinked sweat out of his eyes, and where there had been cheering from the crowd, there was now silence, so crystalline it could shatter.

And he was running right behind Atalante. She was stripped like a youth, wearing only a loincloth, and he sensed that it hurt the people to see her because she was radiant like the Huntress, and just as sacred. He knew he must catch her. He pushed his legs, lengthening his stride, kicking dust from the track. His lungs struggled for breath.

Something glowed before her on the track—something golden that shot sparks. The crowd gasped in fear. For this was a Thing of Power. It might destroy any mortal who touched it. Atalante scooped it up in stride. Still running like the wind, she held it out to the filled stadium. It shot lightning in all directions. The blinding brightness licked down her upraised arm and into her body until she was alight with golden fire.

Melanion's vision cleared. He was flying past them all, past Nestor and the end stave. The crowd, silent a blink of an eye before, was on its feet, shouting in one mighty voice, like the roar of the sea. "Melanion, Melanion!"

And Atalante stood before him robed in white, princess and priestess of Artemis. While bells rang and people cheered, she crowned him with the laurel wreath.

# Chapter 10

## War

As Melanion entered Hamalclion upon his return, he saw Red Bands everywhere. They swaggered, unchecked by any of the Hundred. In the shade of a market stall, he saw Alex's cousin Clisthenes, but he didn't greet any of them. He nodded once to Melanion and slipped into the flurry of people who flooded the marketplace.

Melanion urged his horse on toward the palace. Even as he handed the black to a groom, he sent a slave to request an audience with his father. Minutes passed like hours until the slave returned. The man looked frightened, and wouldn't meet his eyes. "I'm sorry, sir. The king can't see you now."

"Isn't he in the Megaron?"

"No, my Lord. He's in closed meetings with his generals. He told me to bid you welcome. To say he can see you tomorrow."

The slave bowed low and scurried out of Melanion's chamber. The sense of wrongness that had haunted him all day settled like a weight on his chest. He found it hard to breathe. His father hid from him. The Hundred were nowhere in the city. What the hell had happened here?

At moonrise, there was a knock on his door. Clisthenes stood before him muffled in a cloak.

"Come with me," he said in a low voice.

All of them followed as quietly as they could. They wound down from the citadel and skirted the camp on the exercise field with its hundreds of campfires. Using only the moon to point out their path, they followed Clisthenes into the forest. Shadows shimmered beneath the small new leaves.

Melanion didn't like any of this—the clandestine meeting, his missing troops, his father's disfavor. He pulled Clisthenes back.

"What the hell happened here?" he said in a low voice.

"Things are very bad. When you left, you told us to protect the city and the king. There was a need for us, all right. The Red Band grew more vicious every day.

"They took the women—some as young as ten, just little girls. If their fathers or brothers tried to stop them, the Red Bands slew them where they stood. The people came to us, so we fought the bastards.

"Polymus figured it out. He knew that, when the people called for us, they were really calling for you. So he made a snare to catch us out."

The Companions were so quiet, Melanion could actually hear Clisthenes stiffen.

"There were eight of the Hundred who came on an ugly scene in the marketplace. A young boy had just thrown himself between the Red Bands and his father, because they were beating the man to death. There were ten of them— they took turns with the boy, right in front of the people.

"Our men rushed in to save the lad. All around them, they heard shouts, and whips cracking, and then clubs.

"A troop of those bastards beat the crowd bloody. The people ran away. You can't blame them—what do they know about fighting back? The Red Band troop surrounded our men. It was an ambush—Polymus sent them, may he rot in Hell. They killed three of the Hundred and disarmed five, dragging them to the exercise field for judgment."

"But my father—he must have heard of this!"

Gray light seeped into the sky, enough of it for Melanion to see the bleak line of Clisthenes' mouth as he stared down at his hands.

"The king gave judgment," he said.

Bands of iron squeezed Melanion's heart. "What happened?" he whispered.

"All five of the survivors were hanged that day in the square. As a warning to the people."

His father had betrayed him. He had betrayed the Hundred—boys, with their dreams of honor.

Poisoned, Melanion thought in horror. My blood is poisoned with his filth. He staggered, felt someone holding him upright.

Theas leaned close and said something, his hand beneath his elbow, but Melanion couldn't hear him for the pounding of his own heart. He looked away from Theas' troubled face and kept his eyes on Clisthenes, because Clisthenes wasn't his friend, and Clisthenes would judge him properly, like any other man with a murderer's blood running through his veins. It was what he deserved, after all.

Moments passed, maybe years. "What then?" he asked finally, because some part of him still went on as though he was a man and not a monster's spawn.

"All of us, the whole Hundred, gathered in council beyond the farthest reaches of the city. We took our heavy arms. We figured if they followed us, we'd give them a fight they'd remember.

"Some argued that we should return home, arm our vassals, and rebel. Some said we still owed you loyalty,"

Clisthenes said staring at him, his eyes bitter. "Others said we owed you nothing. They said you played at honor, but you were your father's son.

"Linos spoke then, only a few words. He said there was a great battle ahead between free men and slaves. That you wanted to bring to Macedonia what you'd found in Thessaly, and we had to trust you to give us the signal. While you were gone, we had to trust him to make us ready."

Clisthenes shrugged. "That day, we moved to the foothills and lived in the caves. Linos taught us how to forage game and spring roots. We sent scouts into the city every day.

"The Red Bands don't threaten the people much now." Clisthenes smiled grimly. "The first, who murdered the eight—they were found one by one on the exercise field, their throats slit. Another Red Band was idiot enough to stab a farmer for the oat cakes he brought to market. That one fell to his death from the Citadel. Soon, rumors sprang up in the city."

Clisthenes looked at all of them in the growing light. "They say the Mother avenges her people. She's summoned a band of ghosts who rise at night. People have begun to leave offerings at the edge of the city, near the woods— honey cakes and wine. We eat better than we expected to, and the soldiers never come after us. Polymus is too busy planning his war to rout us out of the forest."

Clisthenes' face was drawn and pale in the gray light. "Melanion, if you're loyal to the king, set us free. But if you lead us against him, let us know. Tell us what you want, before we return to our homes and lead our own people against your father."

They shamed him, Melanion thought, as he followed

Clisthenes into a forest clearing. He had been a child hiding from the truth, hoping his father would love him and do right for his sake. All of that was gone now. There was only his vow to his mother to consider before the final act.

The sun rose, blinding in a hard blue sky. At first, he saw nothing ahead of him. Then a spear tip glinted in the sun, and another, and a third. A meadowlark called close by, and then, in the distance, another answered, and the song repeated again and again, farther away.

Young men poured into the clearing, hundreds of them, until they filled the large space. They sat in the mouths of caves in the hillside above Melanion, legs dangling over space—all clear-eyed and straight. Some looked as though they trusted him, some as though they'd as soon spit him through.

Melanion blessed Iasus for teaching him so much in so little time as he vaulted up on a high, flat rock in the middle of the clearing. With a deep breath, he called forth the voice of power.

"The gods sit with us in this assembly," he said. "When I look at you, I'm proud, not to be of the House of the Lion, but to be Macedonian. To the south lies Thessaly, where we can learn about the sacred law that keeps men free, and about the highest good in ourselves, to preserve and teach to our children.

"Between stands Polymus, our enemy and the scourge of Thessaly. Polymus lured Kryton to destroy the best of his country. Against my father I cannot speak, for I must follow my moira. But today I'll bring charges against the beast who preys on us all. I'll try one last time to convince Kryton to avert carnage and ruin."

He took a deep, steadying breath, and looked about him at his men, *his* men, with their serious, clear faces. "If he

kills me, Theas will bring word. Slip away to Thessaly.
Offer yourselves to Iasus—he has need of heroes. Know
when you fight for Thessaly, you defend your own homes
and your honor.

"If I fail and still live, I'll try to escape and lead you into
Thessaly. In this sacred place, with the gods as witness, I
swear by the Mother and the River that I will commit
treason against my father and my king to save the people of
Macedonia and Thessaly. Whatever, the cost, so be it.
There's no turning back now."

The air rang with sound. Youths cheered, swords banged
against shields, boys of eighteen clapped each other on the
back or helmet. Amidst the commotion, Linos leaped up
beside Melanion on the great rock and knelt, offering the
ring with the lion's head.

Melanion slipped it on his finger and raised his fist as his
men grew silent and knelt about him. The symbolism of his
words, his action, weighed heavily on his shoulders, as he
realized fully what he'd just done. He had declared himself
commander and king.

Kryton sat alone in his chamber drinking warm spiced
wine. The chill night was old. He cupped his chin in his
palm. He had been trying to drink himself into a stupor all
night so he could sleep. But sleep had eluded him since the
day he'd hanged those boys.

Kryton gritted his teeth, reminding himself that he had
to do it. The whole campaign hung on Polymus' good will.
Without his troops, Kryton could never take Thessaly. After
Thessaly, he thought. After the battle, he'd get rid of
Polymus. Then he'd be able to reward those boys of the
Hundred properly. All but the eight . . .

He'd refused to see his son again tonight. Damn, but

there was no way to explain to the boy so he'd understand. Better to talk to him about it when he could hand him the Serpent Throne. Kryton took another deep draught of wine. Thank the gods they were to head out for Thessaly on the morrow.

A cry split the air. The heavy door slammed in, followed by a skittering slave who announced his son, and then almost ran out the door. Melanion strode in, sheathing his sword. Kryton stood up. His cheeks burned with indignation. Nobody—*nobody* pushed his way in to the king's chambers.

"Watch yourself, boy. You dare too much."

Melanion looked at him like a stranger. "Master Juggler. You dropped a sword or two."

"This is about the five who were hanged, is it? You ignorant whelp! Where were you when your troops were at the Red Band's throats? What was your advice when my veterans were thrust into the middle of their fights—when the mercenaries went crazy? You were off in Thessaly, playing *games*, boy."

He warmed to it, the anger fed him, helped him justify what he'd done. He heard his own voice, a snarling whine. "You dare to judge me? I've ruled an uneasy kingdom for twenty-five years, seen it seethe on the brink of revolution five times. I'm the only one strong enough to hold it together. And all for you, I might add."

Melanion's lip curled in disdain. "Do you want my gratitude—my respect? Condemn Polymus. Stop the war. Avenge the innocent you've slaughtered, and give me leave to marry Atalante. Now."

Kryton stared at his son. Some time in the last year, the boy had lost any youthful softness. He looked like an avenging god, or a madman—eyes burning in a white face, hand gripping his sword hilt, legs braced apart. He must be mad to challenge his king and his father.

Kryton tamped down his rage. His son couldn't throw away his life like this, not after all his plans and dreams. "Do you think I'd allow you to go on your knees for the chit? They'd have a good laugh on both of us as they kicked you out of Thessaly like a cur begging for scraps. You don't know them. They'll refuse you and make me the laughing stock of Greece."

"But I do know them," Melanion said softly. "I've known them for a year. Iasus is a great and brave king, and he's taught me wonderful things. He'll honor my suit. And honor you because you stayed your hand."

Kryton jerked back. His thoughts tumbled through his brain, hurting him. "What have you done behind my back?"

The boy stood straighter, narrowed his eyes, and gave him a look of such arrogance, it smote him through. It was like looking in a mirror.

"I did nothing dishonorable. Atalante brought me home with her many months ago. She hoped I could learn about them, learn enough to show you how pointless and destructive your plans—"

"Traitor!" Kryton could feel the vein in his temple beating fast and heavy. "I gave you everything—protection, honor, my *love,* damn you. And you betrayed me to my enemy. Did you tell him how many troops I have? Did you tell him which is my weak side, so he could kill me in battle? Gods!

"To think that each time you were away, I was sick with worry. Some mountain lion might have gotten you, that monster boar might have gored you, Iasus might have taken you hostage at the games. And all that time, you plotted with that bastard."

Kryton turned his back on his son. His shoulders shook

so hard, he feared he might humiliate himself. "I did everything I could to keep you safe, to give you a kingdom worth ruling. You didn't give a damn, not for what I've done for you, not for me. You're just like your mother."

A hand touched his shoulder, tentative, gentle. "It was never like that, Father."

Kryton thrust him off, wheeling to face him. "You've chosen your father. He rules in Iolcus, until I send him to his last sleep." His voice rose to a roar he couldn't control. "Get out of my sight before I kill you!"

Melanion's face was ghostly white. He held out his hand to Kryton.

Kryton strode to the great gong standing beside a tapestry and crashed a rod against it. "Guards!" he bellowed. A troop of thirty men sprang into the chamber from an inner door behind the drape.

"Take him to his rooms. Chain him. Then find his Companions. Bind them and bring them to me."

Three of the guards grabbed Melanion and bound his hands together behind his back, pulling him out of the chamber toward his rooms to the left. The rest raced into the corridor to the right, where the Companions had been waiting a short distance away.

Muffled sounds of confusion and alarm reached Kryton. Men shouted, metal pounded on metal, bodies scuffled and slammed against stone walls. He heard running footsteps growing fainter and fainter. When the commander of the guards returned, he was bleeding. Kryton caught a glimpse of the corridor before the man closed his door. It was full of his guards lying dead or wounded on the flagstones.

Melanion shut his eyes and leaned his head against the stones on the wall of his room. He had failed. Failed to change Kryton's mind, failed to escape. He supposed they'd come and kill him soon.

Had Theas escaped? How many of the Companions got away safely? Would the Hundred find their way to Thessaly, or would Kryton's army find them first? Thoughts swirled, and then horror gripped him.

Atalante!

He was numb to his own death, but fear for Atalante tore at his entrails like a vulture. All he could picture were the flood waters swollen with doom, rushing, rolling over her.

His wrists and ankles chafed and his arms ached from the heavy chains. He heard men talking outside this one small room, some on the balcony, some beyond the locked door. He felt like the helpless boy in his recurrent nightmare—too weak to save anyone, not even himself.

Toward morning, the guard came in. They marched him into the silent courtyard and unlocked the leg shackles. He stood like a man at least, ready for the spear he anticipated any moment. He hoped the man who would kill him would face him, so he didn't have to die like a coward from a spear in the back.

The courtyard slowly filled. The generals entered first. They mounted and rode forward. Polymus gave him a calculating glance, then looked away. Xuthus, resplendent in gold trimmed armor, looked at him and licked his grinning lips like a jackal. Kryton came next on a prancing war horse, leading the black he'd given Melanion the year before.

He stopped before Melanion and spoke softly. "You're going to live, traitor, at least for a little while. You will stand chained on the plain of Iolcus and watch me kill the man you worship. It's a fitting punishment for the snake you are.

"When I've won Thessaly, I'll dispose of you as I see fit. Mount." He held out the reins. Melanion raised his bound hands, gripped them, and mounted. The black skittered at the weight of the chains on his back, but settled at the sound of his voice and the touch of his hand. Kryton touched his heel to his horse and moved ahead. Immediately, the guards from the night before surrounded Melanion, and they set off from the citadel into the town.

The rough Macedonian hills surrounded them as they made their way down. Melanion stared at them, loved them suddenly, with their olive trees and their apples, loved the stubborn land, its heart-stopping softness in spring. Loved the people who lined the road as far as he could see. He had wanted to give so much to his country, and he'd failed. He saw his father a little way ahead of his guards. Kryton's head bent toward Polymus, listening carefully, Polymus' creature entirely.

On each side of the road, the common people stood, silently watching the army pass on their way out of Hamalclion. A sound began around him, like the sigh of the ocean against the shore, wave upon wave. A guard on his right drew in his breath. Kryton must have heard it, for he turned his head to look. As Melanion passed the crowds of people, they went to their knees, heads bent, fists on hearts. Melanion's eyes stung. He tried to look at each man, woman, and child who knelt for him, to acknowledge each one. What could he do but accept the homage and the burden of their love?

The army traveled light in order to travel fast. By the time they climbed the foothills of his southern mountains, Kryton knew something was wrong. The air smelled bitter, like charred ash. As they drew near the first farms of the Macedonian helots, the alarm rang back at them from the vanguard. A scout, without regard for the narrow, rocky path, galloped back to him.

"They've burned the fields. There's nothing left!" the man cried.

"Damn the traitors to Hades," Kryton said. Ever since that terrible night when Melanion had looked at him with such . . . contempt, Kryton had felt his luck slipping away. He clenched his fist, as though he could hold the rest and keep it from fleeing.

It would hurt too much to see the boy again. "Keep him chained day and night," he'd told the guards. On the morning of battle they were to surround Melanion and make him watch the killing, until Thessaly was beaten.

But it ate at him, the things Melanion had said, as though Kryton were the child and Melanion the father who knew better. He thought of Iasus, his old enemy, teaching the boy everything he had wanted to teach him once he'd given him a kingdom to rule.

"Tell the men to take heart. We'll have food aplenty across the border. Thessalian farmers are fat and eager for profit. They'll side with us because they know who's going to win this war."

On the fourth day, they descended into Thessaly, and the men stood straighter. But again, bitter smoke swirled toward them on the wind. The army rode past fields blighted from fire. Worst of all was the silence. No birds sang, no life stirred in the blackened fields. The men grew deadly quiet.

Kryton had to do something. He called all the army together. They came, but he saw their faces, some sullen, some frightened. He forced his shoulders back and struck a heroic pose.

"Their defiance will make us stronger, fiercer in battle. We need a quick victory, and I swear to you, we'll get one. There are many of us and few of them. We'll come down on them like Ares in his battle rage. Fight to win. Take no prisoners. Make them know they'll pay with their lives for further rebellion.

"Our victory will be sweet and swift. Instead of burnt fields, we'll reap the rich crops of the south. Be of good heart. Set your sights only on the task at hand. Victory, and the land of Thessaly will be ours for all time!"

They shouted, banged their swords against their shields, eager again for the battle, forgetting for the moment the specter of famine. Kryton stood a little taller and grinned. He had grabbed hold of his luck, and he would keep it close, for he needed it most now.

Atalante walked the battlements toward her father. Below, on Iolcus Plain, the Macedonian's watch fires burned. Iasus smiled when he saw her, but there was so much pain and uncertainty in his eyes. She couldn't speak for fear of shaming herself with tears.

"Atalante . . ."

"Don't, Father." She backed away. She didn't want him to tell her what she'd already realized by staring down at the massive Macedonian army camped around them.

Her father gave her a look of such love, she wanted to throw herself into his arms, but he held his hand up. "The king must speak to his warrior," he said quietly.

A lone tear escaped her. Her father rubbed it from her cheek with his thumb. "When the battle is joined, take your troops to the far end of the plain, just before the woods leading south. When you see the king fall—"

"No!" She flung herself into her father's arms.

242

His arms were steady while she trembled from head to toe. "When you see me fall, Atalante, take your people into the woods and retreat into the south. There you'll join Miletus and half our army. You will harass the enemy from the cover of the forests, until you've beaten him back to Macedonia."

Anguish buffeted her. "I can't leave you."

Her father took her arms from off his neck and held her away from him. His eyes were stern. "Tomorrow, you will be Queen and war leader. The people are in your hands. Have faith in Melanion, as I do, for he's right. The only way to save Thessaly is to divide the army."

In spite of their trembling, she forced her lips to move, to plead with him. "Come with us, Father. You can lead us better than I. You don't need to die."

Iasus covered her hand with his own. "I am King. My duty is to die, just as yours is to live. There's no way to avoid our moira. Accept it, and lead your people well."

They stood in silence on the ramparts and looked down at the enemy. Her father was right. There were too many of them. Tomorrow's battle would be lost.

Her father studied her face, a stern and formal question in his eyes.

She swallowed painfully and straightened her shoulders. "I accept."

"The gods be with you, my daughter."

"And with you, my father."

Iasus smiled down at her, his eyes full of pride and love. "Thank you, my dear. Now go ask your mother to come to me here."


Clymene came up behind Iasus and laid her head against his back. Her hand stole up his shoulder, kneading. He felt the knotted muscles loosen a bit. After a moment, he turned to her and pulled her into his arms.

"You'll be wanting to ask me something, love. Don't waste your breath. The answer is no."

"Dear Heart," she said through the thickness in her throat. "It would be so much easier."

"Shall I go out there tomorrow, knowing you'll leap from this wall as soon as I'm slain?"

"Then don't die."

"Clymene. Look at me." He tipped her chin up and she met his gaze, her own eyes spilling over with her tears.

"First Atalante and now you," he said softly. "What is it with the women of this family?"

"I can't laugh, Iasus." Her voice quavered and broke.

He sighed. "You can't blame me for trying, can you?" He stroked her hair. The sensation of the warmth, the softness of each curl, was precious. "Dearest love, it won't be over tomorrow. You have to be strong for Atalante and Hyperion. You have to live."

She held on, as though she could hold him against fate's decree. "The only time I've been away from you was when I took Atalante to Arkadia for the testing, all those many years ago. Each night, I was so cold without the warmth of your body beside me. How am I to live without you?" She buried her face in his chest.

"Clymene. Listen to me." His hands smoothed over her gown and rested against her back. "You must be braver than I. Your work won't be done tomorrow. As king, I cannot give you permission to leave this life with me, no matter how much I wish it."

"It's not fair."

"Life is seldom fair. Would you rather have wed without love, so you wouldn't miss your husband?" Sniffling, she shook her head against his chest.

He smiled, bittersweet memories of the young girl she'd been filling his mind. She was strong, his Clymene. Stronger than she knew. "Then come with me now, love, while we can. I need you tonight. I want all the memories I can get to take with me to the next land."

When she lifted her head, he saw that tears coursed down her cheeks. Angrily, she dashed the back of her hand against them. "Wait for me there! If you don't, I'll knock down the very walls of Hell looking for you. When I find you, I'll scream like a fishwife, and humiliate you in front of the heroes."

Iasus' voice broke on a laugh. "My love. I'll wait, no matter how long. The gods wouldn't have given us to each other if we weren't meant to be together forever."

Clymene laid her head on his shoulder. As he led her down the stairs, he uttered a silent prayer of thanksgiving that the gods had given him such a woman.

Long after the camp slept, Melanion rose from his skins and stared up at the stars. For the last days, the guards who now followed him across the plain never let him out of their sight. Tomorrow, these same thirty men had orders to surround him, to keep him from slipping away.

By the gods, he would escape them. The heat of battle confused things, and he'd take advantage of it. If Theas and the others had escaped, they'd be looking for him. But even if he was alone, he had a chance as soon as the chains were off, and he'd take it.

His mind was filled with dread visions—of Iasus dead on the plain, of Atalante killed, or worse, captured, and Polymus' prisoner.

Was this the place? Was it here that he finally fulfilled his fate? In order to protect the people he loved, would he be forced to kill his own father?

His thoughts scuttled to escape that possibility. He climbed higher on the hill at the edge of the plain. His chains clanked, betraying his every movement to the vigilant guards. At least they stood off a little, leaving him alone with the night. A star shot across the sky in a brilliant shower of light. He raised his face to the sky and lifted his hands.

"Artemis, hear me," he whispered. "Give me a path to follow for the good. Only for the good."

He knelt and placed both hands on the earth. "Mother, help me. I must keep this ground free." From the depths of the earth came a tingling to his palms, a kind of rolling vibration. His mind was swept clean of struggle and it slowly opened outward. He heard a voice, neither woman's nor man's—very quiet and full of power.

*"Son of the Lion."*

"I am here," he whispered.

*"Remember the sacrifice."*

The voice receded from his mind like the slow ebb of the tide. The vibration beneath his fingers softened into night movements. He felt everything. Crickets, earthworms, beetles shuttled about in the cool turf, a bat winged past and dipped to catch a moth.

His mind returned to this world and its turmoil. What sacrifice? Hyperion's words sounded in his mind, doom-filled. *Shame, exile, a deep pit.* He remembered his first meeting with Hyperion, and the boy's subsequent interpretation of what he had seen—the stag and Melanion as one. A chill caressed his neck, like a sigh from the grave.

"I am the sacrifice," he whispered. "Now is the time."

As Melanion turned to descend the hill, the chains

binding his wrists clanked together, a reminder, if he'd needed one, and an affirmation of his fears. He returned to his bedroll and lay down, not to sleep, but to plot his escape. He'd asked the will of the gods, and they'd answered. But before he accepted his moira, he would defend this ground and those he loved, even against the father he wished he could love better.

Dawn came bright against a clear sky. Kryton's great army shook itself awake and made a quick breakfast. The cavalry bridled their horses and gathered together on the bottom of the hill. The infantry grouped behind them in two phalanxes.

The black beneath Melanion pawed the ground and snorted, eager to be off. Melanion held him back, chains slapping against his forearms, bruising him and the horse. He wore no sword, no shield. The fool guards had given him only his armor, thinking they were enough to protect him. But he knew his fate today, and only wished there were some way to make his death a good one.

His father rode before the men in his painted war chariot, its wheels studded with cruel bronze spikes to cut down Thessalian horses. His charioteer reined in the horses and Kryton spoke.

"Fight like the lion today and you win the south—all its wealth and all its land. Fight with your greatest strength and there'll be food, and warm beds, and women to make your rest easy. Above all, fight for your fame. In time out of mind, bards will sing of Macedonia's great army and its soldiers' brave deeds. Do you set forth for glory?"

The earth shook with the cheering of thousands. At that moment, Iolcus' heavy gates opened beneath the Serpent Arch and an army poured out, painfully undermanned. But it rolled bravely across the plain like a flooding stream. Kryton gave the paean and unsheathed his sword. The charioteer cracked his whip. The king led his charging army down the slope to clash against the small tide of Thessalians.

Melanion spurred the black forward and pushed toward the front. If only he could slip the guards and reach the other side, someone would free him and give him a sword. But his guards surrounded him, holding him to a slow advance.

The first lines of cavalry clashed against each other. Shouts and curses, the clanging of metal against metal, the cries of the fallen filled the air. Here, a horse went down, its belly slit. There, a man slowly toppled from his mount, his helmed head severed from his neck. Melanion shoved and thrust his horse against the guard, searching for Atalante and the Hundred.

Amidst the confusion and sound, a line of Macedonian cavalry wavered and parted like water around an onrushing troop of Thessalians. They galloped in a thundering roll toward Melanion and his guards. The standard bearer held aloft a flowing tapestry. Melanion's gaze leapt to it. In bright gold thread, a lion and a lioness reared within a circle of serpents.

The riders surged forward. They were so fast the guards had time only to raise their swords. A rider whose long, braided hair caught the sunlight and gave it back in brighter gold, shouted "Melanion!"

Astrid, he realized. "Here," he called in the voice of power. He shoved with all his might against the closest guards. The men, harried on both sides, gave way a little, and it was all he needed. He broke through, and Philip had his big hands on the black's reins while Astrid felled a guard to the ground with the sweep of her sword.

Her gaze swerved from Melanion's chained wrists to the guard's waist as he lay prone on the ground. Astrid dismounted at a run, caught up a key on the guard's belt, and flung it to Philip. Philip caught it and unlocked Melanion's chains as she grabbed the guard's sword and shield.

"Where is she?" Melanion shouted, taking the sword and shield from her. Astrid leaped on her horse and pointed left, where the Red Band fought ferociously.

Melanion threw the black into a mad gallop and crossed the plain with Astrid and the rest streaming behind him. His heart pounded in his chest almost loud enough to muffle the battle sounds as he hacked a path toward Atalante. Polymus' apes surrounded her and her men. He cut them down as he came. Men on both sides grabbed at him and almost unseated him, but the black swerved to catch him up again. And all the time, the red heat of battle rage filled Melanion, made him want nothing more than to destroy everything threatening Atalante.

His sword sliced through flesh, his shield countered heavy blows. A Red Band came at him from behind. His leg pressed the black's side. His stallion wheeled, reared and slashed out with his hooves, screaming, leaping forward. Melanion leaned low as the Red Band raised his weapon too late. He fell beneath the arc of Melanion's sword and Melanion broke through. He'd reached Atalante.

Side by side, they fought together as though they'd been doing it all their lives. Their horses shifted weight at the lightest touch of leg. Together, they leaped over fallen soldiers and pivoted, breaking from entrapment.

By midday, they'd won the wooded hills on the edge of the plain. Melanion and Atalante stopped to breathe and rest the horses. He wanted to take her in his arms, to tell her how he loved her, to tell her she was his wife in truth, that she had to live, to remember him as he was, and not as they'd brand him after today. But he had to get her to safety.

He scanned the battlefield to find the Hundred. In the heaving mass of men and animals, he found them on the right wing of the much smaller Thessalian line. Their standard of lions and serpents rippled high above them.

He grasped her arm and pointed to them. "If I fall today, go to them. Tell them to fade from the battlefield. Take them south and regroup there. Linos must lead them. Promise me."

"If we go now, we can reach them together," Atalante said. She showed him the break in the infantry and Melanion spurred his horse forward. Ahead, he spotted movement before the gates of Iolcus and abruptly halted. He saw his father and cried out in anguish.

Kryton sliced through Thessaly's defenders toward the Serpent Gate, where Iasus fought on a white war horse. Polymus and Xuthus rode directly behind him, urging on the Red Band. Clothed in shining armor, Iasus cantered his mount toward Kryton. The white's breastplate blazed in the midday sun. Melanion's limbs froze as he watched Iasus strike the first blow. Kryton's sword arm shuddered against the force of the attack, but held.

"Father!" Melanion shouted. He didn't know which man he called. But Kryton looked toward the hill where his son stood beside Atalante. His face contorted in rage. With renewed strength, he advanced on Iasus, hammering blows on the older man. Iasus retreated beneath the assault. Then Kryton slashed out with his sword. Iasus' weapon fell from his hand. He swayed in the saddle and slid to the earth.

Kryton leaped off the chestnut and stood over the king.

Blood gushed from Iasus' shoulder in bright spurts. Kryton shouted in triumph and raised his sword, both hands on the hilt.

With a groan ripped from his heart, Melanion thrust his sword into its scabbard. He drew his bow, nocked the arrow, and took careful aim at his father's throat. He willed his fingers to release the arrow. In his mind, it flew unimpeded and his father lay dead on the battlefield. But his fingers froze on the bowstring.

Suddenly, something jostled his elbow and threw off his aim. He heard the twang of the bowstring's release, and then two things happened at once. A foot soldier to his father's left grabbed at the air and fell forward, an arrow in the heart. A bowstring beside him thumped in release and Kryton fell, another arrow lodged in his shoulder.

Polymus knelt above Kryton. When he rose, he had the feathered end of the arrow in his hands and held it high for the Macedonians to see.

"Patricide!" he screamed. His voice sounded across the field, thin, high like the hawk before it plummets and strikes. He pointed across the plain toward Melanion's little group.

"Death to the traitor!" he screamed again. "He killed his own father, your king!" The army joined as one under the Red Band banner. Their hoarse shouts rose from a thousand throats and they thundered forward, mad for revenge. Polymus led them across the field at a gallop.

Xuthus hesitated before Iasus' fallen body. The king lay face down. Xuthus dismounted quickly and grabbed a spear thrust down in the earth close by. He kicked Iasus until he rolled over. Licking his lips, Xuthus thrust the spear into Iasus' body again and again. Finally, grinning madly, he leaped on his war horse and charged for Melanion and Atalante on the hill.

They held with what strength they could against the battering wave. Atalante and Melanion fought back to back. Maybe they'd die together, he thought. He only regretted that he would never see her again; his hell would be separation from Atalante. He deserved it for what he'd almost done, and what he'd not been strong enough to do.

Three Red Bands harried him at once, hampering his sword arm. Red-hot pain shot through his thigh. He fell. His blood mixed with the earth where last night, he'd offered himself as the sacrifice.

"Get the princess first before you finish him," Polymus shouted.

And he heard Philip sound the paean somewhere to the left, and felt hands grabbing roughly at him. The darkness descended. He saw and heard no more.

# Chapter 11

## Racing for Time

Atalante stared out the window in her mother's chamber at the plain of Iolcus. The earth lay churned up and black with blood. Snarling hyenas fought each other for the spoils—the severed limbs of soldiers and horses rotting in the sun. The stench of decay wafted toward the palace so that at night, she couldn't have slept if she wanted to.

By the Macedonian king's command, they'd buried her father with all honor and ceremony. They placed Iasus' golden cup in his hand and a golden crown engraved with his name and his rank upon his head. They put gold coins on his eyelids for the Ferryman, honey cakes in the coffin for the beast, Cerberus, and a tablet recording his deeds so Rhadamanthas, the immortal judge, would give him passage to the Isle of the Blessed. She'd stared dry-eyed as the priests performed the ritual.

They hadn't buried Melanion. Polymus had spread the story that he'd tried to murder his father, and so they left him in a pit, without any of the observances. His soul would wander for eternity on the far shore of the River, begging for a deliverance that would never come.

She wasn't grateful for Kryton's respect, nor his careful protection of her mother, her brother, and herself. She wished her arrow had killed him, but she'd been wide of the mark. Melanion wouldn't have missed. She could tell that when she jarred his arm. But in the end, she couldn't unleash the Daughters of Night upon him, even to save her own father.

After Melanion had fallen, four of the swine had captured her. They carried her to a small, windowless room where she had neither light nor sound for what seemed a pain-filled eternity.

When the Macedonian king regained consciousness, his first command had been to release her.

The guards had treated her with courtesy as they ushered her to Hyperion's door. When it opened, she had gazed at him with despair. His eyes were clear and calm, and his arms went around her waist and held on while she shuddered.

"What are we to do, Hyperion? Has the Mother forsaken us?"

"She will never forsake us, Atalante."

"It's my fault," she whispered, holding him tight. "Father told me to run as soon as I saw him fall, but Melanion was wounded. I should have left him, but I couldn't let him die alone."

"Of course you couldn't." Hyperion's voice was filled with tenderness.

"And then it was too late. I couldn't save anything— Father, Melanion, the kingdom."

He led Atalante to a bench. "You must not torment yourself, my sister. You must be strong."

She sank onto it, choked back a sob. "Have you seen the streets?" she asked him. "Erytes snuck into my room and told me the Red Bands torture the people with looting and worse. And Polymus made a decree. It's treason to worship the Mother."

"Polymus may make as many decrees as he likes. We will still worship her," Hyperion said grimly.

Her voice cracked. "They will hurt you if you do. Like they did Melanion." She jumped up from the bench, wringing her hands as she paced.

"You must stay safe, Hyperion. Because I'm going to avenge Melanion. I'll find the monsters who killed Melanion and I'll kill them. I'll find the pit they threw him in. I'll bury his body and pour libations on his grave, so his soul can go free. I don't care if they kill me. I can't stay here and weep like a woman. I want to fight back until I die of it."

Hyperion grabbed her hands.

"Stop it, Atalante! You must do everything you can to survive. The whole future depends on it. Listen to our mother, do exactly what she says, even when it goes against what your heart tells you to do. Mother Dia showed me this in the flames above you on the battlefield." His sea-green eyes held the stern conviction of a priest.

She bit her lip to keep it from trembling. A moan escaped her. It sounded like a helpless animal caught in a snare. "How can I bear it?" she whispered.

"You'll bear it because you must," said Hyperion, reaching up to smooth her tangled hair. He took the corner of a linen towel and wiped her face, and then he looked at her for a long time.

"It's your moira. You watch and wait, and you hurt so badly you want to die. In your pain, you'll transform yourself into something stronger than you ever thought you could be. The people will see it and gain strength to resist. Maybe for ages, they'll remember you not because you fled and fought, but because you stayed with them and met your fate."

"Oh, gods," she sighed. "I'm not made for this, Hyperion."

"Rededicate yourself, Atalante," he said in his deep priest's voice. "Your task is to give us time. Remember, with time, the gods can show us wonders."

A low knock sounded at the door. Clymene entered, followed by Erytes carrying a tray of herbs and potions.

"Atalante," her mother said. "Come with me. You can bring some of these. I don't know what Kryton will need."

Atalante's face went white. She stared at the tray. "You can't mean to do this, Mother."

Clymene glanced from the tray to Atalante. "The Macedonian has summoned me. Take the jars of willow bark and rosemary." Her voice was cool, expressionless.

"He's the pig who killed my father." Atalante felt the bile rise in her throat. She wanted to run from the room, to scream her outrage, but all she could manage was this choked whisper.

Clymene's voice cut through the air like a knife. "This is no time for foolish emotion. We have one weapon left, and that is our intellect. We have one goal, and that is Thessaly's freedom. You will obey me in every way until that goal is achieved. Do you hear me, Atalante?"

Atalante looked from her mother to her brother. Both wore the implacable visages of priests. She bit her lip until it bled. With a long shudder, she met her mother's gaze. "I hear you."

When she followed her mother into Kryton's chamber, Atalante was shocked to see the Macedonian. He lay shivering with fever. A purple hue formed around his mouth and on his fingertips. Clymene probed and smoothed his skin with her hands, sniffed his breath, felt beneath his arms and in the area of his groin.

When she gently palpated his abdomen, Kryton groaned. "What did Polymus say when I sent him to find you?"

"If you die, so do I," Clymene said and continued her examination.

"So why'd you come?"

Clymene shrugged, her face inscrutable. "I'm a healer. Besides . . ." She cast a long look at the Macedonian. "Do you think I care whether I live or die?"

For some time, Clymene continued her examination in silence. Kryton lay with his eyes shut. He made no noise except for one harsh, in-drawn breath. Clymene finished with him and turned to a serving maid.

"Leave us," she said. She turned to Atalante. "Guard the door. I want no eavesdroppers."

Atalante nodded and put her ear to the door as her mother sat back on a stool, smoothing her skirts around her.

"How much do you want to know?" Clymene asked Kryton.

The Macedonian looked at her with fever-bright eyes. "Everything."

"You've been poisoned, King. It's a slow worker, used to imitate a natural death. I can slow its course, but I can't cure you. In time, more or less depending upon your will, you'll die. The medicine I can give you will make you wish you were dead. The pain will last for several hours after each dose. However, if time is what you want, the potion will give it to you. You must decide."

Kryton turned his face to the wall. The room was so quiet, Atalante could hear his sigh. "Did my son do this to me?"

Clymene made an impatient sound. "Search your heart, Kryton. Could Melanion have done this to anyone?"

The king shook his head. Before he passed his hand before his eyes, Atalante thought she saw a drop of moisture in them.

"I was with Melanion when you murdered my father," she said softly from the doorway. "Only my arrow touched you, and I don't dip my arrows in poison, either." Atalante hoped he could hear the scorn in her voice.

However, Kryton seemed oblivious to everything but the import of her words. Tears coursed down the creases of his cheeks. Clymene dipped a linen towel in warm water and bathed his face. Kryton wept on.

"My son, my own son," he whispered. "He warned me, but I thought I knew better. They cut him down in the dust and they buried him without the rituals. They've made him into an anathema. Oh, gods, what have I done?" Kryton put his hands to his face and sobbed.

Before the war, Atalante had feared Kryton, but at this moment, she hated him. Because he made her cry, too, because he wasn't really a monster, but only a . . .

"Fool," she said with a catch in her voice. "How is it only now you see what my father knew, what Melanion . . . ?" She choked and rested her forehead on the hard oak of the door.

"Go into the hallway, Atalante," her mother said. She opened the door and walked into darkened corridor. Torches guttered, casting shadows. The wind rose from the sea and whistled through the darkness. What was once a haven of peace and light had become Hell.

Kryton stared up at Clymene after she'd wiped his face. He remembered her from his humiliating wedding day. She'd been a pretty little thing, then, childless at the time, and soft as a kitten. She wasn't soft now. No, she had a look of iron about her—unbending, tempered, cool. He guessed she'd be as hard on him as her daughter had been, and with good reason.

Her voice was quiet, though, not judgmental, when she

spoke. "My daughter and your son were lovers. I suspect the goddess may have blessed their union many months ago, at her altar in the mountains. Atalante mourns his death as much as she mourns her father—probably more. Had you offered for her, we would have consented, for his sake as well as hers. We loved your son, Kryton. In spite of what we knew was coming, we loved him."

The old hurt rankled, in spite of this, or maybe because of it. "Why did you hate me so much?" he asked, and wanted to squirm at the peevishness he heard in his voice.

Clymene sighed. "Iasus and I didn't hate you, Kryton. We just knew what would happen if you wed Althea. She was my cousin—we'd been raised together, and I understood her. That delicate body held a very proud and stubborn spirit."

"She hated me, hated everything about me."

"You're wrong. She hated you and she loved you. She wanted things from you she couldn't ask you for."

"Gods! Like what?" If he hadn't felt ill before, he did now—sick with regret.

"You're a hard man, Kryton. You wanted a queen who would be there when you wanted her, would never judge you, would never object to your concubines. Althea knew this from the beginning and dreaded your marriage, because she'd resent your wars, your other women, and your lack of respect for her.

"Althea could be very cold when she was angry. She could keep it up for a long, long time. I took one look at you and knew she'd drive you mad with it—maybe make you furious enough to kill her."

"I didn't kill her! She died because she ran away from me. I was frantic to find her. By the gods, I had men searching for months before they found the boy." But even as Kryton defended himself, he remembered his actions on the last night he'd been with Althea, and shuddered. He'd been running away from that night for years, and he shrank from facing it now.

Clymene pulled back and then stood up, fiddling with her jars and vials. "Still, you have much to answer for, Kryton of Macedonia," she said without a hint of inflection.

A low rap on the door caught their attention. Atalante slipped into the room. "Somebody's coming," she whispered.

A few moments later, Kryton heard a tentative knock. "Enter," he said.

Atalante opened the door and ushered old Myron, Kryton's general, into the room. His one-eyed gaze went from Kryton to Clymene to the medicine on the table near the bed. Kryton motioned him closer, and he knelt by the bed, his face screwed up in an effort to hide his worry.

"Majesty, that damned commander sent me with a message for you. The bastard's in the Megaron playing king. He says in front of everybody that he's waiting for your answer and wants it quick. Then he sends me like a slave to bring it to him. By the gods, you've got to get well. And then, order me to kill that snake."

Kryton laid a hand on his old friend's shoulder. "I'm not done yet, Myron. Give me the tablet." When he finished, he gave the tablet to Clymene. "Wait for me outside, friend," he told Myron, who rose with creaking joints and left.

Clymene finished reading and returned the tablet. Her eyes were bleak.

"Send the girl away," Kryton said, with a nod in Atalante's direction.

"Go, now, my daughter. Find Hyperion and stay with him until I come." Clymene made a small motion of her hand, and Atalante slipped out the door. Beside Kryton's bed, the charcoal hissed in the brazier.

He took a deep, painful breath. "Now there's good reason for me to live as long as I can. Tell me everything about the princess Atalante."

Kryton took the drugs. Then he and Clymene spoke for two hours, between fits of agony such as Kryton had never known. Clymene wanted him to rest, but he had so little time as it was, and there was much to accomplish. When the pain lessened a bit, he called for Myron. As the old general entered, he sniffed the air like an old hound who knows when something's amiss.

Kryton knew he smelled the sour odor of drugs and vomit in the room. Myron took one look at him and cried out. He ran to the bed and hovered over him. Kryton waved him away impatiently. He didn't have time for sympathy.

"Tell Polymus the king is pleased to have heard his *petition*. I call assembly in the Megaron for tomorrow morning. The king *commands* him to summon not only the Macedonian generals but also the people of Iolcus to hear and accept his proposal. Can you do that, Myron?"

"Of course, Majesty," Myron said in a shaky voice, wiping his good eye with his sleeve. He was unable to meet his king's eyes. Poor fellow. Kryton would wager Myron had never broken down in his entire life before, and was damned ashamed to have done it now.

Myron walked slowly to the door and opened it. Then he turned and looked squarely at Kryton. "The gods keep you, Sire," he said, and bowed himself out.

"So we all hope," said Kryton as he fell back on the bed. He was sweating so much he'd soaked the sheets. Clymene changed them herself. When he protested, she explained she didn't want the servants to know how bad it was.

By morning, Kryton felt stronger. Although his bowels still griped painfully, he could breathe without gasping and the purple hue about his mouth and eyes had dimmed. Clymene called men into the chamber, trusted servants who brought materials for a litter. As soon as the corridor door was shut, they assembled it.

"I can't be carried through the halls like an infant," Kryton thundered at Clymene. "Do you want the whole world to see how weak I am?"

"Don't be a fool, King. I understand only too well what's at stake here."

Well, he thought as the men placed him on the litter, the kitten has claws.

Clymene stood at the far wall, in front of a chest. She motioned for help, and two of the men pushed it aside and lifted the colorful wool rug beneath it. Clymene bent down and raised a small trap door in the floor. The men swept up the litter and carried Kryton down the ancient stone staircase leading to cellars beneath the palace.

They wound through a maze below ground. The only light was from Clymene's torch. Kryton caught sight of treasure rooms and storerooms to his left and right. He saw a great door to one side. It was closed, like a hand pushing him away. He dimly felt there was something behind that door he wanted to see. Something comforting and accepting. But he felt like an outcast. Whatever was there didn't want him.

When they'd carried him past that place, they climbed a stairway and came to a small door. The queen put her eye to it, looking through a peephole, no doubt.

"It's empty," she told the men. "We can enter." They brought him through the door. He realized this was the Megaron, with its frescoes, shining shields, and swords. They set him on the marble throne of Iolcus.

He felt like a thief. He felt the gods of the place knew Iasus, not he, should sit here.

Well, hell. He had work to do, and only he could do it now. The gods would have to accept him, just like Clymene. He was all they had.

Clymene stood just behind him on his left. Atalante climbed the few stairs to the dais and took her place at his right hand, wearing the ceremonial sword buckled on her hip. She gave him a cold, distant look.

"You know what you're to say?" he asked her.

Atalante nodded solemnly. He could see she hated him, but the girl was no fool. She'd do the right thing. Gods, she was a beauty. No wonder Melanion wanted her.

Melanion . . .

He shut his eyes against the sting and shook his head to clear it of foolish thoughts, all of them too late. When he opened them, the first generals were walking into the Megaron. Polymus came last, of course, draped with his medals of honor. Obviously, the bastard assumed Kryton was too ill to attend. Polymus must be looking forward to presiding over the assembly. Well, he had a surprise or two coming.

As he crossed the Megaron, Polymus read a document and spoke to a Red Band guard at his side at the same time. He didn't even look at the throne, but made straight for the dais. The traitor had his foot on the first stair when Kryton decided to put an end to his complacence.

"Greetings, Polymus." Kryton was pleased to hear how strong and deep his voice had become.

Polymus' head lifted at the sound of Kryton's voice. His mouth dropped, but he recovered in a flash, shoving the tablet at the guard and dropping to one knee, his head bowed.

"Rise," said Kryton in the most majestic tones he could muster.

"How good to see you've improved in health, Majesty," Polymus said. "I am overjoyed at this change."

"I am aware of your deep interest in my health." Kryton underlined the irony of his statement with a smile that was little more than a snarl. "With the help of Thessaly's queen, I am at last recovering quite well from that cursed wound."

"Wonderful news, for which we are all grateful," Polymus said in silky tones.

The seasoned Macedonian generals who crowded the Megaron grinned at Kryton with open relief. To one side, the faction that had thrown in its lot with Polymus glanced around uneasily, pondering which way the wind blew now.

Watching carefully, the artisans and merchants of Iolcus stood together to the left of the throne. With the barons' retreat to the south, they had become the leaders of the city. Kryton looked carefully at these men. He could see the loneliness in their eyes, and the dedication. After all, he understood their thankless task. They had no power, but still had to keep order under a hated conqueror's rule. The best they could do was warn their daughters to hide at home and keep their sons from taking the kitchen knives, killing a few Red Bands, and hanging for it.

Meanwhile, so Myron told him, their nobles camped in the mountains, harassed the army, and captured the people's adulation.

Kryton raised his hand for silence. "Polymus has requested an audience to present a proposal. I command him to speak."

Polymus strode forward and faced the gathering with a theatrical flourish of his cape. "Macedonians and Thessalians. The bitter war is over, thank the gods. The

Macedonians are eager to show mercy to King Kryton's new subjects. We wish that his two states will unite in peace."

Polymus' voice was pulpy as an overripe orange. "I want to strengthen the bond between us—to symbolically unite our people. Thessalians, you have a princess, the daughter of an ancient and noble line. I have a son, a young and brave man, who would protect her as we Macedonians wish to protect all of you."

Xuthus sidled forward. Gods, the boy was a disgusting specimen, with his scraggly goatee, his flushed, mottled face, his furtive eyes. Xuthus looked gaudy enough to be a monarch from Crete or Egypt. His tunic of white silk was embroidered with gold threads. Rubies lined the sleeves and the hem. He wore a heavy chain of gold wrought of serpents, head to tail. Xuthus moistened his lips in anticipation, bowed to the generals, and turned toward the dais.

Kryton's loyal generals had never seen anything quite like Xuthus' display. They stared with amazed frowns. In the silence that gripped the Megaron, one Thessalian hissed to another. "That necklace belongs to the royal house. I repaired it for our king just months ago."

Guards moved in the speaker's direction, but the Thessalians closed ranks. Kryton held up his hand, stopping the guards in their tracks. He'd be damned if he let Polymus punish the artisan.

"I ask that the king and the assembly approve the marriage of the princess to my son. Let us unite our lands now and forever. What say you?" Polymus continued as though all was well.

The Thessalians began to mutter. Their furious whine rose, reminding Kryton of hornets from a trampled nest. The Macedonians waited stoically for Kryton's judgment.

Kryton held up his hand and the hall fell silent. "Your *sincere* desire for peace is admirable, Polymus. But the princess is a priestess of Artemis Agrotera. She must, like the goddess, go a maiden. She can't wed your son."

"For the good of the state, our priests will find a way to appease the goddess," Polymus said carelessly.

"Now, Polymus," said Kryton. The humor in his voice overlay a layer of steel. "Here we sit, two old fellows with our Macedonian attitudes and beliefs. If we want to merge the two kingdoms, we must pay attention to Thessaly's customs and respect them. In Thessaly, the women speak for themselves.

"Of course," he continued smoothly, "if you plan to change Thessaly's deeply honored customs, announce it here in assembly, in front of our army. After all, they'll be responsible for enforcing the law. Come on, let's put it to a vote, and treat with the princess in the Macedonian way. In other words, we'll speak around her, about her, any way but to her. What say you?"

The hornets' whine sounded again, louder. Polymus' gaze slid from one Thessalian to another. Kryton guessed the snake was frantically tallying the numbers of Red Bands slaughtered in the last week in forays for supplies. Polymus was comparing that number to the dwindling supplies in the city, and concluding that the army would starve if it didn't break through soon to Arcadia and Dimeni in the south.

Kryton watched Polymus puzzling it all out. If the townspeople rebelled, who knew what they'd do—burn the rest of the grain stored in the city, pour out the wine and oil? Polymus needed the people quiet until the south was in his hands. For now, he had to be careful. Polymus bowed before Atalante like a humble courtier.

"I ask pardon, Princess. Before this assembly, I ask you

respectfully. Please consider my son's suit."

He pushed Xuthus forward. The paunchy redhead strolled up to the dais. Atalante watched his approach with cold eyes. When Xuthus reached her, he knelt and offered something to her. Kryton took a look at the intricately wrought box worked in enamel and gold. The figures on it illustrated the tale of Zeus overthrowing his father Uranus and strewing parts of his body—particularly his cock and balls—into the sea.

Kryton had seen a hell of a lot in his life, but this "gift" disgusted him.

Xuthus whispered so only Atalante and Kryton could hear him. "Only a god can murder his father and get away with it," he said. By the fires of Hades, he referred to Melanion!

Xuthus grinned at their shocked silence. With a broad gesture, Xuthus opened the case. Inside lay a golden diadem encrusted with jewels. Atalante's face was pale but expressionless. She barely glanced at the gift, then stared for a long time into Xuthus' mottled face.

Polymus' voice cut through the silence. "Since he first saw you, my son has been mad with love for you. Dear Princess, his heart is in your hands. One word from your lips could make all the difference . . ."

Then his pleading tone hardened into a threat. "Consider your people. Those in Iolcus as well as the south, which we'll surely take."

Polymus' mouth twisted and his eyes narrowed. "So many you love have died. Don't endanger countless more by this foolish maiden's whim to remain unveiled. Think how the Macedonians—my Red Band in particular—would react to this affront. I couldn't answer for the safety of the women in the capital."

Atalante drew herself up. "If this is my destiny, let it come," she said with a power that was cold and bright and a little cruel, like the moon goddess she served. "But I made a vow to the goddess when I saw the Macedonians amassed on Iolcus Plain. I will marry only a man who will meet me in the stadium and race me for my hand. If he wins, I'll go to my marriage bed without complaint."

She pointed to Xuthus standing a step below her. The snake's spawn actually trembled beneath the shadow of her hand. As he stumbled back, the case fell and splintered against the floor tiles.

"Beware, Xuthus," she said. "For any man who runs against me and loses will die. I'll run before the people; they'll judge that all we have agreed upon goes according to the law we set down today. That is my bride price. Death to him who can't beat me."

In the silence that followed, Polymus blinked and cleared his throat. He turned to Kryton. "My son's a soldier, not a runner. Let a proxy race her. If that man wins, he'll have gold beyond counting, and my son will wed Atalante. Remember, Kryton, you sent a trusted general to sign your wedding contract to a Thessalian by proxy. By this old Macedonian law I make my claim."

Atalante felt the bile rise in her throat at Polymus' words. Kryton had told her that Xuthus would never have the courage to challenge her, but neither he nor her mother had anticipated Polymus' knowledge of Macedonian law and his agility at twisting it to his ends. She glanced at Kryton for help. Surely, there was a legal argument to supercede Polymus' claim.

But Kryton gripped the marble arms of the serpent throne, his knuckles white. The pain must have returned, and the Macedonian king was struggling against it. Any moment, he might reveal his weakness if he had to speak. She couldn't allow that—Kryton was their only hope against Polymus. She had to hide the king's agony from the assembly.

With a quick stride, she blocked Polymus' view of the king. "I agree, Commander. Before the assembly, Macedonian and Thessalian, we're sworn." She turned her back on the assembly and looked carefully at Kryton, who nodded at her as he caught his breath. His face was pale, but smoothed over. The pain had lifted, if just for the moment.

"It will be as you say, Atalante," Kryton said in a clear voice. A priest approached, holding a bowl of blood from a pure white bull sacrificed this morning. Dipping his finger in the bowl, the priest made the sign of the Huntress' arrow on Xuthus' forehead and on Atalante's, as well.

"You're sworn by the rules of assembly and the gods who watch us this day," said Kryton. "So be it."

"Quick!" Clymene said to the litter bearers. "Get him into bed." Atalante followed her mother into Kryton's chamber, worriedly watching the servants lower the king onto soft linen sheets. He groaned with relief.

Clymene grabbed a towel and blotted the sweat running down Kryton's face.

"Did you see the look on his face? What an ass, to think he'd gotten rid of me," the king said through chattering teeth.

"Yes, yes, quiet now. You've got to rest." Clymene kneaded the muscles in the king's neck and shoulders. She called for hot towels. Atalante guessed they were for his arms and legs, to stop the shaking.

"By the gods, I'll show him," Kryton said.

Clymene's lips pressed into a thin line. "Your pulse is

weak and thready. You vomited twice on the way back here. If you don't rest, you won't have a chance to show anybody anything. Understand?"

"Yes, yes . . ." Kryton gave her an airy wave. But he did close his eyes.

Moments passed as Clymene sat beside Kryton watching him carefully. She glanced at Atalante and smiled a little. "His pulse is strong again, and the shaking's stopped. This is good."

"Clymene?" Kryton said.

"Yes?"

"Send Myron looking for the traitorous bastard who tended my wound. I want to question him."

Clymene shook her head. "You won't find him. Polymus wouldn't leave any loose ends."

"No. Still, we have to try. In the meantime, find out all you can about the runner they'll hire."

Clymene left immediately. Atalante sat beside the king as he dozed, watching for any signs of stress. She looked at the weathered face, trying to find any resemblance to Melanion. There were a few—the same jaw, square and strong, the same high cheekbones, but not the sweetness of her lover's smile, or the teasing glint in eyes gray as the dawn sky.

She had dreamed of Melanion last night. The dream was so real, so comforting, she woke convinced he still lived. And then reality hit with such a painful wrench that she rolled over and stuffed a pillow into her mouth so no one would hear her sobs. Even now, staring at his father for glimpses of Melanion, she couldn't quite believe he was dead, and cursed herself for being a fool in a world where cleverness meant everything.

As Kryton stirred and woke, Erytes slipped into the

room through the trap door, followed by Hyperion. Erytes' eyes danced with excitement.

"I know everything," Erytes said proudly. "Queen Clymene sent me to be her eyes and ears. They never pay attention to servant boys."

"Did you run into any danger?" Atalante asked him as she mixed the sleeping draught into some warm wine.

"Nah, some of them remember my brother. They think I followed the army to Iolcus with dreams of glory and plunder. Guess where I got a job," he said, then paused dramatically.

"I can't imagine," Atalante said with half a smile. It was difficult not to respond to Erytes' spirit and general delight in life.

"I'm cleaning the rooms of the vulture, himself. I heard it all firsthand."

"Who's the runner?" Kryton asked, rising on one elbow.

"Dion. He's the son of a sheep farmer from the mountains around Hamalclion. He's a good sort—everybody likes him. He ran in the spring games, but Melanion passed him in the first heat. He's got long legs and an easy manner. The soldiers are betting on him, but they don't know anything about Atalante. Yet."

Atalante felt sick. "How old is he?" she asked him.

"Young. Maybe even younger than Melanion. His mother's sick. If he wins, he'll send the money home to pay for a wise woman."

"Oh." Atalante's stomach knotted. Young. An easy manner. A sick mother, by the gods. She hated this.

"You can't go soft on him," Erytes said—Erytes, who nursed every injured creature he found. "They're not forcing him, after all. And he should be ashamed of challenging a girl. He doesn't know you're faster than the wind."

271

"But afterwards, Erytes. Polymus will kill him," Atalante said with a catch in her voice.

Erytes stared at her, his expression set in a white face. "Win, Atalante. I was there when Polymus gave Xuthus a lecture. He told Xuthus he couldn't give in to his 'perverted appetites' until you'd delivered his first grandson and another babe, just in case the first one didn't live. Then, he said, Xuthus could do what he wanted with you and Polymus would 'dispose of you' afterward. He plans to put the baby on the throne as the rightful king, and he'll be the regent."

Atalante crouched over her belly, stomach roiling.

"There, my girl," Kryton said softly. "There's nothing for it but to win and sacrifice this . . . Macedonian."

"I have to go," Erytes said, moving toward the trap door. "He'll want me running errands soon."

"I'll stay and take Atalante's place," Hyperion said.

"You can't do that, Little Owl. You'll wear yourself out." Atalante stroked Hyperion's thin cheek. After all the other losses she'd suffered, the thought of losing her brother was too much to bear.

He just shook his head. "You've got to rest for the race tomorrow. And Mother told me I could."

As Atalante slipped into the stairway beneath the trap door, she heard the king and her brother talking.

"I wish . . ." the king said with a groan.

"What?" Hyperion asked in the voice she'd heard so often, that rich, kind tone that made her want to tell him everything, because Hyperion still wouldn't hate her for whatever she revealed.

"Nothing," the king said with a sigh. "I just regret Melanion only saw the cruelty in my decisions and not the complexity of my choices."

When Atalante reached her room, she realized it was night. She bathed and ate a light supper, too miserable to eat more than half what a maidservant brought her. She couldn't sleep and stood by the window looking out into the moonless night. It must have been midnight when she heard a rap on her door. Her mother entered and handed her a long black cloak like the one she was wearing.

"Put it on," Clymene said. "Raise the hood. I want to see if these still work." Atalante slipped the cloak about her shoulders and raised the hood, following her mother into the corridor. They wound through the palace in silence. Occasionally, a torch in a wall sconce sputtered, throwing a flickering light on the hallway. They passed soldiers who didn't seem to notice them at all. When they stood outside the king's room, the guards stared straight through them and didn't move a hair as Clymene silently opened the door and stepped through.

Atalante handed her mother the cloak and stared at her, questioning.

Clymene carefully folded the cloaks. "They're very old, made by priestesses of your goddess in her incarnation as Hecate, High Sorceress. I wanted to make sure the spells protecting them were still strong. Someday soon, we may need them." She pointed to Kryton lying restless on the big bed. "He wanted to see you."

Atalante looked at the king. His hands pulled at the blanket. A searing pain slashed her heart.

"What is it?" Kryton asked gruffly. Her staring must have made him self-conscious.

"I didn't realize," she whispered. "Melanion had your hands. It's just—hard to look at them." She bit her lip to stop its trembling and turned away, fighting for control. It took her a while to regain it and face him again.

"What do you wish?" she asked him.

"To give you some advice," he said evenly. "Your rebels need time. With your help, I can give it to 'em. Come here into the light."

She stepped forward. As he studied her, his scrutiny was so intense she flinched.

"Pure beauty," he mused. "What sculptors try for in stone and bards in words, in one face, one form. No wonder my son loved you."

She scowled at him. He knows nothing about it, she thought bitterly. Nothing at all. "Melanion saw more in me than mere beauty."

"I know you'd stick me through in a minute if it'd help your country," he said as though he'd read her mind. "But you need me, so forgive my unenlightened musings. I'm just glad he had some happiness before he died." He broke off and grasped the wool again, and worked it, worked it in silence.

With a sigh, he raised his gaze to her again. "Hyperion told me you run like the wind. Don't run full out tomorrow, or the next time, or the next. Play Polymus like a trout—don't tug the line until he's hooked deep. Keep him hoping the next man will be fast enough, until your troops have destroyed enough of . . ." Kryton choked, swallowed, "my army to take Iolcus again. Do you understand?"

Atalante nodded. Kryton's eyes were weary, his cheeks grooved from suffering. She felt her heart soften a bit.

The king lifted his hand, in blessing or dismissal, perhaps. "Go. Sleep the sleep of the honorable. Pray to your gods for victory. But, by heaven, go slowly tomorrow."

She nodded and walked to the door, where her mother helped her into the cloak. Atalante's hands trembled as she tied the strings about her neck. She did not want to like

Kryton. She needed her hatred, her anger, to make her strong enough.

Clymene's low voice broke into her thoughts. "I've sacrificed to the Mother, Atalante. There is something more you must do tomorrow."

She lifted her gaze to her mother's face. Clymene looked stern, the way she had when she'd told Atalante bad news in the past. What now, she thought with dread.

"You must run. Immodestly."

Atalante stared at her. Her blood went cold. "What do you mean, immodestly?"

Her mother looked down at her hands. "Unclothed," she said. "Like a man."

Atalante's fists clenched. "No! Everybody will see. The Macedonians. That cur who thinks he'll own me—with his eyes on me, I'll be desecrated. I'll be filthy."

She raised her hand in supplication. "Don't make me do this, Mother. All I have left is my pride. It's the only thing keeping me alive."

Clymene grasped her hands and held her when she wanted to flee. "There's no mistake, Atalante. I asked three times, and three times She answered me. You must do it."

Atalante went cold beneath the insistent clasp of her mother's hands. From the time she was five, Clymene had asked her for more and more, and she always gave it. With the hope that someday, it would be enough to make her mother's eyes soften when she saw Atalante. Now, beneath the weight of this last ignominy, she seethed with bitter resentment.

"Would you make Hyperion sacrifice himself like this for the people?" she whispered.

Clymene's expression turned grim. "He already has.

275

Who do you think risked his life to worship Mother Dia with me last night?"

Atalante shoved herself away. Ashamed, furious, she wrapped the cloak tightly about her and flew down the hallway. Still running, she crossed Iolcus Plain to the wooded hills above it. She wanted to cry, to wail and shriek at the moon-deserted sky. But what would it serve to call on a goddess who'd forgotten her?

Atalante turned and stumbled back to the palace. She had one thing left beside her pride—her duty. Until Thessaly was free, she'd do it. And then, she'd die.

The morrow dawned bright and clear. The stadium was packed with a strangely silent crowd and enough soldiers to keep order. Atalante entered through the Athlete's Gate and walked to the track. A white alabaster altar stood on the grassy plain in the center of the track. Four recently erected columns rose around it. They were wreathed from grassy base to high capitals with maidenhair ferns, hyacinths, and narcissus. The scents of spring assailed her nostrils. The altar where she was to be purified now would be her wedding altar after the race, if Polymus' plans came to fruition.

A priest waited for her beside the altar. She knelt before him. He'd sacrificed a dove moments before and now read the entrails. Then he placed the sign of Aphrodite, the goddess of love to whom Polymus dedicated this race, on her forehead and blessed her.

The man Dion came forward. While the priest purified him, Atalante studied him carefully, noting his stride, looking for swelling or other signs of injury on his legs. As she watched him, she felt torn between contempt and pity. The man didn't even bow his head in respect after he'd received the goddess' mark.

Atalante took a deep breath. She stripped and gave the robe to an attendant, ignoring the shocked gasps of the crowd. Instead of the modest chiton, she wore nothing but a small loincloth. As she walked, she could feel her breasts sway. It made her hot with humiliation. Then, within the time it took to breathe, she forgot how she looked, and what her pride demanded. All her senses became heightened. When she turned and looked directly at Xuthus, she saw everything behind his gape-jawed stare—his thoughts, his fears, his desires. And understood why the Mother had insisted she run naked. Stripped of her clothing, Atalante received the gift of Sight.

Xuthus' thoughts winged to her through the air between them. As he looked his fill at her, he was seized with a terrible longing. He felt as though he were dying of love. The Mother had meant her to pierce him through, to enslave him, and Atalante had succeeded.

She could hear his thoughts, his plans for her. Xuthus would keep her as a treasure, would shower her with jewels and silks from the east. He would enclose her, guard her from men's eyes, except when he brought her forth for the court's adulation. He grew almost faint at the thought that he could claim her after the race. He would never let his father destroy her, never!

Atalante could hear his heart thunder in his chest, could feel his desperate adoration build. She almost felt sorry for him. Almost.

The low moan of pity from the crowd comforted her. Some of her people knelt in the stands; others hid their eyes from her as though she were a goddess disrobed. Atalante took a deep, calming breath and fitted her foot against the starting block.

A trumpet pierced the silence. Dion sprang forward.

Atalante ran a length behind, watching his movements. There were four turns around the stadium. She must gain imperceptibly.

They circled the course once. Atalante crept up on Dion until she ran in his shadow. By the third lap, she ran almost even with him, but at the sound of his ragged breathing, she fell back. She could feel him taking heart, assuming she was spent. He lunged forward at the turn for home, churning his legs faster, thinking he was leaving her behind. Vaguely she could hear the women sobbing in the stands.

When she could see the final stave, Atalante opened her stride. Slowly, she allowed herself to pull ahead. People in the stands leaped to their feet, screaming, laughing, and hugging each other. She whipped by the end stave and turned to see Dion lunge for the finish, gasping.

A handmaiden ran across the field to her, holding out her chiton. Atalante slipped into it, and just that quickly, her enemy's thoughts were closed to her. A bouquet of narcissus pelted her and she realized the crowd was throwing flowers. She laughed, looking around. The winner's pavilion was thick with them—irises and wildflowers, all white and purple, formed a carpet of hope beneath her feet.

Polymus stood by the altar beside Aphrodite's priest. His face was dark with rage. His eyes were two slits, like the masks the Bacchants wear when they perform their unspeakable rites.

He gave a signal and a gong boomed out, silencing the crowd.

"The princess Atalante pronounced judgment on the loser of this race earlier this week in the Megaron. She who judged him must dispatch him."

Chilled, Atalante looked at him. "But I never agreed to this."

Polymus smiled, a slow, poisonous lift of his lips. "You gave the penalty. You carry out the punishment. Unless you want to forfeit the race, instead."

Gods, she was to kill a man in cold blood?

Aye, she thought. With Kryton too ill to overthrow Polymus, this was her punishment for outmaneuvering the commander in court.

They dragged Dion before her. He fell, covered his eyes, and choked back a sob. She raised him up as gently as she could.

"Listen to me," she said softly. "You'll face Charon, the Ferryman, and Hades, the King of the Shadow World. Show them you can die like a man and they'll reward you. I know you don't believe in the gods, but they exist. If you trust them, you'll be happy soon.

"I'll be quick," she promised him. "Make peace with the gods, then give me the sign when you're ready."

As Atalante walked to the green oval inside the track, her hands shook, and she remembered Melanion lying bleeding in the meadow that beautiful autumn day. A servant handed her a bow and arrow while they brought Dion to the altar and stood him against a column. She wondered how she'd manage to nock the arrow and her gaze flew to Dion as the sick nausea welled up inside her. His lips trembled, but he stood upright and he looked to her for some sort of salvation. It was his look that steadied her. She owed him all she could give—speed and accuracy. Dion raised his arm, hand outstretched toward her in salute. Never shifting his gaze from her, he took a deep breath of the flower-scented air. She let the arrow fly. He fell instantly.

Atalante dropped the bow to the ground. She walked the long path to the Athlete's Gate and through the stadium to the palace. Everyone she passed drew back from her with sighs and murmurs of pity she didn't deserve.

She wandered into her room, removed her chiton, and donned a robe. Hyperion entered silently as she belted it.

"Now I know why the Mother told me to run without this," she said in a voice that sounded dead to her ears. "See," she said, holding it out with shaking fingers. It's white, for purity. Murderers don't dress in white."

"You're not a murderer." Hyperion held out his hand, but Atalante turned away. She didn't want to soil him with her touch.

"It's going to happen every time, you know. I'll have to kill them all." She laughed, a high-pitched, hysterical sound that rose to a breathy scream. "The witch from Kalydon— her curse. I didn't tell you about it. Melanion knew. He tried to protect me from it, but Melanion's dead, isn't he?" Her gaze skittered around the room, searching.

"I keep forgetting he's dead," she said with a sob. "I wake up in the morning and I think, Hurry, Melanion. Come back to me. Isn't that absurd?"

Her voice rose in pitch. "I'm glad he's dead. I couldn't live if he heard what I did today. He would have found an-other way—he would have outsmarted Polymus, or started an uprising—anything, other than killing a decent man in cold blood. And he's the one whose soul is damned. Gods! Where is he?"

"Sit down," Hyperion said in a calm voice. "They'll hear you and report to Polymus."

Somehow, she managed to find the bench and stared into nothing. Hyperion sat down beside her and stroked her hand. She pulled it away.

"I killed the runner with that hand."

Hyperion took it up and placed it in his lap, holding it quietly. She shut her eyes and felt something wet and warm on her hand. His tears were washing it.

She shook her head. "You can't understand."

"Look at me," he told her. Slowly, she opened her eyes and turned to him. His gaze was calm, tender. His clear eyes told her he knew exactly what Polymus had forced her to do.

"My sister. This is your suffering. This is your sacrifice. I can't take it from you, but I can share it. Atalante, no matter what happens, I'll always love you."

She couldn't accept the absolution Hyperion offered, along with the balm of his love. The trust on the runner's face and the death rattle in his throat would haunt her for the rest of her life. She deserved no less.

With a sigh, Atalante rose and walked into her small garden, staring at the thin sliver of the moon that hung in the dark sky. Light from the room shone on a dark pile of small shapes beneath the shadows of the high wall.

"What are those?" Hyperion asked quietly from the doorway.

She picked some of them up and returned to her chamber.

The lamp disclosed many small, inexpensive treasures thrown over the wall that day. Honey cakes garnished with nuts, ribbons, a pretty veil someone's daughter had woven of fine wool.

"Think, my sister. Think who left them for you," Hyperion said, carefully picking up a child's worn wooden doll.

Atalante's eyes filled with tears. "My people," she said in a dull voice. And knew she had to go on.

# Chapter 12

## The Land of the Dead

For a time, there was only red. The red heat of pain, red blood throbbing against something tight that blocked the tide of life from ebbing. Then black again, and then the fire, a heat that left him raging. At last, they came for him out of the darkness. The dread Daughters of Night, the Erinyes, their claws unsheathed, their faces too horrible for a mortal to look upon. He turned his head and begged to die.

They affixed their claws to his leg, slashing at his entrails, his head, until the pain was unbearable. They whispered a word. At first, he couldn't make it out. Eventually, he heard it clearly above the pain.

"Patricide," they whispered. He screamed and knew no more.

The darkness covered him for an eternity. Then he heard a familiar voice and made out the crackle of fire. With a great effort, Melanion opened his eyes.

"He's alive," someone said.

A long braid of gold swung above Melanion's face. "Drink," a woman said—maybe Astrid.

He tried. The wine tasted bitter. He managed only a few sips.

"We've got to keep him moving," another said.

The voices grew angry, tense.

"By the gods, he needs rest!"

Melanion turned his head dizzily.

"If you want him to live, follow me." Was that Nestor, grimed and slashed from battle? He looked nothing like the careless young fop of last winter.

Melanion felt a jostle. He was rising in the air—floating. On what? He felt the tilt downward, more jolts, and smelled . . . water—fresh lake water. The pain rose to a white-hot crescendo. Someone muttered a curse. Melanion slid into darkness again.

He awoke in a small room. An oil lamp threw a glow on clean white walls, the linen sheet covering his body, and the folds of a woman's blue robe. She was sitting beside his bed. Her gray hair was held in place at the back of her neck by a gold rope. Her wrinkled face had a timeless quality, old as religion and young as the birth of spring. Her blue eyes were brilliant, like Atalante's. Strength radiated from her, including him in its field of force.

Melanion gripped the sheet in panic, realizing he could reason again. It was just a matter of time before they came for him, clawing, speaking the unspeakable. Melanion tried to say something. The woman bent to hear him.

He tried again. "Please. Keep them away from me."

"They're gone," she said. Her voice held safety.

"Where? What?"

The blue eyes crinkled. She picked up a wine cup. "First you drink," she said, cradling his head so he could. "Then you sleep. Then we talk."

The potion tasted pleasant—honey and something else. He could swallow fairly easily. When she laid his head on the pillow again, he closed his eyes.

This time, there was nothing but the cave, his mother's voice, and her stories of the gods and heroes, until even that slipped away. Layers of sleep covered him, and he knew peace.

When Melanion woke again, the woman was there, bending over his thigh. Two young girls, acolytes in white gowns, stood behind her. One of them held a lamp close to his leg as the woman removed a bandage. She reached into the bowl the other girl held for her and rubbed some yellow salve into his wound. His leg throbbed with an angry beat, but he didn't faint. The raging heat, the pain in his head, was gone.

The woman gave him a long look, then went back to bandaging the wound again. "You're looking much better," she said. "You'll carry a long scar. You'll limp on that leg. But you'll live."

She held out a gold cup with images of the Mother sitting in judgment, young rams locking horns before her. He drank deeply.

So the Furies had left him with only this punishment. He was to be a cripple, then, for the rest of his life. It was a bitter sentence, to send others off to fight, to give up all hope of leading the people. A man blemished in that way could never be king.

The woman gave him a long look. "This is hard for you to bear. But you can still save two kingdoms, if only the gods and your moira are with you."

He shook his head to clear it, and a thousand questions filled it, begging to be asked. "Thessaly?"

She set her mouth in a line. "Taken."

His heart pounded a tattoo in his chest. "Atalante?"

"Alive. But that's all I can tell you."

Xuthus, he thought in a maelstrom of panic. He struggled to rise. "I have to go."

She touched his chest with one finger and he slumped back, the wind almost knocked out of him. "When the gods will it. You're a lucky man, Melanion. Had your companions been a few hours later, I'd be offering honey cakes at your tomb right now. So you'll sleep and mend. Then we'll plan how to proceed."

He felt the drug take him, or perhaps her voice wove the curtain of night descending on his vision. "Who are you?" he whispered.

"I am Arete, Queen of Arkadia. You're in my palace beside the Lake of Sighs. Sleep, Son of the Lion. There's much for you to accomplish here."

He shook his head. "I should be dead," he whispered as his lids drooped. "I was dead, and damned to the deepest pit of Hell. None of this makes sense."

He heard a musical tinkle of laughter. "In Arkadia, you must learn to accept what makes no sense."

Bright morning light shone in Melanion's eyes. He rubbed them and slowly opened them with an uncomfortable feeling that someone had been looking at him for a long time. The queen stood beside his bed, a bowl of steaming porridge in her hand. It looked delicious, with flecks of butter and milk and honey. He pulled the sheet up from his waist to his chest.

"Be easy," she told him with a smile. "I'm more interested in your character than your physique."

"It's a powerful priestess who can explore a man's soul while he sleeps," Melanion said, hoisting himself higher against the pillows.

"I'm a healer. I can find out a lot about you while you sleep—how much of a stoic you are, for instance. A man in pain will groan or cry out in his sleep. Will he do so awake? And another thing—the state of his conscience, perhaps. Are his dreams full of demons who torment him?"

Melanion felt the blood stop in his veins.

Arete's blue eyes softened. "The demons could be of your own making. You might berate yourself too harshly. But demons seldom leave a man in peace unless he makes expiation."

She smoothed the sheet over his chest. "Eat. Your friends wish to see you."

The door swung open. Theas, Philip, Nestor, and Astrid crept in, looking subdued and anxious.

"At least you look better than you did the last time we saw you," Theas said.

Melanion waved his hand, dismissing their concern. "What news?"

Philip drew a chair close to the bed and sat. "Thank the gods Iasus left half his army in reserve under Miletus. They're in the southern hills, along with our Hundred—what's left of them—and the young Thessalians. We don't know about the rest of the war leaders."

"Reports are coming into Arkadia slowly," Nestor said. "They've taken Atalante." His voice broke. "But Queen Arete says she's alive."

Nestor's fists clenched and he took a deep breath, almost a hiss. "Our king is dead."

Astrid put an arm around Nestor's shoulders. He was taut as a bowstring, but at least he didn't move away from her. Her face was grave as she looked at Melanion. "You're all that's left of our commanders. Tell us what to do," she said.

He shut his eyes. "Go back to the hills south of Iolcus. Find what remains of the nobility and the Companions. When I'm ready, I'll come."

"It's suicide," Philip said. "How can you fight when your leg—who will protect you?"

"I'm giving you an order." Melanion fixed him with a fierce look.

"The king gave me an order, too. Long before you did. It's my duty to keep you alive. The only reason you're still breathing is because I reached you in time." He folded his forearms, beefy muscles rippling. "I'm not leaving. Even you can't make me go."

Theas gave the giant a long look and shrugged. "Let him stay, Melanion. He won't be good for much, otherwise."

Melanion shook his head. "The rebels need every man."

Nestor took one look at him and motioned to the others. All four gathered around Theas. Melanion heard his soft voice as he told them what to do.

"Nestor, you see us back through the mountains. When—if—the queen calls for you, return to Arkadia and lead Melanion north. Philip, you remain here."

Melanion levered himself upright. "Philip will not stay!"

The four stared at him as though he were daft, then turned again to Theas.

"Astrid," Theas continued. "How many horses can we lead back?"

"One to ride, and one to lead carefully. The trail's too treacherous for more," she said.

"All right. Queen Arete, can you spare two mounts apiece for us, twenty of your men to accompany us, and forty more of your best trained horses?"

Arete nodded. "One word of caution. Tell nobody that the prince is alive. Each one involved in the resistance, most especially Atalante, must make his sacrifice without hope. That is the will of the Mother. Furthermore, our enemy must never guess our strength."

"Yes, Majesty," they said.

"Good. The gods preserve you. There's so much work to be done." She quickly left the room, presumably to give more orders, Melanion thought.

They were all content to give orders without consulting him, taking their leave with fond wishes for his recovery and promises to send word.

So. It was already begun. He was no longer the man they looked to as war leader and future king. The Furies had done their work well.

When Arete returned later that day, he attempted to greet her courteously. None of this was her fault, and she had, in fact, saved his life.

"Why?" he asked.

Arete gave him a long look. He had a sneaking suspicion that her eyes saw more than he wanted to show her.

"Why did I bring you back from the Land of the Dead?" she asked as she checked his leg. She took her time bandaging it again. Then she motioned to Philip, who had just entered his room, and he pulled up a chair for her. With calm deliberation, she sat and smoothed her skirts.

"You may not be ready to fight your enemies, Melanion, but you are an honored guest," she began. "A hero sent to us by the gods. We looked for your coming many days before you arrived. Indeed, many months ago, the Mother spoke to me through the movements of the House Snakes, foretelling your coming. What you do may well save the two kingdoms—and our world as we know it."

A skeptical laugh escaped Melanion's lips. "My lady Arete. I respect the gods and their oracles, so I must conclude that you've misread the omens. I am no hero, but a man deserving of the darkest corners of Hell."

Arete shook her head. "Where do you get your ideas, Prince? You think a hero is pure as snow, always certain when it comes time to choose? Nonsense. A hero is human. He understands what evil is. He knows sometimes neither choice he can make is good. His glory comes from the struggle against evil, and he acts in spite of his uncertainty, because not to act would be worse. Save your cynicism for another time. Now, you need faith in the gods and in their choice to preserve this land—Melanion, Son of the Lion."

Arete's gaze mesmerized him. Her power shimmered in the air, reached for him and then surrounded him, until he felt it surge inside him. He listened for more, rapt in the moment, waiting for her voice to break the silence and call him to action.

"You're here to perform a grave, some say an impossible, task. From the beginning, only women have taken on this labor, and only a few have succeeded. Most met their death attempting it.

"The Mother has never before called a man to try. You are looking at almost certain failure." Arete leaned toward him, her gaze kind.

"If you refuse the trial, you may cast your lot with the rebels. Eventually, with a horse beneath you, you'll be able to fight, and our soldiers can use your advice. This is the way most men fight, Melanion—with other men, not with spirits. We'll understand—nay, we'll wish you well if you choose this path. But I believe against all the traditional barriers pertaining to your gender that the Mother will accept you. And I know the best chance to destroy the barbarians lies with your accepting the ordeal."

Arete sat back in her chair, shoulders relaxed. Slowly, the sense of power that had enveloped Melanion lifted like a mist. He was himself again, the same doubt-filled man with a strangling sense of his own unworthiness.

"Before you decide anything, rest and regain your strength. The odds against you are overwhelming, and you might save Atalante from Xuthus' tender mercies if you return to the north and fight with your comrades. Take your time."

Panic roiled in his belly at the thought of what Xuthus might do to Atalante at any moment. He held on to himself, pushing the panic back, needing to think.

"You must be a mighty priestess," he said. "You know things about me—about Iolcus. Are you certain the Mother, and not some cruel god, shows you these things?"

"I am certain She does," said Arete, her gaze serene.

"And you believe the ordeal is the best chance to save my lady?" He grabbed her sleeve, too filled with urgency to behave in a courteous manner.

Her gaze bored into his. "Yes. I believe it's the only way."

He took a deep breath and struggled to sit up. He had to make Arete understand that he was free enough of the drugs to know what he was saying. "I consent to the under-taking."

Arete narrowed her eyes. "It makes sense to return north and fight Polymus with the others."

Melanion shook his head. "You told me I must accept what makes no sense. I have no choice. For Atalante, I accept."

Philip, who had stood silent through all of this, made a muffled sound of protest. Melanion tried to give him a re-assuring grin, but realized his mouth trembled. Actually, he shook all over. What a hero, he thought. Arete eased him back against the pillows. A lock of hair hung over one eye, clouding his vision. He was too weak to lift his hand.

Arete brushed his hair back as though he were a small boy. "When the time comes, you'll have what help we can give you. Because you've consented to your fate, the Mother will protect you from your demons.

"Try your best to quell any doubts you have about your worthiness for the task. Believe me, you are the chosen one.

The Mother has accepted you as hero or sacrifice, for the good of the people. Hold to that understanding. It will keep you safe from whatever drives you."

Melanion tried to summon serenity. But his mind returned to Iolcus Plain. Two swords flashed again in the sun. Two kings faced each other again.

"Did Nestor speak truth? Is Iasus dead?"

Arete nodded slowly, the pain evident on her face.

Melanion stared down at his hands. "And my father?" His voice trembled as he waited for the answer.

Arete's gaze was compassionate. "I cannot say. The Mother didn't show me his fate."

A sick misery filled Melanion. He stared at his hands as they plucked at the linen sheet, wishing for a sign, trying to remember anything that meant he hadn't murdered his father. It was useless. He remembered nothing but his fingers on the bowstring, his arrow pointed directly at his father's throat.

A week passed, then two. Melanion heard vague noises outside his chamber. The queen told him of the messengers and envoys from the rebel troops arriving from and departing to the hills south of Iolcus. Women rushed by his open door with clothing. "For the refugees from the north," Philip said. Soldiers came and went. Every day, he chafed at the eternity it took to heal.

But Arete was adamant. Until his strength returned, Melanion remained a prisoner, undisturbed by any but Philip, somnolent most of the time, but confined to bed like a child. Each evening, Arete brought him a potion tasting of wine and honey and something that had a wild tang blended with a scent of lavender. He suspected the brew made him sleep overmuch, and his sleep was full of dreams.

In some dreams, his leg no longer ached and pulled. He ran long, without strain. Atalante ran with him, laughing, her beautiful face full of mischief. The dreams brought comfort. But each morning he woke disoriented, wondering for that first moment how he came to lie alone, with an aching leg and a vague sense that he'd committed an unspeakable crime.

Some dreams made little sense. In one, he saw two lions yoked, pulling Artemis' chariot. In another, a hunter stood before the great, round altar stone of Great Artemis, his face in shadow. The man held a lusty baby and raised it above the altar. Silver bathed the child in blessing.

One morning, Melanion woke knowing he was healed enough to rise. When Arete entered his chamber, he was standing beside the window looking out at the flowering almond beside the Lake of Sighs. Arete's smile was worth the struggle when he walked—well, limped, actually, toward her.

Philip stuck his head into the room and grinned. Just in time, Melanion thought. The leg was beginning to fold on him. He hobbled to the bed with as much dignity as he could master and lowered himself into a sitting position.

Arete handed him a square of linen and he wiped the sweat off his face. "You've done well, Prince," she said. "I've never seen the drug work as quickly. With effort, you'll be ready within a fortnight. Philip will help you, of course."

Overnight, Philip changed from a man with a delicate sense of understanding to a tyrant. His training made the years at Myron's school seem like an idyll in the Isle of the Blessed. Philip pushed him to work strained and weakened muscles until they screamed for release, and then he pushed Melanion harder. One morning, he entered Melanion's chamber holding a javelin.

Melanion flexed the muscles of his back and arms, grimacing. "More exercise, eh? At this rate, I should do well as a wrestler, that is, if I could use my leg properly."

Philip fixed him with a narrow glance. "You've got to compensate for it, or you'll never fight well enough to win, not even on a horse. And the queen insists that you must strengthen your arms, shoulders, and back."

Melanion shrugged. He hated himself for caring so much that he'd never again move with a warrior's strength and quickness. It was unseemly to want what he didn't deserve. Arete had told him he could contribute something of value if he lived through the ordeal. That was enough in itself for a man still haunted by self-contempt.

Philip, seeing what must be a grim expression on his face, clapped Melanion on the back. "You can ride and walk, swim, even. What the hell, you've got both legs still. Not many men who've taken a sword like you did can say that."

"Not many men have a friend with your loyalty," Melanion said.

Philip reddened and smiled. "Wait till after javelin practice before you say that. I'm still your worst nightmare."

If you only knew, Melanion thought as he limped toward the door.

"You've muscled up in the back and arms more than you ever were," Philip said following him out. "Astonishing you've done it so fast. I think it's due to that stuff Arete brings you to drink every night. You're almost as strong as me. Almost."

Melanion eyed the javelin and grinned. "We'll see soon enough."

"What about a little wager to make my win even sweeter?" Philip laughed. He slowed his stride to match Melanion's as they left the palace together.

★ ★ ★ ★ ★

Shortly after this, Melanion knew his body had healed as well as it could. Aside from the leg, he felt just as he had before the battle on Iolcus Plain. Requesting an audience with the queen, he followed a maiden through the ancient corridors of the Lake Palace to the Megaron. As he entered, Arete looked up and gave him a regal nod. He limped forward and slowly dropped to his knees.

"You are prepared to face the ordeal?" she asked.

"I'm ready."

"Good. The Mother is waiting."

Arete bade him follow her past the Lake of Sighs. They wound down a wooded path to a small sanctuary beside a grove of trees. An old priest took him by the hand and led him into a clean, whitewashed room. The man was tall and thin with beak nose, a set of heavy jowls, and long white hair. He looked a bit like a pelican.

"Spend the next three days in contemplation and fasting," the old man said. "Nothing will pass your lips but the water of the Stream of Remembrance. Then you'll be purified and make the sacrifice. Remember, you do this to honor the Mother and the Cthonioi, the Sacred Dead."

My dead? Melanion wondered, and saw two kings with raised swords.

The old man grasped his forearm. "I am charged to warn you. You can still turn back. The waters of the Lake show no victory. This trial will be terrible. You may die any moment. If you make a mistake, your spirit will wander forever on this side of the River, calling for rest. Even if you succeed and win the Mother's consent—even if She allows the god to give you the treasure, it will be only the first step. Do you wish to accept or reject the undertaking?"

"What treasure?" Melanion asked.

The priest shook his head. "I cannot say. Do you accept or reject the undertaking?"

Melanion thought of Atalante, brought to Xuthus' bed. If he was all that stood between her and that fate, so be it. His fists clenched in determination.

"I accept," he said clearly, so all the gods and Mother Dia could hear him. The priest patted his arm and left, apparently satisfied. Melanion thought the old man ought to have some definite reservations. After all, the priest had just put his nation in the hands of a cripple who didn't understand and wasn't the least bit prepared for the battle ahead.

At sunset on the third night of his fast, Arete came for him with two young boys of perfect physical appearance, dressed in black wool chitons. They bathed him in the Stream of Remembrance. The water was chill. In the darkening gloom, he could just make out its path into the Lake of Sighs. The old priest stood on the bank and sang the hymns in a light, dry voice as they led him out of the water. He anointed Melanion with oil and the boys dressed him in a chiton of black linen, festooned with ribbons of all colors. They slipped black pigskin sandals on his feet.

The boys led him back to the hut where Arete waited. Nestor, newly returned, arrived with Philip to bid him farewell. Both were dressed in black. While Philip gave him a brave smile, Nestor looked grave. For the first time, Melanion saw complete respect in his gaze. Nestor held out his hand and grasped his arm.

"The Mother chose well," he said. "May She keep you through this journey."

Dim, cloaked shapes surrounded him and brought him through the depths of the great forest and into a torch-lit grove of ancient oak trees, each more thick than the arm spans of three men. He felt the people as one warm force, a single, rich pulse of life.

Arete motioned him forward and he stepped down into a pit where a black ram lay sacrificed upon an altar. The queen stood beside him studying the entrails.

With a sigh, she shook her head. "I see nothing—no reassurance," she said.

Grimly, Melanion took the cup she held and poured out a few drops of the wine as a libation. He drank the rest of the bitter brew.

"Take these weapons," Arete said. She buckled a sword of finely wrought bronze on his hips. A serpent twined about a vertical grapevine was hammered on the sheath. Next Arete gave him a small knife made of bone. It felt very old and fit perfectly to his hand. He slipped it into his girdle.

Next, she gave him warm honey cakes for the serpents guarding the tunnel into the Land of the Dead.

The people began a soft chant. "Cthonioi, heroes of our people, hear our supplication. Intercede with the Mother. For our sakes beg her to release him again to us with the instrument of our salvation."

Melanion walked to the opening in the pit. It looked like a cave's mouth. Arete embraced him and handed him the torch, pointing silently to the steps leading downward into the cave. "Follow the smoke," she said.

As he entered, he realized how small and alone he was. He could barely hear the peoples' voices. The smoke and darkness seemed to cut him off from all life.

There was nothing to do but go on. Melanion held the torch aloft and walked into the bowels of the earth.

At length, he reached a circular room. The walls seemed to glow an eerie white in the torchlight. A bronze gate circled a dark hole in the center of the room. Serpents lay curled before it.

When Melanion set down the honey cakes, the snakes came at once to eat.

Following the queen's instructions, he placed his torch in an empty wall sconce and opened the bronze gate. Going to his knees before the round hole, he rested his hands on the marble floor.

"Lady Mother, I'm only a man, and a guilty one," he whispered, "but it seems I'm all they've got. For their sakes, accept me, so I may bring back their salvation."

He made a secret sign, a holy one of deep respect, bending his head to the cool stone. As Melanion lay at the mouth of the cave, he felt a thrill of fear race along his nerves. A noise like the pulsing of the ocean filled his ears in rhythmic waves of sound. The rhythm quickened. It surrounded him like a giant heart beating, squeezing the blood in his veins faster and faster. He only had time for one thought.

"Birth and death," Melanion whispered. Air whooshed, sucking him into the hole feet first. He slid down a long tube. Helpless, he clenched his body against the force pushing him from above and sucking at him from below. Suddenly, he crashed through the end of the tunnel, landing hard on all fours in a dim cave. His leg wrenched so painfully he cried out, his voice echoing hollowly. He shook his head to clear it, realizing he was so deep below the earth's crust that he was lost from the land of the living.

Melanion struggled to his feet, looking around. The cave was a high one, but the air in it was warm and dry. Flecks glittered in the walls. Gold, silver, and precious stones blinked in the half-light. He saw an opening at the end of the cave and limped toward it into another cavern full of dim glories. Ignoring his throbbing leg, he walked, it seemed, for a lifetime.

At last, he came to a stone corridor. Torches guttered in wall sconces on either side, as far as he could see. As he walked the long hallway, a sense of foreboding gripped him, and tendrils of fear curled up his spine. The ceiling seemed to rise higher and higher above him. The walls seemed to expand outward. He looked at his hands, his feet.

*He was shrinking.*

His heart pounded like a drum as he approached a tall door made of oak with four panels on it. Suddenly, with a clarity of vision he'd never possessed before, he understood the full extent of his task.

*There was a monster waiting to meet him in the room behind that door, and he had shrunk to the size of a six-year-old child.*

He stiffened his spine. He had consented. Whatever came, he had to face it. And in that moment of acceptance, he went back, back to the time before the nightmares, back to the vulnerability and confusion of his six-year-old self. The door latch was higher than his head. By stretching his arm, he could just reach it with his hand. Carved on each panel was a wildflower indigenous to Macedonia. A sense of great joy spread through him as he pushed the door open.

"Come in, Melanion," his mother said. "I've been waiting for you."

He stood inside his mother's room. There were the large bed covered in a fine wool blanket, the burnished shields and swords on the wall, the rich tapestries.

His mother sat at the great loom. She was so pretty. Her clear gray eyes were touched with sorrow, but she gazed at him with all-encompassing love. She motioned toward him and he came forward with a grin. He'd been out playing at quoits with some of the soldiers, proud that they included him in their men's games.

His mother bent to hug him and smoothed his hair back from his face. Melanion looked down at his hands, feeling bad he'd stayed away. She might have needed him. The slaves weren't nearly as respectful as they should be to her. They thought she was out of favor with his father, and that was enough to keep them from her door.

"Sit beside me and tell me of your day," she urged, and he sat at her feet, describing the hawk's nest he'd found high up on one of the hills surrounding Hamalclion. She laughed and laid her hand on his head, pressing him against the warm, solid strength of her leg. Then she picked up the shuttle and began to weave, singing a Thessalian song.

Footsteps crashed outside the door. Melanion's mother broke off her song. The door flung wide and a monster stood, broad, thick legs braced apart, enormously tall. He held a large wine cup in his hand, and he swayed. Backlit by torches, his face was shadowed.

His mother flung him behind her, but this time, for the first time, he understood her every word. "You're a fool, Kryton, to come here when the boy is with me. A barbarian with no sense of decency."

The beast reared, as though her words pierced his flesh. "What have I done to make you hate me? I gave you honor. I took no other women. And still you turned your face away from me, as though I were some sea monster, and you a maiden chained to rock!"

"No other women! That was years ago," his mother said.

"Not so many," the monster growled. "I waited. I begged for your love and got only your scorn."

"You came to me drunk and reeling, telling me how you'd destroy my homeland, how you'd make my kindred sorry. Did you really expect I'd greet you sweetly?"

"They hate me. They turned you against me." The monster rubbed his eyes, huge shoulders hunched. His voice softened. "Even now, I would dismiss my mistresses for you, Althea. You know it. You jeer at me out of stubborn habit, and like a fool, I court you, as though I could change your mind. I still want you, and only you." He loomed over her, a huge man, one hand gripping her arm, the other stroking her hair, kneading the soft skin of her shoulder.

"Open to me, Althea," he whispered. "Send the boy away and give to me. I need you so much."

His mother's eyes glittered in a white face. "Think again, you drunken sot."

The beast-man grabbed her shoulders, shaking her until her teeth chattered. "You never loved me. You must love another . . ." He whirled, releasing her so quickly she sagged and caught herself against the loom.

"Althea, I've never touched you in anger before. But by the gods, if you don't protest your innocence now, I'll kill you. I swear it. Or him." The monster reached behind her and grabbed Melanion.

Held fast by the powerful arms, Melanion choked in fear.

"The boy," the monster raged. "Is he mine, or did you get him from your lover? Tell me, before I go mad!"

His mother rose slowly, pulling Melanion from the beast-man's hands. She lifted her chin and her mouth curved into a mocking smile.

The beast exploded. He roared and sprang for Melanion's mother, lifting her against the wall, throttling her. His hands convulsed on her throat. He would tear her to pieces.

Melanion leaped on the monster's back and sank his teeth into the thick muscle of his shoulder. The monster howled and threw him off. Melanion crashed against the wall. Shields clattered and fell to the floor with him. He took a breath and felt the clutching pain in his ribs, knowing he was too little, too weak to stop anything. And then, he remembered what he'd said aeons before, when this happened for the first time.

*"When I am a man, I shall kill him."*

Lightning flashed outside the windows. Thunder crashed. A grown man's horror gripped him. This was fate. This was Hell.

In a crystallized moment of silence, everything in the room was caught and suspended in time. Like figures on a frieze, the beast-man, the tortured woman, and the child froze. Then the very air in the room fragmented, like shards of glass. When the jagged components came together again so clearly his eyes hurt with the sharp outlines of objects and forms, everything was curiously smaller than it had been before.

He looked down at his hands, thick with calluses from his recent practice with spear, sword, and javelin. The monster had shrunk, had become only a man, although still a warrior in his prime, with heavy muscles and a rage bordering on madness. Melanion's mother was really a delicate slip of a girl, slender as a child, easily snapped in two.

The muscles of the warrior's back and arms rippled as he turned on the woman again.

"Oh, gods, how must I deal with such a father?" Melanion cried. His voice sounded in his own ears like a beast's scream. But he wasn't a beast. He had consented. And this time, after all the frenzied nightmares, he had seen the truth.

*"What you saw was more a battle than it looked,"* his mother had told him long ago, after that brutal evening,

301

when they made their escape from Hamalclion. And then he saw his father as he was—a man, tormented to the point of madness.

Melanion filled his lungs and called on the Voice of Power.

"Father." The word filled the room. "It ends now."

Kryton turned from the woman he had loved and abused that terrible night. With a roar of pain, he came at Melanion, his massive arms flexing, his sword unsheathed.

Melanion drew his sword and raised it. The king watched him, measured him. Melanion looked, really looked for the first time, and saw something in Kryton's eyes beyond the rage and blood lust he had seen as a child on this doom-ridden night.

He dove deeper into his father's soul, past the cruel task of gaining and keeping a throne, past the mockery of his neighbors, past the hurt and bewilderment because he wanted his wife so badly and didn't know how to reach her. Deep into the core, into a pool of pain Kryton put aside every day to get on with the business of life.

Melanion re-sheathed the sword and unbuckled the belt, letting it slip to the ground. He took the ancient knife from his girdle and laid it beside the sword.

"Father," he said softly. "You're a man. Years ago, you kept yourself from finishing it. Stop now, and redeem yourself."

Kryton gave him a look of longing. But he shook his head. "This is my punishment. I must hurt your mother, over and over. And you must try to end it. The only way is to kill me."

The incipient sting of tears burned Melanion's eyes. He tried to smile while his heart twisted at the sight of Kryton's ravaged face. "If this is my fate, then I'll fight to stop you, to save you. But I can't kill you, Father. You suffer just like I do. Come to me."

Melanion opened his arms. Kryton dropped his sword and came into them. Their bodies closed, seeking weaknesses, seeking dominance, refusing to yield to the other in their pain-wracked embrace. Hours, maybe years passed as Melanion strained against an opponent bent on his own destruction.

This must be his moira, he thought—to lock with his father in eternal agony, the leg shooting needles of pain through his body. He fought through the long, dark night in silence, gasping for each breath, reeling with searing agony, moved by a helpless compassion for his father's torment.

A cock crowed. A faint glow appeared at the window. His father grabbed Melanion's thigh in his two hands and squeezed. White-hot pain flashed through his head, blinding him. Melanion collapsed against his father.

Kryton laid him gently on the ground and kissed his forehead. "It's over," he said. Melanion felt searing tears brand his thigh and heard Kryton rise heavily to his feet. A deep sleep settled over him like a warm blanket.

At the edge of sleep, his mother's voice sounded in his heart. "Tell your father when you see him again. I will wait for him. Forever."

*Atalante knelt beside him, smiling although tears swam in her eyes. "I love you," she said. "I miss you every day. Come to me."*

*His arms reached for her and pulled her down against his body. She opened for him as sweetly as a flower to the sun. And he sank into her, wordless thanks for the blessing of her scent, her light weight resting in his arms, the living warmth of her body. Deep, deep inside her, he felt the tug*

*of her love and her passion. Easily as a river flowing to
the sea, he gave her his seed, and with it, everything he
had—all the loneliness of the nights without her, all the
doubts and the fears leading up to the ordeal, all his
longing for peace in her arms. Sated, filled with a quiet
joy, he slept.*

At first, Melanion heard only birdsong and the tinkling
play of water. There was light—not much—a dim, rosy
glow on his closed eyelids. He opened them and found himself in a walled garden of incomparable beauty. A stream
flowed past him, glinting in the sun.

Daffodils, roses, columbine, and phlox all bloomed together. Perfectly pruned fruit trees grew in different stages
of fruition. Plum and peach blossoms filled the air with pink
and white clouds of scent. A little beyond them, apple trees
grew, full of fruit. The apples were shining gold.

Melanion rose at the sound of footsteps. A young man
approached, graceful as a lynx, and entered the garden
through an intricately wrought bronze gate. A wreath of
grape leaves that held three of the golden apples garlanded
his dark locks. His beautiful dark eyes smiled when he saw
Melanion.

Dropping to one knee, Melanion bowed his head.

"You know me, Son of the Lion?" the shining youth
asked.

It was Atalante who had told him, of course. Who had
made him understand when he had wanted only to condemn. "Great Bacchus. You suffer death for us. You come
again to show us that we will live forever."

The god smiled at him, pleased, it seemed. "You, too are
the sacrifice suffering for your people. I bring you their deliverance," he said, slipping the wreath from his head and

placing it on Melanion's brow. It was light, easy to carry. Bacchus lifted the bronze sword from the ground where it had lain and buckled it on Melanion with his own hands. He held out the ceremonial knife and Melanion took it.

"Go in peace," the god said. "Try to free your people." He disappeared, and Melanion was left alone in the garden, facing a gate made of gold in the garden wall. It swung open, beckoning. Melanion walked through.

He walked for miles on a road lit with rosy light through a rich, fruitful country. The road wound upward. He kept going, never tired, never hungry. His thigh didn't ache at all. The road ended before a cave. He walked into it on springy moss, listening to night sounds. An opening yawned ahead. He squinted against a bright, red-gold light, shielding his eyes from the brightness. Walking into the light, he came out of the cave and stood in the midst of a torch-lit circle. The force supporting his body drained, and seemed to take the marrow of his bones with it. He felt himself falling to the ground as people pressed forward. Dimly, as the black curtain came down around him, he heard Arete's voice.

"All gods be praised," she said. "He's brought the signs."

When Melanion awoke, he was lying in the cottage where he'd been purified before he attempted the ordeal. Everything was ordinary—the light from the setting sun, the linen sheets, his own hands as he held them up to check that he was still a man. Had he dreamed the whole adventure? It seemed like a dream now, his mother alive, his father younger, his understanding of their love for each other and the battle raging between them.

The old priest called to a young boy, who immediately

ran out the door. "I am relieved you have awakened at last," the priest said, pushing Melanion back as he struggled to rise. "The drug you took is very strong and the journey centuries long. You must lie quiet for a little while, to get used to being alive again."

The priest clucked about the cottage, heating a brew of wine over a brazier and straightening bandages.

With a rustle of skirts, Queen Arete swept in, followed by Philip and Nestor. Philip had obviously forgotten his manners, as he almost ran Arete down in order to get a good look at Melanion. The priest lifted Melanion into a sitting position and gave him mulled wine to drink and gruel to eat. The pleasing spices hid whatever medicine the old man might have put into the food and drink.

Philip watched him closely, his gaze following Melanion's hands as he ate and drank. "Can you speak?" he asked. "Are you really yourself?"

"Pay him no mind. He's crazed," Nestor said.

Melanion shook his head, warmed by Philip's loyalty. "I feel the same. Don't worry, Philip. I was in more danger on the battlefield than I was—wherever I was."

Philip grimaced. "Nestor told me what happens to a man who seeks the Cthonoi. If he had to listen to me rave, it was his loose tongue that set me off."

Nestor shrugged. "He kept at me forever. I only told him when he threatened to bother the queen about it."

Arete looked from one to the other. "Enough, both of you. You've seen him, Philip. Tomorrow you may talk with him all you wish. Nestor, take him sailing. The Lake of Sighs will soothe his worries."

Philip reddened. Bowing hastily, he followed Nestor out of the cottage.

In the quiet moments afterwards, Arete checked

Melanion's life signs. Her eyes widened as she gently pulled the muscles of his legs.

"Melanion," she said slowly. "I want you to walk to the door."

"All right." He felt good. It was easy to rise and walk about.

"Now back to me," Arete said. She stared at his legs as though they'd sprouted feathers.

"Sit before you're too tired to hit the bed," she told him, and he landed on the bed with a thud. He hadn't realized how little strength he had.

Arete bit her lip. "I'm sorry. I shouldn't have made you get up so quickly, but this is very odd. I wanted to see what would happen."

Melanion stared at her in confusion.

"At the time of your return, with all the confusion and relief, what I saw with my own eyes as you walked out of the cave didn't register. Have you wondered at all about your time in the Land of the Dead? Have you asked yourself how much you experienced was a vision brought on by the drug, and how much was real?"

Silently, he nodded.

She laughed, a sound both joyful and broken. "Look at your leg, Melanion. Look for the scar."

He took up the chiton and studied his left leg. The skin was smooth, muscled, tanned. There was no sign it had been slit to the bone just a month ago. His gaze leaped to Arete.

"My dear," she said as tenderly as his own mother, "you'll walk upright as any man. You'll run again. The Mother has chosen. You'll be the one to take the signs north to Iolcus and lead the people."

Melanion felt his heart expand until it was so full he

thought it might burst. Atalante, he thought. He could fight for her now, he could free her. He could set right his father's mistakes.

He could be a king.

Arete clapped her hands. At that sharp sound, men came running—messengers, by the looks of their traveling capes and the pouches slung over their shoulders.

"Send the word forth," Arete said in the formal tones of a monarch. "To the north, through the passes, into the villages surrounding Iolcus. Tell all whose homes have been plundered, whose wives and daughters have been raped, whose husbands and sons have been murdered. Tell them, 'It has come.' Tell them, 'At the sign.' "

They sped off. The cottage was empty and silent. Arete turned her face to the wall, and Melanion heard her sobs.

# Chapter 13

## The Runner

*It has come. At the sign* . . . In those weeks, the whole countryside stirred to life. On the road from the south to the villages outside Iolcus, crude drawings appeared overnight—three circles intertwined.

*It has come. At the sign* . . . The rebel soldiers whispered the words when they raided a group of Red Bands pillaging a village, and then the villagers whispered them to the merchants and their wives in Iolcus.

*It has come. At the sign* . . . People went about their business with a catch in their throats for fear the Red Bands would notice the hope on their faces and grow suspicious.

Kryton had begun to lose flesh. He insisted Clymene give him more of the drug, even though he writhed in pain each night from it. But he was determined to preside at court.

"As long as my presence is felt in the Megaron, you, Hyperion, and Atalante are safe," he said when Clymene argued against such large doses.

"Foolish," Clymene muttered as Atalante followed her from Kryton's chamber to the queen's rooms. Clymene went about now with a set face, even more remote than she'd been with Atalante before. Atalante knew she worried constantly. She understood her mother believed the end was near. She was colder to everyone but Hyperion, who opened the door to greet them now.

As soon as she had shut the door against any curious guards, Clymene pulled Hyperion close. "You should be resting, my love."

"I'm going to sit beside Kryton for a while, Mother," Hyperion said.

Clymene frowned and stroked his hair back from his pale forehead. "You need rest, dear, not the weary work of keeping Kryton's mind off his pain."

Erytes slipped into Clymene's rooms, grinning like a little brigand. He knew every warren and hole in the palace, and had brought word of each rebel victory to cheer them. Atalante needed the hope he brought. She was a virtual prisoner in the palace, allowed out only to run across the plain or into the wooded hills. Polymus knew she'd never leave her people, but he didn't want them to see her. Atalante suspected he was afraid she'd foment revolution simply by walking among them.

"I can help the king tonight," Erytes said.

Clymene shook her head. "I don't dare send you to help him. If anybody saw you and reported your kindness to Polymus, the gods know what terror you'd face. I've half a mind to send you back to your family, Erytes. It's a terrible risk for you to work so closely around Polymus and Xuthus."

"I'm too scrawny and little to attract their notice," said Erytes, his black eyes shining with mischief.

Atalante watched her mother turn her mind to the present problem. "Atalante cannot do it. She must face the next challenger tomorrow. I'll do it."

Hyperion shook his head. "He does better with me. We're used to each other, and he knows he doesn't have to be brave."

Clymene bit her lip. "You're giving the last of your

strength to comfort him. Why do it when you know it was Kryton who killed your father, who set loose the evil afflicting us?"

"He has a soul, too, Mother. I sit with him in the dark, when he faces his pain and the consequences of his actions. He suffers more than any of us because he sees what he's done."

Hyperion laid his hand on Clymene's knee and closed his eyes. He looked so thin and weary that Atalante wanted to gather him up, to run with him to some happy place far away, where he could rest.

"I think that's why we do well together, Kryton and I. He knows I forgive him, and it makes him free to look truthfully at what he's done."

"I saw the little couch he had brought to his room so you can lie comfortably beside him. If it weren't for that, I'd order you to stay here and sleep. But Hyperion, you must promise me. You will rest."

"I promise," Hyperion said with a smile. But Atalante saw only his luminous eyes in a wasted face. Her heart caught in fear at a vision of men lowering his small, thin body into the grave for his final rest. Automatically, she made the sign against evil and saw her mother did the same. Hyperion simply smiled again and closed his eyes.

Atalante's hands trembled. Hyperion must have sensed her distress, for he opened his eyes again and gave her such a look of love and understanding, she felt tears gather in her eyes. With a quick step, she bent over Hyperion, kissed his brow, and hurried from the room, to emerge moments later on the plain and begin her practice run.

As the next morning dawned, it brought some respite after a long, painful night. Kryton turned his head toward Hyperion and asked in a fit of self-loathing, "How can you listen to me? I've destroyed everything you love."

"The gods and the Mother will judge you, not I."

Kryton stared at the young face, so sober and so pale with his own suffering. "Such a young boy to be so wise."

Hyperion looked down at his hands with a frown. "I'm not so wise all the time. I get mad enough about things I can't change."

"About every sorry plague I've brought on you?" Kryton asked.

Hyperion rolled his eyes. "Why do grown-ups always think it all comes back to them? Sometimes I just . . . wish things could be different for me." He lay back on the little couch, his hands stacked behind his head. How the boy reminded him sometimes of Melanion in his gestures, his thoughts, too.

"For instance," Hyperion continued, "I wish I could live to grow up. The world's such an interesting place, and I'd like to see a lot of it. But since I'm going to die soon, I wish I could be a great warrior, like Achilles or Hector, and leave a name for myself." He let out a deep sigh. "But I'm just a boy-priest that nobody will sing about." A long moment passed as he stared at the ceiling.

"I wish I could die defending my home."

Kryton cleared his throat and turned his head, rubbing the sharp sting in his eyes. Little whelp, so full of glorious dreams. So unaware of what a hero he was.

Hyperion's soft voice went on. "I can't talk to mother about dying. She can't face it, so she thinks there must be something she can do about it. She's convinced that if I get more rest and eat more meat, my heart will heal.

"And Atalante has all she can do to face the next race and the next man she has to kill." Hyperion's eyes grew wistful. "Melanion knew how I felt. He brought me a bow.

Not a baby bow, but light enough for me to bend. And a quiver of arrows."

"Melanion," Kryton said, and his heart wrenched. "Such dreams I've had of him. If only they were true."

"He showed me how to use the bow. I still practice every day." He gave Kryton a hesitant look. "Would you like to see it?"

The lad was killing him. In another minute, he wouldn't be able to hide the tears that threatened to overflow. "I would. My son did that for you, did he?" Kryton asked, staring at his hands.

"Uh-huh. He was my friend. And he never treated me like a little boy."

Kryton fixed his gaze on the plain beyond the window while Hyperion got his bow and arrows. He saw the tents of his soldiers. He saw Polymus' Red Bands swaggering about. The pain from the drug began to lessen, but the guilt battered him harder.

He pushed it down, knowing it only weakened him. He had the boy to think of, and his mother, and his sister, and all their people. He had to keep up the pretence of strength, no matter how much he wanted to give in to the shame and the longing for what he'd never have now.

When he'd been young, long before assassins killed his father, long before he made it his business to be tougher than his enemies, he'd wanted to be a hero. Too late for that, he told himself. But not too late for Hyperion.

The boy came back, the bow slung across his back. Kryton called in a servant and told him to get the target from Hyperion's room.

"I want to see what you can do with it," Kryton said. "I know a few things about archery too, lad."

The days passed, and Kryton taught Hyperion everything he could. He drilled the boy the way he'd drilled his regiments, and Hyperion improved steadily. In return, he told Kryton stories about Melanion—stories that filled him with pride and sorrow. Now he knew how Melanion had met Atalante in the mountains. He knew the Huntress had chosen them both, and he heard all about King Stag, and the sacrifice Melanion had agreed to be.

The sickness ate at the blood flowing in Kryton's veins. But with the sapping of his strength and the battle he fought to protect Thessaly, Kryton's soul expanded until those who knew him well could see it shine in his eyes. And those who knew nothing but their own ambition paused in its pursuit when they felt his gaze.

Xuthus entered his chamber unsteadily, his eyes unfocused. "Father," he slurred. "What're you doing . . ."

The back of Polymus' hand cracked across his face with enough force to make his sorry excuse for a son totter and fall into a heap at his feet. He looked down at Xuthus in furious contempt. Xuthus felt his cheek gingerly. Polymus was pleased to see the slash in it from his signet ring. He wanted to mark the little swine. If he'd had any other choice for an heir, he would have killed Xuthus, right then, and felt only satisfaction.

"What was the only thing I asked of you, you fool?" Polymus said, clamping his jaw so tight he thought he might break off a tooth.

"I . . . I can't think when you're so mad," Xuthus said. "I didn't do anything."

Why did he have to grovel and whine like a damned slave? Polymus bent over and hauled Xuthus to his feet by the front of his chiton. "This boy—the one who cleans my rooms. Who gave you permission to use him like a whore?

To beat him into unconsciousness when you were done?"
Polymus pointed a finger at Erytes, who lay in a bloody
heap on the tiles of his antechamber.

Xuthus shrugged, nervously licking his lips. "He's just a
little slave boy, some Helot from the mountains. You can't
have meant him when you warned me about my lust. He's
nothing."

"Idiot!" Polymus saw Xuthus cringe and cower at his
soft hiss.

"If word of this gets out, those damned Thessalians will
use it to make more trouble. The king hangs on, the bitch
runs faster every time. And now this!"

"Father," Xuthus pleaded with him. "I swear to you, I
couldn't help it. I thought it would free me, to have him, to
make him suffer, but it only enslaved me more."

Polymus felt the fury mount again. "What in hell are you
raving about?"

"Look at me!"

He stared at Xuthus in surprise. His eyes were blood-
shot, his raw body wasted. "What's wrong with you? Are
you ill?"

Xuthus gave him a look of anguish. "I can't think of anything else but having her."

"Atalante?"

Xuthus nodded, swallowing hard. "The boy was just . . .
I took him to rid myself of the fever, but it just got worse. I
need *her* or I'll die of longing."

"I can't deal with you now," Polymus said as impatience
took him. He pointed to the young boy. "Finish him off.
Get rid of this . . . mess tonight and come to me in the
morning." Polymus swept out of the room. He had to get
away from the sick ass he'd spawned. He had to end this
little game Kryton played with him and find a man who

could beat that vixen in a foot race. Was that so difficult—
to find one man who was faster than a girl?

Xuthus ran out the door of his chamber and headed for
the Red Bands' quarters as fast as his legs could carry him.

"Quick," he whispered to two of the men he remembered from last night's orgy. They followed him down the
hall as he explained his father's orders.

When Xuthus threw his door open and re-entered his
room, he stared, startled, and let out a yelp of shock as he
looked into the empty corner where the boy had lain. The
little slave was gone. The men behind him looked around
uneasily in the eerie silence.

"What do we tell the commander?" one asked him.

Xuthus shuddered, knowing if his father heard of this,
his own neck might end up on the block. "We say we took
care of it."

The men stared at him, mirroring his own terror in their
gazes. Then the guards slowly nodded and crept out of the
room.


In the queen's chambers, Atalante jumped to her feet ut-
tering a startled cry as her mother strode into the room, her
eyes blazing. Erytes lay in her arms, his head arched back,
blood dripping from the cloak wrapped around him.
Clymene laid him on her bed and gently cradled his head.
He whimpered as he tried to move and lost consciousness.

"Bring pure water and my herbs," Clymene told a white-
faced servant. "Atalante, lift his head. We've got to get this
poppy extract into him before I set his leg."

"Mother! It's badly broken—so is his left arm," Atalante
said, perusing the damage.

"See where the bone presses against the flesh?" Clymene
said grimly. "I'll try to set it first, while he still has a little

strength to bear the pain."

Hyperion slipped into the room and stared at his friend, horror and pity etched on his face. "Who did this?" he whispered.

"Xuthus." Clymene turned her face and spat. "Leave us, Hyperion. I have much to do and no time to answer questions."

Hyperion nodded and slipped from the room.

Atalante had never heard her mother sound harsh with her brother before. Something else was troubling Clymene, she thought as she brought her mother bandages and splints. Clymene worked in a fury of concentration, pulling the fractured bone of the calf back into place. In spite of the opium, Erytes screamed twice in a shrill, high voice.

As she set Erytes' arm, sweat broke out on Clymene's forehead and ran down her back, staining her gown. Finally, she sat back on her heels for a moment and rubbed her neck.

"Thank the gods he fainted after I set the first break. I didn't know if I could go on hurting him, and I had to." Clymene took a knife and cut away the bloody chiton, turning the unconscious boy on his stomach.

Atalante gasped and felt her gorge rising in a wave of nausea.

"Oh, yes," Clymene said in a bitter voice. "He's been used—with a sick cruelty that offends both the gods and every decent man who lives."

Atalante bit her lip until she tasted blood. "Will he recover?"

Clymene cast her a weary look. "With time, the pain will be gone. But his mind—who knows?" In silence, she cleaned the boy and covered him with a snowy blanket.

Atalante stared at her mother, seething with a fury she'd

never experienced, even on the battlefield. "Give me permission to lose the next race, Mother. Let me marry Xuthus and have him to myself in the bridal chamber. All I need is a moment alone with him. I promise you, I'll make him suffer."

Clymene shook her head. Her gaze softened as she did so, but Atalante knew with a sinking heart what her mother would say. "You have to win every time. That's the strength we need from you, Atalante. That's the burden you carry."

The queen bent over Erytes, stroking his hair back from his face. "And I have to take this guilt upon myself," she said in a quiet voice. "I didn't send him away when there was time. I was selfish. I wanted Hyperion to be happy for as long as he could, and I chose that over this child's safety. That's my burden to carry."

Polymus called Xuthus to him a week after the incident with the slave boy. He was inundated with problems and the news just kept getting worse with every day. A report had just reached him that the rebels had massacred a cavalry unit of a hundred men sent south to commandeer wheat. The damned Thessalians had taken the horses and thrown their bodies on a mass pyre and burned them without ceremony. The news was spreading though the camps like a grass fire. The superstitious mercenaries who believed cremation was forbidden had almost rioted.

As for Atalante—he'd been lenient so far, hoping to marry her off to Xuthus so he could take the full force of the army south to subdue the rebels. But the bitch was still winning. How did she get a little faster each time? How had his hands become tied regarding her? The merchants—that was it. They'd give him hell to pay if he forced her to marry Xuthus. He'd have a major rebellion on his hands unless he found a man who could beat her.

A servant pounded a staff against the oak door of Polymus' chamber and Xuthus entered. He looked like a man slowly dying of starvation. His eyes were hollow in a bony face. Obviously, he hadn't recovered from the strange torment Atalante brought him.

"Just how sick are you?" Polymus asked.

Xuthus' gaze shifted to Polymus' face, then the floor, then the window. His body was as restless as his gaze. He tried to sit, then he stood and paced, then he sat, only to stand again a moment later. "I can't sleep. I can't eat. Some god has cursed me."

"Hold yourself together. We have the makings of a disaster on our hands." Polymus grabbed his son by the shoulders to give him a shake and felt bone beneath slack skin.

And with that vile sensation, that feeling he was holding onto a corpse, Polymus lost control. "It's the little Thessalian whore, you fool, not some god who's bewitched you! I'm getting rid of her, and her sickly brother, and her witch of a mother, keeping Kryton alive when he should have died long ago. Kryton, too. I'll kill them all, damn their souls!"

"No!" Xuthus slipped to the floor and clutched Polymus' robes, almost pulling him to his knees with desperate strength.

"From the moment she stripped to run, I was smitten. It's worse every time, but I can't look away. If you kill her, I'll die of grief."

Xuthus writhed on the floor, sobbing. "If I could have her, I'd be a man again. Why can't you find me a runner? In all Thessaly, there must be one man who can beat her."

Polymus' dream was slipping away and the woman was

the key to all of it. "Just drag her to your bed and take her," he said in disgust. But Xuthus' hands clung to him, like a monkey's paws.

"I can't. It would be like bedding a dead woman. I'll die if I don't have her by her own consent. Find me a man, for the sake of your damned dynasty you want so much. Find me a man!"

The hollow rap of a staff echoed through the chamber. Xuthus crawled to his feet, his eyes skipping from shadowed corner to the door. He shuddered. "What a sound! Like iron against marble in a tomb."

"Control yourself. It's just a guard."

Polymus poured wine and pushed the cup into Xuthus' shaking hands. "Enter," he called.

The Red Band stepped into the room with a swagger, and gave a crisp salute. "There's a man come, Commander. A Macedonian. They say he can run like the wind."

# Chapter 14

## A Week Earlier

Melanion reached the end of the mountain pass at evening and called a halt to make camp. He'd been climbing for three days, following Nestor, who seemed to know the tortuous forest paths as though a map were tattooed on his brain. He stretched shoulders sore from hacking brush and thorn bushes and patted the neck of his mount.

"I'll water the horses," Nestor called, leading them to a creek not far away. Melanion and Philip built a small fire while he was gone, speaking only when absolutely necessary. Their silence wasn't due to any danger lying about. The Macedonians huddled farther north of these woods. Rather, Melanion had developed an affinity for silence ever since he'd returned from the quest. As he stood, he automatically checked the pouch that hung on his hip. He could feel the reassuring solidity of the signs—the golden apples from the magical garden that rested in the pouch.

A branch crackled to his left. He whirled, too late. Ten men threw themselves at him. His dagger flashed white in the setting sun as a soldier wrenched it out of his hand, and then screamed, dropping the ancient stone. The man's hand glowed as though he'd been scalded.

A young blond stood over him, only eighteen by the look of him.

"Your first command, is it?" Philip said insolently as he struggled against the five men who held him.

"Shut up!" the blond cried, back handing him hard across the face. "I'll ask the questions, Macedonian pig." The youth held his hand against his chest. Melanion tried not to grin. The boy would be lucky if his blow hadn't broken a bone in that hand. Philip had a jaw as hard as a horse's.

The youth must have noticed something in Melanion's expression. He wheeled back at him. "Where are the rest of your men?" he shouted. "How many? Answer or you'll die."

"Next time you command soldiers, Cousin, make sure your men watch their flank." Melanion heard Nestor's lazy drawl and looked to his right. He strolled into the clearing and gave the young blond a long, assessing look. "And the man you're threatening with death is the same one who brings the signs to Iolcus."

"Oh, gods." The boy and his men hastily turned him and Philip loose. To Melanion's surprise, they all dropped to their knees and laid their fists on their hearts, a sign of utmost respect, shown only to a god or a king.

"Sire, I, my apologies. I had no idea—I wasn't expecting you. I—how can I make it up to you?" the boy stammered.

"Perhaps you could hand me my knife," Melanion replied, rubbing his wrist. The boy reached out a cautious hand to the gleaming white hilt. With a deep intake of breath, he grasped the knife and held it up to Melanion, who took it, re-sheathing it carefully. As the boy looked in wonder at his unscathed hand, Melanion felt a pang. He hadn't thought when he'd asked for the knife.

"With your permission, Majesty, I'll find my commander and bring him to greet you," the youth said. As soon as Melanion gave a nod, he was off through the woods. A few minutes later, a contingency of warriors crashed through the brush into the little clearing, Linos at the head. He took one look at Melanion and fell to his knees.

Melanion pulled him to his feet and held him at arm's length. A huge, relieved grin split his mouth until his face ached with it. Here was one of his own, still alive after the slaughter on the plain of Iolcus.

Linos blinked hard against the sheen of moisture gathering in his eyes. He shook his head slowly. "I saw them carry you off the battlefield, bleeding like a sacrificial ram. I was sure you were dead. When Nestor told me otherwise, I feared . . ."

His gaze traveled down one side of Melanion and up the other. "No scars, nothing. How's it possible?"

"They took me to Arkadia," Melanion said, as though that one word, evoking magic and mystery, explained it all. Linos looked thoughtful for a moment, then let out his breath in a rush of understanding. Perhaps it did explain everything.

"Send for the others," he said. "They'll want to greet their king."

Men poured into the clearing, filling it to overflowing. Melanion saw Alex, Nikos, and Korone among them, smiling and crowding around him.

One face was missing, and Melanion felt cold dread. "Theas?" he asked, and Alex's eyes grew troubled.

"Scouting around Iolcus—trying to get into the palace to speak to Queen Clymene. But he should have been back half a week ago."

Melanion sucked in a deep breath. "He has too much intelligence to get caught. I know he'll make it." The glow of his homecoming dimmed. *Gods spare him,* he thought, remembering the calm gray gaze, the cool intellect, the cutting words that held him back from more crazy, rebellious risks, when he tested his limits and danced on the edge of death. *I need him so much.*

Melanion looked around him. The Hundred and the young Thessalians had massed together and formed a redoubtable army. Linos raised his hand and absolute silence immediately ruled. The entire contingency dropped to their knees.

"Sovereign of Macedonia and Thessaly, who rules by the decree of the free peoples of both lands," Linos intoned formally. "We have pledged ourselves to you from the moment we knew you lived."

Miletus brushed through the clearing, shining with beads of sweat from his run through the forest. "All gods be praised," he said. "You alone can lead us, as though you were Iasus' true son. Do you consent?"

Melanion touched the pouch at his side. It radiated warmth and solidity, the gift of the gods. He looked about the circle of kneeling soldiers, with the hope shining clear in their eyes. He knew what he had to do. "With my life and my soul," he said, "I consent."

That night before dinner, Melanion consulted Linos and Miletus. He found out that the command he'd assumed wouldn't be an easy one—not that he'd ever expected it to be so.

"There are only about two thousand of us camped in the forest. The rest were killed on Iolcus Plain," Linos said.

"How many Red Bands and Macedonians?" Melanion asked.

"Ten times our number," Miletus told him with a grave look.

The tent flap moved to the side and Theas walked in.

"Thank the gods," Melanion said rising to his feet and throwing his arms around Theas in a rough hug. "Nobody knew whether you were dead or alive." He held on tight with such relief in his heart that he didn't know whether to laugh or cry.

"I came straight away, as soon as Korone told me you'd come."

Melanion finally dropped his arms and Theas his. He then turned to Miletus and saluted.

"We've taken out a troop of Macedonians on the way back."

"We heard of vicious fighting from peasants fleeing that area. How many of ours died in the battle?"

"Ten—all brave men and strong fighters. We'll miss them," Theas said.

"What news from Iolcus?" Melanion asked Theas, holding out a full wine cup and his breath. Theas gave him a look of such empathy, Melanion wondered whether his friend knew how deeply he yearned for Atalante. All through the time he'd been gone, she had been with him— in the underworld, in the mountains as he ran, before he slept and upon his waking.

He imagined her, struggling each day to do her duty when her every nerve and sinew screamed to her to run and fight with the rebels. He tortured himself with visions of Xuthus touching her, kissing her, hurting her, until he thought he'd go mad. Yet he'd managed to come this far, and the time for battle was so close. And afterwards, if the gods gave them victory and if they lived, he would find a way to make it up to her—a way to see her smile, and maybe even laugh again.

Theas took a deep drink. "Supplies are running low in the capital. Atalante still holds the people together, but we'd better make a move soon, before the artisans and small barons give up. Polymus has levied a crushing tax on them. It's just a matter of time before they join him to ease their suffering."

"If we hold the south and train more men, we could fight them more effectively in autumn," Miletus said.

"If we strike now, we have surprise and the townspeople on our side," Theas said.

"It's your decision," Linos told Melanion.

To his own surprise, Melanion didn't hesitate. "We go now, while the gods are with us."

Theas grinned. Linos nodded.

Miletus stood up and gave him a solemn bow. "As my king wishes," he said, and strode from the tent to notify captains and lieutenants.

They feasted together on fresh killed boar. Theas left Melanion's side for a moment and strode to the front of a tent several yards away. In answer to his low call, Korone parted the flaps and stood before him. They spoke together softly, but Melanion could see in the dimming light Theas' face flushing hotter by the moment. His ever calm gray eyes snapped with his repressed fury.

"Theas," he called. "Come to the fire and let us all know what this argument entails."

Korone skirted about Theas and strode to the fire, shoulders quivering with anger, skirt slashing the forest floor. "I have a good plan, and Theas says it's stupid. Even more insulting, he forbids it. What right does he have to make objections? I'm as good a soldier as he is, and it's a good plan."

"It's doomed to fail, Korone. If you'd just listen to me, you'd realize how much danger you'll be in and—"

"You think everything I do is too dangerous," Korone broke in. "You think I should sit at home and weave, like your meek little Macedonian women. You think—"

Melanion had heard enough. "What's the plan?"

Korone flashed a triumphant glance at Theas, grabbed a stick, and knelt to draw in the dirt. "We know a column of horse soldiers is coming south about . . . here, two day's journey south of Iolcus and half a day from us . . . here." She drew an X with a circle for the troop and another for the rebel camp.

"They plan to ride into a few villages and burn them down. We know this because they've sent out a call for a couple of guides, and one of the men who answered the call heard them planning the raids. They figure they can go back to Iolcus afterwards and brag that the south can be conquered. If we let them get away with it, they'll sap the spirit from our people just before we get to Iolcus.

"We can stop them, with no losses to ourselves. We can take their horses and whatever arms they've got afterwards. All we need is a couple of guides to lead them into a very vulnerable spot, where they can't fight back."

"I say we raid them, like we've done so well in the past," Theas said.

"Like your last raid?" Korone asked him with a frown. "We can't afford to lose another ten men, Theas. We need every one of them for Iolcus. Astrid and I can go as boys. We'll say our father was killed in the big battle, that we want safety for our mother and sisters after Macedonia has conquered the south."

Theas grabbed her arms. Theas, always the gentleman, Melanion knew, shook Korone. Hard. "They'll know you're a woman. By the gods, no man could look at you and not realize that. They'll know right away you're a spy and they'll kill you. But first—first . . . they'll do unspeakable things to you, Korone. I can't permit it. Not ever."

Korone flung free of his arms. "Who are you to permit

327

me or not? I'm a warrior. If I were Nestor, you'd give me a strong handshake for luck and send me off. I demand the same."

"You think I can *shake your hand, damn you?*" Theas shouted.

"Theas." A boy's calm voice overrode the fury in Theas' voice. "They'll never guess we're women." A young boy stepped into the circle of soldiers. He looked like Alex's younger brother, down to the short, shining hair and the blue chiton he wore.

"Astrid," Melanion heard a Thessalian maiden cry in horror. "Your beautiful hair!"

Astrid shrugged a shoulder beneath the blue chiton. "It was too much trouble in battle."

Melanion was impressed. He never would have guessed she was anything but a twelve-year-old lad of good family. Lacking Theas' good judgment, which had obviously gone the way of his even temper, Melanion turned to Linos and Miletus.

"It's just crazy enough to work," Linos said. "If Astrid and Korone stay together at all times, they might pull it off. But I still don't like it."

"Korone's right," Miletus added. "We'll need every man we've got by next week."

"My father died at Iolcus," Astrid said. "And Korone's brother . . ."

"My brother is my own concern, not anyone else's," Korone said. "As is my revenge."

Melanion gave her a long look. "So be it," he said at last. "Come to me later tonight. We'll plan the details."

Korone let out the breath she hadn't known she was holding. At a muffled sound behind her, she turned to see Theas stride off into the forest. She ran as fast as she could to catch up with him. Now that she'd won, the thought of leaving him without making peace disturbed her deeply.

She caught up with him at a little stream that ran past the clearing where the horses grazed. He stood, legs akimbo, his rigid back to her, staring out at the rushing water.

She put out a tentative hand and touched his arm. "Please, Theas. Let's part friends. Who knows when we'll meet again?"

Theas stiffened at her touch. His whole body seemed clenched against her. "You've made your choice," he said.

"I should never have said that about your losing ten men on the last raid, Theas." Korone's voice broke. She felt so guilty, disparaging him like that when he didn't deserve it. She'd just wanted to win so badly, she'd used any argument she could think of.

"You were up against too many soldiers, and they were so well armed. We've all lost more men than that. You know all of us would rather serve under you than anyone else, Theas. You've kept more of us safe than any other commander." She wished he'd turn around. She wished he'd give just one sign that he could forgive her.

When he wheeled on her, she was so startled she stepped back into the unyielding trunk of a tree. But it was softer than the hard muscle of his set jaw, and cooler than the fury flaming in his eyes.

"You think I'm upset because my *pride* is wounded? Brainless woman! I'm not upset. I'm furious. While you're off on your little adventure, you think about why."

So, he thought she was a fool, did he? She blinked hard against the sting of tears and set her jaw. He was letting her leave without a good-bye when he might never see her again, and she would never, never forgive him for that.

"I don't have to think, Macedonian. You didn't get your way over a woman, that's why. When all this is over, go back to your hills, you ignorant male. Your slave women can have you, for all I care."

She cried all night, deep, gulping sobs that left her breathless and shocked at her own foolishness. When morning came, she rose and donned a white chiton, without borders or embellishment. Astrid had cut her hair the night before, quietly handing her a linen strip to blow her nose and blot her tears, and telling her they'd make it back safely, that she could give Theas another piece of her mind then.

She and Astrid knew where to lead the Macedonians and when to arrive at the ambush. There was nothing left to do but mount up. Astrid already sat on her horse—the very same one that was champion in the spring equestrian games. Korone looked around the clearing once more, peering through the dim light for a tall, gray-eyed man who might have changed his mind about saying good-bye.

Nestor appeared at the edge of the pasture instead, leading Theas' gray.

"He says to take him," Nestor told her, looking unhappy.

"I can't. If I don't—well, nothing can happen to this stallion. He's one of the best from Queen Arete's stables, and Theas will need him next week."

"He said to tell you to stop arguing. He said 'take him and may he and the gods keep you safe.' You'd better do as he says, Korone. You do know he'll be no good for anything unless you come back in one piece, don't you?" Nestor asked her gently.

Stupid tears! Korone blinked them back again. It seemed she'd cried forever. She gave a choked laugh. "He knows how bad a rider I am. How can he give his beautiful horse to me when I don't deserve it?"

Nestor scratched his head. "How did he know you'd say that, Korone?" He sighed. "I'm to tell you to think about it."

Korone took the reins Nestor proffered and leaped up on the gray. The horse snorted and pawed the ground, eager to be off. "Tell him thank you," she said to Nestor. "Tell him . . . just tell him good-bye."

As the sun rose, Korone rode beside Astrid in silence. Why would Theas hate her so much last night that he couldn't even look at her and then, this morning, give her his prize possession, his beautiful horse? Why was he so furious? She had never seen rage like that before, except maybe once. She furrowed her brow remembering. She'd been a very young child, maybe three years old.

Her father had found her reaching for a snake. She'd thought it was one of the House snakes, who guarded the walls and the green, grassy courtyard from danger, and she'd wanted to pet it. Right before she could, her father had slammed his staff down on it and sliced its head off with his knife. Then he'd shaken her until her teeth rattled and held her so close she thought she'd never take another breath again. Apparently, she'd reached out to pet a viper.

Korone shook her head. But her father had been angry because he loved her and she'd put herself in terrible danger. Whereas Theas . . . Theas couldn't possibly love her. It was absurd. He hated her dancing. He hated the way she flirted, even though she never flirted with him. He hated the way she walked, by the gods! He couldn't possibly love her the way she'd wanted him to, almost from the beginning.

Could he? Her heart gave a wild lurch. And if he did love

her, could she finally admit to herself how very much she
. . . ? "Oh, gods," she whispered. "I don't care if he never
says a word, if he never feels the same. Just let me tell him I
love him before I die."

An hour, maybe two passed as they rode north. Then
Astrid raised her hand and they halted at the top of the
mountain pass, looking down at the path the Macedonian
troop would take.

"They'll stumble on us soon," Astrid said as they dismounted. Korone could hear the tension in her voice. It
had been easy yesterday, warmed by her cleverness and surrounded by comrades, to talk about this plan. But her
nerves were as tight as bowstrings now.

Astrid must have sensed it, for she gave her a hug. "Let's
have something to eat. It'll cheer us and chase away the
goblins."

"I couldn't eat a thing," Korone said with a sigh. "My
heart's stuck where I swallow." She watched the trail in
brooding silence.

A few minutes later, she heard hoofbeats. A hundred
horses struck iron against rock as they climbed the narrow
path. Astrid took Korone's hand and squeezed it. Together,
they raised their heads to the sky and bowed them to the
earth in one last, silent prayer.

A moment later, the captain of the unit appeared from
around a bend. Grizzled, scarred across his cheek, and
large, he caught sight of them and halted some feet below
them.

"What's this?" he called up in a gruff voice.

Astrid raised her hand to the captain. "Hail, Macedonian. We beg a moment of your time."

"Speak, boy," the man said. "And hurry up about it. We
don't have all day."

"We heard you're looking for scouts, sir. We can help you. We know every inch of these hills. You won't be sorry if you give us your protection."

"And why would two Thessalian whelps want it?" The captain had climbed the rest of the way and stared down at them both from his horse. His face was a blend of suspicion and interest. At least he wasn't dismissing them out of hand. And he hadn't drawn his sword on them, either, Korone thought.

"We're sons of Myron, freeholder in the Marsh village very close to this pass. He was killed at Iolcus. My mother and sisters can't keep the land without a grown man—that's Arkadian law. My brother and I figured if we help you, you'll remember us when you conquer the south. And you'll let our mother keep the land." She shrugged. "Not all Thessalians are happy with the old laws. We'd like to be on the winning side, and help change things for the better, at least for us."

The captain rubbed his beard. "You know the rebel camps?"

Astrid nodded. "We know two near our village."

"How many in each camp?"

"About fifty. Your men could take them easily tomorrow at dawn," Korone said.

The captain nodded crisply. "Lead us into the rebel camps, and you'll get your land, boys. Polymus rewards those who help him, just as he punishes those who lie to him. Understand?"

Korone grasped the reins so hard her knuckles hurt. "Yes, sir."

A beefy, thick-set soldier with narrow eyes and a twisted mouth had ridden up beside the captain and sat his horse, listening. Korone suppressed a shudder. "Captain, I say kill them and take the horses. It's easier than trusting a damned Thessalian."

"When I give my word, I keep it," the captain said sharply. "See to the men." He looked at Astrid. "Can you lead us to a good spot? We'll make camp for the night and set out tomorrow to snuff out the rebel offal."

"Yes, sir. About an hour's ride from here, there's a good clearing, big enough for all of you."

"Lead me to it, lads. And tonight," he said with a long look at the soldier who'd ridden back down the hill out of earshot, "you sleep right outside my tent."

Later, as the stars glittered in the night sky, Korone unrolled her blanket and placed it as close to the captain's tent as she could. She huddled close to Astrid, her hand on the knife at her belt, afraid to shut her eyes. The men were brutes, mostly Red Bands. There was only one decent man, the one who led them.

In the darkness, she heard jokes of such crudity she wasn't even sure she understood them. Some, like the one a man made in reference to the two of them, made her shudder in fear.

"Shut your traps," the captain shouted, and the camp grew quiet. But Korone couldn't sleep. She had never been so frightened in her life.

At dawn, Korone froze when a Red Band approached them. It was the animal who'd suggested the captain kill them yesterday. She shook Astrid awake just before the bastard slammed a foot into her back. "Get up, little priests. Time to butcher the rebel scum." He gave a snort and walked away.

"Gods, what filth," muttered Korone.

"Quiet," Astrid whispered. "The captain will hear you. Come and get the horses with me."

"All right." She started after Astrid and brushed aside a bush at the edge of the camp. A hand clamped down tight over her mouth and beefy arms hauled her up, kicking and flailing. The raw odor of sweat told her who had her, but no matter how much she struggled, she couldn't break the Red Band's iron grip as he hauled her into the woods at the edge of camp.

The Macedonian's hammy paw held her clamped to his side. She bit the other hand he'd pressed so hard against her mouth. She had to scream for Astrid. The bastard cursed and slapped her so hard her head snapped back against his arm. Then his hand came down over her mouth and nose as well. She struggled, lungs straining, terrified as she choked against the heavy, murderous hand. She lost consciousness.

When she came to, she lay sprawled on the ground. The Red Band knelt over her, a gleam in his nasty little eyes. She raised her knee and her fist at the same instant, trying for his nose and his groin. He dodged her knee, grunting, but her fist landed squarely on his nose. He bled like a stuck pig, howling and shaking her like a rag doll.

Think, she had to think. Of a way to reach her knife, sheathed at her waist. But he grabbed her arms and raised them over her head, holding her down with a knee on her chest. She was helpless against his monstrous strength. He grabbed his knife and laid it at her throat.

"One sound and I slit you from end to end," he said.

Her chiton was pulled up to her chest. If she managed to scream, the whole troop would be down on them, and even though this idiot hadn't seen she was a woman, the others would in the growing light.

The Red Band made lewd movements with his hips, thrusting toward her pelvis.

"Let me go, you pot-gutted, stinking pig," she hissed.

"I'm hungry for fresh meat, little eunuch. Go ahead. See if you can stop me." His sneer, his stinking breath, his strength maddened her. She struggled. The knife slit her chiton open from neck to thigh, just as the first ray of the sun shot through the trees.

The Red Band stared down at her breasts and roared. "Whore! Spy!" He thrust her to her feet and dragged her toward the camp. "Do you know what we do to lying bitches? We pass them around, to one man after the other. We'll have you any way we want. If you don't die of that, we'll slice you to pieces. First these," he said as he squeezed her breast so hard dark welts formed immediately.

She kicked and fought him, but by now, he had her in camp. Men stood at the other side of the smoldering fire, saddling their horses.

"She's a lying, whoring spy!" the Red Band roared.

Korone felt a whoosh of air behind her. The Red Band tottered and fell away. His head rolled off his body to the ground. She whirled to find Astrid, mounted, brandishing her bloody sword.

"Up and follow me!" she shouted, throwing the gray's reins to Korone.

Korone flung herself onto the gray's broad back and wheeled, galloping out of the camp, along the narrow trail, over stone heaps, down, down into creek bottoms and up again. Horses thundered behind her as she clung low over the gray's neck. His mane blew into her eyes. Out they flew into a clearing surrounded by log walls a man's height. And at the end was another wall, impossibly high. The Macedonians raced after them into the clearing.

"Take my lead," Astrid screamed over her shoulder. "Grab mane and jump!"

She grabbed tight. The gray's powerful haunches thrust off and she sailed high over the wall to land with a bone-jarring thud on the other side. She looked back over her shoulder in terror.

The Macedonians milled in the clearing. With a crash, the last logs fell into place behind them and neatly stacked up into a wall as high as the others. The trap had shut. The whole troop rushed at the walls, and the killing began.

It took no time at all. The rebels in the treetops let their arrows fly. Within minutes, the entire unit lay dead.

Korone watched them lead away Macedonian horses that hadn't injured themselves in the panic and dispatch the rest. They made a funeral pyre of the fallen logs and burned the bodies.

Slowly, Korone became aware that she stood naked near the huge clearing, grimed with dirt and sweat. Something soft and warm fell over her shoulders. A himation covered her to her feet. Hands grasped her shoulders, tender and strong. She knew whose they were without looking.

She turned to face him. She was afraid to speak because she was so wracked with emotion she didn't know whether she'd cry or just begin to cackle madly. Theas swallowed hard, looking at the welts on her neck. All of a sudden, she was ashamed, and desperate to get clean. She pulled away, but he took her gently by the hand and led her into the forest to a clear, pure stream.

When Theas lifted the himation from her shoulders, he looked carefully at her breasts, her arms, her cheek. He swallowed a sound that might have been a groan, like a man who had received a death wound trying to be brave about it. Without a word, he began to gently sponge the dirt from her body. Each careful touch seemed to rid her of the shame, if not the horror of what the Red Band had done to her.

When she was clean, he wrapped her in the himation as lovingly as a mother would wrap her babe. She found she could speak without gagging.

"Thank you for the gray," she whispered. "He saved my life."

He touched her cheek, sensitive fingers just brushing the dark bruise. "Why," he asked. "Why did you risk yourself?"

She took a deep breath. "You would have loved my brother, Theas. He was full of dreams of honor, just like you. He went to hunt with a friend, in the mountains well south of the Macedonian border. When a troop of soldiers found them, he managed to get his friend free before Polymus entered the camp.

"His friend hid in the forest and saw everything." For a moment, she couldn't go on. "They tortured him, of course. They thought he might be a spy. When Polymus was done with him, they left. His friend crept back into the camp and carried what was left of his body home so we could give him the proper rites."

For the first time, Korone let her anguish over her brother show on her face. She wanted Theas to understand her, to know all of her.

"I had to do it. We have to win back our freedom—for my brother, and all the others who died because of Polymus. If they had killed me, I wouldn't have minded so much, except for leaving you, Theas. But I had to fight them. Evil cannot stand."

Suddenly, she felt them—traitorous tears, spilling over her eyes, down her face. Tears for her brother taken much too soon in a horrible death, tears for her country, tears of sorrow that she hadn't told Theas earlier, that she had wasted so much time they could have had together.

Theas pulled her close and held her against his chest

stroking her hair. "I understand," he murmured in a voice so low and sweet, Korone thought it sounded like music. It felt so good to cling to him, to use his strength, to sob out her fury and her agony for the first time. She lost track of minutes, hours, it seemed, while she cried. Until finally, her tears were spent.

He held her still in the circle of his arms, but a little away from him, so she could see his face.

"I need you to understand, too, Korone. I fought against you, not because I wanted you to go home and weave with the women. I know you have to fight, and I'd be proud to fight at your side. I've thought about it, lying awake at night. How we'd never retreat. How we'd know each other so well, we'd fight as one mind, one body. If you were wounded, I'd stand between you and the enemy." He laughed, a little ragged catch in his breath.

"I've even thought that I could help you die, even speed it for you, so you'd begin the journey without more pain. I could bear that. But when I knew you wanted to go away from me, where I couldn't protect you from the most vile acts men can do, not knowing the agony you'd be in—don't ask me to do that again, Korone. Maybe Melanion can do it without turning into a lunatic, but I can't."

He closed his eyes, those wise eyes that had judged her in the past and found her a flirt, and a foolish, haughty creature. When he opened them and looked at her again, his heart shone within their clear depths.

"Korone, I love you, better than my life. And I'll die before I see you go into such danger again."

She flung her arms around him and kissed his gray eyes, and his mouth that trembled. Steady, laconic Theas, in whom all feeling ran so deep—that he should love her!

"I was supposed to tell you first," she said, laughing and

crying at the same time. "I love you, Theas. Only I'm more selfish than you are. I want my whole life to show you how much I love you. I want our children. And if I can't have that, I want to live every moment I have left with you and for you. Come." She held out her hand.

He looked at it, dubious. "After what that animal did to you, do you really . . ."

She smiled, and even if her smile trembled as his did, she felt certain inside. "Come and make me whole again, Theas. Give me back my joy." He took her hand and followed her deeper into the forest.

"Keep to yourself," Miletus said to Melanion as he packed the last of his supplies. The general rubbed his beard. "Did I tell you that already?"

Melanion grinned. "Twice."

"I must be getting old," Miletus said. "Remember, keep the patch on at all times."

Melanion touched the black patch covering one eye. "I'll remember."

The general sighed, then threw his brawny arms about him. "Go with the gods," he said, and held the black until Melanion swung himself up on the horse.

The moon had just risen. Melanion rode quietly behind Nestor, following the light. It seemed to be a visible string pulling him closer to his fate, either for good or ill. He felt clean, free from the doubts and remorse that had plagued him all his life. Whatever happened, he was on the gods' path.

He longed for Atalante. Wait for me, he silently called to her. Know I'm coming.

But he, himself, knew that was impossible. Atalante thought he was dead. Part of her suffering was to think she would never see him again. And part of his suffering was to realize he could do nothing to change it until the signs were revealed.

As they came to the wooded hills above Iolcus, he dismounted and looked out at the enemy campfires, numerous as stars on the plain. Gods, he thought. My own people are the enemy.

A twig cracked in the underbrush. Melanion and Nestor backed into the safety of the trees and waited. A young boy stepped into the moonlight. They could just make out his dark curls. Melanion signaled to Nestor. In an instant, he had a knife at the boy's throat and a hand clamped over his mouth.

"Scream and you die," Melanion said. "Who are you? What are you doing here in the middle of the night?"

"I'm Erytes, son of Amphytrion," whispered the boy. "Are you rebel or Macedonian?"

"Rebel," Melanion said softly. Nestor slackened his grip and the boy stood tall. The moon shone straight down on Erytes, revealing a boy painfully thin. There was a hesitance to the body that had once jumped and run without a thought but bliss.

"What are you about here?" Nestor asked.

"Queen Clymene sent me. She had a vision three nights ago, and since then, I've been watching for you. I'm supposed to escort a Macedonian runner into Iolcus."

"I'm your man," Melanion whispered.

Nestor clasped his arm hard. "The gods watch over you until we meet again."

"And you," Melanion said. He slipped on the cloak Erytes held out to him and stepped down the hillside into the plain, past the sleeping army of Red Bands, Macedonians, and mercenaries. As the moon slipped behind a cloud, he could hear their grunts, their sighs, their night-mare cries in languages he didn't understand as they beseeched their foreign gods. Heavy-lidded guards stared through him as though he didn't exist, and he wondered at the cloak and its powers.

He looked toward his destination, the great, serpent-crowned wall of Iolcus rising from the night. Erytes touched his arm and led him around the wall to a hedge. Feeling his way, Melanion crept to the door behind the hedge and opened it with a push. Silently, it swung open and he slipped inside.

"Come," Erytes whispered, and took his hand. Melanion followed the boy through the long, black corridors. Erytes seemed to feel his way through his toes. At last they came to a halt and Erytes pushed open a door. A small oil lamp shone on a bed laid with clean linen. A tray held food and in the corner, a small table held a wash bowl and ewer.

"The queen bids you eat and rest," Erytes told him. In the lamplight, Melanion got a clear look at Erytes' pale face and haunted eyes. The boy stood straight, though, shoulders back, chin up, like a small soldier.

"Tomorrow, a messenger will come to take you to Polymus. Prepare yourself. There will be a trial."

"There are always trials," Melanion said in a low whisper. "If the gods have chosen their cause, they'll be watching."

The boy shrugged. "I leave you to their care, stranger. Keep the lamp lit if you want. Nobody comes down here." Soundlessly, he left the room, more a specter than a child.

What had happened to the carefree boy with the dark, laughing eyes? Melanion wondered. How much anguish had he suffered here? He looked around the room and felt his heart twist. He was in the room where he and Atalante had lain together through warm nights of love. He slipped into the bed and blew out the lamp, commending himself to the gods. Within a short time, Melanion slept a deep, dreamless sleep beneath the silver caress of the moon.

In the chamber above Melanion's, Kryton and Hyperion spoke in low voices waiting for the dawn.

"It won't be long now," Kryton said. "I can feel it coming like a great drum beating. I'm glad it's soon. I can't hold out much longer."

"Are you afraid?" Hyperion asked him.

"Not of anything as long as I can hold back the evil until the appointed time."

"But of going beyond this life?"

"Oh, that." Kryton attempted a grin, but it must look more like a grimace of pain, for that's what he felt inside. The boy was such a believer, and worked so hard to comfort him. "No. My punishment will be upon me soon enough, I reckon. What good is it to imagine the worst when you know you deserve it?"

"But with the Mother's love, you don't have to fear the next life, Kryton."

Kryton wanted to be easy on the boy, but he had never been anything but honest with him, and he wasn't going to start lying now. "Hyperion, lad. I've never been a believing man. Mortals invent their gods so they can bargain with 'em. They pray to Ares for victory in war, or Phoebus Apollo if they need to know the future. They bring bribes and hope they'll get favors in return. Much like men do with kings, you know."

Hyperion slowly shook his head. "It's not like that at all," he said in his priest's voice, the one that compelled Kryton to listen. "Our stories of the gods teach us about ourselves—that we've got a spark of divinity, too. In the stories, we see the wisdom of Athene, the strength of Zeus, the beauty of the Soul seeking Love.

"But the Mother, She's there for a special reason. She shows us the compassion that flows from the Divine to us, and must continue to flow through us to all we come to know. It makes us care for the creatures of the earth, for the very streams and forests we walk through. For our children and our wives."

*For our children and our wives.* He felt Hyperion's words in the deepest recesses of his heart. What had he ever done for his child, his wife? Kryton looked down at hands that had been given so much to hold and that had destroyed it all. "There are those of us who never cared for anything beyond our own selfish desires," he said low. "The sooner we leave our mess for someone else to clean up, the better."

"The Mother forgives, and thus teaches us to forgive. For without mercy, there's no chance of joy between man and woman, father and son. For me, if not for your own boy, go to her."

Kryton let out his breath in a jagged sigh of pain. "What can she give an old fool, Hyperion?"

The boy merely stared at him, with calm, bright eyes. For a long moment, Kryton tried to fight against the pull of the boy's conviction, but to no avail. He smiled and shook his head.

"I give up. If she'll have me, take me to her."

As the bearers carried Kryton's litter through the labyrinth beneath the palace, he thought of the edicts Polymus had decreed against the Mother's worship. No garlanded maidens had brought offerings of the first crops to Her shrine. The great festival She shared with Bacchus had not been celebrated this year. No playwrights entered Her contest of tragedies, no athletes competed, no bards sang to Her.

But when the bearers carried him into the Mother's shrine, Kryton saw that someone had cleaned the walls and the votive bowls of meal and milk were fresh. He stared up at the great statue of the Mother, standing with sinuous serpents and trustful bulls at rest at Her feet. The shrine gave off a sense of order—order that comes from creation, that tells the seasons when to turn, a seedling when to rise to the light, a womb when to loose a child into the world. In spite of his physical pain and his constant regrets, serenity surrounded him.

They lowered the litter before the statue, where he could see her face clearly. "Leave me for a time," he whispered.

In the empty room, in the rose-tinted light of the torch they'd left behind, he stared at the ancient statue. The artist had captured antitheses: strength and femininity, remote formality springing from a wellspring of suffering that, as he watched, melted into tenderness. He felt like a child faced with grown-up mysteries and passions.

Willing himself to silence, he studied the face of the goddess, going deeper into the stone beyond the ageless beauty of her features until he reached the solid core of compassion at the heart of the marble.

A voice, still and tender, came up to him from the depths of the earth, from the depths of his soul.

*"What do you ask, Kryton of Macedonia?"*

"Nothing," he whispered. "For I've committed unspeakable acts."

*"Speak them."*

He shuddered and forced his tongue to form the words. "I killed my wife, a woman of delicacy and honor whom I should have protected with my life. She died alone on a

345

chill mountaintop. In arrogance and greed, I brought great suffering upon two kingdoms." The last was the most painful, but he struggled and gave it breath.

"I killed my only son."

He sobbed, deep in the pit of despair he'd dug through the days and acts of his life. "I am the destroyer," he said.

*"Child of man,"* said the still voice. *"Come to me."*

He crawled to the base of the statue and grasped the ring of serpents in both hands. Sobs lashed him until each breath tore his lungs, but the pain didn't stop him. The air throbbed around him, emanating from the heart of the statue, through the serpents at her feet. It vibrated against his skin, his closed eyes. He was awash in the hum of it as though he were a drop of water dancing upon a wave in a great ocean.

Softly, the still voice echoed. *"Kryton. Remember the ring."* He collapsed, his body washed by a white mist, and lay at the Mother's feet.

Vaguely, he heard Hyperion's voice and felt bearers lift him. Someone poured a potion down his throat in drops.

But Kryton dreamed. In his dream, the ring of serpents turned into the ring of the lion's head, and he placed it on Melanion's finger and told the boy he was the true heir to his kingdom. The ring shifted its aspect, sometimes becoming the serpents, and sometimes the lion.

Kryton thought in the dream. The men who said they had found his son dead on the battlefield had brought him Melanion's sword and shield, but they hadn't brought him the ring. And if they'd had his son's body, surely it would have been easy to pull the ring off his finger for definite identification.

His skin warmed. He noticed light beyond his closed eyes. Opening them, Kryton saw Clymene bending over him. Her face was full of fear. But the dawn of a new day rose behind her shoulder. He smiled up at her, and knew the joy he felt in his heart must show on his face.

"Don't be afraid," he said. "I'll live long enough to protect Atalante." He gave a laugh that was half a sob. "I must, you know, until I can give her to him. My son, that they told me was dead, is alive." With a great sigh, he closed his eyes and slept.

Hyperion and Clymene conferred while Kryton dozed.

"Is it possible?" Clymene whispered.

"I don't know. He's weak. He wants it to be true so badly. But to ignore a sign from the Mother would be foolish."

"We can't tell Atalante," Clymene said. "It could be cruel to make her hope."

Hyperion frowned. "They've found another fool. She'll have to race him. It's destroying her, mother. Polymus watches with such calculation. He knows every time he makes her kill, she's closer to begging him to finish it."

"To think of the last one! She went on her knees to Polymus—my daughter, Queen of Thessaly, fell to her knees before that animal, because the boy was only sixteen. He laughed, said it was legal, that she'd not made any stipulation as to age." Clymene clenched her fists, furious and aching for her child.

"Mother, please. Take Atalante and go to Arkadia."

Clymene looked at Hyperion in surprise. "And leave our people? Leave Kryton, when I can keep him alive for a little longer?"

"As it is, I fear this will be the last audience he'll attend."

★ ★ ★ ★ ★

The Megaron was packed with Red Bands and mercenaries. Everyone wanted to see the new runner, Kryton realized. Polymus had orchestrated these audiences into a fine show. Slaves softly played citharas and reeds. Courtiers in brilliant silks stolen from Thessaly's treasure chests strolled and conversed in low voices.

They had all begun to ignore him. Kryton figured they'd guessed it was a matter of weeks before he died, and Polymus was the man of the hour.

"Majesty." Myron's voice recalled his thoughts. The old veteran knelt at his feet.

"Rise," Kryton said, and motioned him to step forward.

"I'm reporting the condition of the troops," Myron quavered. He told Kryton how many measures of grain each unit still had, how much wine, what men had died on forays into the south, how many old generals still commanded their troops, how many Red Bands and mercenaries there were left.

Kryton wasn't surprised. He'd been hatching a plot since mid morning and was ready to put it into action. "How many of the old generals would still take a direct order from me?" he asked.

Tears welled in Myron's rheumy eye. "All of us, Sire. We're your men, now and always."

"Good. Come close and listen." Kryton told the old man everything he'd need to convey to the loyal Macedonian commanders. As he spoke, Myron's stooped form slowly straightened, until he stood upright as a man half his age.

"They'll need proof this order comes from me," Kryton told him. He pulled the Lion Head ring, one of only two in the kingdom, from his hand. It slipped easily from his wasted finger.

"Here. Take it to those we can trust and show them that the king commands them." As he gave Myron the ring, he checked the Megaron to assure himself no one had seen this exchange. The courtiers were too interested in Polymus' every move to pay attention, he saw with relief. Only the lowly foot soldier by the entryway, a scarred and sun-baked veteran with an eye-patch like Myron's, was watching. The man was too crude, too newly arrived to be Polymus' spy. As Myron stepped smartly off on his mission, Atalante slipped into her place beside the throne. It was time to present the runner.

A gong rang. Polymus walked with Xuthus toward the throne as though they led a Triumph. Courtiers threw flower petals in their path, and they walked to the strident beat of music. Xuthus' purple robe, bordered in gold, shocked Atalante. Purple was a color only for the gods to wear.

"Hubris," she whispered.

Kryton's mocking smile told her he, at least, understood. "Serves him right, the damned idiot. If they hadn't cursed him before, they've done it, now."

"I hope you haven't tired yourself, Majesty, by presiding over this little ceremony. Perhaps this will be your last appearance before us, if you don't take care."

Polymus must know he's dying, Atalante thought. He'd never risk such effrontery otherwise. She forced herself not to rub arms suddenly chilled.

"The gods decide our fate, Polymus. State your business."

"A new man offers himself to challenge the princess."

"Call him forward," Kryton said. A messenger ran the length of the hall and led a scarred veteran to the throne. "I noticed him before," murmured Kryton.

The man was older—nearing thirty, perhaps, and had obviously lost an eye, but something about him drew Atalante and held her captive. It may have been the spark of joy she swore she saw on his face for an instant when their eyes met. It could be the way he held himself, with a grace and dignity to his carriage. It could be the long, beautiful lines of his muscled legs. He seemed so familiar, and his eye was that beautiful gray she still dreamed of. She looked away from the intensity of his gaze, fighting for control over the sudden ache in her chest.

It was the stranger's voice that brought her back to the Megaron and the people around her. It was deep and gruff, unlike the melodious tones of the man she'd loved. Kryton must have asked the man why he'd sacrifice himself knowing the penalty for losing.

"I've had a life of soldiering," the man said. "I'm getting too old for sleeping on the cold ground, and never a woman of my own. The gold's a fortune to a man like me. I'm good, maybe good enough. If I win, I'll settle down, buy me a farm, find a wife, have sons. If I lose, life's short anyway. All or nothing. It's a gamble, but why not?"

Polymus smiled, folding his arms in satisfaction. "Do you accept this man, Kryton?" he asked.

"I do," said Kryton.

"You race tomorrow, Princess." Polymus was all business, now. "I warn you, he's fast."

"Tomorrow we'll know," Atalante said. "If that's all you want of me, I'll retire, now."

Polymus dismissed her with the gesture of a man so certain of winning he could afford to be generous. Furious, frightened, she turned her back on him and walked out the door.

Kryton felt her fear. He wished he could reassure her

and tell her Melanion would come for her, but Clymene had demanded his silence, arguing that Atalante would never be able to keep her joy to herself if she heard Melanion might be alive.

Polymus gave Kryton a deep, mocking bow. "I must prepare the stadium, Sire. So much to do in so little time. The priests must be ready to marry my son and the princess tomorrow, the slaves must weave garlands, these friends of mine must have the best seats in the stadium . . ." He shrugged and smiled, a man of importance giving a polite excuse to an unnecessary old man.

The veteran paused at the throne. "I've soldiered for the king for fifteen years," he said when Polymus shot him a questioning look. My unit's an old one. We infantrymen have a gift for him. All right if I do it now?"

"I commend you for your loyalty," Polymus said smoothly. "After you're through here, come to my son's rooms. He wishes to talk to you."

The veteran nodded, took the steps to the throne, and dropped to his knees. "A few moments ago, I saw you give something away. I've brought you another to take its place." He put something small, solid, and round into Kryton's hand and closed it tightly around the object. Kryton's heart gave a lurch. The man did something else then—something odd, seeing he was a stranger, and of low birth.

He took the hand in which he'd placed the gift and laid it against his forehead as he knelt before Kryton. It was sign of deep reverence, given only by the nobility and then only when the relationship was close. He held Kryton's hand there for a long time, as though he were loathe to give up his touch.

It wasn't until the Megaron was empty that Kryton

opened his hand and stared at what lay on his palm. Against his wasted flesh glowed a shining gold ring fashioned with the head of a lion—the ring of Macedonia's crown prince.

When Melanion entered Xuthus' quarters, he found the commander's son seated on an inlaid chair, plucking the purple robe as though it burned him. Melanion hoped to hell it did.

But he bowed and said in the gruff voice of a foot soldier, "What's a man like you want with a man like me, son of Polymus?"

Xuthus jerked upright from the cushioned chair and paced the room like a rangy beast in a cage. "Nobody's fast enough. I want you to do something, anything, to win the race."

He turned and clutched Melanion's hand with his bony fingers. Xuthus had wasted away to nothing. "You don't want to die," he said in a whine. "You want the gold, and I want her. Can you trip her?"

Melanion shook his head. "Can't do that. The crowd would see. They'd tear me to pieces. But I've got something that'll do the trick—gold, from an old priestess of Astarte, the love goddess. Your favorite deity, I heard. I can get close enough to throw it out to the princess, and believe me, she'll pick it up."

"Bah! She doesn't give a rat's ass for gold," Xuthus said. "I'd have her by now if that was so."

"But this is magic gold, my lord. Take a look. You'll see what I mean." Melanion opened his pouch and lifted one of the apples just far enough for Xuthus to fall beneath the metal's warm seduction.

Xuthus cried out in longing and reached for it. With a flick of his wrist, Melanion tucked the apple back into the pouch. Xuthus shook his head, seemingly to clear what little brain he had. Once hidden, the glowing apple no longer sang like a siren to him, but Melanion knew Xuthus would have moved heaven and earth to grab it a moment ago.

"It'll work on her like it did on me?" Xuthus asked him.

"Sure, as long as you can keep this secret. Don't say a word to anyone, not even your father. That way, she'll not get a warning, and she'll look at the apples, all right. Once she does, I'll catch her and pass her while she stoops to pick them up."

Xuthus' ravaged face turned solemn. He put a finger to his lips and clapped Melanion on the back. "Not a word to anybody," he said, and licked his lips.

Melanion smiled at him, and Xuthus rubbed his hands with glee, never noticing that Melanion must look as he felt—like a wolf baring his teeth. "Put on your brightest robe tomorrow, my lord, in preparation for the last race. I promise you, you'll finally get what you deserve."

"Run well," Xuthus said. "My fate goes with you."

"Indeed," Melanion whispered to himself as he shut the door on the snake.

# Chapter 15

## The Signs

Atalante heard Hyperion enter the room, but she didn't turn from the window. She stared at the veteran running across Iolcus Plain. He sped by the soldiers' tents like the winged god.

"Look at him," she said softly. "He's beautiful."

"Can you beat him?" Hyperion asked her.

She nodded. "Yes. Barely. But I can't kill him afterwards."

"He's old enough to know what he's doing," Hyperion said in a cold voice, so out of keeping with his usual warmth, it startled her. "He wants a profit, just like the rest. He won't be so difficult to kill."

"Look at him," Atalante pleaded. "Look at the lines of his body. He's so beautiful when he moves."

Hyperion held out his thin hand, and she took it, clinging to his touch like an anchor. "I can't go through with it again," she said, and heard her voice crack.

But Hyperion didn't offer her compassion, the way he usually did. He pulled her away from the window. "Listen, Atalante! I've heard Her speak. You must run. This time, you must."

"Little Owl," she whispered, and felt her tears slip down her cheek, each one a scalding brand. "I can't be Polymus' executioner again." She slid to the floor, kneeling before him, a petitioner to her priest. "Give me leave, Hyperion.

354

Give me leave to marry Xuthus and there will be two more deaths on my wedding night. Please. I can't kill this one."

Hyperion gently pried her hands away. "As priest and prince, I command you, Atalante. Once more, you must run."

At the appointed hour, Erytes led Melanion through the dark corridors into Kryton's chamber. Melanion crossed the room and knelt at his father's bedside. In the Megaron, watching Polymus out of the corner of his eye, he'd barely had time to look at his father. Now, his heart twisted as he saw how thin and wasted Kryton had become. His father's skin stretched across his bones like wrinkled parchment. The bruised blue veins showed through the back of his hands.

But Kryton's eyes were mild, shining from his ravaged face with the serenity of a holy man. And his gaze roved over Melanion's disguised form with a kindness he'd never seen before. His father had suffered much in the last months, but it had changed him in more ways than the physical.

Kryton motioned Erytes out of the room. As the door clicked shut behind the tapestry, Kryton stared at him for a long time. Occasionally, he grimaced, as though he were in terrible pain.

"Where did you get the ring?" he finally asked.

"First, Sire, tell me how you fare," Melanion said.

Kryton's brow lifted in the old, ironic gesture. "I'll be dead by morning. I wish to know while I still have my senses, what became of my son. If you have any compassion at all, tell me what you know so I can die in peace."

Melanion slipped off the eye patch. The dark ointment and the painted scars wouldn't fade for several days, but at least his eyes were the same as they'd ever been.

"Black-fringed," Kryton said in a hushed voice. "Althea's eyes. Melanion's eyes."

"Father," Melanion said, and heard his voice break on the word. "Here I am."

Kryton pulled his head down to him. His hands traced Melanion's face, sensing that way what he couldn't seem to see clearly, touching his forehead, his hair, his hands. "My flesh and Althea's. My beloved son, alive." His breath hitched. "Forgive me," he said.

Melanion felt the sting of tears. "Father, I'm the one who must ask your forgiveness. On the plain of Iolcus, I pointed my arrow at your throat."

His father smiled with such reassurance that Melanion wondered if he knew a great truth. "And could you have loosed the arrow, even to save Iasus' life?" he asked.

Melanion remembered the long battle with the monster who was in reality a blessed spirit. "No, Father. Not even for Iasus. I've been places . . . I can't even talk about them. You probably won't believe me. I know you were never much for spiritual matters."

Kryton smiled and shook his head. "You'd be surprised," he said. "For such dreams I've dreamed."

"I saw Mother," Melanion told him. "She said, 'Tell your father I will wait for him. Forever.' "

Kryton lay back against the pillows and took a deep breath. "She said that?" He smiled, unshed tears glittering in his eyes. His thin face glowed. "I'll see her. Althea . . ."

A heaving cough racked his body. Kryton drew a harsh breath, motioned for the wine cup by the bed. After he drank, he dashed away the moisture in his eyes with his hand. He fumbled with the ring on his finger and dropped it into Melanion's hand. "Put it back on. You're king, now. And listen to me, for time grows short," he said in a business-like manner—Melanion's pragmatic father again.

"These are the men you can trust." Kryton listed those still loyal to him, beginning with Myron and his sons.

As the stars wheeled in the night sky, Kryton gave Melanion an understanding of the men he'd ruled—which would need prodding, which would do their duty quickly, which he could trust for sage advice. His voice grew weaker, until Melanion had to lean over, his ear close to Kryton's lips, to hear his words. But Kryton's mind stayed clear, in spite of the obvious pain that came with each breath he drew.

Melanion listened, every word engraved in his mind forever. He knew this was the wrong time to indulge in regret, but as Kryton lay, drawing in shallow breaths, his thoughts were tinged with a deep sorrow for what might have been. There was so much he wanted to tell his father that would never get said. If the gods were good tomorrow, he would live to marry Atalante. They would have children his father would never see.

At midnight, Kryton lay silent, his chest barely moving. Once, he opened his eyes and smiled at Melanion. "It's time," he said.

His eyes closed again. He was quiet for a space. "Live through tomorrow," he breathed. "You're our immortality."

A little later—"I love you," he whispered. His breath caught once, and he breathed no more.

Melanion studied the still face. He took Kryton's hand from his and placed it gently on the blanket. He felt clean and spare, as though what he'd shared tonight had dispelled the last vestiges of the conflict that rocked him from birth. His hand closed upon the lion-head ring on his finger and he kissed his father's hand. Rising, he gave the sign of respect to his fallen monarch.

"A good journey, my father." He replaced the eye patch, slipped through the hidden door behind the tapestry, and softly called Erytes to him.

Atalante stood by the window watching the runner cross the plain. As soft footsteps paused outside her door, she turned to see her mother entering the chamber with a tray of food. She bade the serving girl who followed her in to carry out Atalante's untouched dinner.

"You have to eat," Clymene said in her dry, practical voice. "It may be a very long day."

Atalante picked at a warm oat cake.

"The Mother sent me a vision," Clymene said. "You must be purified before the people today."

Atalante's eyes widened in surprise. "It's death to worship Her. Who will carry the signs if they kill me?"

"She will shield you. And another thing. You must lose this race."

Atalante felt her knees buckle. She sank into a chair. "Thank the gods," she said. "It's over."

In the city and the country outside the palace, the word went out on the wind.

*"It has come. At the sign . . ."* Farmers dressed themselves in pure white, as if they were going to a sacred festival. They kissed their wives and children good-bye with unusual tenderness, and picked up what tools they had to do the job.

In the city, people gathered in the marketplace. Wives had demanded to go to the stadium with their men. Their older children took charge of the younger ones, hurrying them out of the city.

The Thessalians entered the stadium in a great wave.

The Macedonian courtiers and their women already filled the seats nearest the track. Soldiers strolled the aisles to keep peace and to push the townspeople and farmers into the upper decks. Robed in white himations, the Thessalians watched and waited.

Shrieks of laughter reached them from the lower seats. Macedonian hetairas gotten up in jewels and gowns plundered from Thessalian nobles rubbed up against Polymus' men, chattering and laughing. None of them seemed to notice the priests who walked onto the central green and began a sacrifice.

But the people in the upper stands watched with growing excitement. A pure white bull walked beside a pure black one. Rose garlands wreathed their gilded horns.

The priests led the white bull to a high altar and the black to a low one in the center of the running track. Silently, they called upon the Great Artemis and the Mother. They were quick in the killing. The bulls sank to their knees without a sound—a good sign. The smoke of the fire rose into the air above the high altar, giving off a goodly aroma. The black bull's blood soaked into the earth.

Some of the hetairas, scenting the sacrifice, told their officers they were hungry, and demanded sweetmeats.

The shrill voice of the flute drew the crowd's attention. Young boys dressed in white formed a train of dancers. They sang the old melodies, without words. It didn't matter—the ancient words were engraved in every citizen's heart. They were the songs that called the people to battle.

Atalante followed the line of boys winding in and out like the Mother's serpents in an ancient dance. She tried to calm herself, but her heart beat hard against her chest like the beat of the drum. She looked for Xuthus, so she would remember where to send her first arrow. He sat surrounded by courtiers and women, dressed in purple again, heavily weighed down in gold chains. His gaze devoured Atalante and he licked his lips in a sickening gesture of anticipation. The henna-stippled hand of a courtesan offered him a honey cake. He pushed it away.

As she stripped to run, Atalante felt his hot gaze and glanced toward him in disgust. He was watching, stroking himself. As she felt the bile rise in her throat, she saw his lips move and understood his one word. "Mine," he said across the distance.

Not on your life, she thought, and walked naked toward the high altar.

Hyperion ran into his mother's chamber. She sat at the window watching Atalante walk toward the altar in the stadium.

"The king is dead," he told her.

They went together into Kryton's chamber. He lay still and distant, his face a dignified mask. Somebody had placed the lion crown of Macedonia on his gray head and crossed his hands on his chest. His sword and his ceremonial golden cup lay beside him.

Hyperion stared at him—Kryton, the cause of all the terror and loss, the conqueror he couldn't hate. He turned to his mother. "I must give him the sacred rites," he said.

Clymene's face went pale. "The punishment for performing the Mother's rites is death, Hyperion. You know that. And he didn't even believe in Her."

Hyperion nodded slowly. How could he make his mother understand? "She loved him in the end. As High Priest, I must honor Her choice and this man, by giving him the proper rites."

Clymene's hand trembled as she touched his cheek. "She

wouldn't ask you to do this. It may well mean your death."
Her voice broke and she drew him close to her.

"Mother, you demand a great deal of courage from
Atalante," he reminded her gently.

"She's a warrior, my love. A queen if she lives. You're
still so young, and you're not strong. Please, Hyperion."
Clymene's hands clutched at him, as though she could hold
him against what they both knew was right.

He understood her fear, her possessive love, even as it
hurt him, even as he knew it had hurt Atalante. He pulled
her hands off him and backed away. "I know what my future holds, Mother. I accept it. But I can't hide during the
short time I have. Don't make me ashamed of my life. I
have so little of it left."

Clymene reached for him. For the first time since the
subjugation of their country, she cried, great, gulping sobs,
holding him tightly, rocking him. He didn't know what to
do but to let her finish. She wiped her tears with the edge of
her robe and stared at him bleakly.

"Why do I have to go on living?" she asked.

He gave her a long look, revealing every bit of the shock
and horror he felt. "You have another child," he said in his
priest's voice. "Don't you realize how much Atalante needs
you—has needed you all along?"

"Atalante?" Clymene's eyes widened in surprise. "She's
as strong as the rocks holding up this fortress."

"How much more do you think she can take, Mother?
The Macedonians killed your husband, but he was her
father, as well. They killed Melanion and didn't even bury
him. Polymus has made her murder ten men whose only
crime was to race against her. She loves me and she knows
I'm dying. Only now do I understand that she's had to face
every ordeal all alone."

"She hasn't been alone," Clymene protested. "I have worked with her every day, consulting with her, telling her the visions the Mother has sent me."

Hyperion was so angry, he wanted to shout. "When was the last time you held her, let her cry to you, told her you loved her? You think Kryton was the only parent to make mistakes?"

He took a deep breath and grabbed Clymene's hands in his. "Maybe the gods will be good to you, Mother. Maybe they'll let you live beyond this horror for one reason. If Atalante survives, you'll have the chance to love the daughter you were afraid to love all these years, and to help her heal."

Clymene put her hands over her eyes, effectively ending the conversation. Hyperion prayed she wasn't hiding from what he'd just told her, but rather was saddened and moved to do better. When he rose to attend the king, Clymene asked to accompany Hyperion to the Mother's shrine. With a handful of loyal servants, they bore Kryton's body there and began the ceremony that would free his soul to cross the river and journey to the Land of the Dead.

Xuthus lolled back in his seat, the heat in his loins throbbing as he watched Atalante doff the little loincloth. She walked across the grass toward the funny looking low altar with the grace of a queen. A priest spoke to her and she nodded her consent. The man dipped his finger into a golden cup and drew with blood on the palms of her hands. Xuthus squinted to get a better look. A waving circle decorated both palms of her hands.

In a fluid motion that made him lean toward her in longing, Atalante dropped to her knees and laid both palms against the earth. Then she rose and walked to the high altar, where Artemis' priestess daubed her forehead and shoulders with the blood from the white bull. She raised her arms to the sky and seemed, for a breathless moment, to burn like a flame before Xuthus' eyes.

"What's happening?" he asked, staring in fear that Atalante would disappear in a puff of smoke.

Anteas, a son of the old general, Myron, leaned toward him from two seats away. His white robe brushed against Xuthus' arm, and he shivered in the warm air. "I believe she knows she'll marry you today after the race. They've just purified her of the blood she's shed, so the ceremony won't be tainted," Anteas said in a smooth voice.

"I see," Xuthus said, leaning back in his chair. He played with the heavy gold chain, filled with anticipation. He knew the rules. Four times around the track and the veteran would take home a heavy pouch of gold while he . . . Ah, he would claim the greatest prize of all. Aside from the heavy tug of his loins, Xuthus felt a curious and pleasurable lack of energy, an almost drugged state of relaxation.

Xuthus turned his head and watched the veteran enter the stadium through the Athlete's Gate. The Macedonians cheered him as he walked up to the priests, dressed in a white chiton and a chlamys over his shoulders. His pouch swung at his hip. The one-eyed veteran went through the same strange ritual Atalante had gone through—obviously, another Thessalian rite Xuthus would do away with after he'd finally drowned himself in Atalante's body. The soldier stripped off the chiton but kept the chlamys.

Courtiers in the stands began to flutter like a flock of brightly colored birds. Xuthus roused himself enough from his lethargy to notice that his father entered, looking dark as a thundercloud. His escort of guards pushed hetairas out of the way and ushered Polymus into the seat beside Xuthus.

"Damn it," Polymus muttered, smoothing his robe. "Myron and those old men kept me behind with complaints about dwindling supplies. Did anything happen of note while I was gone?" he asked.

"No," Xuthus said, settling back in his seat with a smile of satisfaction. "Except she's going to marry me, and she knows it."

"Don't be an idiot."

Xuthus looked from the veteran on the track to Atalante, her beautiful body stretching in the sun, the red blood on her shoulders glowing like liquid rubies. When both she and the veteran stood up straight, they stared at his father for rather a long time, almost as though they were memorizing his place in the stands. Xuthus almost leaned over to tell his father, who had turned away from the track to speak to his bodyguard. But the sun was so warm, and he felt so peaceful, he immediately forgot what he wanted to tell him. A cymbal sounded, and the runners took their places.

As she readied herself against the block, it occurred to Atalante that she hadn't yet looked at the soldier who had challenged her. She had been concentrating too deeply on the fulfillment of her charge.

How would the gods send the signs to her if she were to raise them today? Her whole body tingled with anxiety. Her heart pumped. Her senses were so acute, she felt the blood course through her veins. Her ears were so sensitive she could hear individual voices in the stands. She felt as though she could react swiftly enough to catch a gnat zipping past her.

She felt the soldier's hot gaze brand her back and she wanted to turn, to face him down. But the warning gong sounded, and then the bell.

Atalante broke free of the blocks and flew along the

track. She let him know he'd challenged a runner. As she sped along the oval, Atalante felt his even breathing a shadow's breadth behind. She sprinted faster. He stuck with her, matching the rhythm of her footsteps. They came around the track to the Macedonian's cheers. The upper decks, full of Thessalians, were silent.

Again, Atalante tried to increase her stride. But again, the runner clung until they were halfway around the track. Then he flung something across her path, something that glowed like a thousand suns. Her heart lurched. She swerved, reached for it, had it in her hand.

*The first of the signs.*

He was even with her. As she ran, Atalante commanded herself to stay steady when she wanted to shout for joy. It was only the first of three, and she had to catch the others. But she raised her arm high to the crowd and held the golden sphere aloft. The sun hit it and sparked golden lights from her hand into the air around her.

Xuthus smiled dreamily. It was just as the veteran had promised. Atalante had swerved to pick up the golden apple, and she'd lost her advantage.

"What's that?" Polymus muttered.

"She's carrying fire in her hand," Xuthus said. "Isn't it beautiful?"

The Thessalians in the stands above swayed forward, sighing, transfixed.

Atalante circled again for the third time. The soldier flung another of the signs her way. She swooped in stride and caught it up. Raising her hands, she held both globes aloft to the crowd.

The white-clad Thessalians surged to their feet. As she ran, Atalante heard their voices tinged with fear and awe. "Not yet," they murmured. "Wait for the three."

Atalante raced on, rounding the track for the final lap, turning her head to watch the runner. He ran right alongside her as though they were a perfectly matched pair of chariot horses. But halfway through the final lap, the soldier threw out the last apple. Pausing a pulse beat to pick it up, Atalante sank behind him. She didn't care. She had them all, and held them high above her head.

The people stared as the apples dripped gold down her arms, over her body. She was a leaping golden statue, shining, liquid, throwing off a glory like the sun. The people shaded their eyes against the light. The Thessalians in the upper decks roared, like a mighty ocean matching its strength with the storm about to break in an instant.

"Behold!" they cried. "Atalante, Sign-bearer!"

She ran on, the golden sparks striking the dust of the stadium as her feet thrust off with each step. Just ahead of her, the soldier ran. His cape came loose from its clasp and fell from him. She saw the back of his left shoulder. Glowing like the white crescent moon against the dark tan of his body was a scar—her brand on the body of this runner who had the grace and beauty of only one man.

As he crossed the finish line ahead of her, she screamed with all the lost nights and days of her grief.

"Melanion!"

He turned and opened his arms a split second before she fell into them. His lips clung to hers as fiercely as his shadow had just moments before. In spite of the tumult around her, she felt only him, the strength of his arms around her, the hard heat of his body, the scorching tenderness of his love encircling her. Then he pulled away and thrust the wreath upon her head. Taking the apples from her hands, he lifted them to the wreath. They sent out a glory the roaring crowd could follow.

She heard the resounding notes of the paean.

"Thessaly!" she shouted. "To me."

The young nobles and the Hundred poured into the stadium through the Athlete's Gate, swords raised, already dripping with blood. The white-clad people in the stands threw off their robes. Roaring Thessalians ran down the silk-robed Macedonians, who stared in confusion and terror at the mob falling upon them with pitchforks and axes. Mothers of murdered sons, husbands of despoiled wives screamed vengeance. Armed with kitchen knives and short blades, they attacked.

"Atalante!" Melanion shouted above the crowd. He pointed to the stands. Xuthus stood alone, his eyes wide with terror, clutching the purple silk close to his body.

Atalante gave a full-throated battle cry and leaped to the top of the marble altar decked with wedding garlands. As someone thrust a bow and arrow into her hands, she scanned the row where she'd last seen Xuthus. But the Thessalians streamed into it now, and Xuthus had disappeared.

Erytes climbed up behind her. Throwing one arm around her waist to steady himself, he pointed out a purple-clad figure shrinking back into the higher seats. She nodded, eyes narrowed, and took aim carefully.

Like an eager lover, the arrow flew to Xuthus' throat and plunged through the flesh. He clutched the shaft, gasping like a drowning man. Blood ran down his robe, red on purple, an impious sacrifice. Atalante watched until he fell face down, only to be trampled by shrieking Macedonians trying vainly to escape.

Strong arms reached for her. Melanion lifted her down and the Companions instantly surrounded them. As she ran forward the others surged around her. The people followed the bright rays of gold in the air above her. There was no stopping them now, she thought right before the battle rage took her.

In the milling crowd of Macedonians, Polymus was nowhere to be seen. "Gone," she shouted to Melanion as he ran beside her to the Athlete's Gate.

He leaped on a low wall beside the Gate. She saw him draw a deep breath. "To the Plain," he cried in the Voice of Power.

"Melanion," a thousand voices cried. "Follow the King!"

When the mob howled for blood, Polymus had scoured the stadium for a means of escape, but there was nowhere to run. White-clad soldiers filled the Athlete's Gate, and armed peasants packed the stands. One of them lunged for him, screaming his name, his pike raised. Polymus snatched a sword from a paralyzed Red Band guard and ran the scurvy bastard through. As the peasant crumbled at his feet, Polymus grabbed his white cloak and covered himself. In the confusion, any man in white had a better chance of getting out alive.

Polymus clawed his way toward the Athlete's Gate and ferreted through the surging soldiers. He had made it to Iolcus Plain. Heart pumping, he ran toward a contingency of Red Bands. With a roar, he organized the cavalry into a striking unit. A soldier brought him his stallion and he leaped atop its back, raising his hand in the signal to cut down the rebels racing out of the stadium. They charged at full gallop behind him. Polymus gritted his teeth in a grin of triumph as he urged the stallion forward. The peasants faltered, looking for a way to escape the thundering army.

At a wild shout from the right, Polymus turned his head and gasped in outrage. Myron and his sons charged toward his Red Bands, leading a troop of cavalry. Polymus could see that the soldiers had tied white ribbons around their arms. The manes of their horses flowed with white. Similarly identified infantry marched in quick-step after the Macedonians—Kryton's loyal soldiers had sided with the rebels.

"For your King!" Myron shouted as he charged, and the others answered in one voice. "Melanion!"

Polymus screamed in fury and raised his sword, wheeling his horse about to face the greater threat descending upon him. The Macedonians charged the Red Bands and the deep line of mercenaries behind them. They sliced through with their swords, and the Thessalians raced toward Polymus' men from the Athlete's Gate, falling upon them from behind. Polymus heard his men groan and smelled blood all around him—a river of blood—as the Macedonians decimated his men in a full assault. The Thessalians grabbed shields and swords of the dead and slaughtered more Red Bands from behind.

A small contingency of his men raced toward the battle from the palace. The last of his guards had proved loyal, at least, Polymus thought in relief. But as they turned north on the plain, Polymus realized they were fleeing before the rebels could kill them, too. But no, Myron's cavalry harassed them, pushing them toward Polymus and his dwindling troops.

"A horse!" Polymus heard the clear cry of a woman and wheeled around. One of the Thessalians cantered up to the princess Atalante leading a pure white stallion. As Polymus watched, she leaped upon the charger's back and touched his flanks. The gold from the wreath crowning her head flowed down her golden body into the stallion's white coat. His hooves struck out fire on any man who drew near.

Polymus' hands trembled on the sword he carried until he almost dropped it. The woman had become a Thing of Power.

Polymus' heart hammered in his throat watching his Red Bands quail before Atalante. Her bowstring vibrated gold against a blue sky. Men fell one after the other from her deadly arrows. Damn them all, he thought bitterly. His gaze skittered about, found an opening. He shouted an order to half his remaining Red Bands to charge Atalante. The fools obeyed, he saw with satisfaction. As they galloped toward her, he signaled the other half to follow him. As Thessalians and Macedonians converged around Atalante to protect her, Polymus escaped with his little army. They thundered across the plain and raced through the Serpent Gate.

"Shut the gate!" Polymus shouted. "To the walls!" The great doors swung shut behind him. A contingency of Red Bands ran up the stairway to defend the walls.

Atalante searched the plain in time to see Polymus enter Iolcus. She raised her arm to the Hundred massed about her, and pointed. Her brother and her mother were inside the palace. Gods knew what Polymus would do to them. She pushed the golden war horse forward. The Hundred surged after her. She had to get in before Polymus hurt them.

Melanion fought beside her on a black stallion. She gave him a look encompassing every bit of the fear she felt. He nodded grimly and spurred his horse forward, taking the lead. The army followed them, eating the distance to the palace.

At the gates of the city, Atalante pulled up short. A deadly shower of arrows rained down from the wall above. Melanion slid the black to a halt and backed him away from the wall. "Stay behind me," he shouted, turning his head toward her. Love swelled inside her at the protectiveness of his gesture. She studied the walls, saw a man aim, and screamed, her blood chilling in her veins.

"Melanion!" A Thessalian cavalry soldier, one of high rank from the looks of his armor, thrust himself between Melanion and the deadly shaft.

"To the hedge," Melanion shouted a second later, and they wheeled, galloping to the side of the palace. Erytes stood before the hedge, motioning them toward the door. She threw herself from her horse and plunged into darkness, giving off golden fire for the others to follow.

In the corridor of the ground floor, Polymus thrust his way through his chamber door, barking orders to the Red Bands. "You—take my chest and place it in a wagon. Hurry." He stopped, looked around at all that should have been his, all that the little she-demon and his bastard king had taken from him.

"I'll make them remember me," he whispered. Turning to his guards, he smiled, planning just how they'd pay. "Take a few men," he said to the captain. "Find Kryton, that whore of a queen, and her loathsome seed. Bring them here."

He sat and caught his breath. Running his hand down his sword, he checked it for sharpness and then re-sheathed it. He poured himself a cup of wine and sat awaiting the men. They were taking an inordinate amount of time to find a dying old man, a woman, and a sick child. Moments passed. He pounded his fist against the palm of his hand and paced.

A hesitant rap sounded at the door. "Enter," he shouted. The contingency he'd sent out filed in, staring at their feet. "Well?" he demanded.

"My lord, we can't find them," the captain said with a quaver.

"Idiots," he hissed, slapping the captain across the cheek with the back of his hand.

"May-maybe they're hiding in the storerooms," said a Red Band. "Where they keep the oil and wine."

"Show me," said Polymus, his fury mounting. He had to find them. They had to pay. "Keep your weapons at hand. They're dangerous." The men looked at him as though he'd gone mad, to think a dying old man, a woman, and a weak boy could be dangerous. But they *were*. Kryton had lived in spite of the poison he'd ordered the physician to rub into his wound. The woman was responsible, with her witchcraft and her spells. The boy should have died by now. He was a ghost of himself. But he too, like his mother lived on, to revel in Polymus' defeat.

By all the hounds in hell, he wouldn't have it. Polymus followed the men through the maze below the palace, until they came to huge, closed door. "Open it," he ordered them. The men tried the latch. The door was locked from the inside. He heard sounds beyond it, the soft chanting of men and women.

"Open it," he shouted, and his soldiers put their shoulders to the door. A moment later, it shuddered and crashed open. Polymus stood in the doorway, writhing in fury. The boy and his mother stood at the front of the room beside a bier holding a reclining, wasted body. Kryton, Polymus thought in triumph. The bastard had finally died.

Hyperion's head shot up and his back straightened. He wore white, like every other damned traitor in the kingdom today. As he turned to speak softly to the men and women around him, Polymus saw the boy had a quiver of arrows at his back and a small bow over his shoulder.

"How dare you desecrate this place? You risk the Mother's anger, and her curse."

Polymus glanced from his prey to the great statue of the Mother on the dais. She seemed to loom over his soldiers at the front of the room, and they whispered to each other, closed ranks, and began to back up away from the boy.

Polymus gave a harsh shout to break the spell settling over his men. "Blasphemers! You know the law I set down against this evil worship. The punishment for this traitorous act is death. Kill them. Then burn down this abomination. Burn it all down."

"My lord, the oil stores," one man objected. "We'll set the palace afire."

"Do it." Polymus felt a kick of savage satisfaction. "We'll leave them a funeral pyre fit for a king."

As he shoved the men ahead of him forward, he heard his own feral growl. The Red Bands were still moved more by fear of what he would do to them than what a mere boy could manage with that toy bow.

The first Red Band got halfway across the shrine when he gasped and fell forward, the shaft of Hyperion's arrow plunged into his chest.

# Chapter 16

## The Tablets

Melanion fought his way through the narrow corridors. The Red Guards impeded his progress with desperate force, blocking his little army at every step. He unsheathed the Arkadian sword he'd carried through the Land of the Dead. It winked ferociously in the golden light that was Atalante. Following him step by step, she unleashed her arrows behind the shelter of his shield.

The sword flashed and arced. Men fell before him left and right. The sword seemed a blur of gold in the darkness. He didn't tire or slow. But the hair on the back of his neck prickled.

"Hurry," he urged the Companions. Stumbling over fallen bodies, slicing through standing men, he made his way to the Mother's shrine. Loud shouting and confusion met him as he shoved through the door. His gaze flew to the altar at the far end of the room.

"Polymus," he shouted in the Voice of Power. There was a lull in the noise, a parting of the troops.

Polymus stood at the altar, his sword raised over Hyperion's prone body. The prince lay with his back arched upon the white marble. Clymene struggled behind him, her arms pinioned by two Red Bands. Polymus turned his head toward Melanion and his eyes gleamed with a red-tinged hatred. He resembled the monstrous Kalydonian boar more than a man. An animal sound rose from his throat and his lips twisted in a malevolent grin. He raised both hands high above the small boy, and thrust down with all his might.

"No," Atalante sobbed at his side. Melanion heard his own groan, and surged toward Polymus, hacking at the Red Bands impeding him.

Polymus pulled the sword free. He shoved the prince's body over the edge of the altar. His gaze held Melanion's as he motioned to the guards holding Clymene to bring her forward. The men raised her up on the altar stone.

A bowstring sang behind Melanion. One of the guards holding the queen on the altar plummeted forward off the dais. The other pulled his hands from Clymene's struggling form and scrambled behind the altar. Clymene tried to roll off the stone, but Polymus grabbed her by the throat and forced her down again, raising his sword.

"Mother!" Atalante screamed and sprinted past Melanion. Her quiver was empty. Grabbing a sword from a dying Red Band, she thrust it through the soldier blocking her path. But she was too far from the altar, Melanion knew. They'd never reach it in time.

"Clymene!" he shouted. "The knife." He pulled out the ancient stone dagger and flung it through the air to the altar. It soared through space like a hawk diving for its prey. Clymene reached out a hand, grasped it, and thrust with all her might into Polymus' belly.

Polymus' fingers loosened on the sword and it clattered to the floor. He grunted and doubled over, clutching his stomach. Clymene pulled the knife free. It came easily back to her hand. She rolled off the altar and stood beside it. Polymus sank against the marble, confused, clutching at the wound. Blood seeped through his fingers.

Clymene rolled him over, until she looked directly into

his eyes as he lay on the altar staring up at her. She thrust the knife into his chest.

"This is for Iasus." Again, she thrust into his side.

"This for Hyperion." Again, and blood spurted from his belly.

"This for Erytes." One last time, she stabbed.

"And this for Kryton."

Polymus choked. Blood dribbled from his mouth. He staggered to his feet and fell backwards, again lying on the altar. Clymene bent and pulled back his head by his hair, exposing his neck as though he were a sacrifice.

"This for the people of Macedonia and Thessaly," she said in a voice as formal as a ritual. She slit his throat, end to end.

Atalante, sobbing and bloodied, ran through the last dying men to the altar where her mother knelt beside Hyperion, cradling his head in her arms. A spark shone in her brother's eyes.

"Atalante," he whispered. "Be happy for me. I am a warrior."

The light went from him. Clymene pressed him to her body and raised her head to heaven, keening the high, timeless song of grief.

"Atalante. Let me hold you." Melanion knelt beside her as she stared at her mother and her brother's body. Hyperion's blood covered her mother's gown. His arms were limp.

Whose arm would be so gentle around her shoulders now? She longed to lay her head against Melanion's chest and give up all of it into his care.

But she couldn't. She couldn't ask for love or acceptance from anyone other than Hyperion. She didn't deserve that.

Atalante pulled herself to her feet and staggered away from the altar. She must leave before she desecrated the Mother's shrine. She wished she could stop shaking.

A strong compulsion filled her—to run until she was out of the city, in the wilderness somewhere. She must hide with the beasts and the trees and the mountains, away from the pity and the terror of men.

"Hyperion's dead," she whispered. "Oh, gods, who will absolve me now?"

Something drained from her body, like sand from an hourglass. She felt it, licking like flame, drying out the marrow of her bones as it left her. She slumped against the altar, felt strong arms lift her, and sank into darkness beyond sleep.

Melanion carried his precious burden to the chamber beneath the Megaron. His heart froze in fear as he laid Atalante on the bed they'd shared with such passionate delight. He leaned over her pale, limp form as the last of the golden flame flickered out of her.

"Don't die," he told her over and over again. "Don't you dare go away from me now."

He didn't know how long he held her, surrounding her with his strength, his heat. Some time later, Theas came with a physician.

"She still breathes," Melanion said without looking up. He wouldn't let the man come between them. He was sure the only thing keeping her chest rising and falling was his own hand covering hers and his body bent above her, defying death.

The physician seemed to understand. He allowed Melanion to stay where he was. But after examining Atalante for injuries and wounds, he shook his head. "This is not a mortal sickness. I don't know what to do for her," he said in a voice choked with tears. "If I could give my own life in place of hers, I would."

Korone came with a bowl of warm water and cloths. "I'll watch her while you wash the grime of battle from you," she said.

Melanion motioned her away. "She's still breathing," he said fiercely, and clutched Atalante's hand.

Korone lit a lamp in the little room against the growing darkness. Hours had passed since the battle, he realized, bent over Atalante's still form. For a moment, his heart stopped beating. Her chest lay still. Frantic, he put his cheek close to her lips and felt it, the faintest exhalation of air.

"Where's the queen?" he asked Korone.

"In her chambers. I think she's in shock," Korone said.

"Get her down here, now."

"Melanion," Theas said in a quiet voice. "What more can she do?"

"She kept my father alive." He was so cold inside. He couldn't take his eyes off Atalante. He was afraid to stop talking, for without the sound of his voice she might slip away.

He barely heard the click of the latch. Then Clymene was at his elbow, bending over her daughter.

"Gods," she breathed. "Why did no one tell me sooner?"

"Perhaps they thought you were too busy mourning your son to care." He rubbed his eyes wearily with his hand. "Forgive me. I should never have said that."

Clymene pushed him aside and took Atalante's wrist in her hand. "This is very bad." She pointed to a bag behind her. "Bring it to me, and call for some of my priestesses. Now."

Melanion did so. He watched while Clymene poured a

medication into a small cup and held it to Atalante's lips. Drop by drop, she gave it to her. At a quiet rap on the door, he rose to his feet again and opened it. Several women entered. Some were in the first flush of womanhood and some were old. All were dressed in white.

"Leave us," Clymene said. "Quickly, Melanion. There's little time."

He wanted to spend every minute she still breathed beside her. But he knew a sacred mystery when he saw one. He went to the door, opened it, and paused, turning again to Clymene. "Save her."

Clymene jerked her head in a nod. He walked out, closed the door behind him, and sank to the floor. Covering his head with his hands, he prayed harder and longer than he ever had in his life.

Melanion had no idea how much time passed before the priestesses slipped from the room. As he rose, one of them gave him a tremulous smile. He strode into the chamber and to the bed where Atalante lay still and pale. Clymene was seated beside her. She smoothed back her daughter's golden curls and gave Atalante a smile that held that special warmth Melanion had never seen her give to anyone but Iasus and Hyperion.

Clymene looked up at him and rose from the chair, motioning him into it. "She'll live," she told him as he sat and took Atalante's hand. "It will be slow—slower still for her soul to follow her body's healing." In the pause that followed, she studied him carefully.

"You love my daughter very much." It was not a question, but a statement.

"She is my life," Melanion said.

"Then I owe you, and my daughter when she is ready to hear it, an explanation. Are you willing to listen now?"

He looked down at Atalante. Her breathing was more perceptible, and her pale face had a bit of color in it. "For what you have just done, I would be willing to hear the entire history of the world from you."

Clymene smiled briefly. "Very well. First, you must know that for many years of my marriage, I was barren. Then the gods blessed me with a beautiful child. Atalante was so . . . alive, so vibrant, from the moment of her birth. Iasus and I had nothing from her but joy.

"When she was five, the Mother appeared to me in a dream. She said to me that Atalante would be the Maiden that year."

Melanion looked at her blankly. "The Maiden?"

"Each year, a young woman is chosen to bring a sacrifice to the House Serpents—meal and milk to feed them. She carries it along a treacherous forest path full of roots and rocks, and she must walk it at night. If she spills one drop of the milk, or one grain of the meal, there will be a great famine in Thessaly. And even if she brings the dishes safely to the House Serpents, they must accept the offering. Only then is Thessaly safe for another year.

"The sacrifice takes place in Arkadia. Usually, the Maiden spends a year in my mother's kingdom, learning how to walk the path blindfolded, carrying the dishes. Usually, the Maiden is at least fifteen summers old. But this year, the Mother spoke a scant week before the ceremony. And she chose my only child—an innocent barely out of the nursery, who had no time to learn the necessary skills." Clymene stared first at Atalante and then at Melanion.

"I was there for the testing. I was given the same drug my mother gave Atalante. I became . . . one with her. I felt my daughter's fear, her worry as she lifted the bowls and began her walk. I found out things I never knew about her that night.

"She was afraid of tall monsters. I realized that when I saw the shadows deepen and the trees loom up before her like her nightmare figures. At that moment, huge wings whooshed by her, so close they almost touched her cheek. I felt her start; saw the meal and the milk roll and almost spill. I felt her force herself to be still, to be calm. Above her, a great hawk settled on an overhanging branch. I heard its voice in the darkness, a whisper on the wind.

" 'Give it up,' the voice said. 'Such a little girl—and the dishes are too heavy. You'll spill them, for sure. Then they'll come for you, those women who watched you begin your journey tonight. They'll tear you limb from limb.'

"She tried not to listen. She started to cry, very softly, because she was afraid she'd spill the meal and the milk. The voice went on. 'Come away. I'll take you back to your father. He wants you safe to grow up, so you can be queen. When you're queen, you'll be like him. You can do just what you like, and the people won't be able to tell you what to do.' "

Clymene gave him a fierce look of pride. "Atalante was too smart for that. Even at five, she knew that to be king is to be first in the midst of danger. She knew the voice lied. So she called out to the hero-goddess who protected her from the nightmare monsters. She asked Artemis to light her way."

Clymene gave a laugh that was part sob. "Wouldn't you know, Melanion? The moon came out from behind a cloud and shone on that path. Atalante could see every rock and root on it. She carried the dishes safely to the House Snakes, and called them out as though they were her brothers. They came, twining around her, resting against her. They accepted her completely.

"Just as I thought the ordeal had ended, a lady stepped into the clearing. The air crackled around her. She was radiant, beautiful. She carried a quiver of arrows on her back and a bow in her hand. She smiled at my daughter.

" 'Well done,' she said. 'The Mother wishes to claim you, but you are mine. Keep faith and I'll not fail you through the fire and storm that await you.' The goddess touched Atalante's forehead with the tip of her finger. I felt the bolt of fire that went through my little girl. I saw the darkness take her.

"While I waited for her to recover consciousness, I thought of many things. I thought of how brave she was, how wise. I thought of Artemis' words, and I knew terrible trials were in store for my beautiful child. So I made a decision to help her, to make her strong."

Clymene glanced at him and shrugged her thin shoulders. "You should know, Melanion. How old were you when you lost your mother? Heroes are forged in adversity."

Clymene put her hands over her eyes. "I gave her all I could, demanded of her all she could give in return. But I made a terrible mistake. Atalante needed a mother's love, unconditionally given. I forced myself to deny her that and thanked the gods each day because Hyperion could give that to her. Now all I can do is pray she'll accept that love from me in his stead."

After a long moment, Clymene wiped at her eyes, took a linen square, and blew her nose. She straightened her shoulders and gave Melanion a smile of sorts. "Go and rest. Or bathe the muck of battle off you. She should waken soon, and you want her to see you at your best."

He hesitated, and Clymene waved her hands at him.

"Go on, Melanion. I'll watch after her while you're gone. Never fear. I'll keep her safe."

Melanion made his way slowly down the long corridor. At that moment, all he wanted was to take Atalante in his arms and hold her against all the misery of the world. The queen said she'd recover, but how long would it take to heal the inner scars she carried?

Quick footsteps behind him made him turn. Theas caught up with him, a grave expression on his face. "Come," he said.

Melanion followed him to the Megaron. It was filled with the wounded lying on cots in long rows. In the center of the room, Nestor lay on a cot surrounded by his friends. His eyes were shadowed, and his face drawn. The broken shaft of a javelin was embedded in his abdomen.

He smiled when he saw Melanion and weakly motioned to Philip, who knelt by his head. Philip lifted him up and held a wine cup to his lips. Nestor sipped at the potion and sighed as Philip gently laid him back against the pillow.

"She lives?" he asked Melanion in a whisper.

Suddenly, Melanion remembered that moment beneath the palace wall and the javelin a cavalry soldier had taken for him.

"Yes," Melanion said. "Nestor, you gave your life for me. Why?"

Nestor smiled and Melanion saw a transcendent sweetness that must have lain beneath his cynical façade forever. "She loves you," he said simply.

He gasped, swallowed convulsively. "Tell her," he whispered. "Tell her she was always beautiful to me."

The light went from his face. Philip bent his head. Korone sobbed quietly in Theas' arms.

"He waited all night to hear that Atalante would live," Theas said.

Melanion put his hand on Nestor's head. "Where is his armor?"

"They had to cut off his breastplate to get to the wound," Astrid told him.

"Have the smiths make him another even finer. Find his jewelry. We must bury him with honor."

They had buried many heroes in the next days, Melanion thought as he returned to the palace at Iolcus. He had accompanied his father on his last journey to the mountains, where they put him to rest beside his wife. Melanion had looked down at the graves and felt serenity flow through him. His parents were united at last.

Now, as he hurried down the corridors of the palace, he wondered how he would find Atalante. He had been gone for five days, and worried every one of them. Would she still have the haunted look in her eyes that he'd last seen? She had been too quiet, too guarded at their last meeting.

At the door of her chamber, he paused, torn between giving her time to prepare herself before their meeting and barging in, insisting she let him fight whatever demons tormented her. The hell with it, he thought. He had never been subtle. He knocked twice and, at the quiet call from inside, entered the room.

She sat at the window. The sun caressed her hair, making a halo. But the light emphasized the shadows beneath her eyes and the delicate cheekbones in her pale, thin face. She gave him a ghost of a smile, but he could see her hands, listless on the fabric of her plain blue gown.

"You've arrived back safe," she said softly. "That is good."

He walked toward her slowly, almost afraid that if he approached all at once, she would bolt. And he knew that even weak, Atalante would run faster than he.

"Dear heart," he said when he had come close enough. "You must let me take some of the burden."

She looked at him in surprise. "I had hoped that you would take more than some. I have asked the council to make you king of Thessaly, as well as Macedonia."

A chill crept down Melanion's neck. "You are to be queen, Atalante. You will rule Thessaly."

She rose swiftly and backed away from him, holding out her hand to keep him away. "Oh, no. I am unfit."

He crossed the distance between them in two strides, backing her against the wall. She cowered there. His Atalante who had faced monsters and fought beside him twice in battle, shuddered and covered her face at his approach. He felt sick at the pit of his stomach.

"I'm going to hold you now, Atalante. I am only going to hold you," he said quietly.

"No!" she screamed and flung him off. And then she did bolt, straight out of the room. Melanion ran into the corridor and after her, but she'd had a head start on him. He took to his heels, tearing down the stairs and into the courtyard.

Where would she go? he thought wildly as he raced through the city. Across the plain to the forest and the hills? To the ocean? Fear skittered up his backbone as he pictured her simply walking into the sea until it closed around her. He came to a halt at the stadium, breathing hard, his stomach muscles cramping, and sank to his knees.

"Help me," he whispered to whatever god listened. From the dust of the earth, an answer came, and he knew where she'd gone.

When he approached Hyperion's tomb, he saw Atalante

lying prone on the new mound of dirt, her head in her arms. He sat on the ground very close, but not touching her.

"What does he say?" Melanion asked softly.

Atalante heard Melanion's voice and tried desperately to keep from reaching for him. She shook her head from side to side, trying to find an explanation for him—for herself. "It's always the same answer," she said in a weary voice. "I have to. It's my duty."

She felt his hand hover over her hair and wished for his touch. But she didn't deserve it, didn't deserve another moment of happiness in this life. His hand and all the warmth of his love retreated.

"Would it be so terrible a duty to marry me in front of the people? To have our children?" he asked her in a stiff voice.

Didn't he understand?

She pushed herself up into a sitting position, ashamed he'd caught her at all, wanting to run again until she had no more breath. Instead, she had to make the supreme effort of convincing him to leave her alone. It was so hard to fight him, when every part of her still wished for him.

She rubbed her tears from her cheeks with the back of her hand and looked him in the eye so he'd know she told him truth. "You'll never be able to look at me without remembering what I've done. I'm filthy with it."

"Oh, gods!" Melanion grabbed her—simply grabbed her and pulled her hard against him, wrapping his arms around her like a vise.

Stupid, childish tears started again. Atalante couldn't seem to hold them back, nor the wrenching sobs that shook her. But he just held her, stroking her back, letting her cry, as though he cared about her, even when she made him see nothing could cleanse her. In the face of his tenderness, she was helpless.

"I let him make me into a monster," she whispered.

"You'll carry the scars he inflicted forever, Atalante," Melanion said in a gentle murmur. "You'll never be the same again. But if I came back to you limping, unable to defend you properly, to rule beside you, or to run with you, would you love me less?"

She shook her head against his chest, feeling his warmth, hearing the strong beat of his heart.

"Then how can you think I would lose one little bit of the love I have for you because of those scars you carry deep inside?"

He stroked her hair, soothing away the tight band around her heart. "You're not an innocent woman. You had to choose against honor and conscience to protect your people. The gods ordained it. Your brother advised you to do it, every time.

"Do you think Hyperion would have ever insisted if it hadn't been the only way?" Melanion pulled away for a moment, holding her shoulders. His gaze held her, compelled her with its power.

"I am awe-struck when I look at you, Atalante. I see your suffering and your boundless love. I beg you in all humility, give me the right to stand beside you." His beautiful mouth curved in an uneven smile.

"And if, for a time or forever, there's a part of you that limps—well, I never could beat you in an honest race."

He meant it, all of it. She knew that as she very carefully wrapped her arms around his neck and nestled against him, letting him surround her, letting his strength support her. Maybe, just maybe, it would not be such a burden to live.

It was sunset when Melanion led her back to the palace. He had done no more than hold her, stroking her back, his touch a loving feast for a starved soul. She was at peace with the decisions they'd made. They would marry before the people within the week. They would rule both kingdoms together, sending Theas and Korone to Macedonia to represent them until Thessaly's worst problems were solved. Melanion insisted upon two promises. She agreed to trust that he loved her, and to never leave him.

Korone met them with a worried look as they entered the palace. "The queen has been asking after you these last three hours," she said. "She waits for you in the library."

"What now?" Atalante whispered.

Melanion squeezed her hand, leading her to the library door. "Let's see. Together."

At their knock, Clymene opened the door and drew them into the room. Her face was pale and she looked as though she'd been crying, but she embraced them both with a quiet smile.

"I remembered Hyperion's request and looked in his room." She gestured to the library table, piled high with tablets.

"Behind the tile at the head of his bed?" Melanion asked, thinking back to the day he'd visited Hyperion and seen him writing.

"Yes. He'd hidden them there." She took Atalante's hand and led her to the table. "They're a record, my love. A chronicle of your father's reign and of your exploits. He's written down everything—the time you went to the mountain and met Melanion, the boar hunt in Kalydon, what you endured during the occupation. Tomorrow, you must read them all.

"But I think it will help you to read the letter he left behind for you. I want you to read it now. Will you do that?"

Ever since the night she'd awakened to find her mother

watching over her, Atalante had sensed that something fundamental had changed between them. Clymene looked at her now with a shy warmth that glowed to life at times like these. Whenever she was close enough, she would raise her hand to touch Atalante—on her head, or her shoulder, as she did now. After Clymene handed her the tablet and left the room, Atalante turned to Melanion.

"Why does she do that?" she asked him, closing her own hand over the lingering warmth of her mother's.

"I suspect it's to make up for all the time she felt she couldn't," he said, smiling down at her.

Atalante stared blindly at the tablet in her hand. "I would have been happy to feel her touch any time in these many years."

"She would have been overjoyed to give it. But that's another story, my love. One you must promise to ask your mother to tell you tomorrow."

She gave him her promise willingly. She lived because he had made it bearable. There was nothing she wouldn't do for him.

"Come," he said. Holding out his hand, Melanion walked to the king's great chair and drew her down to his lap. He pulled an oil lamp close. Together, they read the letter.

*Atalante, queen of Thessaly and Macedonia*

*My beautiful, brave sister, I send you greetings across the wide chasm between your world and mine. If my visions are true, you have freed our land from evil. Now free yourself of shame. This you must do, for your soul, for your nation, and for Melanion.*

*Remember, we come from the One, and return to that Creator when our span is over. Our word for Her is the*

*Mother, but it doesn't matter what we call this ineffable Force. Our duty, indeed, our right is to imitate what we understand of Her. We must create, as She does, be it with the careful tending of the land, the lines of the poet, the lullaby of a mother. All of this is an act of love, and that is what you are, Atalante. Love.*

*All that is good is so because we have created.*

*All that is evil is so because someone has destroyed. You remained and suffered to create a beacon for the people. It never destroyed you, Atalante. It only made you more of what you are, and that is entirely good.*

*On this, the night before my earthly death, I dreamed a great dream. I saw Melanion come to you. I saw you ruling together in peace and plenty. I heard poets in another age praising your deeds. And I saw Melanion carry your babes to an altar on top of a mountain and raise them high to the night sky for your goddess' blessing.*

*Joy to you, Atalante, Sign Bearer. You will live forever.*

Atalante rose and walked to the window. The sun was setting in a blaze of crimson and purple. Melanion followed. He stood warm and strong at her back. His arms were gentle as she leaned in to his body. She felt light enough to drift along the currents of air in the evening sky. She took a deep breath and realized that she was free.

"Dreams are wonderful things," she said softly. "When the nights became unbearable, you came to me in my dreams. You gave me comfort, even when I thought you were dead."

"I dreamed, also." His voice was deep and gentle. "My love reached you as yours reached me. Even from the land of the dead."